W9-BHL-830

Tapas on the Ramblas

A Russell Quant Mystery

Also by the author

Amuse Bouche
Flight of Aquavit

Tapas on the Ramblas

A Russell Quant Mystery

Anthony Bidulka

INSOMNIAC PRESS

Copyright © 2005 by Anthony Bidulka

Edited by Catherine Lake

All rights reserved. No part of this publication may be reproduced, stored in a retrieval system or transmitted, in any form or by any means, without the prior written permission of the publisher or, in case of photocopying or other reprographic copying, a license from Access Copyright, 1 Yonge Street, Suite 1900, Toronto, Ontario, Canada, M5E 1E5.

Library and Archives Canada Cataloguing in Publication

Bidulka, Anthony, 1962-
Tapas on the Ramblas / Anthony Bidulka.

(A Russell Quant mystery)
Includes bibliographical references.
ISBN 1-894663-97-7

I. Title. II. Series: Bidulka, Anthony, 1962- . Russell Quant mystery.

PS8553.I319T36 2005   C813'.6   C2005-903402-5

The publisher gratefully acknowledges the support of the Canada Council, the Ontario Arts Council and the Department of Canadian Heritage through the Book Publishing Industry Development Program.

Printed and bound in Canada

Insomniac Press
192 Spadina Avenue, Suite 403
Toronto, Ontario, Canada, M5T 2C2
www.insomniacpress.com

Some things just go better together—like wine & cheese, pizza & beer, champagne & amuse bouche, aquavit & herring, tapas & sangria. Without one, the other is not nearly as savoury.

This is for Herb, aptly named, for he brings such fine flavour to all the days of my life.

The Wiser Family Tree

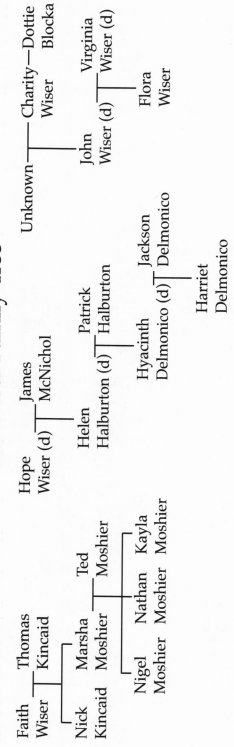

Chapter 1

It was late on a mid-August afternoon. Through south-facing windows, slanted spears of gilded sunshine pierced my office. At the sound of Lilly's songbird voice I gazed up from where I was slouched behind my desk lazily studying the fleeting marvel. "Flora Wiser is here to see you," she told me, a wide smile on her sunny-side-up face.

As I dutifully rose to greet my four o'clock, Lilly moved aside to let the woman through my office door. Flora Wiser, although younger than I'd imagined—in her early twenties—presented herself as a much older woman. But not in any of the positive ways. She lacked the energy and exuberance I generally equate with her age group. Rather, she moved with a nervous hesitation, reminding me of a brown rabbit in a brown field, sniffing the air for danger, not sure if she should dash or stand perfectly still in the hope of remaining unseen. Her face was an oval of colourless skin untouched by sun or cosmetics, highlighted by...well, by nothing. It was a wholly unremarkable face; greenish eyes dulled by the unreflective lenses of wire frame glasses, a nondescript nose, a line for a mouth. Her dun-coloured hair, woven into a thick, bristly braid, hung heavy down her back like jute rope. She was medium height and slender, with bony shoulders permanently hunched forward in the manner of someone who is much taller but doesn't want to be. That was about all I could surmise about her body, well hidden beneath baggy layers of grey-tone clothing: a long-sleeved man's shirt beneath a vest-like tunic and a thick skirt that swung sluggishly about her ankles. At her waist was a bulky macramé purse and on her size ten feet she wore all-purpose, all-weather, slip-on Birkenstocks.

I held out my hand and readied myself for a limp fish or the dreaded fingers-only shake. The unexpected strength and substance of her grasp and full palm-to-palm contact surprised me as her wiry fingers firmly encircled my hand. I offered her a seat in front of my desk and returned to my own. The beams of sunlight I'd been admiring earlier had dissipated, as if they'd been disturbed by our sudden movements and decided to move on to more tranquil realms.

"Can I get you more huckleberry herb tea, Ms. Wiser?" Lilly asked from her spot in the doorway.

Huckleberry? We have huckleberry tea? What is a huckleberry?

Flora gazed back at Lilly with a doe-eyed smile; a smile that told me Lilly had made Flora Wiser fall in love with her, as does anyone who spends any time in the PWC waiting room. "Oh, thanks Lilly, but I think I'm fine," she answered, her voice flat and nasal.

"Okay," Lilly responded. "Make sure you stop by the desk on your way out and I'll have that saskatoon berry jelly recipe ready for you."

Flora nodded so enthusiastically I thought her rope of hair must have been chafing her neck. "Okay, I won't forget."

"Russell, can I get anything for you?"

Huckleberry eh? "Uh, no, Lilly, thanks," I told her.

Lilly left us alone then, closing the door behind her.

I returned my full attention to my potential client, landing a pleasant smile on her. "How was your trip?" I asked, knowing Flora Wiser had driven up from Regina to meet with me.

"Oh it was good," she replied, noticeably less smiley than she'd been with Lilly.

All right then, enough with the idle chit-chat. "In our telephone conversation you mentioned that your..." I made a move as if to check my notes, even though the details of her call were still very clear in my mind, "...grandmother asked you to come see me?"

"Yes, she did. She wants me to hire you," Flora Wiser told me.

"I see." Overstatement. "Do I know your grandmother?"

"Oh, I don't know," she said with a quirk of her head as if she hadn't considered that possibility. "Her name is Charity Wiser. She lives in Victoria."

The name didn't ring a bell. I had thought it would. Why else would someone from two provinces away ask her granddaughter to travel for over two hours specifically to hire me? I was on the eve of my third anniversary as a private detective and I am darn good at my job, but I could hardly convince myself that my reputation had spread as far as British Columbia. Or maybe... "Did she tell you why she wanted you to hire me in particular?"

Flora winced. I couldn't tell if it was because she didn't know the answer or simply did not want to discuss it. "I think you'll have to talk to Grandmother about that, Mr. Quant. I'm sorry."

"That's not a problem," I said, picking up a pen and flipping to a blank page on the pad of paper in front of me, ready to take notes. "I was just curious. Maybe we could discuss why your grandmother is in need of my services?"

"Well," she began, with a hapless expression on her face. "Grandmother thinks someone is trying to kill her...for her money...and she wants you to find out who."

Oh my. I was expecting to be asked to track down a wayward ex-husband behind on his alimony payments or play I Spy with a cheating paramour. Even at that I was being overly optimistic. Many of my cases are about as exciting as a weekend of back-to-back hockey playoffs, eating submarine sandwiches and guzzling beer while the spouse is out of town...for a gay man. You see, most gay men (and most straight women) actually *prefer* to be in the company of their special someones, maybe even a little dressed up, watching *Designer Guys*, and eating sushi.

"Can you tell me why she thinks someone is trying to kill her?"

With some effort, because the edges kept catching in the holes,

Flora withdrew a large manila envelope from her macramé pouch. "Most of what you need to know is in here," she told me. "But I can tell you what I know," she added with a voice that made me think it wouldn't be a lot.

"That would be very helpful," I said, noticing with a decided tinge of dissatisfaction that she wasn't handing over the envelope just yet. Now, I'm a detective, curious as they come. I wanted to get my hands on that envelope and its contents worse than Smeagol wanted that damned piece of jewellery in *The Lord of the Rings*.

"My grandmother owns a company called Wiser Meats," she began.

Aha. Now I recognized the name, at least the Wiser part of it, for it is emblazoned upon the shrink-wrapped visage of my most guilty pleasure—Wiser Hickory Smoked Hot Dogs. Although I rarely admit to it, one of my all-time favourite meals is a Wiser hot dog wrapped in a squishy blanket of processed, pre-sliced, no-grain, white bread. No fancy hot dog bun or even ketchup or mustard or sauerkraut for me. And sometimes...sometimes I don't even cook the hot dog. I had no idea that Flora Wiser and her grandmother, Charity Wiser, were the hot dog Wisers. Wiser Meats is a meat processing and packaging giant in Canada, head officed in Alberta and best known for its smoked hams and bacons. Thanksgiving is not Thanksgiving without a smoked Wiser turkey and a barbecue is not a barbecue without Wiser hamburger patties. I was impressed, and confused. Why would the renowned Wiser company send this whippet of a girl to hire me if a potential murderer was threatening their matriarch?

"Although she's still president of the board of directors," Flora continued, "she retired from day-to-day duties some time ago. She's lived on an estate on Vancouver Island for many years. It's where I grew up after my parents were killed in a car accident."

"You were raised by your grandmother then?"

"Partly. Since I was fourteen," she said matter-of-factly, using her forefinger to push the frame of her glasses back up her nose. "A lot of people say Grandmother is tight with her money, but the one thing she does spend money on is her Charity Events."

"You mean fundraisers, that sort of thing?"

"No. Charity Events is just what she calls them, you know, after her own name. She's hosted one every two or three years for the past twenty or so. And all members of the family are expected to attend."

"Her children and other grandchildren then?"

"My father was her only child, and I'm her only grandchild. But Grandmother's two sisters, Faith and Hope, had children. So the family is mostly my uncles and aunts and cousins. There are fifteen of us in all."

Faith, Hope and Charity. Cute. "So these Charity Events are actually family reunions?" I questioned, trying to understand.

Flora winced again, knitting her furry brows together. "I suppose."

"Well, that's very nice of her to keep the family together like that."

"Welllllll, not really," Flora said with an awkward laugh. "That's not really why she does it." She looked down at her hands, whittling away at an invisible piece of soap. "Or how the others see it."

"Oh?" I could smell a juicy story. Gosh I wanted that envelope. "Why does she do it then? Why does your grandmother hold these Charity Events?"

"She thinks that the only reason the family is nice to her is because they want her money when she dies. Because of that she treats them a certain way. I think for her the Charity Events are entertainment, like a game.

"These aren't just parties or nice quiet family dinners or anything like that, Mr. Quant. Charity Events are grand extravaganzas, sometimes going on for several days, and usually revolving around some kind of theme. I suppose the activities hold interest for Grandmother, but for the most part their goal is to embarrass or make the rest of the family as uncomfortable as possible."

"I see," I said, not wanting to provide any judgement of my own. "Why do they put up with it?"

"I suppose because Grandmother is right. They *do* want to be included on her list of heirs. They *do* want her money. And they're willing to do whatever it takes to get it. It's a weird, twisted, unspoken agreement."

"What kind of activities are we talking about here?" I asked, intrigued and more than a little stupefied. My grandmother was a wizened little woman who handed out onion ring chips, chocolate Wagon Wheels and one-dollar bills (when we still had one-dollar bills) in exchange for hugs and cheek pinches. Come to think of it, she looked a lot like Smeagol in a babushka and shawl.

Flora screwed up her face and rolled her eyes behind her glasses as she recalled past Charity Events. "Let's see, there was the *Star Trek* convention in Las Vegas. And it wasn't sufficient just to be there. You had to come prepared, complete with blue skin and tentacles, or whatever, and attend all the meetings and rallies. A few years ago we spent a long weekend at a nudist beach," and here she grimaced at the memory, "playing sports." I cringed in sympathy. "We've gone whitewater rafting, herded cattle at a dude ranch, learned to drive Formula One race cars."

"That doesn't sound too bad," I observed.

Flora gave me one of those looks as if she were putting up with the naive comments of a little kid who knew nothing. "For some people. But you have to understand, Mr. Quant, most of the family are not what I would call...physically adventurous. They're just not into these kinds of things or aren't physically able to do them. But," she shrugged, "they do. They live from one end of the country to the other, but they all make the trip and take part in whatever it is Grandmother concocts, pretending to enjoy it."

Wow. Charity Wiser must have one very dark sense of humour, I decided. She must, to put her family through a continual circus of events as a means of admission into her will. I was beginning to see why someone might be compelled to put an end to it all. "So somebody is fed up?" I said, hoping to lead Flora into telling me the rest of the story—'cause if she wasn't, I wanted that precious envelope!

Flora Wiser had a habit of quick head bobs whenever she was agreeing with something you'd said, and did it now. "I think so. The last Charity Event was in May, about three months ago and that might have been what finally sent someone over the edge. It was held at the estate in Victoria. Grandmother had the grounds retrofitted to resemble a military boot camp and each of us was expected to spend six hours a day over a four-day long weekend being whipped into shape. She hired a platoon of trainers who put us through gruelling physical training. Nobody enjoyed it, not even the older folks who were given more rest periods.

"Now to be fair, Grandmother was right there with us, sweating and grunting and groaning through it all. The only pleasure was at the end of the day when we'd return to the house. Grandmother had the best chefs and masseurs and relaxation therapists available to cater to our needs. But mostly we were too tired to take advantage of any of it. It was dreadful, truly."

Not my idea of a pleasant time either. "And something happened at the boot camp? Someone made an attempt on your grandmother's life?"

She stared at me for a second or two, as if still shocked at the thought of it, before telling me: "Someone poisoned her tea."

"What happened?"

"I don't really know much about it. You'll have to get the details from Grandmother. All I know is that she thinks someone tried to kill her that weekend, but she can't prove it. That's what she wants you to do."

Very cool, was my first thought. Quickly followed by, how the heck am I gonna do that with my client in Victoria and all the suspects spread throughout Canada? Flora must have read the look on my face and hurried to tell me, "There's another Charity Event planned for next month. Grandmother wants you to attend. She thinks that if she gets the family together again, the killer will make another attempt. Having everyone in one place will make it easier for you to figure out who it is." She did her nodding thing again and added, not very helpfully, "Or something like that."

"But didn't you say these events are usually held every two or three years? If there really is a killer, won't he or she be suspicious of another one so soon?"

"Probably so, except that Grandmother has told everyone that this is a very special Charity Event in honour of her eightieth birthday."

That bit of information took me aback. The woman making her family jump through flaming hoops of fire and play nude volleyball was eighty years old? I couldn't help but give the octogenarian a virtual high-five.

"I think most of the relatives are grumbling about having to put up with another get-together so soon, but they're buying it with the hope that it signals the end. Given Grandmother's age, they're betting she doesn't have many more Charity Events left in her. And besides, none of them would dare turn down an invitation to their meal ticket's eightieth birthday party."

I had to agree. The logic seemed sound, but I was beginning to wonder if the same could be said of Charity Wiser herself. "So where is this party?" I asked, somehow knowing I was going to be surprised by the answer.

"Well, as I said before, Grandmother isn't interested in throwing what you might consider a regular party. She thought it would be a good idea to host this event where you'd have all the family in one confined space."

I was having visions of one of those Agatha Christie TV murder mysteries, prevalent in the 1970s and '80s. The action always took place in a spooky house on a deserted island where all the guests—mostly aged movie stars trying to revive fading careers—arrived on sputtering motorboats with some Crypt Keeper character at the helm who told them he wouldn't be returning for several days...by which time most of them would be dead. Except for the detective. Sounded like a good deal to me. I was in.

"You'd leave in the middle of September," Flora told me.

"Leave?" I asked, trying to blunt my excitement. Oh my gosh, we *were* going to Murder Island!

"That gives you about a month...to do whatever you need to do to prepare and make yourself available for the trip."

"Trip?"

More head bobbing. "The next Charity Event is on a cruise ship. We'll be sailing from Barcelona to Rome. To make it more enticing..." (Like I needed that.) "...Grandmother told me to tell you that you could invite a guest. All the cabins are booked for double occupancy anyway, so you could bring along your wife or whomever you wish."

For a moment I was speechless, not only for the grandness of what was being offered me but, realistically and logistically, I was wondering if I could...and should...accept it. Did I buy Charity

Wiser's contention that her life was in danger? Or was she just some rich wacko looking to add another player to her real-life game of Murder Mystery? And could I get away so easily? It wasn't much notice. For the moment I only nodded.

"Grandmother says you could pose as her business advisor—she'll tell everyone she plans to do some work during the week and that your presence will provide her with a valid reason to write off the trip for tax purposes. Given her reputation for thrift, no one will question it and you'll get a bird's eye view of the family. What do you say, Mr. Quant? Grandmother is holding open two reservations on the ship, so all you need to do is give me your answer and I'll give you this envelope. In it is a retainer cheque and remaining details my grandmother thought might prove helpful."

I eyed the envelope with lust. Suddenly my questions about the validity of the case and my availability to make the trip seemed trivial. I am generally a person with his feet planted firmly in reality, but I do love to dream. I don't believe in the impossible. You never know, do you? That's why I left my stable, dependable career as a cop with the Saskatoon Police Service for a much riskier turn as a small-city private eye. It was my dream, a whole new exciting way to live my life. This case fit my dream perfectly: a swashbuckling adventure on the high seas. It was *Murder on the Orient Express* on water. I'm not convinced my decision would have been different otherwise, but I found myself answering in the affirmative before I'd thought the whole thing through. But really. A free Mediterranean cruise? Come on!

Colourful Mary's is a restaurant-slash-bookstore owned by my friends Mary Quail and Marushka Yabadochka. Its reputation for fabulous food, much of it influenced by the Aboriginal and Ukrainian heritage (respectively) of the couple, far outdistances that of it being the only gay-owned and -run restaurant in Saskatoon.

That spring, Mary had scooped out a portion of the abandoned lot next door to use in an experiment with outdoor dining during the summer months. She pulled together a collection of cheap auction sale doors and windows, set them on their sides to act as a fence to separate the space from the rest of the gravelled area, then filled it with round bistro tables and folding chairs. She set the tables with royal blue linens and purple dinnerware, added some lipstick-red wine goblets and mustard-yellow-handled flatware, hung a few strings of multicoloured bare bulbs in a criss-cross pattern above the dining area, threw in some tattered streamers and a few plastic parrots, and they were ready for business. It vaguely resembled the after-effects of a Mexican fiesta party I'd once attended and was exactly the kind of thing that kept Colourful Mary's one of the city's most unique and popular hangouts.

Except for a cooing twosome a couple of tables away, Errall and I were the only leftovers from the evening's dinner rush. Over the wacky door/window barrier we'd see the occasional passerby heading for a downtown movie theatre, nightclub or late night coffee-and-dessert place and we'd exchange smiles, but other than that we were pretty much alone. Mood music floated above our heads from hidden outdoor speakers; someone had changed it from the spunky dinnertime salsa to something smooth and sensual, not unlike the red wine we were halfway through the second bottle of. It was one of those perfect Saskatchewan summer nights: no wind, no mosquitoes, and hot. The air felt surprisingly moist—given the prairie penchant for dryness—and even at quarter of ten, there was still a sliver of light at the horizon. All this perfection made the evening more languorous and almost heartbreakingly glorious because of the certain knowledge that tonight—or one night very soon—would come the first nip of chill, no stronger than a child's breath, the sure sign of summer's end.

Errall and I regarded each other over a collection of fat candles Mary had come by to light once it began to get dark. In deference to the weather, Errall wore a sleeveless, V-neck white T-shirt, tan shorts and sloppy sandals. With intense facial features and blue eyes to match, Errall is a striking woman. She had recently cut her dark tresses short, to just below her ears where they naturally flipped out in a jagged edge. It was a sportier, casual look for the normally severe-looking barrister. At close to six feet, she is tall and lanky and her smoking habit—reacquired only two years ago

after a five-year hiatus—was undeservedly given credit for keeping her slim. Errall Strane is my lawyer and owns the building,
PWC, that houses my office, which also makes her my landlord.
But our relationship is more complex than that. An apt description
remains elusive. She's argumentative, crass, bossy, opinionated.
She can be manipulative, particularly in business. She can be cold-
hearted. She's a workaholic. She's driven. She'll sometimes say
black, only because I say white. She's smart, sharp, clever and very
honest. She'll always let you know where you stand in her books.
I have seen her be brave, loyal, fiercely protective and empathetic
if not sympathetic. She can be hard. She can be soft…I suspect. If it
wasn't for my high-school chum, Kelly Doell, I don't think our
paths would have ever crossed, or if they had, I doubt we would
have loitered long in each other's company. Kelly and Errall were
a couple—for years.

Now Kelly was gone.

In February, after a year of turmoil following Kelly's diagnosis
with cancer and resultant loss of a breast, the eight-year relationship had ended. Kelly had become a different person, a person
who couldn't be in a relationship, at least, not a relationship that
also included Errall. The storm of it all only ended when Kelly
suddenly and unexpectedly packed her belongings and moved to
Toronto, rarely to be heard from since, by any of us. Not only was
the relationship over, but so, it seemed, were her other friendships,
including the one with me.

So Errall was undeniably the person I knew who was most in
need of a getaway. But, obvious as it might seem, she was not my
first choice for companionship on the Charity Event Mediterranean cruise. The friendship had existed between Kelly and me,
not Errall and me. Errall was not a friend, she was someone who
slept with a friend. Yet, here we were, part of each other's lives,
with no Kelly in sight.

Even so, and shame on me I suppose, I first asked my neighbour Sereena and then friends Anthony and Jared to join me. But
as it turned out, they were already planning to be away in
September. Then there was my mother, but I was hoping she'd
agree to look after my animals and house while I was gone. And

there were other possible choices too, but by the time my finger was moving farther down the list of potential pleasant and fun travelling companions, another thought began to fester... er...develop in my mind: Perhaps Errall *was* a friend, just on her own, without Kelly. I wasn't ready to conclude that I actually enjoyed her company, but I did know that our times together were often invigorating. Fun? I don't know about that. But given current circumstances, she did need to be on this boat. She had a wound and I had the salve.

"I'm going to do it." She spoke after several moments of careful contemplation. "I'll have to reschedule my root canal with John MacPherson—as if that's not reason enough to leave the country—and check with Sheila to see if she can look after my clients while I'm gone...but Russell, I really think I'm going to do this thing. It's crazy. You and me on a cruise? It's nuts. But God, do I need it."

"The cruise is only a week," I encouraged her further. "You won't be gone that long. And after we get off the boat, Anthony and Jared have invited us to their house in Tuscany before we go home. It'll be perfect. And yeah, you need this."

"Okay, quick, before I change my mind, give me all the details. Spain to Italy, right?"

I pulled out the itinerary Charity Wiser had included in her package and handed it over to Errall. "We set sail from Barcelona then do the Balearic Islands, Tunis..."

"Tunis!" she came as close to squealing as someone like Errall can, eyes fully ablaze. "Africa!" Then she went into her best Meryl Streep-Danish-*Out of Africa* accent, "I hahd a fahrm in Ah-fri-cah." She looked to me for applause. Got none. "That's Northern Africa, right?" she asked in her regular voice.

"Uh, yeah," I said, quickly flipping through some tour brochures to check. "It's the capital of Tunisia. Then we do Sicily and finally up the coast of mainland Italy to..." More checking. "...Civitavecchia," I said, outrageously slaughtering the pronunciation of the town's name with something like Cityvicky-ah.

"Huh?"

"Well," I responded, sounding much more knowledgeable than I really was, compliments of the bottle of shiraz in my belly,

"Rome isn't a coastal city. The closest port is this Silly-victor-victoria place." I checked the brochure. "It says here Rome is about a ninety-minute taxi ride from Silly-oh-toe-sis."

"I bet that'll cost a few Euros," she said, wisely paying no heed to my silliness. "And where exactly are Anthony and Jared staying?"

"Tuscany, the opposite direction. But they tell me they're just a few hours from Stichy-Vichy-ah, near a town called Castellina in Chianti." Finally, a name I could pronounce. And how civilized of those Europeans, naming towns after wine.

"Russell," Errall said, her nose deep into the pages of our itinerary. "You didn't tell me we're sailing on the FOD Cruiseline."

I looked up from where I was straining in the dim lighting to find Castellina in Chianti on a map of Italy I'd now unfolded and held over our table—so close to the candles I worried it might catch fire. "Yeah. Ever hear of it? Is it kind of like Carnival or Holland America?" I asked, not adding my real question: "Or Titanic?"

Although I'd told no one, not only had I never been on a cruise before but I'd rarely set foot on a boat, big or small, of any kind—on purpose. Truth told, I was a trifle nervous at the thought of getting on this vessel. I was game of course, but nervous nonetheless, and desperate for as much assurance of safety as I could get. I'm a true prairie boy. If I'm going to be surrounded by something endless and flat and blue, I expect it to be a field of blooming flax.

"Have you been living under a rock?" Errall looked at me with an unattractive curl in her lip. "What kind of gay person are you? It's FOD! It stands for the Friends of Dorothy Cruiseline. It's right up there with the Radisson or Silversea cruiselines. Not only does it cater primarily to a gay clientele but it is top-of-the-line, luxury plus. They win all sorts of awards in the small, luxury ship category."

Small! Whaddaya mean small? How small? That's a friggin' big sea! "What do you mean small?" I asked calmly.

"Well, I think they only have two ships: The Dorothy holds maybe three-hundred-and-fifty passengers…"

I could feel my skin shift. "How many does the big ship hold?"

"That is the big ship."

Oh shit.

"The other one is just a schooner. I think it holds a hundred, hundred-fifteen at most."

Gulp. "Which one does it say we're on?"

Errall checked the papers in front of her. "The Dorothy. Too bad, eh? Wouldn't it have been a blast to be on a schooner, really feel the waves crashing under you?"

"Yeah, really." Yeah, Yody ho hum, and a bottle of rum, or whatever that pirate song says. I wondered if they had a song about gin. Sheesh. Three-fifty, huh? "How do you know all this?"

"Kelly and I looked into a cruise last year." She stopped there and pretended to suddenly be entranced by something on the itinerary. We didn't talk about Kelly much anymore.

I replenished our wine and used the momentary dearth of conversation to reflect on what I'd just learned. Charity Wiser was sending her family on a gay cruise. What a pip! Suddenly it became clear to me why she'd obviously gone to some trouble to track me down and hire me. It wasn't because I'm a particularly skillful detective. Humphf!

It's because I'm a particularly gay detective.

Chapter 2

To the movers and shakers in the meat-processing industry, Wiser Meats was a golden empire under the sole helmsmanship of Abner Wiser. To the privileged members of Alberta's high society—a rarefied group to which the Wiser clan belonged—Abner Wiser was considered a successful, self-made man. He'd come from nothing to provide handsomely for his family of four, all women, including wife Glorie and three daughters, Faith, Hope and the youngest, Charity. In reality he was an abysmal businessman. The bankers and advisors in Abner's inner circle knew that his greatest talent was in presenting to the world an appearance of success, not its actual achievement.

On a day-to-day basis, the fortunes of Wiser Meats rose and fell as surely as an ocean's tide. As much as came in, went out. Not that Glorie, or any of the Wiser daughters, had any idea of this. Abner provided them with everything they could want, at great cost. The price was a thriving business and ulcers for all involved in its faltering fortunes. Abner's managers and accountants were somehow able to funnel just enough funds from each year's meagre profits to make the business appear to be a Fortune 500-going concern when foreclosure and bankruptcy were often only a hambone away.

Charity was the only Wiser daughter to show any interest or aptitude in following Abner Wiser in the family business. As she worked her way up, she was kept oblivious to the true state of the business' woeful financial affairs. Abner, rather foolishly, thought things would go on forever just as they were. But that, of course, was impossible.

When Abner and Glorie passed on—within months of one another as sometimes happens with long-loving couples—it seemed only natural that Charity, showing little desire for either a husband or children, would inherit the reins of the business while her two sisters made do with hefty cash settlements in lieu. For Faith and Hope it was the beginning of luxury, but for Charity it was the beginning of a nightmare.

It didn't take long before the full impact of her father's inability to run a business came to the forefront with only her left behind to pay the piper, including her sister's inheritances, out of coffers that were echoingly empty. But Charity rebounded from the shock with a raging strength and determination far outstretching anything her father had ever displayed, demonstrating to both the bankers and herself, exactly what she was made of. Instead of fleeing what at first glance appeared to be a hopeless situation, she instead dug in her heels. Through a series of smart business alliances and acquisitions, funded only by her father's name (the only thing of value, albeit questionable, left her), she turned Wiser Meats around in under eighteen months, making it into as successful a venture as her father always boasted it to be.

In time, Charity paid off all debts and bought back all the shares she'd been forced to sell in order to finance the restructuring, and she herself became a multimillionaire. Many falsely believed Charity's success was at the expense of her sisters. For Faith and Hope received, by comparison with Charity's eventual riches, a paltry sum from a supposedly vast family fortune. Only a handful of people knew the personal sacrifices she'd had to make, particularly to write each of those cheques that provided quite handsomely for her sisters, at the same time leaving only scraps for herself. But Charity Wiser kept her secrets, in order to preserve her father's reputation and build her own.

It was about then that my reading was rudely disrupted by a neighbour's cat that had leapt up from some crafty hiding spot beneath my hammock, landing heavily on my bare tummy and sending the papers I'd pulled from Charity Wiser's manila envelope fluttering to the ground.

I let out an "oof" and remonstrated with the feline, using a few well-chosen and colourful words that meant little to her but made me feel much better. She buried her fat, flat face into my ear, sharing a spitting kind of purr while painfully kneading my shoulder for a count of six and then, in a flurry, was gone. I sat up in the hammock and glanced down at Barbra and Brutus, my much better-behaved schnauzers. They regarded me with looks that said, "You didn't expect *us* to do anything about her, did you?" then resumed their late afternoon naps in the shade of a nearby White Fir.

Barbra and Brutus are sister and brother. Originally Brutus lived with Errall and Kelly…until things got rough for them. Brutus came to live with us until the situation improved. But that never happened and Brutus never went back. And now, he's part of my home as if he'd always been there and Barbra is happier for it. So am I.

My backyard is a wonderful never-never land of lovingly planted flora, well-placed clay pots, metalwork benches, fountains, birdbaths and trellises, and stone-laid pathways that lead into leafy enclaves hidden throughout the expanse. It's surrounded by a six-foot-high fence that keeps me and Barbra and Brutus in, and others out—except that cat.

Weather precludes Saskatchewanians from enjoying their backyards and gardens for any extended period of time, so when it's summer and the sun is shining, outside is the place to be. I love everything about my yard, from weeding the flowerbeds to trimming hedges to barbecues on the deck to snoozing in the sun. I love the sound of buzzing bees, flittering birds and rustling leaves by day and cricket songs by night. I love the smell of freshly cut grass and planter tubs full of geraniums. Having a good backyard is akin to expanding your home's square footage by several hundred square feet for a few months every year.

Rolling myself off the hammock, I adjusted my threadbare cotton shorts, slipped my bare feet into a waiting pair of flip-flops and collected the papers the cat had sent to the ground, piling them on a table I'd pulled up next to the hammock. I went inside to refill my glass of lemonade and was back in place in less than a minute, rearranging the essay Charity Wiser had prepared for me, the story of her family's past and present. The pages were handwritten in a strong, steady script. Surprising, given the author was nearly fourscore and a successful modern-day businessperson. I'd expected she'd be well-versed with the capabilities of a computer or, more likely, a Dictaphone along with a handy secretary for transcription. But then again, as I was getting to know Charity Wiser through the words she'd put to paper, perhaps the how of it was *just* the thing she'd do, as much a part of her larger-than-life character as anything else. The first letter of every sentence was an exaggerated capital, dramatic-looking with its ends sweeping far above and below the line; the letters that followed were smaller, precise and neat, portraying a certain pugnaciousness I was almost certain I'd find in the woman I had yet to meet.

It was a rather detailed account, warts and all—or at least warts according to Charity Wiser. She'd correctly assumed I'd need as much detail as possible if I was to find out which member of her family was looking to end her life. It was a fascinating read, of epic novel proportions replete with great loves and losses, business successes and failures, tragedies and triumphs, friends and enemies. Danielle Steel would be proud. The more I read, the more I looked forward to meeting the author. Who was this woman who'd morphed from a spoiled daddy's girl into a powerful and savvy businesswoman? How did she become the woman she was today: rich, successful, reclusive, and bordering on abusive towards her family?

Soon after Charity Wiser had established herself as the power-house owner and manager of Wiser Meats, she gave birth to her only child, John. John's father was never named and I surmised that Charity had not been married to him. In due time John left home, married a woman named Virginia and together they had Flora. As Flora had already told me, John and Virginia had been killed in a car accident when Flora was fourteen and she was there-after raised by Charity and a woman named Dottie Blocka, Charity's housekeeper. Flora, now twenty-two, stayed at the estate in Victoria until, as a young woman, she moved to Regina to take a job with Ducks Unlimited.

The balance of the Wiser family consisted of the progeny of Charity's two sisters. The eldest sister, Faith, joined a convent as a young girl where she remained until she met, fell in love with, left the church for and married a priest, Father Thomas Kincaid. Although both were nearing forty at the time, the two were desirous of a family and quickly had two children. The first born, Marsha, is forty-four, and married to Ted Moshier. Marsha and Ted have twin boys, Nigel and Nathan, twenty, and a girl, Kayla, seventeen. Faith's second child is Nick Kincaid, now thirty-seven and single.

As two middle-aged, disgraced soldiers of God, Faith and Thomas had difficult times finding new careers, spending more time searching for gainful employment than being employed. So, in supporting their new family they worked through Faith's inheritance pretty quickly. Yet, although now poorer than church mice, pun intended, by all accounts they were deliriously happy and never for a day regretted their choice.

I was about to learn about the other sister, Hope, when the portable phone rang. It was a voice from the past.

"I thought I'd call and save you the postage on the thank-you note you're going to send me," she started off.

Grrr. The first time I met Jane Cross she'd attacked me from behind and did her best to grind my face into the carpet of a New York City hotel room. She's a fellow detective who lives and works in Regina. Short, squat, cute, likes to swear and wrassle, physically and verbally. Spitfire comes to mind when I think of her—which I prefer not to do. "Why would I ever send you a note, least of all to say thank you? For what?" I took a sip of my lemonade which had suddenly turned sour.

"For getting your sorry ass out of the unemployment line. I assume Flora Wiser has been to see you?"

I pulled myself into a more erect position in the hammock, causing Barbra and Brutus to each open an eye to check out the possibility of a treat being tossed their way. Was this why Flora drove all the way from Regina to hire me? On the recommendation of Jane Cross? "What do you know about it?" I asked, my suspicious gene on full alert.

"You were second choice, bub. Always the bridesmaid, never the bride. Runner up to lil ol' me. You see, bub, Miss Wiser visited me *first* last week."

What was this? And I hate being called bub. "You obviously want to tell me something, Jane, so just spill it." The sun moved behind a cloud throwing the yard into shadow. Was it getting chilly out?

"I just wanted to make it clear that you owe me one. So there'd be no confusion when in the future I call on you for a favour...although I can't imagine why *I'd* ever need *your* help." Smarmy voice.

"Flora Wiser tried to hire you last week?"

"Yessiree. But I was unable to fit the job into my schedule. Very busy y'know."

"I'm sure, what with all the attacking of innocent hotel guests you have to do every day." Smarmy right back.

There was silence while she conjured up a profanity appropriate for the occasion. But I got the jump on her. "Are you saying that after you turned down the job, you, of your own free will, suggested me?"

She cleared her throat and admitted, "Well, not quite. A couple of hours after Flora left my office I got a call directly from Charity Wiser. She'd heard about my meeting with her granddaughter and decided a personal call was in order. She had specific needs and hoped I could help."

Given my past history with Jane Cross, I was beginning to suspect a practical joke at work, but something about her voice kept me from hanging up—for now. "Needs? What does that mean? Do you know Charity Wiser personally?"

"Nooooo," she said unconvincingly. "Not really. But apparently she knows of me through some acquaintances in common who live on the coast. Acquaintances who knew to refer Charity to me when she was looking for a detective who lives in Regina and...who's gay."

I do not recommend snorting lemonade through one's nose, but that was pretty much what I did at that point. That scamp! Jane Cross—a lesbian. I just knew it! Well, I didn't really, but I pretended that I did. I am a detective after all. I'm supposed to detect such things about people. "Oh," was all I said, the model of restraint.

"Charity called hoping to convince me to take the job," she said, admirably ignoring the sputtering sounds I was making over the phone. "I had to turn her down...very busy y'know..." Yeah, yeah, yeah, I get it; you're a busy and successful private eye, busier and more successful than me. Gotya. "...but I promised to do some research for her to see if I could come up with any other gay detectives in the area. And guess fucking what?" The beginning of a mocking tone. "Guess who I found! You priss!" And she laughed; no...it was more of a cackle.

I joined in—for a second.

But, ha ha ha, solidarity, brother/sister stuff to the side, although I do find Cross' bilious sense of humour entertaining at times, I wasn't in the mood to talk personal stuff with her. Back to business. "Okay, I've already figured out that we're going on a gay cruise, which I guess is par for Charity's course of coming up with embarrassing things to put her family through, but why a gay detective and why from Saskatchewan?" I asked.

"Lotsa reasons. First of all, she wants the detective to be gay so she or he isn't distracted by being on a gay cruise. She wants someone who can remain focused on the job. I guess she thought it'd be easier to find a gay detective than a straight one who wasn't a homophobe. Now I imagine her preference was a lesbian, but I assured her you weren't the kind of gay man who'd be sashaying up and down the decks in Lycra short-shorts and a feather boa looking for a good time. Right? You better back me up on this, Quant, and keep your pecker tethered."

I ignored that. Nothing wrong with feather boas. "What else?"

"The only relative she trusts is the granddaughter she raised, Flora. Since Flora lives here in Regina, Charity wanted someone Flora could easily contact. Also, the Wisers are pretty well connected in Alberta and British Columbia, so it's probably a good idea for the detective—who'd have to be undercover—to be from somewhere else."

"I guess that all makes sense." But since it's in my character to be suspicious of everyone at the beginning of a case, I asked, "Why does Charity Wiser trust her granddaughter?"

She made an "mmm" sound as if she'd thought about that too. "Well, aside from the fact that Charity raised Flora since she was a teenager—so they're like mother and daughter—this is all about money."

"So? Flora could want her grandmother's money as much as anyone else."

"True. But last year when Flora turned twenty-one, she received one million dollars from the Wiser estate. So, in a way, Flora already has a big heap of her inheritance money. She doesn't have to whack her grandmother to get it."

"That's a nice birthday present."

"Uh-huh. And…just between you and me and the fence post…I did a bit of research and guess what? There's one more reason she'd prefer a gay detective."

She stopped there, wanting me to beg for it.

I waited her out, sipping on my sour lemonade in the cooling shade created by a bank of slowly moving clouds—all, I firmly believed, somehow caused by Jane Cross.

Finally she harrumphed and added, "Apparently Charity Wiser has lived with the same woman for the past forty years."

"Dottie Blocka," I said as if I'd scored a point. "Sheesh. You gals think every woman is a lesbian. Dottie Blocka is Charity's housekeeper."

"Oh really? A housekeeper, huh? Dottie Blocka is eighty-eight years old, bub. And, Mr. Know-it-all, Charity Wiser has employed a woman named Gladys Kazindale as her housekeeper for the past twelve years, Darlene Compton for the six years prior to that and Cecilia Broughton before that."

"Oh."

"Bub, anytime you want a lesson on how a real detective does her job, you just call on me."

Oooo this woman makes me steam. "I'm interested, Jane, why did you really turn this down? It's a pretty plum job, you have to admit. Sun, water, sand, murder...all the good things."

"Sure, if you're into fruity drinks, comparing tan lines and waist lines and wearing as little as possible. You see, we women-types are a much more serious lot. Sparkly, shiny things do not easily distract us. We're into deeper stuff."

Bullshit. "I know for a fact lesbians can float just as well as gay guys."

She hesitated for just a second, but long enough for me to know she was about to lie to me. "Like I said, Quant, busy here, long roster of clients who need my expert services."

Aha! "You're scared of water!" As soon as I said it I knew I was right. "You're scared to get on that boat!"

"They're referred to as ships, you dunce."

Na na na na boo boo. She wasn't denying it. I was right and loving it. But God help me if she ever found out I was concerned about the whole big-piece-of-iron-floating-on-water thing myself. "I think you'd look cute in one of those inner tube things, y'know, the kind with a little duck's head at the front..."

Disconnect.

I went back to my reading.

I had to remind myself where I was in my study of the extensive Wiser dynasty. There were three sisters, Faith, Hope and Charity. Charity is my client with the longtime female companion, Dottie (read lesbian lover), with whom she raised granddaughter Flora. Sister Faith is the errant nun with two full-grown children of her own which she had with errant priest, Thomas Kincaid. Now it was Hope's turn, the middle Wiser sister.

According to Charity's tome, sister Hope married a man named James McNichol. It was a joyful union while it lasted but, in the end, begot a tragic legacy. A legacy that seems prepared to perpetuate itself indefinitely. It began when Hope gave birth to a daughter, Helen. Up to then James and Hope, with the help of the Wiser money Hope received from Charity, had had a fun and lively marriage, full of laughter and adventure, but sadly short on time. Three days after Helen's birth, suffering from complications, Hope suddenly and unexpectedly died. James, a successful salesman, was a jovial, handsome and athletic man and although nearly inconsolable over the loss of his young wife, gladly raised his daughter alone with little outside help.

Helen grew up to be a quiet girl, slight and pretty. She knew nothing of her mother but cherished her father. She stayed with James in the family home until she met and married Patrick Halburton, a stolid young man training to become a police officer. Nine months into the marriage, Helen died during the birth of their daughter. Unlike his father-in-law, Patrick felt wholly unprepared to handle a baby. He moved in with his widowed mother, named the child Hyacinth after her, and left most of the parental duties with her. Patrick was grief-stricken by his wife's early demise and never fully recovered. He was mentally and physically unfit to continue in the police academy and eventually found a job as a security guard on a university campus—a position he would keep for the rest of his working life, happiest within the predictable confines of routine.

Hyacinth was nothing like her mother...or her father. She was hefty and healthy and most decidedly vigorous. A tomboy as a girl, reckless and mischievous as a teenager, and sultry as a young woman, Hyacinth loved her paternal grandmother and father dearly but was desperate to escape the stifling confines of their tiny home. She eventually met an equally free-spirited mate, Jackson Delmonico, an aspiring jazz and blues musician. She found herself pregnant long before she wanted to be. Although Hyacinth had never met her mother or maternal grandmother, she knew that they'd both died in childbirth but suspected that, unlike her big-boned, wide-hipped self, they were probably weak and fragile. She was confident she could give birth to her baby in between Jackson's sets and would barely need a sip of water to do it. So they got married and continued with their tempestuous, bohemian lifestyle. Except for Hyacinth's expanding girth they mostly forgot about the baby until the day it arrived. They were happy. They were carefree. They were wrong.

Hyacinth Delmonico died giving birth to a daughter, Harriet.

At first everyone, Jackson included, assumed he'd give the baby to someone else to raise, maybe even give it up for adoption. But as soon as he laid eyes upon her, he became a proud daddy who wasn't about to let anybody take away his baby girl with the beautiful cinnamon skin that blended his dark with her mother's light. This didn't stop him from pursuing his musician's life; it simply meant that baby Harriet was now part of the entourage, moving from city to city, missing school, more often in the company of adults and drugs and alcohol than children and toys and candy.

The Wiser curse, as some referred to it, had left in its horrible wake a family of men—none related by blood, James, Patrick and Jackson, each with a doomed wife and daughter—and one female, Harriet, affectionately known as Harry.

On that sad note I closed the book on the Wiser family history. I'd had enough. I'd wait until I met the real people aboard The Dorothy. Until then I'd plan, pack and lose a pound or two. Now, where did I put my ruby red slippers?

An unexpected heat wave engulfed the city the day Errall and I left Saskatoon. It was Tuesday, September fourteenth. At not yet noon, the on-the-street temperature had risen to just shy of forty degrees Celsius and people were digging out shorts and tank tops they'd already mothballed for the season. It amazes me how a superbly clear blue sky, such as we had that day, can provide a less stable flying environment—especially for the zippy, jazzy but small propeller planes used for many of the short-haul flights out of Saskatoon—than say, full-on winter blizzard conditions. It has something to do with air currents, highs meeting lows, warm meeting cold. But we were lucky that day and enjoyed a bump-free ride.

We connected through Calgary to Vancouver where we spent a pleasant and thankfully rain-free afternoon and evening shopping on Robson and Davie streets. We imbibed and ingested at Delilah's—a favourite of mine with its plush red banquettes, soft rose lighting, hand-painted ceilings, eclectic mood music and sassy martini menu—and ended the night in the cozy comfort of the Pacific Palisades hotel. The next day we did the fresh-seafood-starved, prairie landlubber migration to a ridiculously cheap sushi joint I know of and fell upon the tasty fare like gophers on oats. Having eaten our fill, we headed to the airport in plenty of time to catch our 4 p.m. Lufthansa flight. Eight-and-a-half hours later, we arrived at 10:30 a.m. Thursday morning (1:30 a.m. Saskatchewan time) in Frankfurt, Germany. After a short layover we hopped a ninety-minute flight to Barcelona. *Ola* Spain.

By the time we dumped ourselves into a taxicab headed for the AC Diplomatic Hotel in downtown Barcelona, we were rags. I thought it a particularly good sign that neither of us, so far, had killed the other, nor even made an attempt. Errall, as am I, is a logical, matter-of-fact traveller. She calmly accepts the numerous delays and personal indecencies regularly visited upon travellers as an unavoidable consequence of peregrination. Travelling the world is a big deal and should be respected. To get the goods, sometimes you gotta put up with the crap. Now it was time for some of the goods. We tried hard to play the worldly wayfarers, but couldn't help gawking at the scenes passing by the windows of our cab.

Every so often the reality of our good fortune overtook us and we giggled like schoolgirls. I am a self-admitted simpleton when it comes to knowledge of great art and architecture, but that could not dull my awe at the sight of the massive bell towers of the Temple de la Sagrada Familia and other masterpiece buildings that highlighted our route, many the inspired creations of Antoni Gaudí, a name even I had heard of. We'd only be in Barcelona for a day and I became overwhelmed by the realization that there was too much to see. I glanced at Errall and could see her eyes doing the same wild dance as mine, feasting on buildings, people, cafés, shops, fashion, markets, statues…oh my. I knew that in the time we did have, we'd have to try our best to avoid a common downfall of tourists in this situation: trying to see too much, you end up spinning in circles and seeing nothing at all.

The AC Diplomatic Hotel is a fairly unremarkable eleven-storey structure on the corner of Pau Claris and Consell de Cent in the L'Eixample district. Often with European buildings, exteriors and interiors don't match; sometimes they are centuries apart in age and appearance. And this was certainly the case here. The AC is an ultra-modern, style-and-service kind of place with minimalist furniture and décor and cleverly arranged seating areas in the lobby for those who want to be seen and those who don't. Outside the glass-fronted foyer is the typical hectic, dusty, noisy European street corner, yet inside is all peace, beauty and harmony: fresh-scented air, the babble of trickling water, elaborately displayed works of art. Tucked into a discreet corner of the lobby is an inviting lounge of alternating dark and light woods with low-slung, high-back armchairs in matching browns, the perfect respite from a busy world—all quite lovely.

Since we knew we'd have to get used to sharing even smaller quarters on the ship, Errall and I had booked ourselves into one room. Just as hip as the lobby, our suite was very small and equipped with Japanese-style closets with sliding doors. With enough luggage to see us well togged from the Mediterranean to Tuscany, one of us a gay man, the other a stylish woman, we were hopelessly short of space with only our toiletry kits unpacked. On the brighter side, on a gilt-edged writing table squeezed into one corner of the room was an elaborately wrapped basket filled with goodies: chocolate, a bottle of wine, crumbly cookies and paper-thin wafers, jams and crackers, along with maps of the area and a picture book of Barcelona. Feeling a bit peckish, we demolished a few cookies and read the accompanying note:

Russell and Errall,
Barcelona welcomes you. Meet us at 7 at Mikel Etxea for tapas on the Ramblas.
C & D

We looked at each other and blinked, and then studied the words on the note more closely. Mikel Etxea? Tapas? Ramblas? We scurried to unearth our Spanish to English dictionary from our mountain of luggage.

A good concierge is a hotel guest's best friend. And it was our new best friend, Juan Antonio, who helpfully translated Charity Wiser's note and drew us a map for how best to get to where we were going. In Canadian jargon, Charity had invited us for snacks at a restaurant named Mikel Etxea on a street called Las Ramblas. Carelessly ignorant of what we were getting ourselves into, Errall and I, freshened up and wearing the first of our "We have fashion in Canada too" outfits, strolled out the AC's front doors, into the lovely twenty-degree plus weather, with style, panache and about as much smarts as Lucy Ricardo and Ethel Mertz.

We found our way easily enough to a street called Passeig de Gràcia. Juan Antonio told us this was the Eixample's main avenue, home to charming Modernista buildings, stylish shops and graceful street lamps created by some guy named Pere Falqués. Okey dokey. What he failed to mention were the throngs of people. If I didn't know better, I'd swear all of them were scrambling to get away from some Catalonian version of King Kong...with Errall and me the only ones heading in the wrong direction.

Fortunately we only had four blocks of battling our way against the tide before we came upon Fontanella, the cross street to Plaça de Catalunya, a large plaza area that is reputedly the centre of life in Barcelona. Here we found more street lamps, statues, fountains, pigeons galore and, best of all, some much-needed personal space. You never know how much you miss it until it's gone. And there, like astronauts who've just realized, "Hey, those NASA guys weren't kidding—we really are on the moon!" we came face-to-face with the most famous of all streets in Spain: Las Ramblas. From our vantage point on Plaça de Catalunya, the street seemed to go on forever; and it pretty much does, only coming to an end dozens of blocks away at the toes of Christopher Columbus where his massive statue towers above Port Vell and the sparkling Mediterranean.

Although just as busy as Passeig de Gràcia, there was something distinctly different about Las Ramblas. Instead of the whirlwind atmosphere, here the wide, tree-shaded central walkway seemed home to a more elegant, old world type of living, still active but appreciably more sedate and genteel. There was certainly much hustling and bustling, selling and buying, hawking and gawking but, unlike Passeig de Gràcia where commerce and trade look just as they do in any other big city, Las Ramblas is truly a Spanish original. For many moments we held our spot, resisting the urge to jump into the melee, to be a part of the picture postcard. We hesitated, not wanting to lose that first delicious moment, beholding from our relatively peaceful perch next to the Fountain of Canaletes, one of the most beautiful and oldest great streets of the world. It was a picture I stored in my mind, knowing that, even years later, whenever I heard someone talking about Spain, this would be the scene I'd recall.

But eventually we could stand it no longer. Each taking a deep breath, we stepped away from our place by the nineteenth-century fountain and joined the horde. As we strolled down the canvas-ready corridor in search of Mikel Etxea, we passed by bustling shops and cafés, hotels and food markets, honest-to-goodness palaces, sloppy but sturdy newsstands, and collections of vendor stalls selling everything from caged birds to books and fresh-cut flowers. There were tarot card readers, musicians and the most accomplished mime artists I had ever seen. A tender, warm breeze floated through Las Ramblas that day carrying with it a pleasant old-world odour, a smell that mingled the scent of ancient buildings, fermented fruit and the sea. We moved sluggishly as if drugged by our intoxicating surroundings, taking in the exotic sights and sounds until, at last, the spell was broken when I heard someone calling my name. "Russell Quant!" the voice trumpeted. I turned in its direction and Ohmygawdit'sKatharineHepburn!

Well, Katharine Hepburn fifteen years ago.

A lithe creature, all angles and bristling intensity, was calling out to me from beneath a once-white umbrella made dirty by pollution and time. She was perched on a carmine-cushioned metal chair, one long, trouser-clad leg crossed over the other (ankle on knee, not knee on knee). Her hair, a bundle of washed out sunshine, was pulled back into an odd doughnut-like shape, which, along with the upturned collar of her starched, white, man's shirt, is what first made me think Kate was alive and well and living in Barcelona. She was tanned a healthy-looking light caramel with an abundance of freckles dotting the bridge of her thin nose. Her skin was pulled tight on her face, not from a surgeon's scalpel, but rather because it had no choice, what with the patrician nose, sharp cheek bones and razor-edged chin. Her eyes were pale green beneath pale lashes that matched her hair. Although she'd called out my name in its entirety, I doubted this woman, obviously a doyenne of the world, could truly be seeking me out. There had to be another Russell Quant nearby, some sophisticated esquire who would surely be a better match for this fascinating creature. But then I saw next to her someone I recognized, beneath a floppy, fabric hat, a colourless, faded replica. Flora Wiser.

Errall followed me hesitantly towards the table where these two, plus one more woman, had set up temporary camp at the outdoor pavilion of Mikel Etxea.

"And what of my Flora? Isn't she marvellous? Isn't she a lovely?" Katharine Hepburn demanded to know, exclamation mark, question mark, exclamation mark. Without allowing me opportunity to answer, she threw out a hand, as brown and freckled as her face and proceeded to introduce herself...and us. "I'm Charity Wiser. You're Russell Quant, my sleuth, and Errall Strane, the severe, intelligent and I see, very beautiful, legal eagle. You of course know my most wonderful granddaughter, Flora and next to her..." and here she extended a hand to the plump cheek of an aged, square of a woman with thinning beige hair and a pile of knitting resting on her doughy lap, "...is the most desirable of all, my Ms. Dottie Blocka!"

I truly felt, as did several nearby tables, as if I should applaud. And nearly did. The one thing I knew right off about my new client was that she was all about the performance.

"Sit, sit, sit, oh my goodness, you must sit! Jose, my darling, another chair!" she called out into the cosmos. And the cosmos complied. Once we were settled around the table, Charity clasped the handle of a plastic pitcher that was sitting there and raised it into the air as though it were the little lion at the end of *The Lion King*, and called once more upon Jose, who appeared as if out of nowhere. "Another pitcher of sangria, you wonderful boy, but none of that piss you serve the regular customers! I don't want a litre of cheap red wine mixed with sugar. I want the good stuff, with brandy and a splash of Amaretto! And light on the soda water. Pour favour."

Flora leaned over and attempted to correct her grandmother's pronunciation. For her efforts she received the most loving gaze a heifer ever gave her freshly born calf (despite what was about to come out of her mouth). "Oh my good Lord, you are a lovely! You know absolutely everything! Everything! From now on, you will order! Oh my dear, I feel the weight lifting from my scrawny boned shoulders already."

Ouch, I thought to myself. That was a backhanded compliment that had to smart a bit. But instead, Flora smiled indulgently at her grandmother before allowing her gaze to drift aimlessly into the pother of the street. I turned to look at Charity and found that her blazing eyes had fallen upon me like a sledgehammer on an anvil. The time had arrived for me to audition for a part in the movie that is her life. I was gratuitously relieved, however, from making my debut when a frumpy character, somewhere in her forties and sitting at the table next to ours, laid a hand on Charity's forearm.

She said in a lilting English accent, "I couldn't help but overhearing, dear, but is there something wrong with *our* sangria?" She gesticulated toward the pitcher on her table as if there could be some doubt as to exactly which sangria she was referring.

Charity turned on her like a kindly mongoose on prey, then ever so briefly on the prey's companion, a husband likely, a chunky, silent sort of bloke given to inane grins. She addressed the woman, "Oh you fabulous you, wherever did you get that bonnet?"

After swallowing a perplexed frown and fingering an unfortunate piece of tartan on her head that looked a bit like a beret with wings she replied, "Devon, we're from Devon."

"Of course you are. My, I love Devonshire, and the creeeeeeeeeeeeeammmmm. Jose, more of the same sangria for my friends Gwendolyn and Fred!"

"Actually it's Sharon. Sharon and Pete," the woman stammered, now totally confused.

"Of course it is, *dearie*," Charity proclaimed, already giving them her back, bored of her Devonshire creams. "Russell, you'll order for us of course. I wouldn't have an idea what to ask for. Well, except for the jamón serrano and the gambas a la plancha. And we must have some pollo al ajillo. And I love the banderillas, don't you? And maybe some of those chorizo sausage things with a bit of toast? Errall, what of the albondigas? Love them? Hate them? Oh Juan, where is Juan when you need him? But really, Russell, go ahead. Anything will be fine. Anything."

Errall and I were each handed a laminated one-page tapas menu. It was a dizzying array and I finally concluded on the best thing to order. "Perhaps one of everything?"

"You are a genius of simplicity," Charity announced to those who cared. "And I can only add..." And here she studied the menu as if it were a priceless piece of art. "Oh, let's throw caution to the wind and have two of everything. Juan, please...?"

The server appeared with our doctored pitcher of sangria, another for our bewildered neighbours and a pleasant smile. "Two of all, Madame?" he confirmed.

"You lovely," she said to him, placing a smile back on him. "Yes, indeed, two of all."

"I'm so glad to meet you," I said, trying to bring this conversation...meeting...happening...whatever it was, under some control.

"Do you know tapas, Mr. Quant?" Charity asked me with a look on her face that warned me I was about to be tested.

Although I sometimes love making stuff up when I don't know an answer, just for fun, my senses told me this wasn't the way to go with Charity Wiser. "No," I admitted.

"They're sometimes called pinchos," she told the assembled group and about six or seven eavesdroppers. "They originated in Andalusia in the nineteenth century to accompany sherry...ah, exhilarating Andalusia, how I miss it...anyhow, it all began with the lowly bartender, one of the most underrated professions of all, don't you agree?" No waiting for an answer. "You see, the

Andalusian bartenders would ply their trade in these flea-infested Andalusian villages as best they could, serving drinks, sherry, Cosmopolitans and dark beers mostly, I think. But these damnable flies kept getting into the drinks. Probably all the sugar in the sherry, don't you think? Anyway, what to do? Well don't you know, those clever bartenders began to cover the glasses with a saucer or small plate...also known as...a tapa...to keep out the flies! Well, eventually the custom progressed to where the kind-hearted barkeeps would place chunks of Gamonedo cheese, or maybe a nice blue, I don't know for sure, perhaps a few olives—black to be sure, with the pit—on the tapa to accompany the drink. And these bits of food became known as tapas. In those days the tapas were free, but now of course we're charged outrageous fees...for keeping *their* flies out of *our* drinks!"

Everyone nodded appreciatively. I was betting that about seventy per cent of the story was true. Cosmopolitans in the nineteenth century?

"To tapas!" Charity exclaimed, raising her goblet of crimson sangria with hearty pomp. "The greatest cover-up in history!"

We all laughed, toasted and drank to tapas on the Ramblas. The sangria was good; sweet, but strong, and cold. A perfect complement to the balmy day.

"Enough frivolity," Charity proclaimed. "Let us get down to work. Russell...may I call you Russell?...Russell, tell me, is there anything you need before we board The Dorothy tomorrow?"

"Well," I began haltingly, unsure whether this was the best place to be having such a conversation. But the client always knows best, so I went for it. "I was wondering if you could tell me more about why you feel you are being targeted for murder?" I said this low enough so the Devonshire cream couple couldn't overhear.

"It was Morris, dear, dear Morris who paid the ultimate price so that I might have that knowledge, so that I might be warned, so that I might live," she announced, choking back a hint of a tear.

"Morris?" This was something new. Who was Morris? "Are you telling me Morris...?"

"Yes, Mr. Quant. Morris was murdered!"

Chapter 3

"Morris was our cat." This bit of information came from Dottie Blocka who until now had remained mostly silent while she knitted. "All you need have said, Charity," she told her partner with a gentle but reproving look, "is that Morris, *our cat*, died."

"Not just died, my love, but he…" I could almost hear the director instructing her to pause, wait, wait, and then, with dramatic flourish reveal, "…was poisoned!"

Ah, the poisoned tea Flora had told me about. "Can you tell me more about what happened?" I asked. "It was during the most recent Charity Event?"

"That's correct. At first, when I discovered poor Morris, in my bedroom, dead as a doornail and stiff as a fag at a Chippendales show, my suspicions were not immediately aroused. You see, Morris was not a young feline. He'd seen his share of pussies and catnip. I thought it lamentable of course, but not unusual in the grand scheme of things. It wasn't until some time later that I realized what had truly transpired. Dottie and I were idly chit-chatting—as we old lady types tend to do—about habits and how one

41

of ours, for years and years, has been to have a cup of tea before bed almost every night. You'd think we were crowned British royalty or something."

Dottie took the wee-est of sips from her glass of sangria and said, "Which, of course, you are."

Charity came as close to giggling and blushing as a woman of her ilk is likely to do. She fluttered a hand in Dottie's general direction. "No, no, no, it is *you* who are *my* queen." They smiled at each other with fondness over an old joke. Sated with their verbal love-making, Charity kept on. "Anyhow, the evening Morris passed on, I had returned to my room following a particularly invigorating day of boot camp training. That was when I found the cup of tea waiting for me. How lovely, I though to myself, Dottie knew what a trying day it had been and, as she sometimes does, she'd brought up my tea for me. However, as good fortune would have it, I'd already prepared my own cup and seeing as mine was the hotter of the two, that was the one I drank that night.

"The next morning I did notice that Dottie's tea seemed to have half-evaporated, but with the chaos of Morris being discovered soon after, I forgot all about it until much later."

"When we did finally speak of it," Dottie continued the story, correctly assuming she could do so in many fewer words. "I found it doubly odd because, although my physical body is giving out on me and my heart is growing weak, my mind remains strong as a whistle blow, and I recall, absolutely without a doubt, that that evening I had most definitely *not* brought Charity any tea."

"I'm not sure if I understand the significance of the tea to the cat's death," Errall said, at the same time accepting a draft beer from the waiter as replacement for the sangria, which she hadn't found appealing. "Thank you, Juan."

Flora tilted towards Errall and whispered, "His name isn't really Juan."

Errall frowned and said, "But she...?"

Flora did her nodding thing. "Grandmother also called him Jose. She makes up names as needed."

"You see, the *cat's*..." Charity emphasized the word in such a way so as to communicate to Errall that she did not appreciate

Morris being referred to so cavalierly, especially when Errall clearly knew the cat's name, "...death was caused by the tea."

"What?" I asked, unsure how she'd made the connection, myself quite enjoying the sangria.

"Since Dottie had not brought me the tea, suddenly the second cup became suspicious. I recalled how, the next morning, half of the tea was gone. Also suspicious and conspicuously coincidental so close to Morris' death, wouldn't you say? I, of course, immediately had the body exhumed and an autopsy performed." She stopped then, as any good actress would, acting coy as if there was nothing more of import to say.

"What were the findings?" Russell, the straight man.

"Morris," Charity exclaimed, "had been murdered!"

"Oh good Lord," Errall let out. Fortunately Charity read it as shock at the news rather than incredulity.

"The tea had been poisoned. Morris drank it," Charity announced. "That poison, which stopped dear Morris' heart as sure as if it had been ripped from his chest, Russell Quant, was meant for me. But we were left with nothing. I could prove nothing to the police. The cup and its contents were, of course, long gone. As for Morris, well, they had the balls to suggest that perhaps he'd mistakenly eaten some rat poison set out by a neighbour. Happens all the time, they said. Well, my Morris was accustomed to only the finest feline cuisine. No rat-eater him. So, as you can appreciate and no doubt sympathize with, I am left to discover the culprit—my murderer—on my own. And that, my mighty gumshoe, is where you come in."

A dead cat. A dead cat and a cup of tea. That was why I'd been flown halfway around the world to solve a murder—which had yet to be committed. I sat in my seat trying not to squirm, trying not to give credence to the police theory that perhaps the cat had died a mistaken death and a killer was not stalking Charity Wiser. I cleared my throat, ignored the incorrigible smirk on Errall's face, and plowed on, "Flora suggested the motive for someone wanting you dead might be financial?"

"Yes. The terms of my will...generous terms I might add...have been made widely known to the family." She allowed herself an inward smile. "By me. It's what keeps them coming back like lemmings to my little shindigs. Dottie teases me about it, but it's a fair arrangement. They pay a price. I pay a price. I get something out of it, and they—eventually—will too. But someone doesn't want to wait. Greedy bastard. I'm eighty years old for crying out loud. I won't live twenty more years." Another smile. "Nineteen perhaps, but certainly not twenty."

"May I have a look at your will?"

"On the boat, on the boat," she said with a dismissive wave. Next subject.

"Do you have any idea who the killer might be?"

A hearty guffaw. "It's one of 'em."

Helpful. "And you're convinced the murderer will try again on The Dorothy?"

"I've arranged to give our murderer the best opportunity he or she could hope for. Accidents happen all the time on water. And having the rest of the family around certainly helps divert attention and suspicion, don't you think?"

"Charity," I began carefully, "if that is indeed the case, I wonder if perhaps what you need more than me is a bodyguard."

"Can't you do both?"

Growl. "No. I'm a detective. I detect. I'm not a trained bodyguard. I can't assure your physical safety."

She gave me a slow and careful once over. "You look tough enough to me. What are you, six foot plus, wide shoulders, big chest, big arms, what else do I need? Or are you one of those homosexual men who have muscles for show but don't know how to use them?"

"I am not a bodyguard," I repeated. I needed her to understand this. If the situation arises I can whip it up with the best of them but that isn't what I hire myself out to do.

"You'll do," she decided with finality. "What I need most is someone who can find this asshole *before* he kills me, not some piece of sirloin to pull him off me *after* I'm already dead. You'll do." She tipped her regal head to one side and away from me, signalling an end to the conversation and called out, "Carlos, you lovely, more sangria!"

Friday was boat day. Although Errall and I would have dearly loved several more days to explore Barcelona (or Bar*the*lona as the locals pronounce it), we were just as excited to start our adventure at sea. Well, she was excited. I was excited and a little anxious: about the validity of my case, the eccentricity of my client and the seaworthiness of the boat we'd be on.

We were up at 8:15 a.m. to place our luggage outside our hotel room door as instructed by the Friends of Dorothy people who would be collecting it for transport to The Dorothy. Although we probably should have gone back to sleep to continue our jetlag recovery, we instead found our way to a little coffee shop we'd spotted the night before on Passeig de Gràcia. After a light break-fast and heavy coffee, we found our second wind and toured city sights until, exhausted but exhilarated, it was time to return to the AC for the FOD bus to pick us up at 3 p.m.

Although it's not like me, I took almost no notice of the other pas-sengers aboard the FOD bus or the scenery as we were driven to the docks. I was too busy fretting. I was worrying about whether I'd take one look at The Dorothy, turn tail and hop the first plane home to my landlocked prairie home. I was also thinking about my first meeting with Charity. Between that meeting and the dossier she had prepared for me, I should have been comforted by the depth of background knowledge I had about my client and her family, but I couldn't help wonder about what I didn't know. And, despite my protestations, I worried that I had witlessly signed up to play a human shield rather than a detective. To top it off were my concerns about Errall. Had I been a complete numbskull to think she and I could coexist in one room for a week aboard a ship from which there was no easy escape?

I did my best to push aside my worries as the bus slowed and pulled to a stop. I could sense a mounting excitement from the other passengers as the level of chatter rose and they laughed and joked and strained to see out. I wanted badly to feel it too. I looked out the window and for the first time laid eyes on what would be our floating home for the next week—The Dorothy. It, thankfully,

45

appeared to me to be huge. For some reason that made me feel better. Certainly something that size couldn't sink? Could it? It was gleaming white, as if fresh from a giant car wash and wax, six hundred feet long, eighty wide, with a towering smokestack looming over the back end emblazoned with the FOD logo: two gleaming red sequined shoes, ready to click us far, far away from Kansas.

It was only as we filed off the bus and were directed into a large building—kind of like an airport terminal for ships—that I began to take a good look at the people around me. I had expected them to look as if they'd just walked out of one of those gay travel magazines: buff, ridiculously young and attractive, and mostly men—the type who can pull off sarongs with barely-there hips and jaunty sailorboy caps. Who are those guys anyway? And how did these teenagers with hardly a waking hour left over after all the time they spent in gyms, tanning salons and clubs, manage to have jobs that paid enough to afford them a luxury cruise? (One green-eyed monster present and accounted for.) However, in taking a gander around me, although I did see some of the above-mentioned variety, in general this crowd looked as unremarkable as any other assemblage of people gathering in any train station, airport, pier or bus depot in preparation for a grand voyage. With the exception of the fact that most came in same-sex combinations…and the men seemed more excitable than the women…and the trio of drag queens channelling Mary, Rhoda (her heavy years) and Phyllis…this was a pretty pedestrian crowd. Uh-huh, for sure.

Before being allowed on the ship, our passports were exchanged for electronic boarding cards. We were to present these each time we embarked and disembarked the ship. After that we dutifully traipsed through two sets of security, and, that done, the life of salty luxury was finally ours to embrace. We stepped aboard the craft and were welcomed by an endless row of white-gloved, navy-suited crewmembers with broad smiles and good tans. I knew from the cruise information we'd been given that The Dorothy was built in 2000, registered in the Bahamas, and manned with an Italian crew. With a staff of almost three hundred and holding just three hundred and ninety-five passengers, it was nearly a one-to-one ratio. Eyeing up some of the particularly hand-

46

some cruise ship employees, I wondered if we would be allowed to choose the "one" we wanted. One such denizen approached Errall and me, introduced himself and, gently prying our carry-ons from our hands, replaced them with glasses of champagne, and escorted us to our cabin. My kind of welcome.

Our cabin was Room 654, a veranda suite on Deck Six. We gasped at the sight of it, like a king and queen seeing their newly decorated throne room for the first time. The next moments were a blur as we tried to take everything in. Somehow I'd envisioned a dark, dank closet with a single porthole through which we'd see dirty, green, frothy water splashing about, with maybe an octopus or two glaring in at us with malevolence. Instead we found original artwork (mostly whimsical seascapes) hung from brightly painted walls, colourful silk cushions tossed haphazardly about, and sari-inspired damask draperies that could be pulled closed to separate the sleeping area from the sitting/dining area. There was a full-size marble bathroom with a double-sink vanity, bathtub and separate shower, complete with a full line of complimentary Bvlgari bath-room products. We had a fully stocked wet bar with Vera Wang (yup, she does that too) crystal stemware, and on top of a sitting desk were two sets of stationery, each piece personalized in gold calligraphy with "From the room of Russell Quant" or "From the room of Errall Strane." Best of all was a wall of glass with a sliding door that opened onto a private teak-floored veranda.

"What are those?" Errall asked while playing with the remote for a large, flat screen TV. On the crisp Frette linen of our beds was a pile of equally crisp, white envelopes.

I reached for a handily available letter opener and sliced open one of the envelopes which was addressed to me, noticing that for every one addressed to me, was another for Errall. "It's an invitation!" I called out, as if I'd never been invited to anything before in my life.

Errall had settled on a channel dedicated solely to describing the countless things an FOD passenger needed to know while on board. "It says here," Errall answered back, studying the TV screen, "that the dress code for each day applies to all guests in public areas after six p.m. and for the duration of the evening." Then asked, "Who's it from?"

I read from the black-scripted invite: "Cruise Director Judy Smythwicke requests the pleasure of your company at the Departure Party on the Pool Deck at six p.m.," I read.

"How are we supposed to be ready in time for that?" She turned her attention back to the television. "It says here if we want to book tours in Mahón tomorrow we have to do it before six p.m. tonight."

I opened another. "This is from Richard Gray of GrayPride Tours thanking us for booking with him and asking us to join him for dinner tonight at nine."

"Who's he?" she responded, beginning to sound a little frazzled as she continued to study the long list of must knows. "The tour desk is on Deck Five and is only open until seven p.m."

I ripped open the next invite with shaking fingers. "This one says we're required to be at muster station Five A at five p.m. for a life jacket drill."

"The Pool Bar closes at seven p.m.," Errall crowed, sounding increasingly overwhelmed.

"Here's one from Charity and Dottie asking us to join the family for dinner tomorrow...oh, and she's reminding us that tomorrow is the first of two formal nights on board..."

"Wait, wait, I just saw that...yes, here it is," Errall said, rifling through a stack of papers and brochures she'd come across on the wet bar. "Here it is...formal wear is defined as evening gowns, cocktail dresses or dressy pantsuits for the ladies, and tuxedos or dark suits for the gentlemen. My God, Russell, how quick do you think the laundry service turnaround is? My clothes have been squished in a suitcase for days! Wait a second, I saw that too...we need lists, lists and a binder to organize all this...and do any of those invitations require RSVPs? We should get calling on those, and oh gosh I'd like to have a shower before going out, and who the heck is Richard Gray? Do you know him? Do you know the cruise director? Why did she invite us? Did she invite everyone on board? Or just you and me? Is it a party for four hundred or four? What should I wear? How can we find out? My hair is a mess!"

I'd taken the opportunity during her frenzied tirade to open a bottle of Moet and thrust a newly topped champagne glass into her quivering hand. "Just drink this and shut up."

We had just enough time to unpack, organize clothes into piles to be sent to the laundry service, check the laundry service price list, move half the laundry service clothes into the iron-ourselves pile, organize and respond to our invitations, and splash water on our faces when an announcement informed us that it was time to don our life jackets and proceed to our assigned muster station. What followed was a rather light-hearted (but with serious intent) demonstration of what to do in an alarming number of disaster-movie-of-the-week scenarios. They showed us the location of the lifeboats, which looked a little puny to me. Someone asked if the old maritime rule of women and children first still applied on a gay cruise. People made jokes about it, like how there'd be a sudden proliferation of drag queens as soon as the boat showed signs of sinking, or how the lesbians would be too busy trying to fix the leak to save themselves, leaving the guys free to first decorate and then sail off in all the lifeboats. I didn't think it was a laughing matter. Sure, The Dorothy was a spiffy-looking vessel and I was impressed with the free booze and nice towels, but I was still a bit jittery. Once the drill was over, they mushed us into the Munchkin Land Auditorium, the three-hundred-plus seat arena, along with the passengers from all the other muster stations throughout the ship.

As Errall and I searched for two seats together, I noticed the absence of Charity, Flora and Dottie. And that wasn't easy to do. With all of us still bound up in our identical puffy orange life jackets, we were a room full of trick-or-treaters wearing the same Hallowe'en costume. For the next fifteen minutes, we looked and listened and learned as various members of the crew were introduced and then proceeded to give us the lowdown on their particular area of expertise. There was Thera, the glamorous casino manager, Cynthia who ran the boutique where guests could purchase any of the items they found in their cabins, and Danny and Danae, the "gentleman" and "lady" on-board hosts whose responsibilities seemed to revolve around "entertaining" single travellers. The most important part of our presentation, we were told, was a full demonstration of the various hoots and toots and alarms, unique to The Dorothy, used to inform passengers of various events. These ranged from the common to the unlikely, from approaching port of call to setting sail to man overboard.

Although feeling a bit frazzled from the day's flurry of activity, our second wind now little more than a weak puff of air, we deposited our life jackets in our cabin and proceeded to the Pool Deck for the Departure Party. By the time we arrived, the area around the pool, gussied up with streamers and patio lanterns, was crawling with serving staff and ebullient guests.

"I guess this wasn't a personal invitation," Errall correctly surmised as she skillfully led us directly to a buffet table laden with a multitude of hot and cold tapas.

"Sure it was," I reasoned, "Just Judy and four hundred of her closest friends...this week."

We accepted champagne from a passing waiter and heaped a selection of food onto one plate for sharing.

"I don't think everybody here was at the life jacket drill," I wryly observed, comparing my scraggly shorts and T-shirt to the well-pressed, fresh-looking attire of many of the assembled. "Can you believe it? While we were learning survival skills and how to book a bikini wax, they were taking showers and getting ready for this party!" I was mock-shocked. "We look like Tom Hanks in *Cast Away* and they look like Tom Hanks at the premiere."

Errall finished chewing on a cracker topped with gherkin slices and peach-coloured mousse. "But just think, Russell, in case of emergency, you'll be first in line for a good seat on a lifeboat while they'll still be busy shaping their eyebrows and loosening herbal wraps."

I chortled. "And speaking of people who didn't attend the drill, I still don't see my client anywhere. Do you?"

Errall groaned. "Oh why would you want to?"

I gave her a surprised look. "What do you mean?"

"She's horrid, Russell. Charity Wiser is a horrid woman. The way she treated the staff at that restaurant on the Ramblas last night. And how she spoke to Flora and Dottie too. Not a very nice woman."

"Oh come on," I said. "I agree she's a little...loud and maybe a bit irreverent, but I think it's just how she had to be to make it as a woman in a tough business in the nineteen-forties. And I think Dottie and Flora know that and make allowances."

"And everyone else should too?"

"I don't think she's that bad, Errall." I would have liked to have added that some of Charity's traits were not dissimilar to Errall's, but seeing as we were going to be roomies for the next week, I decided that it was best not to mention it.

"Good evening," said a petite woman in a neat sage-green suit as she pulled up next to us, a high-beam smile on her face. "I'm Judy Smythwicke, the Cruise Director and so glad you could join me this evening." She spoke with a Julie Andrews–inspired English accent. She was in the no-woman's land between fifty and sixty, with a pre- cisely coifed bottle-blond do, careful makeup and a manner that made me think she was either going to scold me for not finishing my scone or break into a West End London show tune. "I do hope you've found everything to your satisfaction thus far?"

"Oh yes," I assured her, fighting temptation to mimic her accent. It's one of my less charming habits. "Everything is just scrumptious." Oh my God. Did I just say scrumptious? By the look on Errall's face I was certain I had.

"How wonderful. Well, we have a superb evening for departure. The captain tells me it's smooth sailing ahead." I got the feeling that nothing short of absolutely cheery good news would ever slip from between Judy's lips. In public. "And speaking of which…"

Errall and I turned to greet two men and a woman who had joined our group. Each was wearing a sharp navy suit with the sparkling red shoe FOD insignia on one lapel. Beneath their tunics, instead of a staid white shirt, they wore navy and white striped sweaters with red piping around the collar and sleeves—very sporty. I looked down at my own travel-weary outfit and knew that Anthony, my boutique-owning friend who'd slavishly select- ed my clothes for the trip, was no doubt feeling a cold shiver down his back, wherever he was.

By the look in her eye I could tell Judy had also noted our cou- ture, but gamely went on regardless. "Please meet Mauro Corsaro," she said with unbridled pride, "our Executive Concierge, who we are especially fortunate to have aboard The Dorothy. He is one of only a handful of shipboard concierges who are members of the esteemed International Golden Keys Association."

We shook hands with appreciative nods pretending to know what Judy was talking about and then turned our attention to the man beside him who was introduced as the Staff Captain. Next to the Staff Captain was Giovanna Bagnato, who we learned was the ship's captain since its maiden voyage. Captain Bagnato was a dark-eyed woman in her early forties with lustrous black hair gathered into a bun and covered by her smart captain's hat. My eyes narrowed to see her smile grow noticeably more dazzling as her hand reached out for Errall's. We made inane chatter for a second or two and then they moved off, Judy in the lead.

I eyed Errall and thought I could see a bit of a blush in her pale cheeks. "You know she's going to be too busy driving the boat to spend any time with you, right?"

She shot me a quick frown. "Don't be an idiot. Come on, let's get another drink and head up front to watch the departure."

Oh gosh. I'd forgotten this thing was about to start moving.

I got through the departure with surprisingly little queasiness. A gay men's chorus singing Christopher Cross' "Sailing" and all-you-can-drink bubbly definitely helped. The Dorothy's bulk simply floated away from the Barcelona dock with barely a ripple in the water and before I knew it we were gone, sailing away on the dazzling Mediterranean Sea. Truly amazing.

After a much-needed nap and shower, Errall and I were ready for our first night afloat. It was a casual night so I wore lightweight tan slacks, an open-necked, short-sleeved, fitted white shirt and designer flip-flops. I thought I looked pretty good and hoped Judy Smythwicke would see me and think so too. Errall had on a sea-spray turquoise wraparound dress and low-heeled white sandals. A little early for dinner, we first made a martini pit stop at the Cowardly Lion lounge on Deck Nine before making our giddy way to Yellow Bricks, the main restaurant on Deck Four.

Yellow Bricks was a massive room dotted with round tables of various sizes, accommodating intimate dining for two up to parties of twelve. The tablecloths were gold lamé and decorated with linen napkins of either chocolate brown, burgundy, purple or rust, with colour-matched candles and plate chargers. Three sides of the restaurant were floor to ceiling windows, which tonight showed off a dark sea with an occasional whitecap. As we were led to Richard Gray's table by a gold-suited host, I marvelled at how steady the floor seemed despite the active looking waters. As we approached, three men stood while two women and the Phyllis drag queen remained seated.

"I'm Richard Gray. Welcome," said one of the men. The first thing I noticed about Richard Gray was his hair. It was a startling silver despite his youngish age, probably mid-forties. It was thick and had a burnished appearance. His face was long, with a high forehead, thick jaw and strong chin. His eyes were light as polished chrome behind delicate, silver-framed glasses and he had an easy smile that produced high-definition cheekbones. He was about five-ten with a solid build. His clothing was pure cruise chic: twill cotton pants just this side of cream and a robin's egg blue, short-sleeved shirt with a cream-coloured collar. His glowing tan, offset nicely by his choice of clothing, was impeccable. "I'm so glad you could join us this evening. Please, everyone, take your seats." We did. "Let me introduce the table. Our new additions are Errall and Russell from Saskatoon, Saskatchewan, Canada. To Errall's left are Rob and Scott from Wyomissing, Pennsylvania. Russell, to your right is Miss Phyllis Lindstrom from Minneapolis/St. Paul, and next to me are Cherry and Melissa from San Mateo, California, celebrating their tenth anniversary."

We all applauded enthusiastically for the couple, then began small talk while perusing menus. I made a hurried survey of the room, trying to get my first sighting of the Wiser clan. And indeed, halfway across the room, sitting at two tables pulled side by side, there they were. Charity, I could tell even from this distance, was running the show and dominating the conversation—at both tables. There were fifteen of them in all, only five or six below the age of forty.

"So which of these characters are we...er, you...supposed to be keeping an eye on?" Errall whispered into my ear, doing her best 99 from *Get Smart* imitation.

"Actually, none of the Wisers are at this table," I told her, taking a pass on the buns making their way from guest to guest.

"Oh. Won't that make it difficult for you to decide which one is a murderer?"

I hate it when Errall plays at being sardonic.

"I guess Charity thought it best if we ease into things slowly. We'll meet the rest of the family tomorrow night at dinner." I tossed my head in the direction of the Wiser tables. "But they're all over there if you want to get a look."

Errall did an admirable job of surveying the group without drawing the attention of the others around our own table.

"They're a motley crew," she commented after a moment. "I know Charity, Dottie and Flora," she said. "I'm guessing the rather regal looking woman who looks like Charity is her sister, Faith. And that must be her husband next to her. But who are the rest of them?"

Although the timing might not have been the best, I was happy to fill Errall in. It was a good rehash for me, kind of like cramming the night before a test. I eyed the Wiser troop and took a shot at identifying them. "I'd say you're right about Faith and Thomas. The hunky dark brute sitting next to them must be their son, Nick. Then their daughter, Marsha, with her hubby, Ted."

"The bland-looking couple?" Errall confirmed. "What *is* she doing with her hair?"

I gave Errall a skeptical look. "Are you sure you're a lesbian?"

She held up the back of her hand to me and sweetly asked me to pick a finger. As it turned out, I only had the choice of one.

"And next to Marsha and Ted are their three kids," I kept on. "The twin boys…I forget their names right now, N somethings, and the girl, Kylie or Kyla or something."

"Boy, you're really on top of this case, aren't you?"

And for the millionth time I asked myself, "Why did I bring her along?"

"The other sister is dead, right?" Errall continued, seemingly unaware of the thoughts running through my head.

"Hope. Yes. Many years ago. The other older guys must be her widower, James, and his son-in-law, Patrick, also a widower. And the black guy is Patrick's son-in-law, Jackson, also a widower. He's a jazz musician."

"That leaves one young woman. She's a doll."

I nodded my agreement. "Very pretty. That would be Harriet, Jackson's daughter."

Errall nodded, her eyes still on the not-a-girl-not-yet-a-woman.

With our Wiser tour complete, I didn't want to appear anti-social to our dining companions, so I turned to "Phyllis" and made a bit of a show of admiring her astonishing resemblance to the character played by Cloris Leachman on *The Mary Tyler Moore Show*. She was perfect, right down to the thin, small-breasted body outfitted in a tight top and flared out pants, large bun of hair with a maze of crazy tendrils atop her head and short, unpolished nails. I said, "I'm surprised you're not dining with Mary and Rhoda." Really, what else was there to say? How's Lars?

"Those two bitches," she said in a gravelly growl loud enough for the entire table to hear. "They think they're so much better than me. Mary thinks she's so perfect and nice. And Rhoda...well, please, just look at her and look at me."

"Rhoda *is* pretty funny," Cherry suggested helpfully from across the table, obviously not used to dealing with the sometimes considerable ego of drag queen mentality.

Phyllis turned an evil eye upon the slight woman, her mouth an ugly grimace and one painted-on eyebrow arched high into her hairline.

"You might be wondering how I put this table together," Richard broke in, smoothly diffusing a potential hair-pulling, bastard punch (the lesbian version of bitch slap) situation. "FOD is one of my favourite carriers on the sea, and whenever they try out a new route, such as this one, I like to make the voyage at least once myself so that I can speak knowledgeably about it to our clientele. And when I do, I like to spend time and, if possible, have dinner with the clients that are on board."

"So we're all customers of GrayPride Tours then?" Melissa asked.

"That's right," Richard told the table.

"How many people on this ship are your clients?" Errall asked.

He turned his fine smile on her. "We have eight separate groups, almost thirty people in total."

"Well, we're privileged to be the first seven," I said.

"Completely my pleasure," the dashing Mr. Gray responded with a wink and nod in my direction. Was he flirting or was that just his way? I decided I liked the attention and wanted more. So I thought up an inane question. "Can you tell us, in general, what type of people are your clients?"

"GrayPride caters almost exclusively to upscale GLBT clients…and their friends…mostly guppies…"

"Guppies?" Melissa asked.

He laughed a nice laugh. "Gay yuppies. They've got money and like to spend it on exceptional service, exceptional food and wine and exceptional locales around the world. To answer your question, Russell, my typical client wants a bit of adventure—but nothing too dirty; expects to pay more—but not be taken advantage of; and declares a day perfect when he or she has been called upon to wear scrubby—but brand name—jeans and pricey—purchased not rented—evening wear in the same twenty-four hour period. They want the opportunity to dance, drink and suntan to excess—although in truth, rarely do."

Rob and Scott in particular were nodding appreciatively at Richard's incisive descriptions.

"You seem to know your customers quite well," I complimented, having to crane my neck to see his face past Phyllis.

"It's my favourite part of what I do," he said with a comfortable smile and—maybe I was imagining this part—a bit of a leer. "Getting to know my clients."

At that moment the sommelier arrived and stole Richard's attention from me. Errall leaned into me and whispered, "Help me."

"What is it?" I whispered back.

"We have to switch seats. These two next to me. One's a financial planner. The other is an accountant. Thrillsville."

I grinned at her and stole a quick peek at Rob and Scott. "They're very cute though."

"Which means absolutely nothing to me," she said dryly.

"What are you two buzzing about?" Phyllis plowed her head of curls into our personal space like a Pekinese looking for some kibble. "If it's about me, I'll kill you. If it's about someone else, I want to hear it."

Right then Captain Bagnato appeared at our table. Although gracious and courteous to all and sincerely wanting to know if our evening was progressing well, most of her interest seemed focused on one thing: Errall.

And so the meal progressed in a pleasant manner aided by some nice Italian wines selected by our table's host; first a tangy San Orsola Parallelo Primitivo del Salento from Puglia and then an oaky Frescobaldi Lucente from Tuscany which, according to Richard, was stylish and polished but lacked a bit of concentration. I thought it was dandy. Afterwards Richard suggested we all repair to Munchkin Land for entertainment and after-dinner drinks. En route, Errall pulled up alongside me and murmured into my ear, "You know he's going to be too busy dealing with his clients to spend any time with you."

A smile flitted onto my lips before I could stop it. To offset it, I said harshly, "Don't be an idiot. Come on, let's hurry and get good seats."

And a good seat I got—right next to Richard. The seating in the Munchkin Land Auditorium was booth-style on a theatre-like incline. Errall, Phyllis, Richard and I squeezed into one banquette; the other two couples found another a level down from us.

I made as good a survey of the room as its dim lighting would allow, hoping for another sighting of the Wisers. I found them sitting together in a grouping of booths down and to my right, but too far away for me to gather any useful information other than their presence. Even though I knew Charity wanted to hold off on a meeting until the next day, I was feeling a bit antsy to get started on my case. As pleasant as all of this was, especially meeting Richard, I was here to work. And yet, sitting next to the man, I couldn't help but enjoy the deep, rich smell of his cologne. One of the Creed scents, he told me when he noticed me sniffing around. I, on the other hand, was wearing something light, airy and inexpensive from Calvin Klein. Anthony would shoot me if he knew.

"You seem to be having a good time," Richard said to me, once Errall and Phyllis were entrenched in an argument over the quality of the MTM spinoff series named for the wacky downstairs neighbour.

"Why do you think that?" I asked with what I hoped was a beguiling look.

"You're smiling a lot. Or maybe you always smile this much?"

I shrugged. "Well," I said, "This is my first cruise. I'm really enjoying it."

His warm eyes hugged mine. "I'm so glad you chose this trip as your maiden voyage."

Yup. Flirting. He was definitely flirting. I was thinking up an appropriate response, something with the words "maiden" and "virgin" in it, when the lights dimmed and Judy Smythwicke appeared on stage. She had changed into a dazzlingly red sequined cocktail dress and high heels.

Miss Judy began with a quippy little intro, talking about how great The Dorothy is and how great all of us looked upon her, then smoothly got on with the show. "You are in for a royal treat tonight, ladies and gentlemen!" she called out in contagious excitement. "On this first glorious night of sailing, a truly mystical night, we are thrilled to present to you a most delightful performer! Please welcome La Psychic!"

I laughed off the corny name and exuberantly joined in with the crowd's hearty applause as La Psychic swept onto the stage. But the laughing stopped and my hands froze in mid-clap when I saw the woman's face.

Chapter 4

The short, heavy-set, dark-haired woman who walked across the stage to the introduction of La Psychic was none other than Alberta Lougheed. She runs her...what would you call it? Her psychic business?...out of the office next to mine on the second floor of the PWC building owned by Errall. It seemed the only PWC tenant not on this boat was Beverly Chaney. I wondered if a gay cruise would have need of a ship psychiatrist. Probably not a bad idea. Errall and I exchanged dumbfounded glances but said nothing as we sat back to watch Alberta begin her show, in all her eccentric, bright-faced glory, looking a little bit like Jann Arden as a gypsy.

I'd never witnessed Alberta at work before and I have never come to a conclusion about whether she truly has some special talent or if she's just another nut bar. Psychic powers are something I don't know or think too much about. After a bit of humorous preamble, Alberta headed into the audience, holding her microphone close to her lips to emphasize the breathy tone of her voice. "Would anyone like to give me a personal item...anything...a watch, a necklace…no underwear this time though, okay guys? Unless you're in 'em, I don't want 'em." Laugh laugh laugh. "Just anything you have that belongs to you…no stolen merchandise please." Laugh laugh laugh. "Something I can use to get a sense of you and your life."

She came upon a young woman who handed over a nose ring. Alberta palmed it and bent over in gales of laughter. Once she recovered she asked, "Honey, did you just take this outta your nose?"

The girl nodded, obviously grooving on the attention.

"Oh my, oh my, well don't take anything else outta any other body parts." More laughing. "Ooo weeee, now that I see all you lesbians up close, I can tell this is the wrong crowd to ask for a necklace…no, wait, sir…" She pointed to a nearby man. "What's that around your neck?" He gave her a petrified stare. "Is that a pearly necklace!" she hooted. "Okay, maybe not. Okay, okay, enough of this joshing around. Darlin', what's your name?" she asked the nose ring giver as she headed back to the stage with the piece of jewellery.

"Jamie," the woman answered, brushing back the bristles of her mohawk with one hand and wiping her lips with the other, good naturedly accepting the backslaps and ribbing of her friends.

Alberta stood on the stage where everyone would have a better view of her as she buried the nose ring in her meaty palm, turned her face heavenward and closed her eyes. After a long moment during which the audience was admirably quiet, she said, "There's someone at home who didn't want you to come on this trip."

Everyone turned to look at Jamie, to assess whether the first psychic volley of the evening had met its mark. I realized how important this initial move by Alberta was. If she failed to connect, half the audience might immediately brand her a charlatan and head off to the bar or casino. But if she got it right…

Jamie's face turned a little whiter and she swiped away a friend's hand that was trying to tickle her.

"My mom," Jamie croaked.

The crowd gasped. Really. It was an honest-to-goodness gasp.

"She thought it was costing me too much money, especially since I just started a new job. She thought I should wait a year and save up."

Alberta's head plopped over to one side; her eyes bored into the other woman's. "That's not *really* why. Is it?"

Jamie gulped. She looked at the woman next to her; a willowy beauty with long, shiny brown hair and a matching nose ring. "She didn't want me to travel with Veronica," Jamie admitted.

"She's going to come around, Jamie," Alberta said. "Not right away, but I see in…well, maybe six months…could be as much as a year…but I see you and Veronica having dinner at your mom's house."

Jamie beamed. Veronica hugged her. The crowd went wild.

Alberta was a hit. People loved her, and they loved her easy, self-deprecating sense of humour that kept them laughing in between her fortune-tellings or whatever they were. For me, seeing her perform like that, without her knowing I was in the audience, was an unexpected joy. It was like seeing someone you've known all your life on stage flawlessly singing a song or playing an instrument when you had no idea they were musically inclined. I enjoyed it immensely…until the end.

After an hour of doing the personal item reading, she moved on to the part of her show that she called "To Catch a Thought." To do this she stood stock-still on stage, closed her eyes and, according to her, let her mind roam the audience until she caught a thought. Then she'd share it with the group and see if anyone owned up to it.

"Someone is thinking about their mother," she began. "She lives…somewhere hot…you're worried about her…her name is Etta or Emma…?" And then she opened her eyes and regarded the audience. "You there, sir?" She pointed at a man sitting near the back of the room, holding up his many-ringed hand.

"Could it be my mother?" he asked, hesitant at first. "Her name is Emily and she lives in Miami."

"That's right. What's your name, sir?"

"Bruce." Bruce was maybe fifty or fifty-five. The man sitting next to him, probably his partner, was sixtyish and had a protective arm around Bruce's shoulders.

"You're mother hasn't been too well recently?"

"She's eighty-nine and had surgery last month to remove a cyst," the partner volunteered, patting Bruce's shoulders for comfort.

"I didn't know if I should come on this trip or stay with her," Bruce said, holding back a tear.

"She's okay, Bruce," Alberta told him, her eyes communicating kindness and empathy. "She's eighty-nine and she's no dummy. She knows a thing or two about life and how to enjoy it, and she is very happy you're here with Allan."

"Oh my God! How did you know my name?" the partner yelped.

The audience sat in stunned silence. I was pretty amazed myself.

Alberta shrugged it off by joking, "It was either Aladdin or Allan...I took a shot."

The audience laughed with her and loved her more.

She did her bit a few more times, with varying levels of success, but by that point it didn't matter anymore. She had them. She could have sung a few songs and released a CD and they'd have bought it. But then something went wrong. Errall noticed it too. It was near the end of the show. Alberta had closed her eyes to the audience as usual and began with, "Okay I'm getting a very strong thought, oh yes, I can almost hear it, can't you?" The audience laughed. "Yes, this voice, it's coming in very clear and you're thinking...you're thinking...you're thinking I'm goin..."

And she stopped. Her face froze. Slowly she opened her dark-lidded eyes and gazed out at the room in stony silence.

"What was that all about?" Errall said to me as we filed out of the auditorium with the rest of the crowd. "Did you see the look on her face? She looked shocked. Or frightened."

"I know," I said. "She covered it well though. I don't think many other people caught it."

"And what the hell is she doing on this boat?"

"I don't know."

Richard caught up with us once the crowd had somewhat thinned outside the doors of the auditorium. "Care to join me for a nightcap?" he asked, graciously including Errall in the invitation. "There's a cozy cigar lounge on the next deck up."

I winced because I really wanted to get to know Richard Gray a little better, but I also wanted to find out what was up with Alberta. The curious cat inside me won over the horny toad. "I'm sorry, Richard, I can't tonight. Rain check?"

He smiled and nodded and looked at Errall questioningly. I thought that was very charming of him. She can be such a lumpy pillow sometimes. That's why I was surprised when she took his arm and off they went. I was very glad she's a lesbian.

A few metres away I saw Judy, our cruise director, greeting guests with her pasted-on smile, and headed over. Once I had her attention, I told her my story of knowing La Psychic and asked if she could direct me to where the performers' dressing rooms were.

"Oh, we don't have anything like that, I'm afraid. We don't go for anything too fancy around here." Uh-huh, what about that dress you're wearing. "But if you wait right where you are, I'm sure she'll be coming out this very exit in the next few moments."

Sure enough, Alberta showed up soon afterwards, a coat-of-many-colours shawl draped over her stage outfit, heavy stage make-up still intact.

"Russell, goodness me, what a surprise to see you!" she enthused with a big hug. A surprised psychic? Isn't that an oxymoron?

"What are you doing on The Dorothy?" I asked.

She looked at some passing passengers, distracted, almost as if she didn't hear what I'd said.

"Alberta, is everything all right? What's going on?"

Her face lost some of its roundness as it settled into wariness. She glanced about, her collection of earrings making a jangling sound. "This isn't a good time," she told me.

"Something happened at the end of your show tonight…"

"Not now," she said, suddenly seeming to want to get away from me. "Tomorrow…are you getting off the ship in Mahón?"

"Uh, yeah, I think so."

"Meet me at Ixo, it's a little café, right on the harbourfront. Noon?"

She was gone before I got out an answer. I guess she knew it would be yes.

Hoping to catch up to Richard and Errall…well, mostly Richard…I dashed up the staircase to Deck Five and found the cigar bar…empty. Except for a lone customer sitting on a low couch under a lamp, with a snifter of brandy, a fat cigar and her knitting.

Dottie Blocka looked up and smiled at me. "Care to join me for a nightcap, Mr. Quant?"

I smiled back. "I'd be delighted." I asked the woman behind the bar for a port and joined Dottie on the couch.

"I assume you don't mind the smoke?" Dottie asked, her eyes mostly on whatever it was she was knitting. Something pink. "This is a cigar bar after all."

I'd given up smoking several years ago but still loved the smell of tobacco. "Not at all. What kind of cigar is it?"

She studied the stogie as if she'd never really looked at it before and said, "I don't really know. Charity gets them for me. It's the only naughtiness left me."

"Oh, I'm sure you could think up one or two more," I suggested with a wink.

"I can think of them," she agreed, her hands busily clicking away, "But with my poor heart, I just can't do them any longer."

There was a bit of silence, and somehow, it was comfortable. With Dottie Blocka, just sitting together was company enough. I enjoyed my drink and she enjoyed her knitting.

"I was an athlete once," she announced without preamble. "When I was a girl."

"Oh. What type of sports did you enjoy?" I asked the expected question.

"Baseball was my thing. I thought about playing on a professional team. I was that good."

"Why didn't you?"

She raised her bright little eyes to mine. "It was a different world back then, Mr. Quant. I got married, right after I finished school."

"I'm sorry you didn't get to pursue your dream."

"What makes you think I didn't?"

I sipped at my drink and used the time to reconsider Dottie Blocka. She was a woman shaped like a beanbag chair, and content with it. Hanging from a delicate gold chain around her thick neck was a pair of gold-rimmed eyeglasses I'd yet to see her wear. Her thinning head of hair looked like the top of a half-eaten vanilla ice cream cone and she wore plain clothing, mostly pastel-coloured dresses under matching sweaters and always with a Kleenex stuck up one sleeve, just in case she got the sniffles. But it was her eyes, almost lost in the pillows of skin around them, that showed who she really was. Bright, quick, wise. Her current physical state belied sharp mental prowess. In her mind she still was a mighty athlete.

"My husband and my family became my new dream."

"I didn't know you had been married," I said.

"Lawrence died in our twentieth year together. But in that time we lived a full and wonderful life. We had no children of our own, so we took in foster children. Seven in all. Some were with us many years, some for just a few months, but they were each so precious to us."

I nodded, sensing that Dottie Blocka was not one to talk a lot, so when she did, it was best to simply sit back and listen.

"I was almost penniless after Lawrence died. So I began doing laundry and housework to keep the money coming in. One day Charity hired me. That was forty years ago, Mr. Quant. I've lived with her every day since. I know her. You may be having some doubts about your decision to take on this job, wondering whether Charity is some crazy old woman making things up."

I did my best to keep my head motionless, no nodding, no shaking, but she could see in my eyes that she was right.

"Well Mr. Quant, if my word counts for anything, I'm here to tell you she isn't."

And with that she went back to her knitting, never once having touched her brandy or cigar. I got the feeling she just liked having them there.

"Thank you for the talk. I think I'll turn in now," I said. "May I escort you to your cabin?"

"Thank you dear boy, but Charity will be quite through at the casino in a few minutes. I'll wait for her."

I was about to get up and head for my room when I thought better of it. "Perhaps I'll wait with you. Charity promised me a look at her will. Maybe I could get a copy tonight?"

Dottie looked at me with a sweet smile as if we'd been talking about nothing more serious than the weather, and said, "Of course, dear."

Minorca lies off the eastern coast of Spain in the western Mediterranean. It's the second largest of the Balearic Islands which collectively form an autonomous region and province of Spain, declared a Biosphere Reserve by UNESCO in 1993. As The Dorothy quietly pulled into the seaport capital of Mahón early the next morning, I was nursing my first cup of coffee on our deck and flipping through the surprisingly few pages of the Last Will and Testament of Charity Wiser. She had followed the keep-it-simple-stupid principle. After taxes and all other estate and probate expenses were taken care of, the home in Victoria and all its adornments, including cars in garages and extensive art collection, would go to Dottie Blocka.

All other assets, including ownership in Wiser Meats, were to be liquidated and one half of those proceeds would also go to Dottie. Of the half remaining, fifty per cent would be divided between her remaining sister, Faith Kincaid, and her granddaughter Flora Wiser; twenty-five per cent would be equally apportioned to Nick Kincaid, Marsha Moshier, James McNichol, Patrick Halburton and Jackson Delmonico; and the remaining twenty-five per cent would be shared by Nigel, Nathan and Kayla Moshier and Harriet Delmonico.

I noted on a pad some interesting points I wanted to keep in mind. First, several of the beneficiaries, Faith, James and Dottie, were aged. In the event of their predeceasing Charity, the will remained silent, meaning their inheritance would go to their estate and would filter down to their own heirs. I guessed Charity decided they could best decide where they wanted their portions to go. Second, the document made no mention or adjustment for the fact that Flora had already received a million dollars. This didn't particularly surprise me, given Charity and Flora's relationship, almost mother/daughter rather than grandmother/granddaughter.

Third, in the case of Faith Wiser's family, no money was allocated to those who married into the family, namely Faith's husband Thomas or Marsha's husband Ted. Yet for the family of deceased sister, Hope Wiser, the by-marriage in-laws, James, Patrick and Jackson, were included. Was this a nod to the bad luck that befell the Hope Wiser women or a slight of the Faith Wiser in-laws or simply a best attempt at fairness?

Fourth, I wondered if anyone in the family was upset with their "ranking" in the overall distribution scheme. Niece and nephew Nick and Marsha were grouped with James and Patrick and Jackson who are unrelated by blood. Faith's grandchildren were in a different strata than Charity's own grandchild yet in the same grouping with Hope's great-grandchild Harriet. And finally, fifth, although impossible to determine Charity Wiser's exact net worth, it was clear that even those relatives sharing the smallest portion of the pie were in for a hefty financial windfall—more than enough to kill for.

Despite it being a lovely, sunny day, the sky a palette of mixed blues with the occasional puffy cloud for contrast, Alberta was all in black, from a scarf which covered much of her head down to her boots that reached high up her calves beneath a heavy black skirt. We were sitting across from each other at a wobbly square table on the front porch of Ixo, a small dockside restaurant in Mahón. In the distance we could hear the babbling sounds of island commerce.

Mahón is famous for its daunting sets of stairs one must scale to reach the main streets of town, where more numerous shopping and dining options are available. So daunting are they in fact, that many tourists choose not to make the tiring trip and make do in the harbourfront area. Each day, enterprising locals haul their wares down the stairs and set up a makeshift market at the foot of the steps. Here you can buy locally crafted ceramics, shoes, costume jewellery and other souvenirs, all without doing a *Rocky*...as long as you're willing to pay a premium. As I half-listened to the constant bartering chatter, I became vaguely aware that one of the loudest and most insistent contributors was Errall. She was using her intimidating lawyer voice to obtain the best price for a pair of scuffs and a belt. The vendors, however, had heard it all before.

"Alberta," I said, once a waiter had deposited our lunch in front of us. "Are you all right? What's going on? You seem nervous about something."

"I can't afford to have The Blacksmith catch me," she told me as her eyes scanned the sidewalk.

"The Blacksmith? Who the hell is The Blacksmith?" It sounded like a nickname you'd give a sixteenth-century executioner.

"You know, old Smithy, Smythwicke."

My brow crinkled in disbelief. "Are you talking about the cruise director? Judy?"

"Don't let her fool you, Russell. She's a bowl of sweet and sour ribs. The sweet only disguises the sour."

"What are you talking about? She's Mary Poppins."

"To you and all the other passengers maybe. But to the staff, she's an ogre. It's not even part of her job, really, but she watches us like a hawk, just waiting to pounce should we do anything wrong."

"That still doesn't explain why you're dressed like an old Italian woman in mourning."

"I don't want her to recognize me just in case she happens by."

"Aren't you allowed off the boat?" I was beginning to wonder if life with FOD wasn't all lollipops and cotton candy as I'd imagined it was.

"Oh sure, we get our days off and privileges to leave the ship at certain ports, but we're not supposed to fraternize with the guests."

"Ohhhhhh. You're not supposed to be seen with me off the ship."

"But there was no way I wasn't going to have at least one visit with you. Imagine running into you and Errall so far from home," she enthused, seeming to forget The Blacksmith for a moment.

"We were certainly surprised to see you last night too. We didn't even know you had left Saskatoon."

"Oh well, it's just temporary. For the money," she said, zealously stuffing her mouth with a chunk of the delicious bread our waiter had brought us along with a tasty *calderetta*." And the glamour. A friend of mine, who's a dancer on the boat, has worked for FOD for a couple years and told me about the gig. They have a regular psychic, but she wanted some time off, so here I am, filling in. Isn't it fabulous?"

"Don't you have to be gay to work on The Dorothy?" I asked.

"Nope. Just gay-friendly. And that I am," she said, reaching over the tabletop to give my cheek an elderly-aunt-type pinch.

"Alberta, about last night?"

She was suddenly intent on digging into her Minorcan fish casserole and was taking her time chewing her food into very small pieces. She helped herself to a healthy gulp of bottled water before looking at me. "You saw that, huh?"

"Yes, Alberta. It looked like you got spooked."

She looked at me for a moment then said, "That's a very precise way of describing it, Russell. I've been searching for a word to describe what I felt, and that's it. I was spooked. Spooked by a spook."

"What was it? What scared you?"

Alberta pulled her chair closer to the table and brought her face so close to mine I could see a tiny crumb of bread stuck to her bright pink lipstick. "At the end of the show…when I was searching for thoughts…"

"Yes?"

"I found one…one that wasn't very nice. I tried to ignore it but it kept on popping into my mind, as if demanding to be heard. It was horrible, Russell. I've rarely felt such a strong thought before. When it comes in that strong…well, it can only mean that the person who's thinking it is pretty serious about it. Like a song they can't get out of their head, it's all they can think about."

"So, what was it? What was the thought?"

"Over and over and over," Alberta began, her voice uncharacteristically shaky. I could feel her breath on my cheek as she spoke. "I could hear it as clear as if the words were being whispered into my ear…over and over…I heard the words."

"What? What did the voice say?"

"I'm going to kill her."

Chapter 5

Upon our return to the ship later that afternoon we found a new
pile of invitations on our beds, enough to fill the rest of our
evening and more. We donned a tuxedo (me) and a sparkly cocktail dress (Errall) and headed out. At the Meet the Captain reception, Captain Bagnato kept Errall in close visual proximity while
playing charming host to the other guests. I spent my time wondering when the heck she had time to plot courses, whip the oars-
men and watch out for glaciers and all the other captain-y stuff I
thought she should be doing, what with all the schmoozing
responsibilities she seemed to have. Afterwards we joined Richard
at the Cowardly Lion Lounge for a quick pre-dinner drink until it
was time for Errall and me to head off to meet the rest of the Wiser
family for the first time.

At nine o'clock sharp we entered Tin-Sel, one of three private
dining rooms on Deck Seven, which Charity had reserved for our
use that evening. The other two were appropriately named Roar
and The Haystack. Tin-Sel was what the Tin Man's home might

have looked like if only he'd had a heart…and a well-padded bank account. The colour scheme was predominantly red and silver, with tin (or tin-like substances) used in abundance throughout the heart-shaped room. From tin flower bouquets to a tin-inlay floor, tin sculptures and a well-stocked tin bar where drinks were being served in, what else, tin cups. Even the serving staff was in on it. For comfort and efficiency, none of them wore the clunky tin armour poor Jack Haley had to endure in the movie, but rather, much sexier tin-hued body paint, and little else except judiciously placed oil cans and funnels.

I immediately caught sight of Charity at the far end of the room holding court over about half of the fifteen assembled guests, while the others chatted amongst themselves in small groupings of two or three nearby. As soon as we stepped into her line of sight, Charity stopped whatever she'd been pontificating on and raised her funnel-shaped martini glass high above her head as if in salute. I knew I was in trouble.

"There he is!" she announced in a loud, boisterous voice, in case the rats scurrying along the boat's lowest depths couldn't hear her. Her drink hung precariously in the air, a few drops spilling from its sides as if the boat were lolling from side to side. (It wasn't.) "Behold, my family, Mr. Russell Quant."

At once all Wiser eyes were upon me, a rather unsettling feeling.

"And his charming companion, the dark princess, Errall Strane."

Errall appeared nonplussed but had the good sense to stand her ground in silence.

"And Mr. Quant," she said to me, "behold…my family!" And with this she swept her drink hand before her with a flourish, as if to present to me the human specimens in the room (which about then were beginning to collectively take on the look of a herd of sheep trying to figure out why the farmer was holding a pair of shears). "Family," she bellowed, her voice a bit slurred, "Mr. Quant is my legaaaaaaal adviiiiiiisor!" She let loose a caustic laugh and, with a wink for me, added, "Go get 'im!"

And with that, she resumed whatever it was she'd been saying to the group surrounding her. I'd been properly and completely dispensed of, like a household chore. Those not in Charity's circle gazed at me for a few seconds longer, some with frowns on their faces that I thought wholly inappropriate, but before long they resumed their whisperings and gossiping and left me alone. I looked at Errall and she at me. Was this a play and someone forgot to give us our lines? Fortunately for us, at that very moment an apologetic Flora Wiser trotted up to us, her sad dogface even sadder and paler than usual, her eyeglasses askew.

"I am so sorry for my grandmother," she said, nodding away. "She gets a bit tipsy during cocktail hour. She'll be fine once she's eaten something."

I noticed Flora had done little to cruise-up her wardrobe, her diminutive frame covered head to toe in layers of bohemian-style clothing in colours so drab they looked seasick.

"Don't worry about it, Flora. But what did she mean by 'go get 'im'?" I asked.

She smiled weakly. "Well, I can't be sure, but I suppose it was a bit of a joke." She glanced over our and her own shoulders to check for any possible eavesdroppers. Finding none she said, "Grandmother knows how paranoid the family is about her will and the eventual distribution of her estate. Having a lawyer or advisor of any kind on this trip will drive them insane. They'll be wondering why you're here."

"Did she think they would actually attack Russell?" Errall, the real lawyer in the group, asked, incensed at the thought.

"Not really," Flora said. "They'd never be so forward about it. But she'd think it was humorous to watch their reactions."

And indeed, when I lifted my head from our tête-à-tête with Flora, I caught Charity's cool green eyes carefully scanning the room, a tight smirk on her lips. She met my eye and delivered another wink. This woman, I was quickly coming to realize, was a fascinating yet frustrating enigma.

"But never mind all that," Flora urged. "They're about to serve dinner. I'll show you to your seats. Grandmother arranged the seating plan." Of course.

I offered Errall my arm. "Dark Princess…"

She gave me a scowl befitting her new title.

There were three round tables set up around Tin-Sel, two seating six apiece and one for five. Flora showed us to a sixer, around which stood three men and the stunning young woman we'd noticed the night before. With her toffee coloured skin, heart-shaped face, and bright smile, the woman immediately reminded me of a twenty-one-year-old Vanessa Williams.

"Errall, Russell, this is my cousin, Harriet," Flora introduced us, looking like a desiccated stalk of straw next to a glorious gardenia.

Harriet threw out her hand and a friendly smile. "So nice to meet you. Errall, I just love your name. Mine makes me sound as if I'm a ninety-year-old schoolmarm. Please call me Harry."

"And this is Harry's father, Jackson Delmonico." Flora was referring to a slightly stooped-over black man who could have been any age between forty-five and seventy. His weary, bleary face, yellowed eyes and ruined voice told me that this was a man accustomed to long, hard nights of overindulging. Even so, he was spiffily turned out that evening, wearing a purple dress jacket with black lapels, a black shirt with ruffled front, billowing black pants and shiny black dress shoes. Everything about the outfit was a little worn and out of date, but certainly attention-grabbing. He had an easy, wide smile that showed off large, tobacco-stained teeth and closely shorn greying hair, beard and moustache. I noticed when Flora introduced Harry, Jackson looked about as proud as if she'd just been awarded a Nobel prize.

The man next to Jackson was also stooped, but that's where the similarity ended. He was thinner, shorter, and looked uncomfortable, like he wanted to have his food and get out of there. He was in his early sixties, with a small, oval face blanched white as Wonder Bread. His dull eyes met ours for less than a second as we shook hands when Flora introduced him as Harry's grandfather, Patrick Halburton.

"And this," Flora said indicating the last man, "is Harry's great-grandfather."

"James McNichol," he declared sprightly, barely noticing me but paying Errall an inordinate amount of attention.

Harry, Jackson, Patrick, James. Harry, Jackson, Patrick, James.

H-J-P-J, H-J-P-J, I repeated to myself to help keep the names and faces and relationships straight.

At eighty-two, even though James outdistanced Jackson and Patrick in age by decades, he appeared substantially heartier and healthier and, I must say, was the most attractive of the three. He was tall, with an almost full head of wavy hair dyed a rusty shade of blond, and his large chest, forty-four inches at least, seemed even larger due to an inspiringly small waist for a man of his years. "What an absolute delight to have you at our table, young lady," he said to Errall as he raised her hand to his lips for a lingering smooch. I've never gotten that: hand-kissing. What's that all about? Why the hand and not the palm or left knee? "Does your mother know you're out this late without a chaperone?" he chided.

Errall gave him one of her rare Crest-commercial smiles. "I guess old Russell here is my chaperone."

He regretfully pulled his eyes from Errall's bosom and regarded me pleasantly. "Well, well, Mr. Quant. The legal advisor." For a burning second I felt a sensation of being named the victim in a game of sea-faring Clue: The Great-Grandfather Killed The Legal Advisor in The Galley with The Anchor. "Good to meet you. You best keep a close eye on your young lady here." He bestowed a salacious leer on Errall. "Who knows what type of trouble a fair maiden such as she could get into on this ship? I've noticed a lot of randy-looking young men aboard who I'm sure would like nothing better than to get to know her better." He gave me one of those manly winks that says, "If you know what I mean?"

I exchanged a bemused grin with Errall and nodded thanks for the warning. Didn't James McNichol know what kind of cruise this was? The only thing any of the randy men on this boat might want from Errall would be the sequins off her dress.

Flora made off for her own table leaving us to take our seats just as the wine steward and menus came around. The selection was awe-inspiring and I finally settled on a lamb dish. The steward suggested a Marques de Caceres Reserva 1995, from Rioja, Spain, which apparently was a very agreeable wine enhanced by a menthol note on the finale. The combo sounded so good that two others at the table ordered the same.

After the wine and amuse bouche were served, I reflected on our tablemates. Charity had seated us with what was left of her late sister Hope's family. Seeing these people in person, particularly Harry—the sole remaining woman—made the story I'd read in Charity's dossier more real and somehow more tragic. Each of the men around this table had married a woman who, upon giving birth to a baby girl, had died, leaving him a widower with a small child to raise. And what of Harry, the last of the baby girls? Would she too become a victim of this sad legacy? Or was she doomed, in order to save her own life, to remain childless forever, regardless of what her desires and dreams might be?

Yet, despite this gloomy future, as I watched Harry interact with her menfolk, all of whom obviously cherished her, she seemed a hopeful, happy girl. Would all of that one day be shattered by a lineage that seemed intent on either restricting her happiness or killing her? I hoped for her sake that she had no desire to be a mother or, if she did, would find ways to be one without giving birth herself. The alternative was…well, a risk greater than most.

"I'm gonna check out that deck out there for a ciggy or two," Jackson announced as he pulled away from the table.

"Oh Daddy, they'll be serving the meal soon," Harry ragged on her father good-naturedly. "You stay right in your seat."

Errall stood up as well. "I think I'll join you."

The two of them regarded each other with the relief of having found a fellow smoker in a world where lobby groups and governments were making it increasingly harder for them to indulge their addiction.

"How about we slip by the bar for some scotch to bring with us?" Jackson suggested to Errall, with an expectant look on his face.

"You have yourself a deal, Mr. Delmonico."

He laughed a throaty, raspy laugh and together they set off. Harry rolled her eyes.

"Have you known my sister-in-law very long, Mr. Quant?" James McNichol, seated at my left, sidled up and asked me in a shushed tone that was not meant for the others at the table to hear.

For a moment I was stymied. I couldn't admit to having just met her if I was supposed to be playing the role of her trusted legal advisor, but I also didn't want to be caught in a lie. "For some time," I said vaguely.

"Ah well, good then, in that case I was wondering if...man to man, you know...if you think I've got a chance there."

I waited for more. When I realized there wasn't any I looked at him and said, "I'm sorry, I don't think I understand."

"Oh come on, man, you know what I mean. Do you think I have a chance with her? You know, to court her. You'd have to agree she is one hell of a handsome woman. Wouldn't you say?"

"Ahhh...but Dottie..."

"No, no, no, Mr. Quant. Not Dottie. Not my type. Not at all. Charity. I know it might seem a bit risqué, what with she and I being in-laws and all. You do know that my first marriage was to Charity's sister, don't you? Well of course you do. But well, my goodness, certainly no one could think badly of us now. My dear Hope died sixty years ago. We had a short marriage, Mr. Quant, but oh how we loved one another. I had to move on though, hadn't I? I gladly raised our daughter Helen. And it was hard in those days for a man alone to raise a young girl. But I did it. Happy to. But when she was gone, married, and then passed on herself, I just had to move on. I was still a young man. Still virile, just as you are now."

"You remarried?" I asked, even though I knew the answer.

He gave me another of his famous winks along with a bit of a nudge in the ribs. "Well, not right away. I had a few relationships. Nothing untoward, mind you, not like young men and women do today, but I had some fun let me tell you. The dating life was for me, let me tell you. But, a man has to settle down sooner or later. So eventually, yes, I did remarry. Three times actually."

I winced, hoping he wasn't about to tell me all his wives died on him. Was I sitting next to a modern day Henry VIII?

"Twice divorced and once more widowed. I loved them all. They say you fall in love, really in love, only once in your life. That, my boy, is hogwash. I loved all my wives the same. It was just that a couple of them didn't love me quite as much," he said with a hint of disappointment on his handsome face. I was trying to find the name of the old-time actor James McNichol reminded me of. James Mason maybe.

"Sorry to hear that." I glanced over at Harry and Patrick who were being left out of the conversation. They seemed content to sit mostly quietly in each other's company, with Harry every once in a while telling her grandfather a little story or giggling over something I couldn't hear. I turned back to James and asked, "So your last marriage ended…?"

"Oh Delilah. She divorced me about five years ago. Went off with someone else. It's okay I guess, if that's what makes her happy. And I've been having some fun of my own since then. But I'm still a y…well, perhaps I can't say I'm so young anymore, but I got some time left in me, Mr. Quant, and I mean to use it. I need a good woman to settle down with again." Another "if you know what I mean" wink and nudge.

I was beginning to know exactly what he meant. James McNichol, for all his experience with the ladies, was still a rather old-fashioned gent who lived in a world with rules that few other men adhere to any longer. When he talked about dating and courting and having fun, those activities did not include sex. So when he couldn't take it anymore and wanted to have sex, he had to find a woman who wanted to get married. Given his good looks, I could understand how he'd have little trouble finding suitable candidates. Seemed like a waste of marriage certificates to me, but whatever. What I couldn't understand was how he could be so dim as to consider Charity wife material, especially when she, along with her life partner, had invited him on a gay cruise!

Our meal arrived and Harry left to retrieve Errall and her father. While we waited, I took another look around the room. Charity was entertaining her dinner companions, Dottie and the younger set, Flora and siblings Nigel, Nathan and Kayla (I checked their names in the dossier before I came), two tables over. The boys seemed to be enjoying every minute of their great-aunt's verbal shenanigans, as if they were on a wild amusement park ride that could end at any time. They knew to take advantage of the thrills while they could. At the other extreme, Kayla looked sour and Flora dour. Sitting at the table next to ours, the fiver, was the woman Errall and I had decided last night had to be Charity's sister. Faith was a gentler version of Charity; softer in her facial features, the way she wore her hair, her clothing choices. Every so often, over the usual mealtime ruckus, I heard the mellifluous tones of her voice as she spoke to others at her table. With her relaxed up-do, graceful neck and delicate hands, she was Snow White at eighty-four. The distinguished-looking gentleman at her side was no doubt her husband, Thomas Kincaid. Next to him were their daughter Marsha and her bulky husband Ted—average Joe and Jane hopelessly trying to pull off Ken and Barbie.

Marsha and Ted were looking particularly ill at ease. As much as James McNichol seemed blissfully unaware that he was on a gay cruise, these two were painfully cognizant of the fact. Whenever the solicitous waiter with only an oil can–like apparatus over his charms or the waitress with "Dorothy is my bitch" tat-tooed on her belly happened by, their eyes would protrude from their heads like boiled eggs. Then they would look at one another with self-righteous indignation—or at least Marsha looked indig-nant. Ted appeared rather befuddled, as if he'd just beheld a uni-corn and didn't know whether he should weep at its uniqueness or shoot it as game. And when one of these creatures had the audacity to come near enough to serve them something, they'd lean so far in the opposite direction they'd almost topple off their chairs. Next to them, Marsha's slightly younger brother, Nick Kincaid, was harder to read. But he was one book I'd have no trou-ble taking to bed at night for some deep study. In fact, his dark, hir-sute, handsome, Village People, super-butch façade was almost too perfect to be real. He was GI Joe on vacation.

The rest of the meal flowed by rather smoothly as I asked ques-tions of the others, feigning polite interest when really I was assessing the possibility of each character as a possible murderer. My success in unearthing revealing facts, however, was less than stellar. Although Harry was a delight to listen to for her sheer exu-berance, she talked a lot about nothing. Her father, Jackson, excused himself countless more times throughout dinner to grab a stronger-than-wine drink from the bar and have a smoke on the outdoor deck. (Errall joined him a third of the time.) Patrick Halburton was a quiet man who said little and, unless Harry was engaging him in conversation, spent a lot of time staring at his food. As for James McNichol, well, he was a long-in-the-tooth Don Juan with little on his mind but how to get into Charity's pants, or, in the meantime, how to get a better look down Errall's dress. Was Charity's resistance to his efforts a plausible motive for murder? I was debating this when from somewhere behind me came the sound of singing.

"Happy Birthday to you, Happy Birthday to you..." It was the tin-coloured staff. They were marching, procession-like, from the kitchen, the lead one holding aloft a massive slab of red-icinged cake on a platter of tin and alive with eight sparklers burning bright.

The rest of the family joined in for the last bit of the song, "...Happy Birthday dear Charity-Grandmother-Auntie, Happy Birthday to you!"

The cake was deposited with a thump onto the table in front of the birthday girl. As the sparklers sputtered mightily to their death, their crackling light threw Charity's face into a sphere of otherworldly glow in which she basked like a movie star. She stared deep into the fizzing brightness, as if daring it to blind her. Dottie sat to one side of Charity, a content smile on her plump face; Flora was on the other, her cheeks burning red from the heat of the spitting candles.

"I'd like to propose a toast!" Charity rose from her chair and hoisted her ubiquitous martini glass into the air, which, I was coming to recognize, was one of her favourite poses. She was wearing a peach-coloured pantsuit of a slinky material that flared at her ankles and wrists. Her hair was up in a bun and her eyes were sparkling like gems—from alcohol or mischief, I couldn't decide. "To my family, who have attended, most without fail, each of my Charity Events over these last many years."

There was a general sound of people preparing to raise their glasses for a sip but it became obvious Charity wasn't quite done. I wondered why someone else wasn't delivering the birthday toast, but really, she hadn't given anyone the chance.

She continued. "And particularly I raise my glass to this Charity Event, aboard this stunning vessel of the sea, The Dorothy. An event like no other, not only for its location and luxuriousness, but because, my dear family, it is to be...our last!"

Protestations and sounds of surprise, sincere and otherwise, abounded.

Charity used the moment to rove the room with calculating eyes. I saw in her the look of a woman who often found herself alone, even in a crowd. The noise of the others was just that, noise. She wasn't listening to any of it. The game was playing out as she expected. The family members were playing their part well, albeit completely transparently and more than a little by rote. But there was something new this time—one of them wanted her dead. This time, these people were more than just pawns on her game board—they were adversaries...at least until the murderer was known. Charity knew how to deal with adversaries. She'd been doing it all her life. So even with stakes at the ultimate high, she exuded confidence because this was a game she was certain that she would ultimately win.

"Yes, our final Charity Event," she told them once more. "And let me tell you why."

A collective intake of breath. Me too. What the heck was she up to?

"Over the years," Charity began, taking a healthy sip from her drink. Realizing it was now empty she called out to a nearby server, "Raymond, you lovely, another please."

By the look on the waiter's face I guessed his name was something other than Raymond, still, he sportingly took away her empty glass.

"Over the years," she began again, "I have not been unaware of a certain...oh, what should I call it...a derision amongst many of you, not all, mind you, but many. A derisory attitude toward not only myself—and my fortune—but also toward my dear sisters, Faith and Hope."

A spattering of "no"s and "not true"s echoed throughout the room. I was having difficulty trying to both listen to Charity's words and monitor the family. From what I could see, most reactions were identical: dawning fear of what next would come out of this powerful woman's mouth. Well, except for Nigel and Nathan whose lips were turned up at the edges and whose naughty-angel faces wore looks that said, "She's gonna blow, dude."

"Oh yes, it's true," Charity crowed. "Do you think I haven't heard the rumours that are spread, the rumblings, the grumblings, the stories that are told? My favourite being the one about three sisters, who, although given the sacred names of Faith, Hope and Charity, by an ironic quirk of fate...have none themselves."

The unrest in the crowd was palpable. Out of the corner of my eye I could see that the staff had ceased all serving duties and were standing at attention near the kitchen doors, either through pre-arranged orders from Charity Wiser herself or simple good sense.

"They say that sister Faith is without faith, having turned her back on God to take up with a man..."

I looked at Faith and Thomas. Their heads were bowed low, as if in prayer. Their daughter Marsha, however, appeared almost apoplectic in her simmering rage. Son Nick's face was a motionless dark stone.

"And they say dear departed sister, Hope, was without hope, having died at an early age, leaving behind a cruel curse that would deny all daughters who came after her the exact things she most hoped for and was denied herself...many children and a full and happy life."

I glanced around my table, at what was left of Hope's family. Harry, Jackson, Patrick, James. The men remained stoic in the wake of Charity's words. Harry released a single, shining tear.

And Charity barraged on. "And that I, Charity Wiser, am without a charitable bone in my body. That I am a bitch who has too much money and infamously gives none of it away!" She then called for her drink and a valiant waiter delivered it in seconds. She accepted it with a "Thank you, Roland" and took a deep pull of the gin.

"Well I must tell you, these words—your words—once made me furious." Her gaze burned around the room, sparing few. "Until one day, I was shocked to realize...that you were right."

More random sound bites from the family members, not sure how to respond but assuming they should.

"And so, it is my intention to remedy this situation," Charity told them. "You have already been introduced to my legal advisor, Russell Quant."

Gulp. Oh no. I was about to be pulled into this familial Mixmaster and couldn't reach the Stop button. I was as much a captive of this woman as her family was. Somehow, in a very short time, I'd become a piece in her game of Monopoly, free for her to manipulate. I only hoped I'd end up a top hat or sports car rather than a wheelbarrow or old shoe. All eyes in the room were either glued to Charity or me. Mine were on my wineglass, and I wished it were full of straight rye.

And then she said them, the words that would reverberate from one end of The Dorothy to the other. The words that would become seared onto the minds of the Wiser clan members as certainly as a brand on a bull: "Upon the conclusion of this cruise, this final Charity Event, Russell and I will travel to Rome where we will meet with my lawyers and redraft my final will and testament."

I heard a glass break and others lowered heavily onto tabletops as if the owners had suddenly lost muscle control. I could smell the acrid scent of fear mixed with anger in the enclosed room. Somebody open a window! There was even a whimper. That may have been me.

Charity went on as if she'd done nothing more than announce the time and location of the morning buffet. "Although my dear Dottie's bequest will of course remain unchanged, with her receiving one half of my estate—of which she is more than deserving— the balance of my monies and assets will now be directed to restore this family's faith, hope and charity."

It was their greatest nightmare come true. I heard Nigel let out a "No way, man." Mouths were gaping open, jaws went slack, breathing was shallow. If only I'd known, I'd have arranged for an Emergency Response Team to be on hand, just in case.

"The resources of the Wiser estate shall now be divided up amongst various charities, including medical research on child-birth-related deaths and the Roman Catholic Church."

You could have heard a drag queen lip-synching.

After a pause, during which her brilliant eyes made a circuitous route around the room, she concluded with: "I'm sure this will meet with all of your approvals and put all rumblings and grumblings and tall tales to rest."

Another person might have then left the room in some dramatic fashion, but Charity stood her ground, staring at the crowd, daring someone, anyone, to speak, challenge her decision, take her on. Of course, no one did. In moments the room was cleared with the exception of Charity, Dottie, Flora, Errall, a few well-entertained serving staff and me.

"Do you know what you just did?" I asked, as I approached Charity's table.

"Do you remember what you asked me on the Ramblas?" she shot back with a question of her own. "You asked me how I could be certain someone would try to kill me again while we were aboard The Dorothy."

I remembered.

"Well," she said with a sly smile on Cheshire Cat lips, "I think I've just assured you that they will."

Chapter 6

Sunday was a day at sea. According to Miss Judy Smythwicke's multitudinous announcements over the PA system, the daily newsletter and the TV station that kept us informed about such things, we were heading for Tunisia, located on the northern coast of Africa. After leaving Minorca we had sailed east towards Sardinia and would travel south along its western coast for a good part of the day. Charity had timed her stunning revelation well. There was no getting off the boat in a huff for any of the family—or me—unless we were in the mood for a very long swim.

When I woke early Sunday morning, I was startled to see through the slits of my morning eyes a churlish grey sky and, as if showing off, a narrow bolt of lightning flashing in the distance. A storm! In an instant my stomach muscles contracted and goosebumps multiplied over the mounds of my bare chest. I rolled over to look at Errall, fast asleep in the next bed. Should I wake her? Should we put on our life jackets? At the first sighting of Shelley Winters or Kate Winslet I would surely faint dead away.

Then, like one of those brain-numb, soon-to-be-dead, horror film heroines, I threw back my bedcovers and reached for my housecoat, intent on facing the demon outside. I stood up, slipped my feet into white terry slippers, and placed them shoulder-width apart, in preparation for the swooping motion of the ship's embattled hull. Yet all seemed still. Surprisingly the floor did not sway with a sickeningly slow, dull lull as I expected. I took a baby step forward and then another, making my unsteady way to the windows. With a gentle swoosh I pulled aside the sliding door and gophered my head through the space I'd created. Salt. Spray. Heady wind. They were all there, but not in any immediately threatening way. I opened the door a little wider, allowing myself room to squeeze through onto the deck, dry except for the edges nearest the railing. I stood there, in my luxurious robe and slippers, stock-still, back plastered against the glass as far from the railing as possible, fighting a rising panic. What had I done? Why had I gotten on this boat for an entire week? Couldn't I have had the sense to try out my sea legs in a less dramatic fashion, perhaps in a wading pool or something less, less, less...big?

I stared at the busy sky and roiling waters, almost indistinguishable at that time of day and in those weather conditions. And then I got all philosophical-like—perhaps it was the acceptance of my imminent demise that brought it on. What is the difference between sea and sky, I asked myself? Sea evaporates into air to become rain that falls into the sea. How do I...and this boat...fit into that cycle? Did we too have to be consumed somehow, to appease the god of the sea—whassisname? Morpheus? Titan? Ed? And yet...yet...even though the sky looked angry and the water unwelcoming, we seemed to be...just fine, plowing along with the steadiness of a chip through dip. The sea was holding us up, propelling us to our next destination, as if we were her guest and under her tender care.

For a long time I stood there, staring at our hostess, making friends with her, watching day slowly, softly tinge the night sky with smudges of light, as if to say, "Good morning, it's my turn now."

I heard Errall rustling about in bed. I poked my head into the cabin and was surprised to see by the clock that I'd been communing with mother sea and sky for almost an hour. I pulled in one last lungful of the lusty sea air and, finding myself oddly invigorated, romped into the room and roused Errall with a well-placed pillow to the buttocks.

By 11 a.m. we'd been to the gym and had our breakfast. Although we could still see the storm hanging like a wet, cold blanket far off the port side of the ship (I was beginning to get the hang of nautical terms), the sky directly above The Dorothy was startlingly blue and sun flooded the Pool Deck. Mindful of her alabaster skin, Errall debated slathering on a coating of factor 45 sun block or finding a nice quiet shaded spot elsewhere to read and eventually chose the latter, leaving me to brave the Mediterranean rays on my own. I slipped on a pair of Body Body Wear trunks (I'd given up Speedos last year), cut to mid-thigh, orange with a vaguely Hawai'iana strip of flowers down each side, a bright yellow tank and pair of flip-flops, prepared a beach tote with Frances Mayes' *Bella Tuscany*, Ombrelle, baseball cap and Dasani and headed out.

The Pool Deck was a large, rectangular, open area, glass walls down both lengths, protecting guests from wind and sea spray but allowing an unimpeded view of the water. At the aft end was a festive-looking cantina that offered a wide selection of frou-frou drinks and tasty poolside snacks. At the fore was a hot tub and behind that an area for playing table tennis and shuffleboard. Tables for two or four, each with a ruby-red umbrella, created an outer rim circling the pool; the inner rim was populated with full-length chaise lounges with mats of blue-and-white gingham like Dorothy's dress in *The Wizard of Oz*.

Despite the early morning storm, the sun had brought out the gays as surely as a sale at IKEA (or Canadian Tire for the lesbians). Immediately, I could tell this was a high-class cruise for there was nary a thong in sight. Instead, most of the crowd was outfitted in tasteful, designer swimwear. On the running track, which was actually on Deck Nine and suspended above the circumference of the pool, were several super-fit men and women, in track suits stylish enough to meet any Saskatoon restaurant dress code, taking their morning jog or fast-walk. As I ambled about near the pool, taking in the scenery and looking for a spot, I was glad I still had a tint of summer colouring so I wasn't the whitest white person on board. But I was close. Judging by suntans ranging from almond to mahogany, I guessed the combined money spent on tanning bed sessions prior to this trip could have paid Martha Stewart's legal bills.

"Russell! Alone? Why don't you join us?" It was Phyllis, suddenly standing next to me, looking shockingly spectacular in a one-piece maillot that revealed not a hint of the wearer's masculinity, but rather a lithe, sway-backed figure reminiscent of...who else, Phyllis Lindstrom. "Mary, Rhoda, look who's here!" she called across the entire Pool Deck expanse to where her friends were relaxing around a table in somewhat less revealing outfits. "Oh, stop gawking," she said with a coy smile, her attention back on me and noticing me noticing her shape...or rather lack of one. "A little Scotch tape goes a long way. Except I have to stay out of the sun or else the adhesive starts melting and then whoops! A nasty surprise for everyone!" She laughed and laughed as she pulled me along by the arm. "My, my, you are a piece of beef, aren't you, Russell Quant," she commented, massaging my bare biceps. "I never would have guessed. You seemed so buttoned-down before."

By this point we'd reached the girls' table and I greeted the sitcom stars as if they were just regular folk.

"Oh, Mar, I don't know if we should ask him to stay," Rhoda, a rainbow-coloured scarf covering her head and knotted above her right ear, complained to the Mary drag queen. "With him around, no one's ever gonna notice me."

Mary gave me a smile as big as Minneapolis and as white as fresh snowfall and waved off Rhoda's concerns. "Mr. Quant, please join us. Can we get you anything?"

"Mary!" Phyllis hissed. "Russell is *my* friend." She turned to me and asked deadpan, "Russell, can Mary get you anything?"

"Thank you, ladies, for the kind invitation," I said as graciously as I could. "But I think I'm going to find a spot in the sun for a while; try to darken up a bit."

"Let me tell ya," this from a cynical Rhoda. "It'll kill ya, Russell, all that sun. And even worse, it'll make you look old."

"Now, Rhoda," Mary admonished her friend before turning back to me with that smile. She was really quite a beauty. "Maybe some other time then?"

I gave her a choir of teeth and a wink. "I'd be delighted."

"Oooooooohhhhhhh, Mr. Quant!" she replied in a quivering alto. Perfect Mary Richards.

Phyllis pulled me aside, but not far enough away so the others couldn't hear her. "Don't mind them, Russell. I promised I'd sit with them, or else I'd come with you." She ran a finger down one of my sideburns. "But let me know when you find a spot and maybe I'll sneak away later."

I smiled, bobbed my head and headed off.

I surveyed the sun-washed area nearest the pool and saw there were still a few tempting spots available. Like the one between the gym bunny and the Antonio Banderas look-alike, or the one next to Mr. Pecs with a goatee, but alas, I spotted some of the Wiser clan and reminded myself that this was a working trip and headed in their direction.

It was the perfect group. With the exception of Harry, it included several of the family I'd not yet formally met (since they'd all disappeared from dinner the previous evening in a rush). Playing charming hostess, Harry stood upon my approach and introduced me to her Great-Aunt Faith, Faith's husband Thomas, their son Nick, and grandchildren Nigel and Nathan and Kayla. Apparently Marsha and Ted, parents of the twins and Kayla, were elsewhere.

"Won't you sit with us, Mr. Quant?" Faith offered kindly. "There's plenty of room."

"I'd love to, thank you," I accepted and pulled up a nearby lounger. I deposited my bag, peeled off my tank and began the laborious process of applying Ombrelle 15. I kind of hoped I'd get a surreptitious peek from Nick, but he seemed steadfastly focused on the pages of a paperback, something with "Blood" in the title. However, I did catch Kayla giving me a once-over.

"Are you enjoying the trip so far, Mr. Quant?" Thomas asked.

"Yes, thank you." I answered, applying block to my face.

Thomas was a tall man, although he had that unmistakable look some older men get that makes it appear as if they've shrunk. But for eighty-one, three years Faith's junior, he appeared every bit as fit and trim as his wife. They had the air of people who are steadfastly dedicated to a well-researched physical fitness regime. I imagined them heading out every morning for a several-kilometre walk with their dog, Muffin, wearing matching velour track suits, after which they'd eat abstemious breakfasts and lunches, only splurging at dinner with a drop of wine and maybe a single chocolate for dessert.

"I'm rather surprised we haven't met before now," he said. "Do you mind my asking how long you've known Charity?"

Oh no you don't. I'm the detective. I'm the one who drills for information. Sheesh, you'd think he'd at least give me time to get this damn block on. "Oh, quite some time now." Vague be my name.

He nodded as if I'd given him quite a lot to think about, then, "And, what is it exactly that you do for her?"

"Oh Thomas, the poor man is going to rue his decision to join us if you keep at him like this," Faith softly chided her husband.

"Oh my gawwwwd! Look at them now!" This came from Kayla, making like a 1980s Valley girl, even though the closest she came was the foothills of Alberta. Maybe she was a Foothilly girl? Her hair was mousy brown at the roots but startlingly blond elsewhere and even in the heat of midday she wore dark eye makeup that was beginning to run down the side of her face and coagulate with her suntan oil, which smelled overwhelmingly of coconut. I turned to see what she was referring to and saw that the object of her derision was none other than Phyllis, Mary and Rhoda. They had exchanged their wigs for rubber, floppy-flower-covered swim caps, having neatly placed their hairpieces on three wigstands, one on each of their chairs around their table, and were in the pool attempting some rather shocking synchronized swimming routines.

"My," Faith commented, "they certainly are…agile."

"That is like soooooo gross!" Kayla added her own commentary. "You can see the fat one's thingy!"

Before we knew it, two long, lean, brown-haired bodies dived into the water alongside the trio and began a duelling set of water ballet, much to the delight of a growing group of on-lookers. Joggers on the running track above the pool had stopped and were leaning over the protective railing to watch the spectacle as well. The joiners were Nigel and Nathan.

Harry clapped her hands a few times exclaiming, "Oh those two! I'd forgotten they were such dolphins in the water. They won some swimming competitions, didn't they Kayla?" she asked her cousin.

Kayla's face was curdled in disgust. "Yeah, I guess so. What a couple of freaks. Who knows what's in that water."

"Are you not intending on utilizing the pool this entire week then, dear?" asked Grandma Faith. Nice shot.

Kayla snorted her answer.

After a few more moments, the rabble-rousing in the pool died down and most of the sunbathers went back to the business of cooking their hides and ordering colourful drinks and the joggers returned to their jogging. Nigel and Nathan remained in the pool trading harmless barbs with the girls. I finally completed my blocking, lay on my lounger and welcomed the first delicious kiss of sun on my autumn-chilled skin.

"Where is Flora this morning?" I asked whoever might be listening. Flora was about the same age as Harry, Kayla and the boys. I would have expected her to be poolside with her cousins.

"I called her room to ask her to join us," Harry answered. "But she said she was going to be busy with Charity and Dottie."

And with that, we fell into silence. Even the others around the pool, as if by some unspoken acquiescence, were quiet and subdued, content for the moment to drink in the sun (and their cocktails) in peaceful bliss. I knew I should be interrogating my companions in search of a potential killer, but instead I allowed myself a few minutes of luxury on our floating Easy-Bake Oven set to Broil.

The next thing I knew I heard Faith's voice announce, "We're going in for a spot of lunch. Anyone care to join us?"

I opened my eyes and knew I'd been sleeping. Faith and her

husband were slipping on shirts and shorts over their bathing suits and gathering their things. How long had I been out?

"Sure, I'll come," Harry said, gathering up her things.

With the twins nowhere to be seen, that left me alone with Kayla and Nick, both motionless and silent beneath the black lenses of their sunglasses. I closed my eyes. Maybe just ten more minutes of shut-eye would be okay.

"Flora never sits in the sun," Kayla said out loud after a minute or two. "She's a bit of a screwball, if you hadn't already noticed."

I lay still and said, "Oh?"

I could hear Kayla slither into the lounger next to mine, leaving her uncle to his slumber a couple spots away. I pretended not to notice. "Actually, most of us kids are screwed up," she said, her voice much closer than before. "In one way or another, and it's because of our fucked up parents." I turned my head to look at her. She was facing sunward, pouty lips and nose pointing straight up, but from my vantagepoint I could see that her eyes were rolled to the side, peeking at me from behind her dark shades. She was checking if I was shocked to hear her say the "f" word—I wasn't. "They're the ones who fucked us up."

Perfect. Kayla was a detective's dream. She was a mouthy-Maxine who wasn't afraid to share her opinions of others, no matter how unpleasant they might be. My job was to keep on saying, "Oh?"

"You know about Flora's parents right?"

"Mmm."

"They were like killed in a horrible car accident. That's when Flora went to live with Charity. Her father was like a real bastard."

I did raise my eyebrows at this. "Why do you say that?"

She giggled a bit and adjusted herself on her lounger so she was half facing me, half keeping an eye on whatever half-dressed man passed our way. She was wearing a too-revealing white swimsuit that didn't do much for her figure, which one day could be just fine but was still on the chubby tomboy side. "No, I mean like a real bastard—a kid without a father. Charity wasn't married when she got knocked up. She couldda cared less when she had the kid. Pretty much ignored him, Mom says. She always tells us we're lucky not to have ended up with a mother like Charity. Anyway, apparently

Charity never had nothin' to do with him or his wife, even after Flora was born. They never came to any of the Charity Events. Charity never paid Flora any attention until her mom and dad were killed in that accident. And it wasn't an accident."

My ears grew red. "Oh?" I sat up on my elbows.

"Naw, they were like major drunks, both of 'em. It's no accident when you drink and then drive. That's what Mom always says. I think that's true. Don't you, Mr. Qu...Russell?"

"That's a sad story."

"Yeah, fer sure, like really, and then old Grandma Charity gets landed with another kid she doesn't want."

"Flora."

She nodded. "Oh yeah, Flora." She smiled at a passing blond man with muscular legs shown off to their best advantage in a fetching pair of purple and white swim trunks. He nodded at me and kept on walking. "Oh what's the use! This boat is like a bowl full of plastic fruit. Looks good, but you can't eat any of it."

As I choked back a laugh, I noticed six men on the other side of the pool near the cantina. It was a group I'd seen before, sticking to one another like a gaggle of newly hatched geese. They were pssting amongst themselves and one was pointing in our direction. Did they know me? Or Kayla? Or Nick? I made a point of staring at them; they noticed and scurried off.

"And Harry's dad. He's supposed to have been like this great musician—jazz or blues or something like that—stuff they listened to like a million years ago...what music do dinosaurs like?" She guffawed at her little joke and kept on when she noticed I wasn't laughing with her. "But really, all he's good at now is getting so buzzed he can barely stand. He's so creepy. I can't stand for him to be around me." She glanced over at Nick to make sure he was still asleep then said, "And then there's my mom and dad. I wish they'd get a divorce already. It's not like everyone doesn't know they want to."

"Maybe they're still trying to make it work," I said, only because it was her folks we were talking about for Pete's sake. I was beginning to wonder if half the stuff coming out of Kayla's mouth wasn't more about a teenager trying to impress me with her knowledge of worldly things and how little she cared one way or the other.

"Are you kidding? No way, dude. Y'know, the only cool person on this boat is Uncle Nick."

Kayla snookered down into her chair and closed her eyes, apparently content that our information exchange was complete. Not at all sleepy anymore, I let my gaze wander lazily around the pool like a butterfly, momentarily alighting on this hunk or that until I caught sight of something that really grabbed my interest— Richard Gray.

It looked like he had just arrived, wearing nothing but a snug pair of black trunks and black slip-on deck shoes. Over his muscular right shoulder he had tossed a dark brown beach towel that matched his chestnut tan. His well-defined chest was coated in a smattering of the same thick, shimmering silver hair that covered his head and was now slicked back as if he'd just emerged from a shower. His thighs and forearms were caramel-coated hams and his belly had just a hint of a roll, indicating a man who liked to keep in shape but not so much as to deny himself fine wine and cuisine.

He caught my look, which I had tossed his way, and he smiled. I watched as he made progress towards us, stopping every so often to chat with people he knew. Who were they? What were they saying to him? Get lost you chatty Pattys!

Whoa, Quant, get a hold of yourself man.

"Hello Russell, it's great to see you," he greeted me once he reached our part of the pool deck.

"Hi Richard." I could see that he was letting his eyes do a little roaming and I, after sucking in and sticking out the appropriate bits, did the same. Eventually we had to move on. "This is Kayla Moshier," I said with a nod at the prone girl's body.

She lowered her sunglasses and eyed him suspiciously as if to say, "Show me your heterosexual membership card before I pay you any attention."

"Hi Kayla." And then his eyes moved expectantly to the meaty lump that was Nick.

"Oh him, he's ah…ah…he's Nick." Shit, was he going to think

Nick was my boyfriend? "He's Uncle Nick," I blurted out, trying to ignore Kayla's withering stare.

The look on Richard's face told me he wasn't quite buying my line, but he was still smiling so I bumbled on. "Yes, he's an uncle, an old uncle friend of mine, of Kayla's who..." And that's where it...thankfully...ended, for we were interrupted by Flora who'd come rushing up from somewhere.

"Mr. Quant," she got out between pants. "Please, come right away. Something horrible has happened."

Charity and Dottie's suite was twice the size of the one I shared with Errall, with a full dining area and living room divided from the sleeping area by filmy drapery that billowed attractively with even the slightest breeze. Their deck was deeper and wider, with room for a patio table and significant lounging space, and this was where Flora and I found them, Charity spitting bullets.

"Can you believe this outrage!" she called out to me as soon as she saw me coming, and in the same breath added, "Pour yourself a drink, lovely." She was having champagne. I passed.

"The shameless, brazen audaciousness of it all; the bloody, ballsy little fucker!" Charity shamelessly, brazenly, audaciously showed off her command of biting adjectives with a verve that revealed a grudging respect for the ballsy little fucker. "It didn't even take them twenty-four hours to make a move!"

"What is it?" I asked, looking to Dottie and Flora for more. "What's happened?"

The two women knew better than to steal the spotlight from the star, so they remained quiet—Dottie rocking her head in a taciturn to-and-fro motion from where she sat, knitting in hand, and Flora standing next to her grandmother, but making no moves to calm her.

Charity flung herself against the railing with surprising force, almost dumping the contents of her flute into the water below. She was wearing a tailored dressing gown covered with large, black orchids over white. "Why don't they just toss me overboard! Flush me down the toilet with all the rest of the refuse! That would make them happy!" She turned back to us, noticed I was still empty-handed and said with a level voice, "No drink, lovely?"

She was looking for someone to play with and Flora and Dottie were either too tired or too savvy to oblige her. "Tell me what's happened?" I pleaded.

"Show it to him," she spat at Flora and then looked away as if trying to avoid a slap in the face.

Flora picked up a single sheet of paper from the table and handed it wordlessly to me.

It was a piece of the ship's personalized stationery, ripped at the top so the header read "From the suite of" and there it stopped, as if mocking us with its withholding of information. Below someone had written the words: CHANGE YOUR MIND OR I WILL KILL YOU.

I looked up at Charity and found her gazing at me with a self-satisfied smile on her lips. She raised her glass and whispered, "And so it begins."

"She knew this would happen, Mr. Quant," Dottie said, never looking up from her handiwork. "Have no doubt about that."

"Oh it's true. It's true!" Charity crowed, sweeping her way towards Dottie and affectionately patting the older woman's sweatered shoulder. "You know me so well."

I studied the note, taking in everything I could, from the phrasing of the threat—direct, no nonsense; the instrument used—a blue ink pen; and the style of writing—simple block letters, much different from Charity's flowing script, obviously meant to disguise the writer's true handwriting.

"Do you recognize the writing?" It couldn't hurt to ask.

"Of course not," Charity answered.

I eyed the other two women. They shook their heads. I wondered if they couldn't identify the writer because the writing was disguised or because they simply did not know the handwriting of the other family members. The likelihood of anyone recognizing someone's handwriting has become increasingly remote as the world of electronic communication has taken over. Even so, the author had been careless, no doubt acting on an emotional response to Charity's announcement.

I faced my client purposefully. "You've put yourself in unnecessary danger," I said to her.

She pursed her lips then, and in a very serious manner told me, "You are incorrect, Mr. Quant. You see, I already was in unnecessary danger."

Our table for dinner that night in the main dining room consisted of Ted and Marsha, Charity and Dottie, Flora, Phyllis, Richard and me. It was casual night but you'd never know it by looking at Dottie and Flora who both seemed to have only one type of clothing in a narrow spectrum of bland colours.

"Marsha, dear," Charity declared, "you don't appear to be enjoying the shark."

Marsha had teased her hair until it looked like a see-through helmet of brown webbing. Her face might have been pretty were it not for a pointed chin (à la Wicked Witch) and eyebrows plucked in such a way as to give her a perpetual frown. She wore a navy-and-blue striped dress with shoulder pads befitting a linebacker—which was a fitting complement to her husband, Ted, who looked like a football player gone to pot. His once fine physique had remoulded itself over years of beer-and-pizza abuse into a puffer-fish version of itself, each deflated muscle group covered over by a gelatinous layer of potato chips, deep-fried food and cream sauce. Marsha had outfitted her blank-faced hubby in a matching navy-and-blue striped shirt that was intended to make him (next to her) look adorable but only managed tight-fitting awkwardness. "It's just fine," she lied, her shark in dill sauce untouched. She was too preoccupied to pay attention to her meal or Charity, her eyes across the room where her messy-haired young sons were seated at a table of fawning men who wore beautiful linen jackets and expensive jewellery.

"Really?" Charity kept on. "You haven't touched a bite. We could have saved the shark and served you a minnow." And she laughed at that in an unattractive way.

"I truly love eating shark," Phyllis interjected. "It's like cannibalizing my ex-husband."

Marsha shot Phyllis a look as if she'd just eaten a rotten oyster. And Phyllis noticed.

"What's the matter, honey? Never felt like eating your husband?" she asked with a cackle, shooting meaty Ted a come-hither look. "If not, I might take a bite."

"So tell me, Mr. Gray," Flora twittered nervously, hoping to change the subject. "What do you know about Tunisia? Have you been there before?"

"Do you really expect any of us to believe you had a husband?" Marsha said to Phyllis with a curl of her heavily painted upper lip.

Oh oh.

"I have," Richard began, warily eyeing the exchange between good drag queen and bad drag queen look-alikes. "Tunis itself has a very easygoing, laid-back air about it, certainly liberal by Islamic standards. I think you'll quite enjo…"

"Do you really expect any of us to believe you haven't been checking out every bubble-butted twink passing by our table? Hoping for a little action on the side?" Phyllis cracked back, knowing not what she spoke of, but, as many do when cornered, she was making things up just to get in her barbs.

Marsha rose faster than a towel in a bathhouse, huffing and puffing and pointing a crimson-hued fingernail at her well-armed verbal opponent. "You take that back you…you…you disgrace of a man. You should be ashamed of yourself."

"Aunt Marsha, please," this from Flora.

Ted was looking wholly discomfited, trying hard to keep up with what was going on and not knowing enough to decide what to do or say. Finally he reached up for his wife's hand with a grease-stained one of his own and said, "Don't get them riled up, Marsha." He yanked on her sleeve, encouraging her to sit back down. "We're outnumbered here."

He was right. By this time several diners in our vicinity had abandoned their own sparkling dinner table conversations in favour of listening to ours—some with mirth, others with barely disguised disapproval.

Marsha looked around and, sensing she was a dartboard in a

room full of poison arrows, quickly sat down.

"This is your fault," she barked in Charity's direction. "Putting us on this boat full of fairies and lezzies."

"Fairies and lezzies and drag queens, oh my. Fairies and lezzies and drag queens, oh my." An unamused Phyllis doing Dorothy.

Uncharacteristically, Charity had been sitting back, delighting in the wordplay. But now she made a noisy display of placing her elbows on the tabletop, one hand under her chin, fiery eyes glaring at Marsha. "You're welcome to leave, my dear," she offered in a venom-tipped tone, her other hand flicking Marsha's attention towards the depthless sea just beyond the windows. "At any time."

"Look at you tonight!" a new voice boomed behind Charity, taking her by surprise. "You are a real vision, Char, a real vision."

Charity turned slightly in her chair to face a beaming James McNichol, inexplicably wearing a tuxedo on casual night along with a spit-and-polish pair of black and white wingtips. The entire dining room could smell his Aqua Velva.

"Oh for God's sake, Jimmy, you startled me. Care to join us? I'm sure Marsha wouldn't mind giving you her seat."

Marsha glowered and turned to her husband for support. Instead she found him digging into his meal like a gold prospector into a riverbed. "I'm just going to check on the boys," she sniffed, pushing back from her plate with an upturned nose. "You can take my spot if you want it."

I watched Marsha stalk away and considered where the Moshier family ranked on my list of suspects. Thus far I'd noticed that Ted and Marsha, unlike their twin sons, were rather uncomfortable being surrounded by a boatload of homosexuals. But it wasn't until now that they...or at least Marsha, had shown her true colours as an all-out homophobe. Whereas the couple seemed to have already guessed, probably years ago, that Charity and Dottie were a couple, they'd put up with it to stay on Charity's—or rather her money's—good side. Now, with Charity's announcement redistributing all her wealth to charity, I guess Marsha couldn't hold it in any longer. I wondered if she'd later come to think of her outburst as a mistake. It certainly was if she thought there was any hope at all of Charity changing her mind. Or maybe, it didn't matter...if Marsha knew Charity wouldn't survive long enough to make the change to her will. And Ted, well, I wasn't sure about him. He seemed to be less bothered by the whole thing than his wife. I knew from daughter Kayla that Ted and Marsha were not exactly enjoying marital bliss, so maybe he just didn't really care anymore. And as for Kayla, she was a forty-six-year-old, hard-luck barmaid in a teenager's body. I'd have to watch out for her. She was just the type to pull a few surprises from her bustier.

"No, no, no, by no means," James replied to empty air. Marsha had already run off to rescue her boys from the homosexual conversion ceremony she was sure was taking place across the room. "I don't mean to interrupt your dinner. I just wanted to get a jump on other would-be suitors and ask you, dear Charity, if you would do me the great honour of accompanying me to the dance to be held later this evening."

Charity focused on his face for a moment, as if she could actually see the marbles pouring out of his head. Phyllis let out a squawk but remained quiet after I gave her a little nudge under the table. Flora grimaced sickly, Richard appeared bemused by what was going on and Dottie was contentedly spearing vegetables with her fork, a tiny smile playing on her lips.

"Jimmy," Charity finally spoke. "If I accompany anyone to the dance, it will be my Dottie."

James straightened himself out and smiled beatifically at Dottie who kept on eating. "Oh, well, of course," he said magnanimously. "Dottie is not to be left alone in her room. Of course she will come too." He winked at Charity. Then, before traipsing off, he added, "I look forward to seeing *both* of you there. What a gay affair it will be."

Indeed.

I wanted to make it to the Munchkin Land Auditorium in time for Alberta's act, but I'd dribbled some chocolate dessert on my pale-blue shirt and needed to rush back to the room for a change and fresh spritz of cologne. When I threw open the cabin's door I heard a small yip of surprise. By the look on Errall's face, you'd have thought I caught her trying on frilly clothing. But the truth was bad enough, I suppose. There she was, chair pulled up to the TV, engrossed in a mindless romantic comedy, her face buried in a plate of fried chicken and fries. And she was wearing sweats! Sweats! On a cruise ship. Who brought sweats on a cruise?

I carefully closed the door behind me and approached her like a family pet that may have gone rabid. "Errall? What are you doing?"

She stared at me with big, round eyes, each a pool of blue surrounded with white. In her right hand was a drumstick and in her left a fistful of fries. "What are you doing back so soon?"

"I thought you said you were having dinner with some girls you met up with," I said.

The sheepishness of being caught unawares quickly dissipated and was replaced by Errall's usual briny attitude. She turned back towards the screen and hoovered the fries. "I lied."

"Yeah? Why'd you do that?"

"None of your business."

"What's that supposed to mean?"

"I'm watching a movie here," she replied testily.

"Push pause and answer my question."

"Are you my mother all of a sudden? Just because I agreed to come on this trip with you doesn't mean you can tell me what to do. If I want to dine alone, that's what I'll do. Now fuck off."

"You fuck off."

Now she pushed pause. Criminy. She put the chicken back on the plate. I was in for it.

She turned on me with her best Joan Crawford sans wire hangers. "Maybe I'm sick of you. Ever think of that? Huh? Did you?"

I hadn't.

"You know I appreciate being invited along, I already told you that like about a million times."

Try once.

"But I don't want to be in your back pocket all the time. We're not that kind of friends, Russell. We're not really friends at all. So there's no need to be side by side all day long pretending that we are."

"That's fine!" I retorted, feeling a hot blush overcome my face. Why exactly, I wasn't sure. Was it because I knew she was right?

I stormed towards the closet, yanking off my soiled shirt, balling it up and tossing it to the floor. I made a hasty search for a replacement, choosing a flimsy, red, sleeveless pullover with a too-deep, buttonless V-neck that I'd bought on a foolish whim and brought along just in case I ever found myself in a foolish mood. I certainly wasn't then, but it was the only thing that looked like it wouldn't need ironing. I stamped my feet on the way to the bathroom, gave my hair a desultory fingering, forgot about the cologne and headed for the door. I opened it, halted, looked back at Errall. Her face was back in the TV and chicken dinner.

I opened my mouth, closed it, opened it again. "I was beginning to think that maybe we *were* friends," I said.

She turned up the volume. I left.

Chapter 7

"That's a very sexy shirt."

Richard had saved me a seat next to him in Munchkin Land. I slid into the booth and because I was still a little miffed from my exchange with Errall I ordered a double Canadian Club and Coke to help take the edge off. On stage, a comedian who called herself Suzy Screendoor was just wrapping up her set. By the smiles in the room I could tell she'd been a hit. Or else everyone else was having doubles too. Alberta was next.

"Well thank you, sir," I replied saucily. "All compliments are graciously accepted and stored away for replay in the future."

We smiled at one another, our eyes holding a little longer than necessary, exchanging the mutual message that we were into one another. I wondered if he had a cabin all to himself.

"Sorry about the dinner show," I said, referring to the Wiser clan dramatics we'd witnessed earlier.

He laughed. "Don't mention it. In my line of work, you can't begin to imagine some of the craziness I've seen. That was lame in comparison. I've come to expect it actually. When people travel together, even the closest of families or best of friends, there are always fireworks. There's truly nothing like being at sea, but let's face it, being on a cruise ship is like being stuck in a hotel you can't leave. Most people are sharing rooms smaller than their bathrooms back home. Flare-ups are bound to occur."

I thought of my argument with Errall and wondered if that counted for us too. We worked in the same building, but we'd never before gone away together, never mind shared a room. We were definitely testing new ground. The question was, should we have even tried? "I suppose that's true." But I was too pissed to talk about it. I wanted to percolate a bit longer. So I changed the subject. "Have you known the Wiser clan for a long while?"

He gave me an appraising look before answering. Was he wondering if I was playing the advisor role, looking out for my client's best interests and debating whether his travel agency was the best one to serve her? Or maybe he was just admiring my bare arms. "Not really," he answered. "And only Charity. I helped her with the travel arrangements for this trip. I'd been wanting to try out The Dorothy for some time as you can imagine. I like having first-hand knowledge of whatever I'm suggesting for my clients. I'd been on the smaller FOD schooner, The Toto, and loved it. So I was pretty certain this would measure up nicely. Anyway, it was just good fortune that it worked out for me to travel with Charity and her family and try out The Dorothy at the same time."

"I bet you're sorry now," I said, only half joshing.

"Not all at," he said, quite seriously. "If I hadn't been on this voyage, I'd never have met you."

Oh yeah. That's it, boy. More of that.

My drink arrived and I used it to lubricate my suddenly dry throat.

"I have a confession to make," I said, in an attempt to cool my overheating jets.

Richard's face fell. "You have a boyfriend?"

"Oh no, no, not at all. No boyfriend."

Big bright smile. "How can that be?"

I shrugged bashfully.

"Haven't found any suitable boyfriend material yet?"

I didn't want to go there. I hadn't found suitable boyfriend material because, although I'd never admit it, least of all to myself, I simply hadn't been looking. It was all too complicated to think about on a luxury cruise. "What I meant to confess is that this trip—keep in mind this is something I haven't told anyone—but this trip, this ship...on all this water in particular...kind of freaks me out."

Richard's eyes opened wide in mock shock. "You've got to be kidding?" he guffawed. "A big strong guy like you? Scared of water? Have you been sea sick?"

I shook my head. "Surprisingly and gratefully not. I had some quivers the first day; I'm still sleeping a bit fitfully, but otherwise...well, otherwise it's been pretty terrific."

"I'm glad. I must say that having The Dorothy as your first seafaring experience certainly helps. She's a state-of-the-art beauty. We could sail through a hurricane and you'd hardly feel it. I probably wouldn't suggest The Toto though. Maybe a bit small for you."

I remembered Errall's description and quite agreed. About then, appreciative applause for Suzy and introduction of Alberta ended our conversation. I leaned into Richard and whispered into his ear, "She's from Saskatoon." I was oddly proud.

As Alberta did her bit, we watched in companionable silence, every so often knocking knees or stealing smoldering glances.

Ever the chameleon, tonight Alberta was a flapper, with a sequined band around her head, a drop waist dress and countless strands of beads swaying from her neck. Mid-jaw, she'd drawn a large beauty mark. Once again she worked the stage like a pro, alternating bawdy humour with sincere kindness and displaying shockingly accurate insight into what certain members of the audience were thinking about. And once again it happened. And I knew exactly when, as clearly as if an arrow had hit a bull's eye painted on her forehead. She was making her way down one of the aisles that ran the length of the audience from stage to back doors, kibitzing with people as she passed, and she just stopped, dead in her tracks. Her head jerked back and her eyes grew wide and filled

with liquid so that they shone in the glare of the spotlight that followed her wherever she went.

I'm going to kill her.

I could see her gaze attempt to penetrate the crowded room as
if trying to pinpoint the source of what she'd heard in her head.
She looked shaken, perplexed, helpless and then frightened. I
wanted to go to her but I didn't want to cause a scene unless I was
sure she needed help. Her eyes moved over the crowd until they
found mine.

I nodded, as if to confirm, "You heard it again?"

She nodded back.

Immediately I scanned the room to see which members of the
Wiser clan I could account for. Slowly I counted them off.

They were all there.

Richard and I joined the boisterous flow of people moving from
Munchkin Land to the ship's nightclub, Emerald City, on Deck
Eight. It was just after 11 p.m. when we got there and the place was
already hopping. What kind of gay people were these? Didn't they
know it was against the rules to even show up at a club before
midnight? Like every other area of the ship, Emerald City did its
best to evoke its namesake, well, sort of. There were shimmering
emerald towers, gilded booths of green leather edged with gold,
and green drinks were being served from behind a bar construct-
ed out of giant yellow bricks piled atop one another. High above
the glimmering dance floor were four cages, not for winged mon-
keys (although that would have been cool), but for Dorothy, the
Tin Man, the Cowardly Lion and the Scarecrow—or rather the go-
go-dancer versions. Dorothy's dress was barely there and her ruby
red shoes were five-inch-high stilettos. Her three companions were
taut where it counted and their get-ups came direct from the MGM
Studios wardrobe department—the porn section.

We got great seats in a booth, joining Harry, Faith and Thomas.
From there I could keep an eye on most of the action in the room.
We ordered a round of drinks and sat back to enjoy the music and
watch the action. It was a Cher retrospective performed by a pret-

ty decent impersonator. I felt Richard's arm glide effortlessly around my shoulders, as if it was meant to be there. I gave him a look and wondered what we were waiting for.

"Oh look," Harry said, fluttering her hands in a wave, looking at something over our heads. "It's Uncle Ted and Auntie Marsha. I'm so glad they came. We can scoot over to make room for them, can't we?"

I spotted the couple, standing like sentinels at the entrance, effectively blocking the flow of traffic into the nightclub. They hadn't caught sight of us yet; they were too busy taking in the tumultuous scene before them. The place was a dizzying array of predominantly male-male, female-female couples in full cruise ship party mode. A rather aggressive mob of drag queens and kings and a few Auntie Em/Uncle Henry and Glinda/Elvira Gulch combos came up behind them, desperate to get in. Judging by the looks on their faces, Marsha and Ted realized they weren't in Alberta anymore and didn't like it one bit. Huddling together like two kids in a fright house, they let the revellers squeeze by, trying not to get any on them. Without acknowledging Harry's efforts to guide them over to our booth, they turned tails and headed for high ground.

"Oh drat, I guess they didn't see us," Harry said, and then she let loose a shriek of surprise.

For a second time our gazes followed hers to the entranceway. And there, like a butterfly emerging from its cocoon, posed a new and improved Flora Wiser. Gone were the Birkenstocks, gone were the layers of dull, drab heavy fabrics, gone were the macramé accessories. Instead, Charity's wallflower granddaughter was wearing a smart off-white, one-piece pantsuit with a halter-style top and a gaily-coloured scarf that flowed down her back. The outfit did wonders to compliment her chicken-bone frame and pale complexion. Her hair had been released from its ponytail bondage and her makeup was flawless, if not a little on the dramatic side, giving her usual pallor some much-needed vitality. She looked like a real, live, pretty girl. And behind every good woman, is another good woman…or a good drag queen. Several steps behind Flora, for the time being content to be out of the limelight, stood Phyllis, beaming with motherly pride. Somehow the two had connected and created this mini-miracle.

As the recreated Flora walked towards our table, a little unsteady on her mid-height heels, we all stood to greet and gush over her. She was breathless but excited by the attention. Nigel Moshier, a young stud who knew a good thing as soon as he spotted it, appeared out of nowhere and dragged Flora off to the dance floor. Faith and Thomas and Nathan and Harry quickly followed. Richard and I were left standing with Phyllis when James McNichol sauntered up, still in his tuxedo.

"Might I have this dance, young lady," he said to Phyllis, sizing up her faux breasts.

Phyllis accepted his arm like a seasoned pro and, nose held high, marched into the writhing crowd shaking it to "Gypsys, Tramps & Thieves."

I had no idea if James knew he was dancing with a man. As Richard and I joined the others, I decided it didn't much matter.

After a couple of doubles I switched to water by the glassful as a pre-emptive strike against the hangover I would get if I kept going down the rye-and-Coke-soaked road. The pro was that it would work, the con was that it kept me from Richard's side because of all the time I spent visiting the bathroom. It was on one of these trips that I caught sight of Flora, waiting in line to get into the Emerald City's women's washroom (there was, as usual, no lineup for the men's). I sidled up to her and complimented her once more on her new look.

"I really don't know what came over me or why I let her do this," Flora said, her usual nodding replaced by doubtful shakes of her newly coiffured head.

"Don't ask why," I suggested. "Just enjoy."

She ran a red-tipped fingernail, already showing signs of chipping, down her makeup-caked cheek. "It doesn't feel like me. It's like I'm in disguise or something." She said it with a sad smile and I wondered if being in disguise was a good feeling for her.

I looked around to ensure the gals nearest us weren't paying us any attention—they weren't—before I asked, "Flora, did you know about your grandmother's intention to change her will?"

"No. But it wouldn't have made much difference if I had. She never really listens to my opinion—or anyone's opinion—once she makes up her mind about something, it's full steam ahead."

"So you don't like the idea?" Flora already had a million dollars of the Wiser fortune, but I knew from my review of Charity's will that she had been due to inherit a great deal more, dollars that were now going to charity.

"Of course not. I knew it would put her in greater danger. And I was right. You saw the note."

Flora knew—assuming the poisoning of Morris the cat was indeed a failed murder attempt on her grandmother—that Charity was already in danger, even before she set foot on this boat. But she was right. Charity's plan to rile up her relatives couldn't help matters and might even encourage someone driven to the thought of murder to actually commit it even faster.

"Do you have any idea who could have sent that note, Flora?" I asked her.

"I really don't," she said, wide-eyed, almost as if she thought she should and couldn't believe it wasn't obvious to her. Or maybe she was just having a tough time seeing since Phyllis had made her dump her glasses in favour of glamour. "Do you?"

Flora had reached the end of the line and it was her turn to enter the bathroom. I shook my head. She nodded a bit and disappeared.

It was hours later, long after Cher had wiped the fake tattoos off her butt and gone to bed, replaced by a DJ who kept the crowd awake with mindless thumping tunes, when the scuffle broke out. I don't know what it is that draws me to a fight like a cat to catnip. I simply cannot sit back and watch. It must be my police training that brings only one thought to mind whenever I hear the unmistakable sounds of a brawl: break it up! The commotion began somewhere in the back corner of Emerald City. Richard and I were in our booth, making forays into the "How far up his thigh can I put my hand in public" game, so he was no doubt a little startled when I jumped up like a jack-in-the-box.

Fights in a gay bar aren't like fights in a straight bar. First of all, the chance that the combatants are women rather than men is pretty high. If it's women, the reasons for the fight are usually the same as they are in a straight bar: drunkenness, sports, jealousy over a woman, vehicle envy or just because. If it's men, the cause is likely even more irrational, like the wearing of a certain pair of pants when you promised your boyfriend you wouldn't, a bitchy comment about someone's new haircut, or an overheated debate regarding who has the best pecs: Orlando or Brad or Tom or Mel (depending on your generational preference). If it's women, the fists are out and there is likely to be blood. If it's men, there's generally a lot of slapping and name-calling—as you'd expect from people whose only frame of reference for a good fight is Alexis and Krystle on *Dynasty*. If it's women, there are usually a lot of other women around catcalling, urging it on, taking mental notes for the next time they're in the ring. If it's men, the women onlookers are bored and the men look away with disdain or horrid childhood memories of schoolyard bullies.

"Break it up! Break it up!" I ordered as I bulled my way towards the scrappers, grabbing the attention of the few nightclub patrons in that part of the bar who weren't already observing the action.

I saw that it was two men, both big burly sorts in jeans and Lacostes that were stretched tight over heaving chests. They were doing a wrestling kind of dance while standing up, all entangled arms and legs, pushing and pulling, neither one getting anywhere. They seemed evenly matched. It wasn't until I began inserting one of my own arms between them that I realized I knew one of the combatants.

"Nick, Nick," I grunted as I sluiced my way into the fray. "Just stop it. Come on guys, call it off."

Hearing his name threw him off. Nick Kincaid released his grasp on the other guy and stumbled back.

"You asshole!" his opponent screamed at him. "What's the matter with you? I said I was sorry, okay!"

I looked at Nick and saw he was bleeding from his lip and a cut

110

on his cheek. I'd seen cuts like that before. I gave the other guy a once-over. He was wearing a ring on the middle finger of his right hand that had done the damage, and now he was also wearing a black-blooming eye and swollen nose. A fair exchange of war wounds I'd say.

"That's enough," I said with authority, as if I had any. It was about then that ship security pulled up, a man and woman looking posh in their uniforms and a little surprised. "Just call it a night, would ya?" I suggested, still having no idea what the fight was about.

"Yeah, whatever," the guy with the shiner said, skulking off into a group of waiting friends—the goslings I'd noticed around the pool.

Nick stood there, silent, staring after the guy as if he'd just woken up and was wondering what had happened.

"What's going on here?" one of the guards asked with indignation.

I ignored him and rounded up Nick under my arm and began leading him to the exit.

From the stage came a blaring announcement, "Ladies and ladies, gentlemen and gentlemen, ladies and gentlemen! We're going to top off your evening with a special treat," bellowed the DJ, valiantly trying to refocus the crowd's attention on having fun. As if spontaneous fisticuffs weren't special treat enough. "We have with us on The Dorothy one of the greats of jazz."

Everyone clapped wildly and scanned the room as if they could identify a jazz great by sight. I was still pulling on Nick to get him out of there but we both came to a full stop when we saw Jackson Delmonico take to the stage, looking as clear-eyed and lively as I'd ever seen him. The applause died down and he played a few trilling riffs on his horn, stopped, and searched the audience until he found who he was looking for.

"Harry, honey," he rasped into a microphone. "Come on up here and give these folks a thrill."

Without further urging, Harry joined her father on stage, looking for all the world like a real star. Out of the corner of my eye I could see the two security guards heading our way. I didn't think there was anything they could do to Nick other than ask him to leave. But why give them the satisfaction? Besides, I wanted to find out what happened. So with the sound of Harry's dulcet tones transporting the appreciative crowd somewhere over the rainbow, I pushed Nick to somewhere out of Emerald City. I glanced back only once, hoping to catch sight of Richard, but all I saw was Flora, on the dance floor, arms outstretched, face turned up, eyes closed, twirling round and round and round. All by herself in the middle of a diffused circle of light.

"You need to visit the infirmary," I said to Nick as we made our way out of the nightclub. "You're bleeding pretty good."

"I'm okay, I just need some fresh air," he grumbled, walking so fast it seemed he was trying to get away from me.

Now why would he want to do that?

"Okay, look, at least let me get you cleaned up," I suggested, scrambling to keep up.

There's a scene in almost every romance-slash-action movie where the hero gets hurt and the heroine attends to his wounds. For a moment the woman is the strong one, in a way rescuing the man by nursing him back to health, and the man is the weak one, wincing like a baby whenever she tries to clean the injured area. The whole thing usually leads to a kiss, or even sex, during which all injuries miraculously disappear.

I shook my head to clear away this type of thinking. Hadn't I just been playing the thigh game with Richard? And, Nick Kincaid was a suspect. Surely I could come up with a better way to investigate him than playing doctor.

Nick threw open the door that led to the Pool Deck and strode into the darkened outdoor area, pulling in great lungfuls of air as he went. I followed. He made for the pool which of course led me to imagine any number of "you really should get out of those wet clothes" scenarios. But instead of a midnight dip he did a couple paces back and forth then ended up at the railing, fists tightened around the steel bars, gazing out at the black sea.

I pulled up beside him. "What happened back there? What was the fight about?"

"Can't you just leave me alone?"

Ahhhhh...nope. I studied Nick Kincaid's profile. Strong, jagged, dark, his jaw bristling with pricks of black hair that defied two shaves a day. Was this a man given to extremes of temper? Violence? Was he capable of murder? What would it take? His share of the Wiser fortune? Yup, I could see this bronco of a man as a killer, but I didn't think poison and threatening notes would be his modus operandi.

"How far would you have gone with that guy?" I pushed him. "Break his nose? Arm? Really hurt him?"

"Get lost, would you?"

"Why are you on this boat, Nick? Why did you come? You don't seem to be having a very good time. You're getting into fights. Is Charity's money so important to you?"

"The fight wasn't my fault!" he turned to look at me, his face pushed into mine. "You don't know...you...you just don't know, man."

"So tell me."

"Listen," he said, his deep voice a baritone warning. I could feel his cold words hot on my cheeks. "I don't care who you are. You just stay out of my way."

With that he walked off. I debated following him and decided to do it.

"Why are you here?" I called after him, thinking that if I asked the question enough times maybe I'd get an answer.

He was back at the double doors that would take him inside. He stopped and turned to stare at me, frustration on his face. I stopped too, about three metres away. He closed the distance in a flash and the next thing I knew he was breathing down my neck. As he hovered over me with his extra two inches I noticed something I hadn't noticed about him before. It was a refinement, a look about him that told a different story. He was a big, rugged man, but his skin looked soft, his hair well-cut, teeth unnaturally white and straight. This was a guy who cared a lot about how he looked.

"Why are *you* here?" he growled.

Oooo. Got me there.

And just as suddenly, he backed down and stepped away. "I'm

here same as the rest. I'm playing by the rules. Right?"

I uttered a sound that could have meant anything and watched Nick go, leaving in his wake the scent of expensive cologne...and a secret.

After tailing Nick Kincaid to the cigar bar where he ordered a hefty scotch, I dashed back to Emerald City and saw that Jackson and Harry were still entertaining an enthralled crowd of giddy spectators. Perfect. It looked to me that both Nick and Jackson would be otherwise engaged for a while, hopefully long enough to allow me to do a little spy work.

It was the threatening note Charity received that convinced me a bit of snooping in the Wiser family rooms wouldn't be a bad idea. In particular, I'd be looking for samples of the room occupant's handwriting to compare to the note, but generally I'd be taking a sniff for anything else that might help me confirm their position on my list of suspects, or even eliminate them from it completely. My room searches were going to be difficult. Except for Flora, who had her own room, all the other Wisers shared a cabin on The Dorothy—Charity and Dottie, Faith and Thomas, Marsha and Ted, James and Patrick, Nigel and Nathan, Kayla and Harry, and, my first targets, Nick and Jackson. For a successful incursion—i.e. I don't get caught—I had to ensure that both roommates would be occupied while I was in their room. And, the fact that I was supposed to be with the Wisers during most waking hours didn't make it any simpler. What was simple was the breaking-in part. I'd practiced on my own cabin door with my handy set of lock picks and had the whole thing down to less than ten seconds.

I sauntered up and down the hallway in front of Nick and Jackson's room until I was certain I'd have enough time to get in without being seen by a fellow passenger, then, nine seconds later, I was in. The room itself was identical to the one I was sharing with Errall, so I was immediately familiar with the layout. I noticed the bed had been turned down—good thing, I didn't want a maid interrupting me. I turned on a bedside lamp that I knew to have subtle lighting and began my foray into the world of the dark and brutish and handsome Nick Kincaid and the heavy-drinking, hard-living, jazz-playing Jackson Delmonico. I gave myself ten minutes tops.

Twelve minutes later I'd found several near-empty bottles of vodka (Jackson) decorating the room at strategic locations—as if the drinker wanted to ensure he'd never have to move more than a few steps should he suddenly want a snort; two hefty rolls of cash (Nick or Jackson?); several cartons of cigarettes (Jackson); a bathroom with a dizzying array of expensive men's products (Nick) and some cheapass crap (Jackson); sparkling white bikini undies (Nick, I hoped) and some I didn't want to touch (Jackson); music industry mags (Jackson) and blow 'em up novels (Nick); and, other than wardrobes consistent with what I'd seen the two men wearing—pricey and tasteful (Nick); colourful and dated (Jackson)—very little else. I found writing samples for both men— Jackson had written some notes in one of his magazines and Nick had carelessly left his passport in an easy-to-find hiding place— but neither looked even remotely similar to that of the note.

I glanced at my watch and knew I was running out of time. What had I found out? Jackson was a man with some bad habits. Could he afford them? Was he desperate for money? Nick had expensive tastes. Could he afford them? Was he desperate for money? And one of the two men was hauling around an awful lot of extra cash; especially on an all-expense-paid cruise. Why? Was it to pay for bad habits or the good life? Or for murder?

Chapter 8

"Good morning, passengers!" Judy Smythwicke's singing voice spilled from the ship's PA system like syrup from a bottle. "And what a delightful morn it is here in Tunisia! Now, just a few tips for the day. Remember this is a conservative country, so please dress accordingly. No bare legs, no bare shoulders. I'd keep my expensive jewellery at home today ladies, if I were you."

Oh come on Judy, I thought to myself as I awoke from a deep slumber, it's the guys who have the jewels on this boat.

"And do beware of purse snatchers and pickpockets," she suggested as gaily as if she were recommending arugula salad over Caesar for lunch. "And I must tell you I spy a few clouds lollygagging about, so I do suggest a parasol even though it does appear to be bluing up nicely on the horizon." Parasol? Bluing up? Judy Smythwicke was beginning to irritate me.

Dress conservatively. No bare legs. No bare shoulders. No jewellery. How could any serious drag queen abide by those rules, I wondered to myself, correctly predicting that many would choose to stay on board and get stinking drunk by the pool. God help us all when we returned.

As Charity considered Tunis the most exotic of our stops, she'd requested that Richard arrange a tour guide and bus for the sole use of the Wisers for the day. So after being processed by Tunisian Immigration, while the other passengers were being crammed into a few large buses, we were being met by a little brown man in a freshly pressed brown shirt and brown trousers named Azib who led us to a roomy, air-conditioned minibus.

Even though Errall and I sat together while we waited for whatever it is one waits for before a tour bus can leave, we said little more than two words to each other. I hadn't gotten much sleep and by the looks of it, neither had she. Not until you see someone early in the morning, before coffee, cosmetics and a comb can you really call yourselves friends. Errall was working on all three in a disjointed manner. Her nearly cold coffee was slopping about in a Styrofoam cup while she tried with her free hand to manipulate a makeup mirror, hairbrush and stick of lip gloss. All with little success.

"Truce," I called as I grabbed the coffee and mirror from her, putting the coffee between my knees and holding the mirror up in front of her face so she could finish her ministrations.

"Of course," she quickly agreed, assessing her face in the mirror. "I'm sorry about yesterday. I just wanted to be alone, y'know?"

"Sure," I said offhandedly but saying nothing more. I wasn't in the mood to get into it right then; I just didn't want to spend the day not talking to one another. So while she fixed her face, I surveyed the bus. All the Wisers were on board except Harry's father and grandfather, Jackson and Patrick who'd both decided to remain on board. I also noticed that Flora, obviously heeding the dress code to the extreme, had returned to her former drabness, leaving last night's metamorphosis in an abandoned pile of fabulousness somewhere on the ship. Phyllis would be crushed.

"That didn't mean you had to stay out half the night," she said, a mischievous glimmer appearing in her two blues as she peeked out at me over the top edge of the mirror.

"Can you believe we're in Northern Africa?" I tried for a segue.

"You slept with Richard," she said, digging in a satchel for some cream stuff.

"We were dancing."

"You're walking bull-legged. Where is he? How's he walking? Isn't he coming along on this junket?"

"No." And I was glad. I didn't want to talk about this. "He's with some of his other clients today."

"That so? Or in his cabin recovering?"

"I liked it better when we weren't talking."

"Give me back my coffee and it's a deal."

Over the jabbering of the Wisers I heard the bus grunt to life. The door closed and we began to move. I handed Errall her coffee and she allowed herself to be distracted by the moving landscape on the other side of her window. I began to lay my plans. It was time to divide and conquer. I'd now had a chance to meet all the players in the game. It was time to assess each one's level of suspicion.

I decided to begin with Ted and Marsha Moshier. Of everyone, except possibly Patrick Halburton, and after last night, Nick Kincaid, they seemed to be the most disgruntled of the bunch on this trip. Their dislike—particularly Marsha's—for Charity simmered below a surface of fakery. Her dislike for gay people, like Charity and Dottie, was even more obvious and she appeared to be continuously distressed about having her children, particularly the twins, Nigel and Nathan, under the influence, so to speak, of a bunch of lezzies and fairies. I knew from their own daughter, Kayla, that their marriage was on the rocks. I was curious to see what else I might find out if I spent some time with them. I didn't relish the thought but I was on the clock.

As the bus haltingly made its way through a section of diplomats' residences to the massive Cathedral of St. Louis atop someplace called Byrsa Hill, it became abundantly clear to us that Azib was a clever man who knew English very well and did not suffer fools gladly. As a result, he did most of the talking and, except for a fearless Charity, few of us asked questions. This was okay as he seemed to predict most anything we'd want to know, explaining in depth every structure, rock formation and vegetable we passed, tossing in some rather colourful and, I think, politically fiery conjecture along the way.

Whenever possible throughout the day, I positioned myself close to Ted and Marsha, engaging them in small talk, getting them used to me hanging around, waiting for a chance to do my detecting shtick. Along the way we visited the few remaining pebbles of Carthage, which was once the dominating power in the western half of the Mediterranean until some Russell Crowe–like Romans threw a tantrum and destroyed it all. The Antonine Baths were not at all what I'd reckoned on for a gay tour. Then we stopped in a lovely whitewashed town called Sidi Bou Said which, unexpectedly, looked liked every whitewashed-walls-blue-shutters-bougainvillea-covered Greek isle village you've ever seen on a postcard. According to Azib, long before the Romans came along, the Greeks also tried to conquer Carthage. Although they tried for about two hundred years, yet never succeeded, it certainly looked as if they'd left behind an interior decorator or two.

Our last stop of the day was for a late lunch and shopping in the city of Tunis itself. We drove through rather modern-looking streets clogged with modern-looking traffic jams, and ended up in a parking lot near a massive, flagstone square where sharply dressed businesspeople mixed with schleppy students and housewives with children, none of whom covered their faces with fabric. And there were tourists, lots of tourists.

As we stepped off the bus into this unknown world, Azib raised a yellow umbrella high over his head. Had Judy Smythwicke gotten to him too?

"It is a beacon," he told us in his clipped accent. "Where we're going is very, very crowded," he warned. "If you fall behind, just keep your eyes on the sunshade."

It seemed ridiculous at first as we paraded through the spacious square. We looked like a group of grade school children on a field trip being led by an overly cautious teacher. But then, just as suddenly as dusk can turn into night, the modern world around us disappeared when Azib led us through a doorway. I thought it was the entrance to a restaurant. Instead we were in the medina—the old quarter, a maze of narrow alleyways with patchwork roofs of battered tin and cardboard. It was as if we'd stepped into a tunnel. If any of our group was claustrophobic, I felt sorry for them. Immediately, that once silly umbrella became a yellow lifesaver floating above a swirling sea of heads.

The medina is a place that has lost some of its importance in many modern Arab cities, but many still consider it a sacred place where traditions of hundreds of years are practiced and continue to prosper. In Tunis, the medina appeared alive and well with its bustling alleyways lined with shops (called souks) and eateries offering a mind-boggling array of goods and foods. The air was thick with humidity and the cloying aromas of smoke, leather, ripened fruit, riper fish, old rugs and newly dyed fabric hung in it like smog.

As my head spun on its axis attempting to take it all in, I felt Marsha's small hand attach itself to the back of my shirt, and every so often I heard her whimper as she caught sight or smell of something unpleasant. Shoulders rubbed with shoulders, and elbows and hands seemed to be everywhere. On either side of us, shopkeepers beckoned with promises of incredible deals and fought for our attention by asking us if we were "USA." Often two or more salespeople from opposing souks would start a rousing argument over who was offering what and who had the best deal and even after we moved on we'd still hear them bickering with passionate intensity. The restaurants, with fronts wide open to the street, were the most curious, dank and dirty places filled with smoke from rolled cigarettes that the men inside were sucking back one after another as if they were tubes of oxygen. The furniture was rudimentary, made of rough-hewn, unpainted, untreated wood. Diners ate off cracked plates and drank cloudy liquid from chipped glasses that looked unwashed. No women ate in these restaurants, but plenty of skinny, skanky dogs, all brown, skulked about with a disturbing proprietary air.

My appetite, usually quite healthy, evaporated.

Azib and his yellow umbrella stopped short before a narrow, unmarked door. He spoke something very quickly, which I could not hear as I was too far back. He opened the door, beckoning us to follow. And just as it had when we'd entered the medina, with a step, our circumstances once again changed drastically. We left behind the rubble and rabble and found ourselves in the peaceful sanctum of what looked to be a high-class Arab restaurant, mercifully quiet and foggy with incense. Azib exchanged words with a tall, pleasant-looking man in the ornate foyer who then motioned for us to follow him inside. Azib seemed unconcerned about whether everyone had successfully made the journey from the bus, but I did a quick head count and was relieved to conclude that all were present and accounted for.

Most of the restaurant's tables were in a central courtyard beneath a stunning mosaic-tiled roof two storeys up. Other, more private tables were hidden in alcoves behind arched doorways that circled the courtyard like a row of Ms. At either end of the oblong room was a dramatic staircase leading to an upper level where I later learned was room for even more dining and the bathrooms. I was hoping the restaurant enjoyed a busy dinner hour because right then, the place was nearly deserted. Only a few of the other tables were inhabited; most by small groups that looked like families, their dark eyes following us with mild interest as we passed by. We were seated at the far side of the courtyard at a table long enough to accommodate our entire group. Azib sat at one end, Charity, Dottie, Faith and Thomas surrounding him. I took a seat at the other end, Ted and Marsha and Nick (sporting bruises from the brouhaha the night before like a mighty lion wearily used to such wounds of battle) to my left, and James and Errall to my right. The five young cousins, hungrily exploring the fantastically foreign locale with their eyes and chattering away like excited birds (except Flora, no chatterer her), were squeezed in between.

I've always found that watching someone who doesn't know they're being watched is a good get-to-know-ya exercise. I took a few minutes to assess the group, observe their interactions with one another and the unfamiliar surroundings. At the far end of the table, the sisters, Charity and Faith, seemed wholly intent on listening to the geography and political science lecture being elaborately delivered by Azib. Every so often the women tossed unhappy looks in the direction of the youngsters at the table, disappointed they weren't hanging on to Azib's every word. Next to them, their partners, Dottie and Thomas, were less rapt, but seemingly satisfied to sit there and divide their attention between Azib and, in Dottie's case her knitting, in Thomas' case his fingernails and knuckles.

Nigel and Nathan (the twins) and Harry (Charity's dearly departed sister's great-granddaughter and Jackson's daughter), were thoroughly enjoying themselves and one another's company on one side of the table, while opposite them, Flora and the twins' sister, Kayla, and her uncle, Nick, presented a more sullen grouping, almost indifferent to the restaurant's exotic ambiance and each other. Errall, situated between Harry and Harry's great-grandfather, James McNichol, was having a more interesting time. James, dressed like a 1940s Cary Grant, and therefore apparently thinking he was him (on a bad, bad day), was making clumsy, dotty attempts at charming Errall and at the same time trying to ascertain exactly the nature of her relationship with me...while I was sitting right next to him listening to every gooey word. Errall tried to brush him off as nicely as she could—a stretch for Errall—by focusing on the giggly goings-on between Harry and Nigel and Nathan. But James was not easily dissuaded and Errall was finally reduced to whispering a few, I'm sure, well-chosen words into his hairy ear after which he maintained a subdued silence.

The first part of the meal consisted mostly of polite oohing and ahhing over the elaborate table settings and questioning Azib about what the heck we were eating. Our appetizer consisted of three dishes, one a combination of lemon and hot peppers, another closely resembled salsa and the last was a bowl of chunky tuna salad. This was followed by a salad of olives, peppers and onions mashed together, topped with sliced boiled egg and a side of dry tuna and then a main course of couscous, cooked carrots and potatoes (not sliced, but in their entirety) and an astoundingly massive shank of lamb for each of us.

"You don't like the food?" I whispered to Marsha, even though Azib could by no means hear me over his voracious chewing and lesson-giving at the other end of the table.

She eyed me warily. Despite occasionally attaching herself to the back of my shirt, Marsha'd been playing cool with me most of the day (as Charity's advisor, and therefore an instrument of her diminishing fortunes, I was not on her list of favourite people). She'd been giving me all the non-verbal signals she could think of to get me to buzz off and stop hanging around her and Ted, but I think I'd finally worn her down. She was tired, uncomfortable in this foreign setting and hungry. "What do you think this is?" she asked, poking at the meat with her fork.

I glanced at Ted who was about to take a big bite out of his portion but put it down when he heard the question. He stared at his wife, then the meat, then his wife. "He said it was lamb, didn't he? It's lamb, don't you think? What else could it be?"

"You see all those dogs out there?" Marsha said, hunting between her potato and two carrots for something edible. Did she think she was going to find a Big Mac in there?

Ted blanched. "You don't think...?"

"Just make it look like you've eaten something by moving stuff around," she instructed her husband. "You don't want to offend them. God only knows what'll happen then. We can go to the buffet when we get back on the ship."

"I'm bloody starving over here, Marsha."

"Well you go right ahead then, but don't come crying to me in the middle of the night when your guts are falling out of your asshole."

Ted grudgingly began rearranging the food on his plate.

"You're not having a very good time on this trip, are you?" I asked with as much empathy in my voice as I could muster whilst chewing a rather tasty tidbit of lamb.

Marsha gave me another eye, behind which I could see she was trying to decide whether or not I was a kindred spirit or just baiting her. She must have settled for the former, desperate to find a compatriot in her misery. "No, we certainly are not. Don't get me wrong, we love cruises, don't we Ted? We've done it many times. We've taken luxurious vacations all over the world."

"Ever been to that Disney World?" Ted asked me, his fatty shoulders thrown back in pride at his worldliness. "It's really something. You should go."

Marsha shot her husband a shushing look and quickly added, "Ted's a very successful businessman you know. Oil and gas mostly." She patted down a frizzy fluff of hair over her ear and inspected the white tips of her French manicure.

I nodded, showing how impressed I was. "Really? I didn't know that. Exploration? Development? Investment? Overseas stuff?" I listed the varying possibilities.

"Er, well, no," Marsha sputtered. "We're more in the service side of the industry."

"We own the M&T Gas Bar and Restaurant not fifty minutes out of Calgary," Ted told me. "Worked there for twenty years and now we own the place. A real Canadian success story. You heard of us maybe? We sell the famous Giantess Cinnamon Buns. Marsha's own invention, y'know."

Marsha looked mortified. She was not used to honesty, I guess. "Shut up, Ted. That's just a part of what we do. We just don't like to brag, that's all. Anyway, as I was saying, as far as this...trip...goes, it's just that, well, we prefer to travel in a...a style we're more accustomed to."

I opened my baby greens wide. "Oh? You don't like The Dorothy?"

"Now we're not snobs, Mr. Quant, don't get us wrong," she said, warming to her topic. "It's not the boat, but...well, I'm just going to say it, it's the company. Ted in particular is uncomfortable and the boys, well the boys are so impressionable. They're only twenty, you know, and Kayla is seventeen. Who knows what she thinks about all this."

Ever thought to ask her? I looked over at the twins and Kayla, about mid-table, and they seemed just fine.

"I mean I'm okay, really I am, I can put up with a lot, but really, poor Ted and the twins, on a boat with a bunch of homosexual beings."

As opposed to human beings? I suppose my sharing a room with Errall put her off my homo scent.

"But I don't know why we're surprised. Charity does this every time. Every time we have a family reunion she seems to go out of her way to choose someplace or somewhere uncomfortable for everyone. Except herself of course."

"Then why do you attend?" I asked the million-dollar question. I was betting I was about to get a million-dollar lie.

"Well, family of course. I don't know what kind of family background you come from, Mr. Quant, but our family is a close one. We spend time together. That's what families do. I want our children to know their cousins and aunts and uncles." She almost teared up at this point, so moved was she with the strength of her familial convictions. "In the end, family is all we've really got."

What a Giantess load of manure. "I take it you and your family were at the last Charity event, the boot camp at Charity's home in May?"

"Yes, of course we were, weren't we Ted?"

"What about the kids?" he asked in return.

"What about the children?" she retorted, pinning him with an irritated look.

"They're eating the meal."

"Oh for crying out loud," Marsha huffed. "I can't save everyone. And I don't want to make a scene. Who knows what could happen."

"Did you know that Charity's cat was poisoned that weekend?" I asked, hoping to bring the discussion back to what was important. This gig was proving difficult. I was finding it near impossible to detect whodunit when there was little proof that anything was actually dun. Charity didn't want me to reveal to the others her belief that one of them was trying to kill her, but she didn't say anything about not talking about Morris' suspicious demise.

Marsha looked at me with a blank look on her heavily made-up face. "She had a cat?"

"My, how truly serendipitous!" came the statement from the other end of the table. Charity was making it known she wanted to be heard. And indeed all other conversation stopped and fifteen pair of eyes and maybe more from other nearby tables fell upon her. She adjusted the collar of her shirt and then looked up with a start, giving an Oscar-winning performance in appearing surprised to find the table's attention on her. "You'll never believe the tales Mr. Azib has been sharing with us. The poor of Tunisia need our help. I've concluded that some of my money should also be siphoned off to this worthy cause."

As worthy a cause as it might be, the news fell flat around the table. Charity's well-chosen words, *siphoned off*, reminded the family that their money was about to flow into pockets other than their own. Just, I suspect, as Charity intended.

"Oh good Lord," I heard James mutter under his breath.

Everyone else was quiet for a moment, the young Moshiers searching out their parents' faces for how to react, Nick and sister Marsha exchanging uncomfortable glances. Harriet and Faith seemed to be the only ones nodding their heads as if the idea of helping the poor and destitute might be a worthy one.

"That would be possible, wouldn't it, Mr. Quant?" Charity called across the table, chin held determinedly high.

"It's something we can discuss," I answered, hoping to cut off the discussion.

"Prickly pear!" she responded.

For a moment I thought she was calling me names, until I saw two white-robed servers delivering platters of the stuff along with steaming pots of sweet mint tea.

"So what the hell is this?" Ted asked under his breath, dissatisfied as a hungry lion at a salad bar. "Can we eat this?" he asked his wife with a pleading look.

"Who knows," Marsha replied with a scowl. "They certainly never serve this in any of the resorts we go to."

"It's dessert," I told them. "Prickly pear. The fruit of the cactus."

Ted chortled. "Oh come on, you expect us t'believe there's such a thing as cactus fruit? You think we were born yesterday?"

For a moment, I didn't care whether or not these two were suspects. I just really didn't want to spend any more time with them.

As we filed out of the restaurant, the same man who greeted us when we arrived was at the door to see us off. Following Azib's example, we held out our palms as we passed by our host, into which he sprinkled a few drops of refreshing rosewater. And then we were back in the din of the ramshackle medina. Azib raised his yellow umbrella as soon as we cleared the restaurant. It was time to shop. For the next hour or so, we fought our way through the masses, every so often stopping to visit stores Azib felt were worth our attention (and money) and with whose owners he seemed very familiar.

It was growing late in the afternoon when I heard the scream. I turned to find Flora struggling through the crowd, trying to get to me. I stopped to wait for her, much to Marsha's chagrin. She'd once again attached herself to my shirt and was now pulling on it to encourage me to move forward. Errall and Ted were also nearby.

"We're going to lose the umbrella if we don't keep moving," Marsha complained, at the same time gifting every passerby with an impressive scowl.

"Something's wrong," Errall understated, also having heard the scream and watching Flora's approach.

When my client's granddaughter finally caught up to us, having clawed her way through the dense crush of people, we could see that she was holding on to the hand of a very tired and flustered Dottie. "Back there," she said between wheezes of air intake, "It's Grandmother!"

I put one hand on her shoulder to calm her and tried to use my eyes to steady her own. "What? What is it?"

"She's gone, Mr. Quant!" Flora cried out. "She's gone!"

Errall and I exchanged an alarmed look.

"We're getting behind!" Marsha warned, hopping up and down to keep sight of the retreating umbrella.

"What happened?" I asked.

"Sounds like the ol' lady got lost," Ted contributed unhelpfully.

"It's my fault," Dottie explained, in a voice that sounded calmer than her face looked. "I walk so damn slow now. It's hard for me to keep up. Flora and Charity were helping me along."

"Then something in one of the stores caught Grandmother's eye," Flora added.

"She told Flora and me to keep on moving so we wouldn't lose sight of Azib and that she'd catch up with us. She's as fast as a gazelle that one, always has been, and I'm so slow, because of my heart. She knew she could let us get a head start and still catch up."

"But when she didn't show up after several minutes," Flora continued, "we went back to look for her but couldn't find her and I was afraid I'd lose our way or lose Dottie and we'd certainly lose sight of Azib and the umbrella! Oh gosh, she's lost in this mess. How will we ever find her?"

"I'm going!" Marsha announced loudly. "I can barely see the umbrella." With that she turned heel and stalked off, Ted scrambling after her.

"What can we do, Mr. Quant?" Dottie asked, ignoring the fleeing couple. "Do you think whoever it is that's trying to kill her has taken her?"

Flora looked startled at the suggestion and stared at Dottie. "What are you talking about? She's just lost."

"Listen," I said, after assessing the crowd in front of us and the identical one behind us. "Errall will catch you two up with the rest of the group." I looked at Errall who nodded agreement, even though her eyes looked a little doubtful about whether or not she'd be able to comply. The yellow umbrella was getting further and further away and Dottie was not a fast walker. "And you've got to go now while the umbrella is still in sight. I'll go back to look for Charity." I focused my attention on Flora and Dottie. "Can either of you tell me anything about where you last saw her? Any hint as to where I might look for her?"

"Hats," Dottie said. "She was looking for one of those hats. They look like the pillbox hats Jackie O used to wear, but with a tassel."

"Chechia, I think they're called," Flora said, nodding wildly, her glasses nearing the tip of her nose.

"Russell, how will you get back?" I felt Errall's hand on my forearm and heard an anxiousness in her voice I didn't want to hear.

I stared at her. I had no answer. "Just go," I told her. I knew the bus had to be at The Dorothy in time for a 5:30 departure. I looked at my watch—4 p.m., and it was at least a half-hour ride back to the dock. "Just tell Azib and the driver to wait for us as long as they can."

Errall impulsively threw her face into mine and gave me a kiss on the lips. When she pulled back, she looked deep into my eyes, her own reflecting back two pools of worry, and said, "Be careful, Russell." And with that she grabbed Dottie's free hand and led the other two women away towards a speck of yellow that was now only fleetingly visible. I watched confounded as the medina's scurrying inhabitants swallowed up my travel companions in mere seconds. In slow motion I rotated a full three-hundred-and-sixty degrees, taking in the dusty, noisy fray of my alien surroundings. I saw nothing and no one that looked familiar or friendly. I felt very alone.

Chapter 9

I *was* alone. I had no idea where I was, which way to go, or, if I did find Charity, how we'd ever find our way back to the bus.

And then it began to rain.

This wasn't just a sprinkling shower; it was a torrent of water being dumped from the sky as if a dam had come undone. Even though makeshift roofs covered much of the medina, they were no match for this kind of downfall. Within seconds the rain found easy openings through which to deliver its load and soon the alleyways of the medina were not only dark and dank, but sodden as well; a wet dog smell began to permeate the air. Whereas most shopkeepers were prepared for such an occurrence, their wares well protected inside their shops or quickly covered with sheets of plastic or plywood, the shoppers were not. Almost immediately I was soaked as if I'd just been run through a car wash. Alone, confused, and wet, all I knew for sure was that Charity was shopping for chechias somewhere in the direction opposite the one our group was going in. With no better option, I dived headfirst into the fracas.

The medina's usual fast pace had reached frenetic proportions as people scurried for shelter, but the persistent souk hawkers remained undaunted and continued to ply their trade. A little monsoon was no reason to put an end to commerce. They called out to me in their shrill voices, some daring to pull at my sleeve, wanting to know if I was USA, or maybe interested in purchasing shoes or beading or ivory. I eventually started yelling back over the thrumming of rain on corrugated tin roofs, "Chechias? Chechias? Do you have chechias? Hats?"

"Monsieur!" came a voice, clear over all the others. "Yez, here, monsieur!"

In an opening between two other stores, a space about two people wide, stood a handsome young man. He was looking right at me, beckoning to me. His skin was a translucent brown that turned deep bronze, almost purple, in the spots where the rain hit it. I was growing frantic as the impossibility of my chore was beginning to sink in and I raced over to him hoping for a miracle.

"You're looking, monsieur, to shop?" His English was pretty good.

"I'm looking for a woman," I said. "Tall, from Canada, looks like Katharine Hepburn?" You never know. "Have you seen such a woman?"

"Yez, yez," he nodded enthusiastically. "Shopping woman. Yez, yez."

Oh thank God! "Where, where did you see her?"

"You come," he said, stepping to the side and motioning me inside his store.

It was a long, narrow space, filled with cheap tourist trinkets, jewellery, rugs and clothing that Flora would wear and, best of all, mercifully dry. Indoors, watching our conversation with interest were four others who I took to be fellow salespeople, three men and a woman.

"You come. Woman shop," my new friend said.

I stepped into the store, glad to be out of the rain, and allowed him to gently guide me with a hand that barely touched my arm towards the rear of the space where an even narrower flight of stairs awaited me. I stopped, suddenly wary. "Uh, where does this go? You saw a Canadian woman shopping here?"

More nodding and smiling as he waved with his hand for me to go up the stairs.

I looked at the others who were also smiling and nodding and waving.

The young man stepped in front of me and began to scale the steps, encouraging me to follow. "Yez, good woman shop. Come."

I did. Up we went, the space barely wide enough for my shoulders, up and around and around until I was certain we must have passed by two or three floors. My view was restricted to the young man's butt, which was pretty delectable, but I was in no mood, my apprehension rising with every step. Should I turn around? Run yelling? Was I about to be sold into white slavery? Was someone going to rob me? Sell me drugs then turn me in to the cops? Was this *Midnight Express* all over again?

We finally topped the stairs; the young man stepped to one side and with a flourish invited me to step through a curtained opening. I poked my head through the slit in the fabric and took a quick inventory, all the while flexing my muscles mightily in case I'd need to use them. Behind the curtain four more men were waiting expectantly in a large, perfectly square room. Except for a low bench before a 1960s-style coffee table, there was no other furniture. Every inch of wall and floor were covered with carpet, a kaleidoscope of colour intricately woven into countless different patterns. Soundproofing?

I was directed by one of the new men to sit on the bench. Here it goes, I thought to myself, it's gonna go down right now; whatever "it" is. I sat down, wiping away the rainwater that, even though I was now sheltered, continued to dribble down my face as if an inexhaustible supply had been stored in my hair. I must have looked a sight: wet hair, my Judy Smythwicke–inspired conservative shirt plastered against my chilled, sodden skin like a second skin, nipples standing at unconservative attention.

Somewhere to my right I heard a slight rustling and then an aged woman appeared from an invisible space between two of the wall hangings. She was carrying a large platter on which she'd laid out an elaborate silver tea service. She set the bounty before me on the coffee table, never uttering a word, and poured me a cup of the steaming liquid. All eyes were on me as if nothing could happen until I took the first sip. So I did. It was hot and sweet, like the tea we had at the restaurant. I mumbled my thanks. The woman disappeared.

Like a well-rehearsed play, the smallest of the quartet of men then approached the centre of the room and stood before me. He was carrying something large, rolled up, maybe three metres wide. With a smile befitting a benevolent king, he threw out his hands into a high arc and phhhwwwooop! Spread before him, splayed out from the flat of his palms down to the tips of my toes was a stunning carpet. It was mostly red with a detailed border of browns, purples and yellows, the centre a labyrinthine design of curlicues and fashioned symbols with meanings I'd never understand. In the half-light of the room the sheen of the piece was velveteen, darker in some spots, light in others. It was outstandingly beautiful.

Phhhwwwooop. Phhhwwwooop. Phhhwwwooop. Three more carpets fell from the grips of the three other gentlemen who now formed a semi-circle in front of me. Phhhwwwooop. Phhhwwwooop. Phhhwwwooop. Phhhwwwooop. Another four. It was like a well choreographed artistic performance. Phhhwwwooop. Phhhwwwooop. Phhhwwwooop. Phhhwwwooop. Another four. My eyes barely had the chance to assess the new offerings when, Phhhwwwooop. Phhhwwwooop. Phhhwwwooop. Phhhwwwooop. More.

"Good woman shop," said an enthusiastic voice from the doorway. It was the attractive man who'd brought me here. "Yez? You buy? For woman. Good prices. Best prices."

"We ship," said another.

"You USA?" asked another.

"Any colour," assured another.

Phhhwwwooop. Phhhwwwooop. Phhhwwwooop. Phhhwwwooop. Four more. These carpet merchants had certainly adapted well to modern American sales culture, responding to a video generation that demands countless images per second. Just keep it coming until they see something they like. But as beautiful as the carpets were, I had a job to do and this experience was getting me nowhere. My search for Charity Wiser had somehow turned into *Ali Baba and the Forty Thieves* and I was desperate for a magic carpet on which to make a getaway.

"You buy? Good prices."

I stood up shaking my head and smiling back at the rug salesmen. "No, no thank you very much." But if you've got some swampland in Florida, I thought to myself, unimpressed with my own gullibility, I'm you're man.

Phhhwwwooop.   Phhhwwwooop.   Phhhwwwooop. Phhhwwwooop.

I moved slowly towards the exit. "No, no thanks."

"Different colour? Different size?" they offered, lastly going for "Different price?"

Phhhwwwooop.   Phhhwwwooop.   Phhhwwwooop. Phhhwwwooop.

"I'm looking for a hat. But thank you." And with the sound of more phhhwwwoooping following me all the way, I dashed through the curtained doorway, down the stairs and out of the store.

"You look for chechia?" It was the female salesperson, who probably knew more English than any of the men, but only dared to speak it out of their presence.

"Yes," I said, coming to a screeching halt and turning to face her, desperate for any help I could get. Time was running short.

"I show you."

She led me at a brisk pace through the still soaking passages of the medina. I wondered if I was once more being taken for a naive fool. Not that I could blame her. For all I knew, the woman was taking me to another souk where she hoped I'd buy whatever it was her father or sister or cousin had to sell that day. Still I had little choice but to trust her. If it turned out badly, oh well.

The woman stopped abruptly after rounding a corner into yet another of the seemingly endless, countless, identical streets. But this wasn't just any street. It was chechia central, a street just for peddlers whose sole product was the round, tasselled hat, mostly made of red silk or velvet, but in many other colours and fabrics too. I turned to thank the woman but she was gone. I looked up and although the worst of the rainstorm had passed, it was still coming down quite hard, turning the street into a flowing gutter of water dirty with refuse, drowned insects and abandoned pieces of food setting sail. There was no need to shelter myself. I was as wet as I could get. I looked at my watch. 4:25. Oh God. The Dorothy was set to leave in one hour.

Where was Charity Wiser? I began to shiver and a fever of apprehension settled over me. I feared this was not going to turn out well.

But I couldn't give up. I wouldn't. I started with the first chechia shop to my right. I stood in its entrance, ignored the squawking invitations of the owners and searched the interior for a tall, distinguished, Canadian woman who was likely beaking off at a clerk for one reason or another.

I continued this way down one side of the chechia street and up the other.

I found nothing. She wasn't there.

Fifteen minutes later I stumbled out of the last Chechias-R-Us and, dispirited, allowed myself to be jostled and pushed and manipulated down the street. As I moved along, like a piece of flotsam on a sea of bodies, I felt a glare, like a magnet's pull. I stopped short and found the source like a homing device. I stared, almost not believing what I was seeing. My eyes met his for only the briefest second, but it was enough. I shoved and bullied my way through a gaggle of youngsters blocking my way and rushed to where I'd seen the familiar face. But he was gone.

"Jackson!" I called out just once, knowing it was a useless attempt in the pandemonium of the medina, my voice no better than a whisper in a choir.

In response, several nearby shopkeepers called back, "USA!"

What was he doing there? He and Patrick opted out of the tour and had stayed on the ship. But there was no doubt in my mind; Jackson Delmonico had been in the medina, watching me.

And then, as unlikely as the Red Sea, the crowd parted, only for a moment, but long enough for me to spot my quarry. Charity Wiser was standing under the ragged overhang of an abandoned shop at the far end of the street. Her man's white shirt, knotted at her thin waist, and black narrow trousers worn with a pair of canvas, lace-up flats, looked a little worse for the wear, damp and bedraggled. Her hair did too, strands of it having escaped the haphazard pile on top of her head. But thank God, she was safe.

As I struggled through the bodies filling the street, I saw the look on her face. A look I was certain few have ever seen: uncertainty, anxiety, maybe fear. Even so, she held her angular body in an aggressive stance, chin up, chest out, to ward off anyone foolish enough to take her for a weak woman who could be taken advantage of.

I was halfway to her when the attack began. It was quick, without warning and with wicked intent. I was too far away to hear the sound of alarm that no doubt escaped Charity's open mouth as she fell back against the bowing wall of the shop when the two men rushed into her. They were attempting to subdue her and pull her into a nearby narrow passageway. Was this it? The attempt on her life? What a perfect place to do it, I grudgingly admitted to myself, in the middle of a crowded, foreign marketplace. How hard would it be to do her in then stash the body under a pile of Persian carpets? She wouldn't be discovered for weeks in this disorganized mess of alleyways and avenues. As I pushed and prodded and hopped over people to get to Charity's aid I got a better look at her assailants. My best guess was that they were local thugs, hired to do the dirty deed. When I finally reached the scene, Charity was giving as good as she got. The men had foolishly underestimated the fighting power of *this* eighty-year-old woman.

I had the advantage of a surprise attack from behind on my side. I decided on the classic head bonk routine that works so well in all those Three Stooges movies and surprisingly well in real life. I reached out and got a good grasp on each man's collar, yanked back with as much force as I could manage and smashed their two heads together like I was playing the cymbals in a New Orleans Mardi Gras marching band. The sound, however, was not nearly as pleasant. The men staggered away from each other and looked at one another as if it were the other's fault. Then, with unexpected solidarity, they each thrust their palms into my chest, causing me to let them go, and scurried away into the thousand-piece jigsaw puzzle that was the medina, never to be seen again. I hoped.

Charity's gaze fell upon me as I stepped up next to her. "Russell," she said in a voice that was calm but in which I detected a slight quiver, "I'm rather pleased to see you."

"Are you all right?" I asked.

She nodded. "Shall we make for the ship?" she queried as if our meeting this way had been pre-arranged.

"Charity, are you all right?" I repeated.

"No damage. Thank you." She sounded like Seven of Nine from *Star Trek: Voyager*.

I looked at my watch. 4:45.

"Can you run?"

"Of course. Don't be silly."

I grabbed her hand and began jogging. I didn't know where or in which direction to go, so I just ran and began calling out, "The square? Where is the square?"

Of course, no one could understand a word of what I was shouting. In the end, we found it ourselves. In the same way we first entered the chaotic, exotic world of the medina, with the ease of Alice going through the looking-glass, we stumbled upon the square through an unmarked, arched doorway, as if through a time portal. Somehow, by what good fortune I do not know, we had taken the right turn. That was the good news.

The bad news: our bus was gone.

"You come! You come!" a voice rang out. It belonged to a scrawny man in a rumpled shirt and dark pants running towards us with flailing arms.

Oh man! These salespeople are relentless!

"You come, Canada!" he spit into our doubting faces. With that he thrust a note into my hands.

Russell-The bus had to leave-I paid Azib's friend to wait for two white Canadians and bring them to the ship-we hope he ends up with you! -Errall

I love her. I love Errall.

I hate her. I hate Errall. The door was locked from inside. I was cold, damp, miserable: my clothes were a mess, stained with I didn't want to know what. Charity and I, ably ferried by Azib's friend, had pulled up shipside just as dockworkers were pulling away the gangplank. The FOD security people reluctantly agreed to allow us on the boat and, when we were, proceeded to give us a stern lecture. All I wanted to do was have a hot shower and lie down.

But the frigging door was locked from the inside.

I banged and called her name. I tried some other names. Finally Errall opened the door and had the good sense to look about as bad as I felt.

"Russell," she mumbled, obviously still half-asleep.

I marched into the room and began a little tirade. "How could you fall asleep when you had no idea where I was or if I'd make it back before the ship left port?" I was furious and a little bit grumpy. "And then you lock me out of my own room! Maybe you were hoping I wouldn't make it back?" And unreasonable. "Then you'd have the cabin all to yourself!"

She directed her bleary gaze out of the window. The Dorothy was gently moving away from land. "I guess it turned out okay, huh?" she croaked. "Settle down, would ya?"

I fumed, enough steam coming out of my ears to fuel The Dorothy's departure.

"I'm not feeling all that good, Russell. Might have been something I ate. I must have locked the door out of habit. I lay down and I guess I fell asleep."

"You're sorry?" I suggested.

She smirked. "Yeah, that too. I'm glad you're back. Really."

I calmed down a bit and went to the bar to fix myself a stiff rye and Coke. "I guess I should thank you for hiring that guy to bring us back."

"You owe me fifty bucks. American. What happened? Did you find her?"

Now that I was done expressing my displeasure and had a couple ounces of liquor in me, I took better notice of my roomie. "Are you okay?" She did look a little off. I plopped down on my bed, a collection of unopened white-enveloped invitations crunching beneath my weight.

She waved it off. "I'll be fine. The nap helped. So tell me. What happened with Charity?"

I gave Errall the rundown of my adventure, starting with spotting Jackson Delmonico and ending with the attack on Charity.

"Do you think Jackson was behind it?" she asked. It was a question that had been ringing through my head ever since I returned to The Dorothy.

"It seems like too much of a coincidence for him not be involved some way, especially since he wasn't supposed to be in Tunis at all. And I did find all that cash in his room. It might have been to pay for this hit."

"Or, it could have been a couple of those pickpockets or thieves Judy Smythwicke warned us about."

I nodded but had a hard time believing it. "I suppose."

"Why was Charity all by herself anyway? Why wasn't she trying to find the rest of the group?"

"She says she got lost. That's it. Nothing more sinister than that."

"Do you believe her?"

I gave Errall a perplexed look. "Why wouldn't I? Why would she lie about something like that?"

She shrugged. "I don't know. I don't trust her, that's all."

I nodded but kept my mouth shut. It was a disturbing thought.

Dinner was a quiet affair. Errall, still not completely well, went back to sleep. I ordered in and ate on our deck. I was slowly coming to befriend the dark, sometimes brooding waters, achieving a certain level of comfort with the immensity of our solitude. We were a speck of humanity on a vast sea and we simply had to trust that she would carry us through. I couldn't explain it then or since, but the entire concept was frightening to me and yet exhilarating at the same time.

Once fed and watered and refuelled with energy, I dashed about the ship checking on the whereabouts of the Wisers, hoping to take advantage of some time alone for another round of sneak and peek. The Moshiers were having a late family dinner together, giving me time to pop into Marsha and Ted's room, Nigel and Nathan's and, with Harry visiting the library with her grandfather, I even made it into the room she shared with Kayla. Unfortunately, none of the visits turned up useful clues or handwriting specimens matching the note Charity received. Why oh why are things not as easy as they are on TV?

Returning to the room at 10 p.m. I found Errall still out, but breathing (I checked) and snoring (the things that happen without a tape recorder). After the goings-on in Tunis I was worried about my client and decided, despite the hour, to call on her.

"Russell, come in. Dottie is asleep but we can talk on the deck. Drink?" Charity welcomed me into her suite, resplendent in a pitch black silk kimono which somehow looked just right for the night.

Once we were seated on the deck, martinis in hand, I broached the subject that was no doubt foremost in both our minds. "Can you tell me anything more about what happened today in Tunis? Did you see anyone or hear anything that might give us some clues as to who was behind this?" I didn't want to put any words in her mouth but I was wondering if she'd caught sight of Jackson as well.

"Before we speak of that, Russell, let me express to you my deepest gratitude for what you did this afternoon. You are my brave warrior. I know you had concerns about being cast in the role of my bodyguard and, I must admit, Russell, that was not far from my mind. And, damn it all, I sit here tonight with you, safe, beverage in hand, and I am glad of it. Glad, I tell you. Without you, who knows where I might be right this minute. Perhaps I'd even be dead, the scent of my blood, pouring from my slitted throat, mixing with the exotic smells of that darkest of port cities..."

Oh dear. "Charity I..."

"No wait," she whispered, perhaps knowing she'd gone too far. She laid a gentle hand on mine. "Really, Russell, thank you," she said solemnly and, I think, sincerely.

"You're welcome."

She sipped her drink, her eyes never leaving mine. "Who was it?"

"The attackers were obviously local."

"Hired by one of my own family."

"Maybe."

"Maybe?" Her ire was rising. "What on earth can you mean by that?"

"There's a possibility that it was a random act of violence. Petty thieves looking for whatever was in your pockets or purse."

"Preposterous. Do you really believe that, Russell?"

I looked at her with a steady gaze and admitted, "No."

"Then who, for God's sake, who?"

"I saw Jackson, in the medina, immediately before the attack."

Charity swallowed a surprised breath. "Jackson? But he wasn't even in Tunis...he...oh my, are you certain? It's him then?"

"We can't know that. But it certainly moves him up my list."

"And who else is topping this list of yours? Who?"

"Marsha. Maybe Nick."

"They hate me, don't they?" She gave me a crestfallen look. "Nick...are you certain?"

"No, Charity. At this point, I'm not sure about anything. Your announcement the other day put everyone at the top of the list. All of those people expected to become rich upon your death. With your words, you changed their lives forever. Even Flora. I hate to say it, but if they didn't before, they may very well all hate you now."

"And want me dead." Charity stared away for a few seconds, letting the enormity of what she'd just said sink in. "That certainly was not my intent." Her voice was uncharacteristically brittle. "I just wanted to help flush out whoever it was who killed Morris." She got up, entered the room and returned quickly with a refilled glass. Mine was still full. "To hell with them," she spit out. "Who cares if they all hate me? It doesn't feel any different than it did before."

I chose to remain silent. I couldn't begin to imagine what that would be like.

Leaving Charity with her third martini and her thoughts, I headed for the casino on Deck Five. The casino is only three smallish rooms; one for slots and two for table games, with an even smaller adjoining bar called Curses. When I stepped inside the glitzy parlour of the casino I immediately spotted what I was hoping to find: some Wisers.

Patrick Halburton's grumpy-gus-looking frame was slumped over a slot machine into which he was stingily feeding quarters. Nick Kincaid, handsomely sporting his wounds, was at a blackjack table, along with Mary of the Phyllis-Mary-Rhoda trio, and two other men who seemed to be paying more attention to the dark brooding beauty of Nick than their own cards. I poked my nose into Curses and spotted Marsha Moshier, made up to the nines but looking like a four and sitting on the middle of five bar stools flirting with the male barkeeper. Unsuccessfully, I'd bet. The rest of the family must have left her here after their dinner.

I decided on a tack and ambled over to the slot machine next to Patrick's and sat myself down. He paid me no attention. I searched my pockets for change and came up with a few coins that I fed into the machine. I punched at a button without knowing what I was doing and was rewarded with a jingle-jangle of loot falling into a metal receptacle near my knees. Patrick glanced over at my noisy winnings then shifted his attention back to his own machine, never actually setting eyes on me.

"How are you today, Mr. Halburton?"

He was frowning at the machine and transferred the same look to me. "Hullo," he replied, eyeing me up briefly before returning his grimace to his game.

Patrick Halburton had a distinct smell about him. Was it from a lack of regular bathing or change of clothes? Or was it simply an unfortunate choice of soap? I wasn't sure. "Did you have a good day on the ship today?" I asked. "I noticed you didn't come on the tour of Tunis."

"That's right."

How was I gonna get this guy to shut up? "Well, they say the ship itself is as much a destination as the ports of call. Did you spend the day in the casino?"

"Oh no. Don't got the money for this kind of thing for long. Just sat in the library. Reading."

"I'm sure that must have been very enjoyable. Did your son-in-law Jackson spend the day with you? I noticed he wasn't on the tour either."

Now I got his attention. He shifted in his seat and faced me, at first wordless, assessing my face as if he'd never seen it before. "I know who you are. You're that lawyer fella Charity's gone and hired to change her will."

"Well, not quite. I'm just her advisor."

"Same damn thing."

"Well, not..." Oh to heck with it. "Was Jackson in the library with you today, Mr. Halburton?"

"Sure he was."

Fibber.

"For part of it."

Okay, jumped the gun.

"What else did he do today? Did he go ashore?"

He was back focusing on the slots. "S'pose you should ask him that."

That was it. My machine swallowed another quarter and spit out fifteen more. It was obvious my gambling partner wasn't in the mood to be as generous. I could tell my winning streak was beginning to piss Patrick Halburton off. Out of the corner of my eye I spotted Nick leaving the blackjack area and head into Curses. I decided to collect my winnings and try my luck elsewhere.

"Here," I said, holding out my fistful of change towards the old man. "I hate carrying around a lot of change." I considered it a down payment on possible future information.

"Don't mind if you do," he said, motioning for me to dump my loot into the metal receptacle at the bottom of his machine.

I said goodnight and headed for the bar.

Nick had settled into a low-slung leather-upholstered chair around one of only three tables tucked away in a dark corner of Curses. Marsha was still at the bar and was whispering something wet into the ear of a muscle-bound guy who'd unluckily sat next to her. He pulled away, looked at her with incredulity, stepped back off his stool and stalked out of the bar. (In search of his boyfriend to bitch-slap Marsha probably.) As her angry eyes followed him they landed on me. She pretended not to see me, slipped off her perch and left, her gait a little unsteady.

I went to the bar, ordered two champagnes from a David Cassidy look-alike and delivered them, along with me, to Nick's table. I felt his pepper-flecked eyes wash over me. He was wearing baggy cargo pants, the type that zip off into shorts, and a navy shirt without sleeves that showed off well-developed arms. Encircling the left one was a barbed wire tattoo.

"I don't drink," he said as I offered him a flute full of the stuff.

"Strange place to be then, in a bar. Or was it just getting too crowded around the blackjack table?"

He looked at me with nothing on his lips. Nice thick lips above a cleft chin sporting a rough and ready five-o'clock shadow.

"Were you on a winning streak?"

"Yeah, I guess."

"So why in the bar?"

Grunt.

I flicked my head towards the scene of Marsha's embarrassment. "Your sister knows she's shopping for beer and pretzels in a champagne and dainties store, doesn't she?"

"Wouldn't matter."

Jeez! He was about as verbose as Patrick.

He shrugged. "Actually I'm glad to see you, Russell. There's something I wanted to say to you."

I smiled. "Well then, you won't mind my joining you then?" I don't know how I came up with that conclusion, but it served my purposes well. "Did you enjoy Tunis?" I asked once I was positioned next to him, enjoying my proximity to the man. Unlike Patrick—his much older cousin-in-law—Nick Kincaid did not smell like an old man. He smelled like a virile, sensual, musky young man. And when the bartender delivered a glass of tonic with lime, he accepted it with a big paw of a hand with long, nicely shaped fingers. I am a sucker for beautiful hands. Like Stanley Tucci in *The Terminal*. Yup—those are good hands.

"I did, very much," he answered when the waiter had gone. "I've always been fascinated by the history of the Punic Wars."

Oh, oh, a smarty. Change of subject required. "What was it you wanted to say to me?"

He studied his drink as if looking for the words in the glass. "I wanted to thank you. For breaking up the fight the other night. I got carried away."

"You never told me what happened," I said, hinting. "Did you know that other guy?"

"Nah," he said. "He thought he knew me. It was a big mix-up."

"I see." I say that a lot, even when it's not true—like now—hoping for more.

But apparently there was no more. Nick sat there quiet.

"Do you get along with your aunt?"

Another shrug. "Charity? I guess so. She's a queer old bird, but she's all right."

Queer. Interesting choice of words. Did he mean to tell me that she was gay, or just that she was odd? "I suppose you don't get to see her too often, what with her living in Victoria and you in…?"

"Toronto."

"Yeah, right. Flora tells me you're a fitness trainer. I spend some time in Toronto. If I'm ever in need of a trainer, what gym are you at?" Must be a good one with very rich clients who pay you very well so you can afford all your expensive clothes and bath gels I said to myself.

He gave me a look. Probably wondering why I was asking so many questions. Couldn't blame him but I wasn't about to stop until he shut me down.

"Spink's."

I nodded, though I'd never heard of the place. "I see you came on this trip alone. No wife or girlfriend or partner to bring along?" If he could use queer, I could use partner. Just to see what reaction I'd get. Nick was a thirty-seven-year-old handsome man who wasn't married, worked hard to make his body look good and had a closet full of matching clothes and skin care products for men. I smelled *Queer as Folk*. And I suspected most of his family did too.

"Is Errall your partner?" he shot back, a look in his eyes I couldn't quite identify.

Do I lie, I wondered, or do I give a little to get some back? "No. She isn't. I have no partner."

"Me either," he said. He raised his glass and saluted me with it. "Here's to being single."

Was I so out of practice? Was this whole conversation really a come on? A flirtation? Or was I totally off base about this guy? When in doubt, go with the flow. Keep your friends close and your suspects closer. So I clinked glasses with him. As we sipped our drinks through engaging smiles, Richard entered the bar. He caught one look of us being engaging and left.

First I'd run off with Nick the night of the bar fight and now this. Even I would be suspicious.

Damn.

Chapter 10

As The Dorothy approached the city port of Palermo on the island
of Sicily on Tuesday morning, the entire Wiser clan, a fully recovered Errall, and I were back in Tin-sel for a family breakfast hosted
by Charity. I was beginning to understand why so many members
of the family dreaded these events. Even I was on edge anticipating
what ruckus Charity might have in store for us today. As Errall and
I settled ourselves next to Faith and Thomas Kincaid, I stole a glance
at the mighty matriarch of the Wiser clan. She was a couple tables
over, flanked as usual by Dottie and Flora. She wore an untucked
blouse with bold orange, navy and white stripes, belted at the waist
over wide-bottomed, white pants. Her hair had been restyled into a
becoming pageboy. There was nary a sign of the vicious attack she'd
suffered the day before.

We didn't have long to wait. The eggs had yet to be served when
she rose from her throne...er, seat, omnipresent glass (OJ and champagne) in one hand and a white sheet of paper in the other. She
looked to be in fine form. Completely gone was the diffidence I'd

spied in her eyes the day before when she'd stood alone, quivering like a wet leaf, lost in the medina. That would never do.

"I'd like to read something to you, if I could." As if anyone could stop her. "A note. Delivered under my door sometime last night." She made a production of putting on a pair of half-moon spectacles and finding the exact distance the paper needed to be from her face so she might read it. She leisurely sipped her mimosa, cleared her throat and began, "It quite simply says: Change your mind or next time you won't be so lucky."

There was silence around the room.

"A death threat, wouldn't you say, Mr. Quant?" She directed her piercing gaze my way, but there was something different in it than the challenging sparks I'd come to expect—something softer, something convivial, a connection. Our experience together, my finding her in a compromised state, rescuing her from two ruffians, and delivering her safely from the medina onto The Dorothy had bound us together and elevated me into a category of acquaintance not many were allowed entry.

But that didn't keep me from experiencing a flash of ire. Why did she keep on doing this? Why was she providing me new information, germane to my case, in the form of a surprise revealed in front of the entire family and a bunch of the ship's staff?

I knew why. Charity Wiser was in love with the dramatic. She was in love with power. She was in love with control. She was in love with making her relatives squirm.

What of the note? Obviously it was sent by whoever arranged the attack in Tunis, all but admitting to it. Now it was clear. It had not been a random act. Charity was meant to die yesterday. And here was the ultimatum: change your mind about changing your will, or I'll kill you before you do. The murderer was growing brash, more aggressive, anxious to have Charity bow to his demands.

"And this threat isn't the first!" she announced, adding, partly under her breath (but not really), "which won't come to a surprise to *someone* in this room."

"What are you implying, Charity? Are you saying someone in this room—someone in this family—is threatening to kill you?" This from her sister Faith. "That is absolutely ludicrous!"

Finally, I thought to myself, someone who isn't willing to be cowed by Charity—at least not without asking a question or two.

"I think it's obvious, don't you?" Charity replied, unfazed. "Dottie warned me not to have another Charity Event after Morris was murdered!" She stopped there and glared at her rapt audience for an uncomfortable moment before continuing. "Oh yes, Morris was murdered! Dottie also warned me not to reveal my plans for my will, and of course, she was right, my lovely Dottie. But what's done is done. We are here, and we are on our way to Rome where I *will* change my will as I've already outlined to you. This..." She raised the note high into the air, shaking it like an enemy's neck, "...changes nothing!

"In other matters," she continued as if she were reciting the items off a shopping list. "I was informed early this morning that due to some stupidity I don't care to understand, The Dorothy cannot dock in the Palermo harbour...something about too many ships already parked there or some such silliness...anyway, we will be putting down anchor some ways offshore and utilizing tenders. With Mr. Gray's assistance I've managed to arrange for three local tenders for our exclusive use. As our departure from Palermo is not until eleven o'clock tonight, we have a great deal of time at our disposal, so this will give our family added flexibility in coming and going to and from the ship.

"Further, although there are three tenders, I will be restricting the use of one for myself, Dottie, Flora, Mr. Quant and his companion, Errall. Each tender has room for at least ten people, so the rest of you should have no problem. I'll leave those details up to you." With business complete, Charity lowered herself majestically into her waiting chair and nodded at a nearby staff member to commence serving breakfast.

I turned to Faith who was at my left and said, "Were you surprised by Charity's answer to your question?" I hoped that since there was only Errall and Faith's husband at the table that she'd feel some licence to speak freely...if she was so inclined.

She looked at me, her face bathed in the gentle light of a morning sun. Again I was struck by her similarity to Charity. Nature is amazing in how it can take the same features and present them in a wholly unique way, a millimetre here, a millimetre there, slightly different colouring, subdue this, emphasize that and voila: a new person.

"Mr. Quant, I don't know how long you've been in the employ of my sister, but I've known her for eighty years and nothing she says or does surprises me."

"Did she ever?"

I saw the corners of her mouth turn up slightly. Her lips were painted a soft rose-petal pink. "Oh my, yes. Charity was…well, let's just say she was quite different than the other Wiser daughters. Everyone thought so. In the nineteen forties Canadian women were not expected to take over their father's business. They were expected to get married. To a man or to God."

"Everyone was surprised when Charity took over Wiser Meats?"

Faith let out a small laugh, even sharing it generously with a tin-coloured waiter who had arrived to serve our breakfast: toast and porridge for her, a fruit plate and bran for me. "They weren't surprised. They were shocked. Everyone expected her to fail. And quickly."

"Did you?"

She eyed me again, searching me out for my real intent. She must have decided it was innocent because she kept on. "I must admit I had my doubts about what she'd taken on. So did Hope. But our lives were so full we really didn't pay it much mind. We were rather selfish I suppose, thinking only of ourselves. We received our inheritances and carelessly went on with our lives."

"I wouldn't say becoming a nun is careless or selfish." I dumped the contents of my fruit plate over my bran and added milk.

She gave me a slight nod. "Thank you for saying that. I've always hoped that was true, despite my decision to leave God's service later in life. But poor Charity had so many struggles and worries. She went through it all alone with no one to help her or guide her or comfort her. Our parents were gone, Hope had her new husband and I had my calling.

"You see, Charity thinks I don't know what she went through with our father's business. But I do. I know how difficult it must have been for her to provide us with our inheritances when there wasn't any money. At the time it meant little to me. All I was interested in as a young woman was serving God. Money had nothing to do with that. But of course later, when Thomas and I left the church, married and began raising a family, I was ever so grateful for it. Without it I...well, we wouldn't have survived. No one would hire us: two people in their forties with little on our resumes other than knowing how to say the rosary. We had two children to feed and clothe and school. The Wiser money made that possible. Thomas and I, we are poor now, it's true, but only in dollars. We have our family—children and grandchildren. That is what enriches our lives, every day.

"You can see, Mr. Quant, how important I think that is, family? To me it is the joy of the world. But I've come to understand that isn't true for everyone. So I can well imagine how difficult it must have been for Charity, with her complicated life, to capitulate to our wishes and raise that child."

"I don't understand...she capitulated to your wishes?"

Faith reached for some water and swallowed hard. "Oh dear. I don't think this is appropriate breakfast conversation, do you, Mr. Quant?"

"It would help me," I tried to convince her to go on. "It would help me in my role as her advisor, to understand the parts of her past that she is too...proud, too modest to speak of."

"She didn't want to keep John," Faith said then, careful to keep her voice low. "She said it was because she was too busy keeping Wiser Meats afloat, but really...really...oh, poor Charity, really she was embarrassed at having been impregnated out of wedlock and I suspect...now I don't know this for certain, Mr. Quant...I suspect that the baby's father was a disreputable man who may have forced himself upon my sister."

The words were surprising but made a lot of sense. Charity's dossier mentioned her son, John, but revealed nothing about his father or how she came to be pregnant. Although Faith was only guessing, the chances were good that her guess was accurate. I could easily imagine that in the 1940s, a young woman, attractive, a lesbian, would consider the world of business preferable to marrying the first man (or any man) who came her way. It was a handy cloak of secrecy beneath which to hide. But such a woman, and owner of one of Canada's largest businesses, would have been an irresistible challenge to a certain type of man.

"You believe she was raped?" I whispered back.

Instead of answering my new question, she reverted to my last, less troubling one. "Hope and I convinced Charity to have the baby and keep him. So she did. She named him John."

I didn't know how much of our conversation he'd overheard, but Thomas noticed his wife becoming upset and laid his big hand over her petite, shaking one. "Dear, are you all right?"

She nodded and gave her husband a tight smile. When she turned to me her eyes were damp. "We were wrong, Mr. Quant. I can't believe I would ever say it would be wrong for a mother to keep her newborn child but...Charity could not be a mother to that child. She had no desire or natural talent for it, and that truth haunts her to this very day."

I nodded and gave her an empathetic look. "I know John left home at an early age and that he and Charity didn't have much contact after that."

"That's true. Their relationship was not a close one. She blames herself, but I'm afraid much of the responsibility falls on Hope and me. Charity didn't want to have a child. We forced her."

"But you couldn't have known what she'd gone through with the child's father...if indeed it was what you suspect. You were giving her advice that was the best you knew how to give at the time."

"I thank God for Flora. She was...is like...a second chance. Even though it came by way of tragedy, here was a child Charity could raise and learn to love as her own. I thank the Lord for that."

"Perhaps we should enjoy our breakfast now?" Thomas suggested, looking directly at me with a stern expression.

But...but...but I have one more question to ask. It was time to be insensitive. I tried to ignore Thomas and asked Faith the big one: "Do you think someone in this room could be threatening to kill your sister?"

"Mr. Quant!" Thomas admonished me, his voice low but pressing.

Faith shook her head decisively. "Never. Not in this family.

Whatever it is that Charity believes is happening is all a mistake…a big mistake."

"What ab…"

"Mr. Quant," Thomas cut me off. "I think that's enough."

I nodded and looked down at my bowl of soggy bran, giving in to the ex-priest's suggestion. I considered what I had just learned. I certainly was gaining a better appreciation for the circumstances of Charity's life. Her self-prepared dossier had left out some important facts. What I hadn't learned was whether any of it spelled out a reason for murder.

Charity had chosen her tender-mates with care, only those people she trusted not to stick a knife in her back—literally. I was again being thrust into the role of bodyguard rather than detective. I'd have preferred to spend the day with other members of the family in order to continue my hunt for a suspect. But then again, what better way to identify a potential murderer than being in the hip pocket of the intended victim?

Given that The Dorothy wasn't leaving port until late evening, our group of five agreed to spend the first part of the day on board the ship. It gave us time to visit the spa or gym, or sun by the pool before meeting at the tender launch for a mid-afternoon trip into Palermo for some shopping and sightseeing to be followed by a late dinner.

I had a couple Wiser rooms yet to search and after breakfast I attempted to seek out opportunities to do so but was thwarted at every turn, never able to find ten safe minutes in which to carry out my foraging for clues. I finally gave up and tracked down Charity in a relatively secluded area off the pool deck. She was sitting alone on a chaise lounge shaded by an umbrella and a fantastically large-brimmed hat with a bold red tassel that hung almost to the ground and matched the wraparound she wore. She was reading a business periodical.

"I knew you'd come a-sniffing," she greeted me with a complicated smile that bore little warmth. "Sit if you must."

I did and then stared at her.

She stared back.

Finally, "Charity, you cannot go ashore."

That was all she needed. "Oh for the sake of Salome's seven veils!" Ewwwboy, here it comes, beginning with an interesting turn of phrase. Did it represent Charity's hunger for someone's head on a platter? Mine? "*You* do not tell *me* what I can or cannot do, Mr. Quant. I employ you, do I not? Of course I do. Our contract says it's so. I don't mean to be harsh, I know you are only concerned for my well-being, I appreciate that, I truly do, but I will not be cowed by some cowardly sonofabitch who writes petty notes and hires Tunisian schoolboys to do his dirty work. I am not afraid, Mr. Quant, I am not afraid!"

I gave her words a few seconds to flow away on the morning breeze before saying, "Well, maybe I am."

"What! What? What are you talking about?" she sputtered.

"I've already told you, I am not a bodyguard. I will do my best to protect you, but I cannot ensure your safety. I am afraid that next time...and there will be a next time, Charity...either I won't be there or I won't be able to save you. We got lucky in Tunis, that's all."

"Russell, pl..."

"Charity, understand this: Someone wants you dead. This isn't a game, this isn't just another Charity Event where you control what happens. You have no control here. I know that may be difficult for you to understand, but you have to try. You're right, I shouldn't tell you what you can or cannot do, but I will tell you *I do not want you to go ashore.*"

She nodded, then said. "But you will come with me?"

I nodded too. It was my job.

"And I hope you will try to understand why I must." She searched my face but did not find what she was looking for.

Charity reached into a nearby cloth purse and pulled out a piece of paper. It was the latest note. She held it out to me, her hand as steady as granite. "I thought you'd be asking to see this."

I took the note. Same block handwriting I'd yet to identify the owner of. Same FOD stationery. Same threatening intent, one which we had just decided to ignore.

After a light workout and lunch by the pool I decided to check out the ship's library, which also doubled as a computer room with several internet accessible machines. It was a cozy space, with wall to wall shelves of books, magazines and DVDs that passengers could sign out for use in their cabins.

I selected a computer station that offered some level of privacy and a comfy chair and settled in. I liked it here. Aside from an unobtrusive FOD staffer who manned the room in case anyone needed assistance, there were only one or two other people meandering throughout the room. I liked having a bit of space and quiet time to myself. Sharing a room is not all it's cracked up to be. And I liked being in front of a computer. It reminded me of my office at home, a room that I love spending time in. I pushed a few buttons to get to my favourite internet browser and played around with some research on the Wisers. It's one of my standard investigative techniques: putting out feelers that sometimes return useful information, sometimes don't—but worth a shot. For the millionth time I wondered how anyone ever found out anything before the internet. Encyclopedias? What are those?

I was about done when a voice slithered over my right shoulder, "I know what you're up to."

I felt the skin on my skull shift a few millimetres. I swivelled in my chair and came face to face with Kayla Moshier, looking a bit smug, slouched in front of the computer monitor at a neighbouring station. She must have come in without my hearing her. "Excuse me?"

"You're like a cop, right? Or a spy, a detective? Right?" Her voice was slippery and purposefully sly.

So the teenager was cleverer than I'd given her credit for. "Why do you think that?" I asked with wide, innocent eyes and a tilt of my head.

"I've been watching you." She adjusted one of the straps of the bikini top she was wearing with a pair of too-tight cut-off jeans. "And you're gay too."

I had truly underestimated this girl. "Why do you think that?" I repeated.

"You've been asking questions galore, you've been following all of us around like a dog; you watch us all the time." She grinned. Her teeth were small, square, strong looking. A meat-eater. "Well, what you don't know is that when you're not looking, I'm watching you back. So there. If you really were Aunt Charity's advisor, you'd be spending time with her, not us. You're looking for something. You're looking for whichever one of us is trying to knock her off."

Rightyroo. But I wasn't about to admit it.

"Right?" she pushed in a whiny tone available only to teenage vocal chords. "You're a private eye, right?"

"I'm an advisor to your Aunt Charity. If I've been hanging around your family it's because I'm trying to be sociable."

She snorted. "Yeah, now I know you're lying. Who'd want to be sociable with this family?" She checked her bad makeup in the blank computer screen's reflection. "So what have you found out so far? Huh? Any suspects? I got some for you."

Excellent. "Oh yeah. Like who?"

"Whaddayou care if you're just an *advisor*?" She didn't wait for an answer that was never gonna come anyway. "It's kind of easy isn't it? All you gotta find out is like who needs the money most?" She stared at me as if I was a big dummy. "Like try Harry's dad," she said as if introducing me to the back of my hand.

I still hadn't had the chance to confront Jackson with the fact that I'd seen him in Tunis when he was supposed to have been aboard The Dorothy. Had he arranged the attack on Charity and hid in the medina to see how it turned out? Then, hoping to make something from the aborted attempt, he sends her the threatening note? "You think Jackson is involved?"

"Yeah, dude. He's little better than a skid row bum from what I hear. He needs money real bad. He could easily be the killer." With that bit of slander, she rose from her chair and attempted an ill-advised seductive exit. "And I know you're gay," she told me, throwing her heavily mascaraed eyes over her undulating shoulder, "because you pay no attention to this." She whacked her ass.

"Anyone else?" I asked without blinking an eye, proving her right. "Any other suspects you've identified?"

She stopped mid-step, thought about this, turned back to me and said, "Harry's grandpa too."

Patrick Halburton? Kayla really seemed to have a hate on for all of her cousin's relatives. "Why?" I asked.

She smirked. "Just because he's a really creepy old man."

While the other passengers were subject to the prescribed departure and arrival times of tenders arranged by FOD, we had our own tenders that would come and go as *we* pleased. Lucky us. Or so I thought until I saw them. The FOD tenders were large and modern and resembled mini-pleasurecrafts . The tenders arranged for us by Richard Gray and Charity looked to have been supplied as a result of a late-night negotiation with a shifty, nameless Sicilian who insisted upon being paid ahead of time in chickens. They were little more than wooden rafts, each piloted by a non-English-speaking youth. And as we boarded, our sixteen-year-old captain welcomed each of us with a suspicious gaze, as if calculating whether our added weight would be what finally sunk his boat.

It was a beautiful afternoon. A powerful sun lit up the sky into its brightest hues of blue, the sound of lapping water was playful and cheerful, and the air smelled of salt and spicy meatballs, but all of it meant nothing to me. While the others seemed oblivious to what doubtlessly would result in dire circumstances, I privately feared for our lives. My life in particular. Sure, I can swim—like a cat that's been thrown into a pool by surprise. And sure, I can save my life if I have to…I think…who can account for the panic factor? But why would I knowingly want to put myself into a situation where that possibility was pretty much inevitable? Was I insane? As I gingerly stepped onto the piece of driftwood that was our boat, noted that there were fewer life vests than passengers, and braved the puerile captain's assessment, I certainly believed myself to be so.

I spent the voyage to Palermo silently repeating every Ukrainian prayer my mother ever taught me and promising myself I would make the return trip aboard one of The Dorothy's more seaworthy tenders—all the while smiling like some crazed maniac for the benefit of my fellow passengers. And then, after about a month we reached shore.

When I stepped off the boat-thing onto wondrous, hard, dry land, I experienced my first ever case of rubber legs. I looked like Gumby as I boarded the shuttle that ferried ship passengers to and from town. But I didn't care. I was alive!

A short drive later the bus came to a lurching halt and expelled us into bedlam. Unceremoniously deposited onto an unfamiliar sidewalk, we hesitated to get our bearings. The street itself was one car wide but seemed to support up to four lanes of zigzagging traffic roaring by us at blurring speeds. Cars, trucks, motorbikes, scooters, bicycles, even tractors, rocketed about as if powered by Concorde engines. Pedestrians—no doubt fresh from lunches of amphetamines and undiluted caffeine—moved about like fast forward versions of real people. We felt as if we'd been tossed into a blender set to puree. It was Italy on crack.

In the span of less than sixty seconds we were yelled at, scolded for holding up traffic, one of us stepped into freshly poured cement, and another somehow offended a passing old woman resulting in a rather inventively worded curse against all of our families and pets. Dottie got dust in her eye and Errall nearly lost her shoe in a sidewalk grate. We smelled the competing aromas of freshly baked bread, water that had sat too long in the sun and unwashed bodies. We were honked at and glared at and witnessed an anorexic cat narrowly avoid being run over with little more than a backward glance. All the while our bus driver was yelling instructions in half-Italian, half-English about where he'd pick us up and at what time as he drove away, the door already closing. Of course all this activity caught the attention of everyone within a half-block radius. They began to stare, some catcalled, some laughed at us, one fellow even spit.

Welcome to Sicily.

The five of us instinctively clasped hands and shuffled down the street en masse in search of some small safe space where we could grab back some dignity and unfold a map. With Dottie a bit slow, it was a cumbersome task that took us a fair bit of time and earned us a few more profanities, but we were becoming inured to this new reality in a hurry and Charity even managed to get in a few epithets of her own.

"I absolutely adore this!" she exclaimed when we'd finally found a few millimetres to call our own, at least momentarily. "Don't you absolutely adore this, Flora, Dottie? Oh of course you do! What's not to adore!"

Flora, now completely de-*Pygmalion*ized, looked, if possible, even paler and drabber than usual. Dottie seemed a bit discombobulated by all the clangorous activity. Even Errall appeared as uncomfortable as a worm in a birdcage.

"I couldn't hear what the bus driver said," Flora whinnied anxiously. "Did anyone hear what he said? How will we know when and where he'll pick us up?"

Charity wrapped a protective arm around her granddaughter's bony shoulders as she propelled her forward. "That, my dearie, is what taxis are for." Then in a louder voice meant for all of us she proclaimed, "Let's meet this Palermo and demand of her the time of our lives!"

And so we did.

Many cathedrals, museums, clothing stores and outdoor coffee shops later we ended up at a restaurant called Cucina Papoff on Via Isidoro La Lumia near the Politeama Opera House. After several courses, all including sausage in one form or another, and three litres of a hearty Sicilian red, Nero d'Avola, we had our waiter call for a cab and contact our tender operator to tell him to expect us soon. Over the course of the afternoon and evening, I had settled down and gotten my paranoia of unparalleled danger lurking behind every corner under control. I even managed to eventually enjoy myself. A little. Perhaps Charity had it right.

One of the many wonderful things about alcohol is that it blunts one's fears, rational and otherwise, and as we stepped again into the dinghy that was our tender I was full of manly courage. The dark sky, the choppy water, the fact that our pubescent boat operator did not smile when we joined him no longer fazed me. I did notice there was no sign of the other two tenders. But seeing as it was 9:30 p.m. and we were to be back on the boat by 10 p.m. for a scheduled 11 p.m. departure, I assumed the others had returned to The Dorothy long ago.

Charity and Dottie sat at the front end of the tender, giggling away between themselves as only long-term couples know well how to do. Flora sat on her own just behind them and Errall and I behind her. Our teen captain piloted from the rear. It was a twenty-minute voyage and we settled in with only the boat's meagre running lights guiding our way.

Once we were away from the dock I felt a nudge in my ribs.

"I didn't mean the things I said the other night," Errall whispered into the dark, taking advantage of the protection it offered her. "I just needed to be alone, you know?"

I had been thinking about my argument with Errall and what it really meant. Errall is one of those people who hide their true feelings, often by disguising them as something else—anger, even illness. I was certain I knew the truth. But did I have the courage to reveal it? "She's gone, Errall," I whispered back, biting my tongue at the same time. I hoped I wouldn't say something to raise the ire of Errall's famous temper, enough to cause her to do something rash...like toss me overboard. "She's gone. She left you." The words sounded cold, harsh. But they were true. "She left me too. We both have to accept that."

A muffled sound but nothing more.

I soldiered on. "Kelly was...is my friend. But she's not around anymore. Maybe she needs time away to regroup, think things over, get a new life. Maybe she'll be back, maybe not, I don't know. But you've got to move on, Errall. If you think that because I'm Kelly's friend you can't go out, have fun, meet people, maybe even other women, well, that's my mistake for not making it clear to you. You can. I expect it. Just go for it. Don't hang out in our room moping."

"Why did you bring me on this trip, Russell?"

Oooboy. Good question. I wasn't sure I had the answer. Or did I? "Maybe...maybe during all these years, you and I were becoming friends...and we just didn't recognize it...until now."

She let out a sigh. I could feel her shift next to me. "Maybe," she whispered.

That's where we ended it. Something else came up.

The first sign of trouble was the motor. It sounded as if it were attempting to clear its throat of a mighty huge hairball—unsuccessfully.

It sputtered, it choked and then…fell silent. And so did we.

Our young captain, dark and scrappy and in dire need of a hairdresser, made no effort to speak to us or reassure us, instead focusing on a restart by yanking the motor's cord. Great, I thought to myself, we're stuck on the mighty sea at the mercy of a boat powered by a Weed Eater engine.

"What's wrong?" asked Flora. "Can't you start it?"

Why do people insist on asking the obvious in times of stress? Did she think he'd turn around, suddenly understanding and speaking English, and say, "Well, actually I can, but this is all part of the *Authentic Sicilian Tour Package* you signed up for. I will start the engine in thirty-four seconds as outlined in your brochure. So please be patient, sit back and enjoy your authentic experience."

Our skipper made a show of knocking the side of the gas tank, which I guess sounded full because he followed this up with a scratching of his head as if mightily confused. He dug around in a basket and pulled out a flashlight, directing its face into the blackness around us. It flickered on and off several times, but finally caught. Now I'm no mechanic, but I wondered if the repair process would go smoother if he'd shine the flashlight on the motor rather than off the bow of the boat. That should have been my first clue that all was not right aboard the S.S. Minnow. The next came when the running lights faltered, plunging us into total blackness except for the weak halo of light coming from the flashlight in the Sicilian's hand.

"Do you have a cellphone?" I asked him, feeling foolish doing so. But maybe he really was only pretending not to know English earlier, playing the surly, silent, Sicilian youth. "Telephono?" I tried. "Walkie talkie-oh?"

And then our captain disappeared.

The splash was as horrifying a sound as the shark music from *Jaws*. My stomach tightened, my head grew dizzy and a stampede of clawed insects began a painful climb up the length of my raw esophagus.

"Oh no! He's fallen overboard!" screamed Dottie. "Someone help him!"

Errall and I scrambled to the back of the boat where the youth had been only seconds ago and tried to peer through the inky blackness for any sign of the young man. From behind us I heard a whipping sound and then a "phlop." A wave of terror hit me again like the flat of a hand against my face. Had someone else gone overboard? Or worse…was some dark, anonymous creature of the sea *pulling* us off the boat…one by one?

"What was that? What was that?" Errall demanded of the dark.

"It was me," this from an invisible Flora. "I threw out a life jacket for him. But it's too dark…I can't see where it landed. I can't see where he is!"

Errall began searching the bottom of the boat for the flashlight, hoping the captain had dropped it before going overboard.

Time was precious. I knew that if the boy was in distress, he needed help now. I couldn't allow myself the luxury of thinking too long about what had to be done. Because if I did, I feared I would not do it.

I jumped.

"Russell!" I heard a choir of voices call out after me.

"Russell, you're crazy!" Errall.

"Mr. Quant, can you see him?" This from Flora.

I began by flailing about as the shock of what I'd done nearly overcame me. In my mind I heard one word echoing over and over again: Nightmare. Nightmare. *Nightmare!*

"Russell!" they yelled in chorus.

"Are you okay?" Errall again.

"Be quiet!" I yelled back, at the same time spitting out a mouthful of brine. "Shhh!" I slowed my movements in the water, beginning to trust in my rudimentary but sufficient swimming skills (the dog paddle). "Maybe I can *hear* where he is." It was too dark to see where he'd gone, my only hope of finding him was by sound. I trained my ear into the general area behind our boat. The others complied and sat in silence on the boat. We listened.

And there it was. The unmistakable sound of someone swimming, then thrashing through the water, then, "Aiuto! Aiuto prego!

Aiuto, mister!"

Oh God! He was drowning and calling out for my help! It sounded as if he had somehow drifted quite far from the boat. I took a deep breath and plunged into the direction of his voice, utilizing swim strokes I seemed to be making up as I went. In my subconscious I was very aware of being cold and being scared, but at the forefront of my brain was the desire to save this boy's life. Even if he was a piss-poor tender captain.

"I'm coming!" I managed to call out. "Wait for me. I'll help you." The poor guy. I knew he couldn't understand a word I was saying, but hopefully the sound of my voice would calm him. Salvation was near.

"Aiuto!" he called out again, sending me a verbal beacon for where to find him.

At first it was a thud against my chest. What the hell? Then again. Someone was kicking me. He was panicking! Going under! This wasn't good. I reached out to grab onto him and managed to sink my fingers into his shirt. But it was empty, just a soaken rag in my hands.

Then, from the direction I'd just come, a sound that curdled every drop of blood in my veins. Screaming.

It was Charity. Then the others.

The tender was under siege.

Chapter 11

He hit me again. In the face. Hard. Then he began to yell at me. For a moment I was disoriented, not comprehending what was going on. Why was he fighting me?

I heard the sound of two or three Italian voices, all jabbering at high speed.

And then I knew.

Our captain hadn't fallen overboard.

He'd jumped.

A blinding glare assaulted my eyes as the beam of a powerful light came to life. It was coming from another vessel, not ours but a skiff, less than a dozen metres away from where the captain and I were now pitched in a watery battle, hands about each other's necks. For a moment we stopped and stared at one another, close enough to make out the whites of each other's eyes. He looked scared. I'm sure I did too. A man on the skiff yelled something to him. In a voice both anxious and threatening the captain yelled something at me. I didn't understand his language any more than he understood mine, but I knew exactly what he was telling me.

From somewhere in the opposite direction I could hear the alarmed calls of my shipmates and the excited voice of yet another Italian. Best I could tell, there were three of them: the captain, one on the skiff, and one attacking the tender. What was happening? What the hell was going on? All I could be sure of was that Charity, Dottie, Flora and Errall were in serious trouble.

The man on the skiff called out again to the captain who in turn screamed instructions to the third man who was attacking the women. The Italians seemed disorganized, unsure of what to do, as if something was not as they expected it to be. From the direction of the tender I could make out the sounds of a mighty skirmish: splashing and splattering, high-pitched yelps and calls for help. I had to do something. I released my hold on the captain's scrawny neck, wound back my right fist and ploughed it into his nose. He looked startled. So I did it again. Blood began to flow. I wondered about sharks. The guy on the skiff was going crazy, catching all this in the ray of his boat light, saying stuff in Italian that couldn't have been nice. I didn't have time to wait for a translator. I brushed past the stunned captain and made for the tender with a strength and speed that belied my physical exhaustion. Good old adrenaline.

By the time I reached the tender, the air was alive with a squawking of such intensity that I might have been in a chicken coop right before Sunday dinner at Farmer Brown's. The squawking was both Italian and English so I had a hint that both sides were still in active combat. I spotted one figure (other than myself) in the water. It was very dark and my eyes were beginning to sting from the constant bathing they were getting in salty sea water. All I could make out was that he seemed to have one of the women in his grasp and was trying to pull her off the tender and into the water. The other three women were making this very difficult for him. I grabbed him from behind, getting an arm locked around his throat, and pressed. Who says music is the only language understood the world over? From behind me I could hear the other two goons calling out to him. I was hoping one of the words they were yelling was "Retreat!"

Under pressure from my persuasive forearm on his Adam's

apple, the man let go of his intended captive, who turned out to be Charity, and in return I let him go. Without a backwards glance he swam away towards the light of the waiting skiff and his band of merry thugs. I bobbed in the water and watched until he was received into the arms of his comrades. As soon as he was on board they extinguished their light and I heard the unmistakable sound of oars in water heading, thankfully, away.

I could feel the beginning of the hurt where I'd been hit in the face and throttled around the neck, and then the ache of exhaustion. But worst of all was the feeling when the reality of what had just happened became terrifyingly clear. This was no accident. The tender hadn't broken down. Someone broke it. Intentionally. The flashlight hadn't been flickering because of a weak battery. It was a signal. Our captain was signalling his mates that he was about to abandon ship and for them to begin the planned attack. While I was lured away to save the drowning captain, Charity would be pulled off the boat and more than likely killed. This had been one giant, elaborate set-up. The person who had been threatening Charity had made another move.

I felt several hands and arms reach out for me and hoist me aboard. I fell inside and collapsed against someone's waiting shoulder, wheezing and choking on a few last drops of seawater and trying to catch my breath. At first there was a bevy of questions, solicitude for my bravery and expressions of concern: Russell, are you okay? Russell, what happened? Russell, your face—are you bleeding? Russell, what happened out there? Russell, who were those men?

I answered as best I could. Once I ascertained that Charity was unharmed, I asked questions of my own. It was as I'd guessed. As soon as I was far enough away from the boat, thinking I was saving our captain, another Sicilian, waiting in the darkness, reached into the tender and tried to pull Charity overboard. The women fought him off, using their hands, knitting needles and whatever else they could find in the boat to stop the man, knocking him over the head repeatedly until I returned.

The exchange of information took several minutes.

And then, nothing.

Except for the slap of dirty waves against the side of our boat, an eerie silence descended upon us. It was clear that our duplicitous captain had been ferried away by his compatriots and that we were left very alone. In a way I was glad not to be able to see the faces of the others. I didn't want to bear witness to the terror that was no doubt etching its terrible lines there. Deserted in total darkness, we were sitting ducks, a bobbing piece of black on a sea of black, fair game for any passing craft to cruise right through, blasting us to smithereens, without even noticing. But my greatest worry was that this was not the end-game. Whoever planned this wanted Charity out of the picture and would not settle for the unsuccessful results of the Italians' attack on us. Something more was going to happen; I could feel it in my bones. The flaw in Charity's logic became apparent to me. She'd wanted to keep us, her trusted circle, around her today in light of the most recent threatening note, thinking that this would somehow protect her. Instead, by setting us apart from the others, all she'd done was make herself, and us, her unwitting companions, easy targets.

"Can we swim for it?" Errall suggested after a long period of quiet.

I scanned the horizon for the comforting outline of The Dorothy. She was lit up like a birthday cake, her smokestack's ruby red slippers a glistening symbol that over the last several days had come to mean home. But home was too far away.

"I can't swim."

My heart crunched. It was Dottie. Suddenly I felt silly for giving heed to my own phobias. Not only had this eighty-eight-year-old woman come on a cruise in the first place, but she had gamely sat in this treacherous tender, all without knowing how to swim. That was trust. Trust that things will work out the way they're supposed to. Trust that no one is going to set you adrift in the middle of a foreign harbour with no means of communicating your dilemma or hope of rescue. Me, I was a little more jaded.

"But you four go ahead," Dottie said, unruffled. "I'll wait here. I have my knitting with me."

I wanted to reach out and touch her arm in reassurance, but I only had a general sense of where her voice came from.

"We could give it a try," Flora spoke. "We'd come back for you."

I frowned at the black space where I guessed Flora was sitting. "We won't be leaving you, Dottie. Besides, it's too far away. We'd never make it. Don't worry, we'll figure something out."

"What time is it?" Flora asked. "We're supposed to be back on The Dorothy by ten o'clock. Suppose we miss the boat?"

"Don't worry, dear," Charity said. And something about her voice told me that she knew, as well as I, that missing the boat's departure was the least of our immediate concerns.

"What's that?" an alarmed voice rang out in the dark. Flora again.

"What? What is it?" Dottie called out.

"I...I can feel...oh no, it's...I can feel...wet."

Wet.

"I...can...too," Errall said, the words coming out of her mouth half-speed as if slowed by the weight of dread. "Russell...?"

"I can...I...oh my God!" Flora cried. "It's wet, it's getting wet. There's water in the boat!"

"Oh no."

"I can feel it too."

"Oh my God!"

The voices were indistinguishable, each tinged with a palpable terror that sent pinpricks into my heart. The terror of knowing a horrible truth.

This was how they were going to put an end to us.

We were sinking, with only one life vest left on board.

It was like experiencing a power failure in an unfamiliar room. A room that is filling with water. A room that is moving up and down, backwards and forwards, side to side. A room you desperately want to escape. The next few minutes were a mess. I tried my hand at restarting the motor. Flora and Dottie, doing her best given her limited mobility, tried to locate the source of the leak, which I suspected was engineered by our captain before he bailed on us. Charity and Errall scrambled about in the darkness searching the boat for anything that might help us: flares, a communication device of some sort, containers to bail out the water that was filling the bottom of the craft. But there was nothing. Nothing by design. Except, by some quirk of fate or ignorance on the part of the culprits who put us in this crisis, one remaining life vest (in addition to the one Flora had already tossed into the abyss in a kind but misguided effort to save our captain).

"Wait!" Errall called to me from somewhere near the front of the boat. "I found a tool of some sort. I think it's a wrench!"

"What am I supposed to do with that?" I yelled back, yanking on the motor's cord for about the millionth time.

"Fix the bloody engine! Fix the leak!"

"You're the lesbian, you fix it!"

"We're going to go down!" cried Flora, her voice several pitches higher than normal. "My God! This can't be happening! It isn't right! It's all wrong!"

"I can't swim." Dottie again. This time her statement of fact was even more frightening. If the boat went down, so would she. At eighty-eight, increasingly frail, overweight and with a weak heart, Dottie would never make it and we could never hope to hold her afloat for long.

I could hear frantic attempts at bailing. They were using cupped hands. But I knew it was useless. I could feel the water inching up my calves at an alarming speed. It felt like molten lead, cold, thick, heavy, and hungry for me, wanting to swallow me whole.

"Don't you worry about a thing, Dottie Blocka," Charity said, sounding in full control of all that mattered. "Everything will be just fine."

"You must try to swim for The Dorothy," Dottie declared.

"Don't be ridiculous, dear. You just sit tight with your knitting and we'll figure something out, won't we Russell?"

Uh, sure. But, uh, can you feel the molten lead?

"Charity, I know what's happening," Dottie sounded resolute. "You can swim like a dolphin, as I'm sure these youngsters can. You must all try to save yourselves. And Flora! Oh Charity, you must save your granddaughter! Would you have her drown?"

"Dottie, no." I could feel the strain and raw emotion of Charity's words course through my own veins. "I will not leave you."

"Russell," Errall said, "we have to do something. The boat is filling fast."

I shook my head, exasperated. "It's too heavy. There's too much weight in it."

"There's nothing to throw off," Flora said. "There's nothing in the boat..."

"Except us," I finished the sentence.

Charity jumped onto the idea excitedly. "If we all jump off the boat, hold on to its sides, the boat will stay afloat longer and Dottie can stay nice and dry, won't you, my lovely?"

"Dottie, put on the life jacket," I instructed, passing it down to Charity.

"Why me?" the old woman protested. "We should vote on who gets to wear the thing."

"You're the only one who can't swim," I said. "Charity, can you help her?"

I heard belts and clips and snaps as Charity helped her partner on with the life-preserving device, and then the first splash. Errall had gone overboard.

"Water's great," she reported between spits of salt water. "You should come in." Bless her heart.

I jumped next, followed by Flora and Charity.

And then, one more splash.

"Dottie! No!" cried Charity. "You crazy old woman, you're to stay on the boat! Russell, help me get her back in!"

"No!" Dottie sputtered back, gulping air and liquid saline at the same time. "If you're jumping off, so am I. If we're to go down, it will be together, my love."

A reverential silence followed this grand gesture of devotion between these two women. If I'd been munching popcorn, watching this scene on my large screen TV, curled up on my comfy leather sofa the colour of soft toffee, in the company of my sweet Barbra and Brutus, a blazing fire in the grate, I'd have teared up. But not now, not here. Not in this murky darkness, feeling cold, wet, frightened, hurting from where I'd been punched and throttled. I had other things to think about. Even though we were all in this together, through none of our own faults, I couldn't help but feel responsible for getting us out of this mess. I was the rough and tumble P.I., used to danger, used to beating impossible odds. But who was I kidding? I wasn't *Spenser: For Hire*. I wanted to tell the others I'd been in tougher situations before and gotten out of them without trouble, but that would have been a lie. I should have lied.

"That's very sweet, Dottie," I heard Charity say, softer now. "But not very sensible. I think you should get back in the boat."

"Isn't this what these life jacket contraptions are for, to keep people afloat? I'm fine, Charity. I'm floating. It's really quite lovely."

I love when people fib to make someone else feel better.

We hung on. Our plan, such as it was, was working. With less weight to support, the tender was taking on water at a much slower rate and managed to stay afloat, giving us a temporary buoy to hold on to. As we silently bobbed up and down in time with the waves, I knew that inside, each of us was fighting our own private battle, wondering if every second might be our last.

But none of them were and soon, we became like one with the water, just another collection of flotsam in the sea.

When we heard the foghorn blast of The Dorothy, our hearts began to sink faster than the tender. It could mean only one thing. She was leaving, preparing to depart the port of Palermo. Without us. She had places to go. Tomorrow The Dorothy's passengers expected to be in Messina, just a strait away from the Italian mainland. They couldn't wait for five wayward passengers who, for all they knew (the tender operator certainly wouldn't tell them otherwise), were whooping it up in some Sicilian pub having lost track of the time.

And, after one more blast, we watched in disbelief as the silhouette of The Dorothy began to move away, leaving us behind.

As cheerless thoughts and helplessness invaded our brains like a cancer, the talk around the slowly sinking tender grew sparse. We were growing tired. The wind had picked up and every so often a whitecap would wash by us with a hateful force. The Dorothy had disappeared from our view in shockingly few minutes, as if it had clicked its heels three times and been magically transported away. We were in dire circumstances.

I racked my brain for a way out, for a plan to bring us to safety, but found it distressingly empty. Flora was right: this wasn't right. How had I, a Saskatchewan son, ended up holding on for dear life to a scrap of rotting wood pretending to be a boat, in the middle of the Mediterranean Sea with my best friend's ex-girlfriend and three other women I barely knew? If this wasn't my greatest nightmare come to life, I didn't know what was. I'd had doubts about getting on The Dorothy, sailing the seas when I was so accustomed to dry, prairie flatlands. And now, as feared, I'd been dunked, abandoned, my legs flailing under me in water deeper than I cared to imagine, solid land hopelessly out of reach. But in the end it was the wrong enemy I'd feared. The Dorothy wasn't my enemy, nor was the sea. It was a person, a person intent on killing my client, and me, and several others along with us.

I fought off bitter panic, rising up in me as surely as bile in a throat, threatening to pull me under and drown me faster than any water could. I couldn't let it. There was work to do. The work of staying alive as long as humanly possible. I wanted to live. These women wanted to live. But how? How could we possibly survive this?

I could hear Charity and Dottie whispering sweet nothings to each other somewhere on the other side of the boat. Flora was to my right, and had been silent for a long time. Errall was to my left. Every so often she spoke, mutterings mostly, more to hear her own voice than to offer any real solution to our situation. I too called out every minute or two, like roll call, asking everyone if they were still okay and holding on. I said useless things like, I'm sure someone will come by soon and find us, or the Coast Guard should be by any time, or The Dorothy's captain would have contacted the authorities about our being missing and they'll be looking for us by now. Lies. All lies. The shroud of relentless dark seemed to amplify my feelings of helplessness and fear and loneliness.

I realized I had been wrong earlier.

I wished I could see their faces.

Chapter 12

A searchlight appeared in the distance and quickly grew in size and brightness as it neared our position. Although I'm sure no one could hear us, we began to yell, if for no other reason than to prove to ourselves that we were alive and that we could.

Waiting patiently for my turn to be hauled aboard the luxury yacht, moving up and down with the water like a human cork, I looked up, way up, and spotted three figures looking down at us. One was a man, standing alone on the uppermost deck. I could barely make out the shape of him. He was standing slightly back from the railing, seemingly aloof yet very interested in the activity below him. The other two, on the lower deck, standing just beyond where the crew was valiantly toiling to bring us up, were a woman and a man. The woman was all in white, the light fabric of her clothing fluttering about her like the wings of an angel. Unlike the man on the upper deck, these two were pressed against the railing, intently peering down at us. I stared at them, glad for the distraction. As I did I thought I saw something familiar, something... something...but I couldn't put my finger on it. The ambient light was low, the searchlight having been extinguished and all other lights trained upon the rescue effort. I shielded my eyes to get a better look at the couple and sensed that the woman was staring right back at me. But it was not until it was my turn to be hoisted from the roiling water that might have been our graveyard that I saw her clearly. In disbelief I beheld her face.

"Russell," her rich voice reached down to me like a helping hand. "Glad you could stop by."

I swallowed a mouthful of seawater. I couldn't believe what I was hearing. I couldn't believe what I was seeing. Our saviour was none other than Sereena Orion Smith.

The yacht was a fifty-metre from the renowned Benetti shipyard, one of only a handful in the flagship "Golden Bay" series, designed by some guy named Francois Zuretti. She boasted eleven crewmembers, six cabins including a full-width master on the main deck, a nine-metre beam, and a MTU 396 TE 94 engine with a cruising speed of fourteen-point-five knots. She had a tender all her own, plus a couple of Jet Skis and two clear-bottom kayaks. Or so Richard Gray told me when I was dry and warm and settled in the warm embrace of the boat's considerable comforts. A fan of all luxurious means of travel—be it ship, yacht, jet aircraft or locomotive—Richard was fully versed on all the specifications of the Kismet, as she was called.

"Better?" he asked, as I downed a second snifter of warmed Courvoisier.

I went back to work towel drying my hair, sitting on the bed in my cabin—our cabin?—next to him. It was a trifle smaller than the one I shared with Errall on The Dorothy, but not by much. "Yes, thank you," I answered, giving him a grateful smile. With everything that had gone on, everything that begged for explanation, the stupidest thing came next to my lips. "Listen, about you seeing me with Nick Kincaid last night..."

He held up a hand to my mouth, the pads of his fingers soft on my lips. "Don't. You don't have to explain. I don't know why I reacted the way I did...running away like that...it was stupid, childish. I'm the one who should apologize. You can do whatever you want with whoever you want."

I kissed his fingers and brought them down to my chest, under the folds of my robe. He swallowed hard and I could feel his fingers begin to work on my nipple, as if by instinct. Our eyes were bound together. We pulled the invisible string taut, our lips meeting but not kissing. For a glorious moment we simply took in the smell of each other and basked in the warmth of being so intimately near.

Being completely naked beneath my robe I was either at a distinct disadvantage or advantage, depending on how you looked at it. I decided it was the latter. I stood up slowly and with one easy motion let the robe fall to the floor. He wanted to feast, but I pushed him away. I stepped back and leaned back against the nearest wall, my hands crossed behind me and resting on the shelf of my buttocks.

Unabashedly displaying my wares for inspection, I told him, "Your turn,"

And he took it, standing to peel away the layers that covered his skin. Until the last one, the one that would show me what I hadn't seen around the pool. But before he could go any further I rushed him, throwing him back on the bed, falling with all my weight on top of him. I wanted to make that final discovery myself. It was a tumble for the top, a position of control, superiority, a position we both sought to win from the other. We somersaulted over and over making so much noise I hoped the others had already left their adjoining cabins for the main salon where we were promised food and drink once we'd cleaned up. But Richard and I were determined to get dirty. This was much better than food and drink, even to a starving man. We were equally matched for strength—for a while. He fought me off, but with little of the force I knew his bulging muscles were capable of. And then I won.

He may have let me.

By the time we found our way to the main salon, I was desperate to have him again. Something about the sea air made me...insatiable. I resisted. The salon was empty but through two sliding glass doors we saw an exterior deck overlooking the night lights of Palermo and two women sitting in lounge chairs even though the sun had long ago disappeared. Their heads were close together as they talked, a half-empty bottle of wine on a small table between them.

"I'm pleased you could join us," Sereena's raw-edged voice proclaimed as she rose graciously from her lounger to greet us, dark, romance-novel-heroine hair, eyes and face at their best in the seascape-tinged dim lighting.

I still found it difficult to comprehend that she was really there. She was a long way from her home, the one right next to mine on a quiet, dead-end street in Saskatoon. And, as always when I happen to catch sight of Sereena Orion Smith unexpectedly, I was momentarily taken aback. The rare handsomeness of her features is accentuated by the unapologetic signs of a larger-than-life existence. She has lived next to me for years, sharing, on rare occasion, shards and slivers of a once perilous and exotic lifestyle, and yet, still, remains frustratingly, alluringly, unknowable to me.

"Well," I quipped back, "we were passing by..."

She gave us a rare throaty laugh and guided Richard and me into chairs next to the one occupied by Errall. She too was freshly showered and had donned someone else's clothes, including a light sweater she had wrapped around herself like a blanket to ward off the sea's midnight chill.

"Tonight, I will serve you," Sereena told us. "You poor souls deserve it after what you've been through. Whatever you want, if it's in the larder, it's yours. Starting with some champagne perhaps? Something stronger? And food I suppose?"

I was slightly abuzz from the cognac—or perhaps it was the après-cognac activity—but it seemed neither was enough to sufficiently warm me up after marinating in the sea for so long. As for food, well we'd had a big dinner but that seemed millions of years ago. "If you have some rye...Coke? That would be terrific. And I'm craving something meaty, substantial, like a hamburger or something."

"Richard?" Sereena turned to him, her steel eyes boring into him as if using the pretext of offering a drink to search his soul. "What reward would befit a hero?"

"I think he's already been rewarded." This from Errall, with an irritatingly knowing smirk on her face.

"Will the sex be sufficient for you then?" Sereena inquired dryly.

Richard blushed and bumbled a few words. Errall shook her head in mock disgust. I laughed.

"I'll just have some wine," he finally got out.

"Excellent." Sereena turned to address a figure that appeared out of the shadows the moment she said his name. "Phillipe, did you get all that? Another wineglass for Mr. Gray, and a rye and Coke, make it strong, and a hamburger for Mr. Quant." Her serving duties dispensed with, Sereena lowered herself back on her lounger and the crewmember, in a sporty white and blue uniform, jumped to it.

"Sereena, these clothes," I said, fingering the delicate fabric of the rich navy Yves Saint Laurent shirt I was wearing. It had probably set the owner back about four hundred dollars. Errall's new togs likely cost even more. They didn't exactly fit either of us, but at that price, who cared, and in the dim lighting of the deck they looked way fine. "Who do they belong to? Are you sure they won't mind?"

"Oh, of course not, darling," she said. "Besides, they're all ashore wreaking havoc on an unsuspecting Palermo. They'll never miss a piece or two out of their oversized wardrobes for one night."

At that point Charity and Flora joined us. We all rose except Errall. Sereena did her hosting shtick.

"Actually I've just come to deliver Flora to the young people. She was insisting on staying with Dottie and me but there's really no need." Charity looked spectacular in blazing purple silk, a turban wrapped about her hair and a dressing gown tightly fastened around her nearly non-existent waist with a thick sash.

"How is Dottie?" I inquired, concerned about the woman for whom the frenzy and physical toll of our experience was magnified by her age and body's limitations.

"Her heart is racing a bit faster than normal. But she'll be fine.

She just needs to rest." She turned to face Sereena. "And although we spoke briefly earlier, on behalf of my dear Dottie and myself, I'm also here to more formally express our deep gratitude to you and to the crew of this fine vessel. I don't even want to contemplate where we'd be right now were it not for your efforts tonight. I…well I just can't think about it or even speak of it."

I watched the exchange between these two women with great curiosity: Charity Wiser an imposing, dominating, at times tyrannical and cantankerous force of a woman; Sereena Smith a complex, fantastical creature with a mythical past that no one person knows the whole of. Would the two together result in a detonation of unimaginable power or would they coalesce into some rare exhibit of similitude?

How Sereena ended up in a little house next to mine on an unremarkable street in Saskatoon, Saskatchewan I'm not quite sure. Forty, maybe fifty, she's an imperfect, damaged, raving beauty who lives life without sham or deception and that's what I like most about her. And she has a soft, caring side as, I supposed, did Charity, at least in her dealings with her beloved Dottie and granddaughter Flora. So were Sereena and Charity…the same? Maybe…given thirty more years and a similar life history…but no. No. Sereena is a creature all unto herself. I am convinced one similar never came before nor will ever come after her.

Sereena stepped closer to Charity and clasped the older woman's hands into her own, their eyes communing something private between two women who recognized each other as creatures of a certain sort. Then she asked, "Will you join us for a drink before getting back to Dottie?"

"I would love to and I would love to hear the circumstances that brought you to our rescue," she answered, "but I want to be with Dottie right now."

"Of course. I understand. Perhaps we can have breakfast tomorrow morning?"

"Yes, thank you. Until then."

Charity and Sereena exchanged cheek kisses, the kind where lips actually touched skin. As Charity moved to leave she gave me a look and said, "Russell, may I have a word in private before I go?"

I followed my client indoors into the empty salon where the others couldn't hear us.

"Russell," Charity said, standing very near to me, her expression serious, her voice fighting to keep control. "Who could have done this thing?"

I looked at her with nothing to say and sadly admitted to myself that I had no idea. Any one of her family could have arranged to have our tender driver sabotage the boat, attack us, then leave us adrift and sinking, surely to our deaths. Any one of them could have hired the thugs in Tunis, sent her the threatening notes. All of them were reasonable suspects. If Charity Wiser hadn't managed to piss off every member of her family before this trip began, she certainly had now. Enough to push one of them to murder? It seemed so. Someone was trying their best to kill Charity Wiser. And, damn it, I was going to find out who. I just hadn't done it yet.

Charity read the look on my face and sank into a nearby armchair, letting out a mournful, "Oh dear." She placed a hand on her brow and I was surprised to see it tremble.

I knelt down next to her. She removed the hand that shaded her eyes and looked deep into mine. "This is my fault. I caused this. Bringing this family on this cruise, knowing full well there was a murderer amongst them. Announcing changes to my will. It is my doing." I stayed mum. Briefly she fingered the outline of the faded bruise on my jaw where the tender captain had punched me. "Russell, I told my family that you were my advisor. It was meant as a deception, a cover for your real purpose. But, I've come to think of you as such. An advisor and trusted friend and a man who has saved my life on more than one occasion, and the precious life of those I hold most dear. I am forever grateful for that. I hope you know that. I can be a true mule at times, have been and will be again. But I hope you know that what I say right now is true and will not change."

I nodded. It was a heartfelt and honest speech.

"It was one thing when it was just me," Charity continued tremulously. "But what happened tonight could very well have taken my Dottie's life. And Flora's. I cannot have that. I've only now come to realize that I may have been acting irresponsibly by egging on this killer." *May* have? "It never dawned on me that doing so would put others I love in mortal danger. Tell me what to do, Russell Quant. Tell me what to do and I will do it."

I doubted she would keep that promise, but I accepted it, tried to comfort her as best I could, and finally sent her off to be with Dottie.

When I returned to the deck, Sereena was speaking to Flora. "Please, have a seat. Phillipe will bring you anything you wish."

Flora settled herself into a straight-backed chair slightly away from the group and I marvelled at how on this ship of excess and beauty, she had still managed to find a set of dry clothing that looked dowdy. Maybe it was the wearer. I felt sorry for her. She looked upset, spooked. Maybe the reality of our salvation had not quite set in. Or, perhaps, how close we'd come to death, had.

Phillipe delivered my food and drink and Richard's glass and took Flora's order for hot milk, and then I asked the questions I was dying to know the answers to. "Sereena, what are you doing here? How did you ever find us?"

Sereena filled Richard's glass from the bottle she'd been sharing with Errall and began her story. "When you first told me about your travel plans," she said, instinctively knowing better than to mention in front of Errall that I'd first approached her about joining me on The Dorothy, "I knew of course that I'd also be sailing somewhere in the Mediterranean. But I wasn't sure about the timing and exactly where I'd be. Yesterday I asked our captain to contact the captain of The Dorothy to compare itineraries and by happenstance it seemed we might cross paths here in Palermo. However, by the time the Kismet arrived, you and the others had already gone ashore. So we stayed in the harbour and waited to hear from Mr. Corsaro, your concierge, who kindly agreed to inform us when you re-boarded, hopefully in time for a short visit."

"But we never returned," I said.

Sereena refilled her glass and passed the bottle to Errall.

"The message we received was that you and four other passengers had departed for Palermo on a tender late in the afternoon, never returned and that The Dorothy was preparing to leave port. The captain informed the Port Authority about your status, but of course they had no reason to suspect foul play. Apparently there had been a precedent of certain members of your party returning late to the ship from a previous day?"

Tunis. I gave her a weak smile and gulped my rye.

"At the same time we received a rather strange request from The Dorothy," Sereena continued.

"Really?" Flora asked. "What was that?"

"One of the other passengers wanted to come aboard the Kismet."

"Richard," I murmured, giving the big lug a syrupy smile, hungry for something other than my hamburger.

"Yes. He'd learned about our communications and that I was a friend of yours."

Richard added, "I was worried when you hadn't returned to the boat by nine-thirty and more so by ten o'clock. Someone from your family told me about Charity's announcement that morning at breakfast...about the threatening letter...and I became even more concerned. I knew you wouldn't miss The Dorothy's departure unless something bad had happened. The captain, knowing you were clients of mine, kept me well informed of what was happening. I tried to convince her to send out a search party. Then the Kismet kindly offered its assistance."

"How did you know to search for us in the water?" Errall asked.

"Richard eventually managed to contact the people who supplied the tenders," Sereena told her. "Although they won't admit to any involvement in the matter, they did concede that they were indeed missing one of their tenders."

"And one of their tender drivers?" I asked, my voice tinged with anger. The little shit.

"So, with Richard aboard, we went searching for you and here you are."

"What now?" Errall wanted to know.

"Our captain has informed the Palermo authorities that you've been safely recovered, and Captain Bagnato of The Dorothy has agreed to take you back on board when we rendezvous with them tomorrow. So, once my travelling companions return, we are off to Messina to put you back where you belong," Sereena concluded with a smile. "Until then, you are guests of the Kismet."

"Speaking of which," Errall began, "Who owns this tub?"

"It belongs to a friend of mine. He has sportingly gone along with this adventure every step of the way."

"The man on the deck?" I asked. "The one I saw when we were being pulled up from the water. Is he the owner?"

"That was Richard, darling," Sereena told me.

"No, not next to you. The man on the upper deck, watching us."

"Perhaps then. All the other guests are ashore in Palermo."

I nodded and then, emboldened by liquor, took an uncharacteristic further step into the veiled labyrinth that is Sereena's world. "Who is he? Who is the man who owns the Kismet?"

Sereena's face was as immovable and unreadable as the Mona Lisa's. She said, "He's a wonderful story best left for another time," she answered lightly, adding, "Your food is getting cold, Russell. Eat it."

Shut down.

Wednesday morning arrived in a blaze of citrus sun and cerulean sky, and the scene on the main salon deck was much different from the night before. It was crowded for one thing. I couldn't imagine where all these people, maybe seventeen or eighteen in all (including we five), had slept. And the boat was moving, fast. But that didn't seem to deter the group from partaking in a leisurely mid-morning breakfast party beneath the toasty Mediterranean rays. The guests, sitting, standing, lounging, were spread throughout the area in haphazard groupings—couples, threesomes, foursomes, some singles—oriented towards the sun or the tuxedoed musicians playing light classical pieces at the far back end of the deck. I later learned the musicians had been convinced to come aboard in Palermo (at the urging of the Kismet's onshore rabble-rousers) and would disembark in Messina. From my *CBS*

Masterworks Dinner Classics: Breakfast in Bed CD I recognized the current piece: Peer Gynt Suite number 1, opus 46: Morning. Perfect. Off to one side was a buffet table dressed in gauze white and faint blue, and laden with chafing dishes, immense serving platters, champagne buckets, coffee urns, samovars and candelabras that somehow remained lit in the vigorous breeze created by our speed. Nestled in ice were crystal jugs of colourful juices made from native berries and fruits, there were heaps of caviar, eggs, scones, pâté and delicate pieces of curled meat too beautiful to be called sausages, right alongside bottles of chilled Bollinger, Krug and Veuve Clicquot sweating fetchingly in the sunshine.

No one paid me much attention when I stepped onto the deck, back in my original outfit that had miraculously been laundered overnight. I caught sight of Richard sitting with Flora at a table for two, drinking coffee. Richard and I had spent the night together doing research on one another, but he'd woken early and left behind a note saying he'd see me later. My cheeks involuntarily pinked at the memory, like I was friggin' Audrey Hepburn mooning outside Tiffany's (when the only Tiffany's I'd ever known was a long-defunct pizza joint on Saskatoon's 8th Street). Sereena, Charity and Dottie were at another table, deep in conversation. Errall, ever the schmoozer, was amidst a group of three I did not recognize: a sixtyish man with a trumpeting voice, a thin wisp of a fellow wearing a Speedo that just covered the required bits and who had the face of a beautiful but bedraggled street urchin, and a large caftaned woman with countless strands of colourful wooden beads hanging heavy from her thick neck. I waved a cheery hello that went wholly unnoticed.

I shrugged and approached the majestic smorgasbord. The rich-looking coffee urn was a classic, resting on a stepped pedestal base and adorned with a band of scrolling grapes, leaves and vines at the foot, midsection and lip. The handles were carved with waterleaf thumb rests and held in place by cornucopia devices. I selected a white cup from an arrangement nearby, fingering the emblem on its side and filled it with coffee. I picked up a matching plate and, while having my first sip, surveyed the considerable breakfast pickings. Just as I was about to scoop a couple helpings of eggs Benedict onto my plate a voice at my right said, "Are you enjoying the coffee?"

I turned to find a dashing man posing next to me. He was Greek, I surmised, based firstly on his accent, secondly on his dark features (that had had a longtime love affair with the sun) and thirdly on my in-depth study of the movie *Summer Lovers*. He might as well have been bare-chested, for his unbuttoned shirt was made of something I can only describe as cotton chain mail. He wore tight black shorts and black sandals.

Actually the java had a bit of a musty smell to it, but, just in case he'd been the first one up on the yacht that morning and had made it himself, I said, "It's good. Strong, just the way I like it."

"Kopi Luwak," he said, with a knowing nod.

Okay, maybe he wasn't Greek. What language was that? Kopi Luwak? Sounded Indonesian or something.

"You know Kopi Luwak then?" he asked.

Silly me. Kopi was obviously someone's name. "Oh, no, I don't. I...well I just got here." I smiled brightly. "I'm afraid I don't know most of these people."

He smiled too, wide and long, toothy and somehow lascivious. Yup, he was Greek. "No, no, my friend, the café, Kopi Luwak. It is the world's rarest."

I looked suitably impressed and took another sip of the earthy, rich liquid. There was something about it though....

"You may be considering Jamaican Blue, Kona, Tanzanian Peaberry...true, all exceptional coffees...but Kopi Luwak beats them all, wouldn't you agree?"

I nodded and slurped.

"Perhaps only as little as five-hundred pounds available per year, sometimes seventy-five dollars per quarter pound..."

I spit up a bit then.

"But it is more than the unique flavour that sets it apart."

Yeah, the ridiculous price. "Oh? What's that?" I inquired, adding uselessly, "It's very tasty though."

The Greek laid his large, dark hand on mine, bringing it and the coffee cup it held up to his healthy nose. He closed his eyes and whiffed. His face transformed into an expression of orgasm, but only for a second. "What makes this coffee so rare is the processing," he told me.

Oh gawd! I have a cousin who roasts coffee for one of those ubiquitous GottaDrinkMe coffee spots with stores on every corner. Don't get me wrong, I like the product, I just don't want to spend two hours learning how it's made. Just pour it and let me drink it. How was I gonna get away from this guy?

"Kopi Luwak comes from the islands of Sumatra, Java and Sulawesi." Here it comes. "On these islands is a small mammal called the *Paradoxurus Hermaphroditus*. You've heard of this *Hermaphroditus*? A musang, a toddy cat, a palm civet?"

Uh, no.

"They are tree-dwelling animals belonging to the civet family. Most Indonesians consider them pests." Ah-hah, I was right about the Indonesian thing. "They climb into the coffee trees and eat only the ripest, reddest coffee cherries."

"That is a shame," I sympathized. Maybe an omelette instead of eggs Benedict?

"But," he smiled winningly. "What goes in must come out. The locals gather the...beans...which, amazingly, come through the digestion process fairly intact, still wrapped in layers of the cherries' mucilage."

Wha...? Now he had my attention.

"You see the enzymes in the animals' stomachs add something unique to the coffee's flavour through fermentation. And," he added with a hearty laugh, "the farmers get to harvest the coffee without climbing the trees."

"Wait," I said. "Are you telling me the world's priciest specialty coffee comes from the partially pre-digested...excrement of some tree-hugging animal?"

He laughed again. "Shit. Yes, it comes from shit. Pass me the Towle please?"

Towel? He wanted a towel? "Uh, how about one of these serviettes?" I asked, passing him a white linen napkin.

Aristotle (as I'd come to think of him) stood back and gave me one of those looks. I've been around obscenely rich people and know the look. It wasn't the "I'm better than you, get out of my way" look, but rather, the much less common, "You're not like me, I could teach you a thing or two" look. He started off slowly, "I meant the flatware, a fork and knife and spoon please. They're Towle Sterling Chippendale. Four-hundred-and-seventy-four-dollars for a five-piece setting. Retail of course."

I fought a blush I did not want and handed him the cutlery.

"Your plate and cup are Versace, Rosenthal Meandre D'or, also about the same price for five pieces. Marvellous, yes? You'll always know it by the Gorgon's head leitmotif. The crystal is Dartington; Christina I think." He shrugged then, lesson over. "I've been waiting for someone to go for the Bennies. Care to share one?"

I forgave him for calling the eggs Benedict "Bennies." He was cute and trying to be kind—in his own way. What did throw me off was that he wanted to *share* an eggs Benedict. I took a closer look at him. He *was* a big man—but a big man with a twenty-nine inch waist. On his Versace plate were a quarter of one piece of unbuttered toast, a single wedge of cantaloupe, half a beautiful sausage and three slices of tomato.

"Uh, sure," I agreed, rethinking my plan of having two all for myself.

"You're one of the stowaways," he commented as he proceeded to separate one of the "Bennies" into two equal portions with the precision of a surgeon.

"Yes. We were fortunate that Sereena and the Kismet came along when they did."

"Sereena, as you call her, has a habit of that," he said, ladling over my meagre benny ration.

As you call her? What did he mean by that? "Are you the Kismet's owner by any chance?" I asked, recalling Sereena's reluctance to share that information with us the night before.

He laughed a deep, rich laugh. "Oh no. I, too, am a stowaway of sorts." With that he walked off to join a young woman sunbathing topless at the opposite end of the deck.

After loading up the rest of my Versace, Rosenthal Meandre D'or— sorely lacking with only half a Bennie on it—I surveyed the deck to find a place to sit. The thought of joining Richard entered my head—right move or wrong move or dumb move? I looked over to where he was sitting with Flora and noticed things had changed between them. If I didn't know better I'd have guessed that these two were having a rather heated argument. Sure enough, as I made my way over, hoping to overhear, Flora rose to her Birkenstocked feet and fled, looking red-faced and unhappy.

"Richard?" I said questioningly as I pulled up alongside his table.

He looked up at me, not having noticed my approach and, gentleman that he was, half-rose and indicated the seat just vacated by Flora. "Russell, please, join me." His smile was pasted on with a weak adhesive. "Lovely day."

Lovely day? Lovely day? We'd spent the night together; he'd just had some kind of altercation with my client's (and his client's) granddaughter and he wanted to comment on the weather?

I sat, laying my breakfast and coffee before me. "Richard, I just saw Flora run off as if something was wrong. Is it? What happened?"

His brow shrugged into three horizontal lines. "You saw that then? I'm sorry."

"What were the two of you fighting about?" As far as I knew, Richard and Flora barely knew one another. What could they have to bicker over?

"It wasn't a fight, it was..." He looked at me, pained. "It was an accusation."

Ding, ding, ding, ding, ding, went my sensors.

"Flora is under the impression that all this is my fault, the fault of GrayPride Tours. As you know, GrayPride helped Charity organize this family trip and, more specifically, organized the tenders for the transportation into Palermo yesterday."

Ah. "Certainly she can't believe you're responsible for what happened to us?" I asked sympathetically, always hating to see anyone wrongly guilted.

"Well, it was one of my associates who made most of the arrangements, but in the end, yes, she believes I am at fault."

I silently hoped GrayPride Tours had good insurance. "She's upset right now," I told him. "She's been through a lot in the last couple of days. She's young, and she's worried about her grand-mother and Dottie."

"Yes," he nodded slowly. "Yes, she is very worried about her grandmother."

With every one of us who'd been on the tender feeling subdued and more than a little worn down from our harrowing experience, most disappeared into their rooms after breakfast for more rest. Sereena seemed preoccupied and there was little else for me to do for the balance of the trip but exchange banalities with the other Kismetites, which was pleasant but ultimately futile. So I settled into a semi-secluded spot on a side deck and scribbled away on a pad of paper. I drew the Wiser family tree, three-pronged with the sisters Hope, Faith and Charity at the top, and stared at it for a long time wondering which was the thoroughly rotten apple. I made notes on each of the relatives, what I knew about them, what I suspected about them and why each of them could be the killer. We were on the sixth day of the cruise and I felt frustratingly far from figuring out who the culprit was. I had ideas, growing suspicions, but little concrete evidence. There'd been plenty snooping around and fisticuffs, but all I'd been left with were a sore jaw and raw throat. As I unconsciously rubbed the spot where the tender captain had grabbed me about the throat, I saw Richard and Flora in the distance, leaning over the yacht's railing and talking calmly. At least *they* were making some progress.

We'd had less than a day aboard the Kismet, a luxury yacht whose guests proved to be companionable, pleasant, colourful, bordering on eccentric, generous in allowing us to share their space for a night and a day…and wholly unrevealing. They were like a pen of magnificent birds, usually preferring to be elsewhere, but every so often congregating to compare their plumage and relax in the com-plaisance of sameness. Who were these people? Where had they come from? Where did they belong? Why was my Saskatoon neighbour amongst them?

We left the Kismet, Sereena, and her playmates, at 4 p.m. Wednesday afternoon, well within curfew for The Dorothy's 5:30 departure from Messina. As I strode away from the yacht and Sereena's farewell embrace, I glanced at the upper deck. No one. I lowered my gaze to Sereena who was eyeing me carefully, her face a granite mask.

Chapter 13

Although we missed the earthquake-prone, three-thousand-year-old city of Messina, we were glad to be reunited with our shipmates on The Dorothy, not to mention our luggage. When Errall and I finally made our way back to our cabin, our beds were white with invitations—missed ones from last night and new ones for tonight. Also in the pile of communiqués was the trusty ship's newsletter that reminded us that tonight was a formal night. If we were planning to go out, we had once again to pull out the tuxes and gowns.

I hurried through my prep. Despite what we'd been through in the past twenty-four hours, our time aboard the ritzy Kismet had put me in the mood for more champagne and fancy bib and tucker. I left Errall barely out of the shower and, jaunty in my tux, made my way to the ship's library to check e-mails and do a bit more electronic snooping before we commenced our evening plans. I had just reached the Deck Six lobby area when I heard arguing voices. They were coming from a small area adjacent to and slightly behind the grand staircase, there for the use of passengers who didn't want to wait for one of the four guest elevators. The arguers had backed themselves far into the corner space beneath the stairs and were therefore blocked from my line of sight. Unless I marched right up to them and asked to join in, I couldn't get close enough to make out what they were saying. But I *was* close enough to identify one of the voices. It was James McNichol, Harry's great-grandfather and Charity's witless suitor and brother-in-law.

I tiptoed closer, approaching the staircase at tortoise pace, listening for whatever bits and pieces I could catch before my presence became known to them. It sounded as if the unknown voice, a man's, was angry with James, accusing him of something. Something to do with his mother. And then, lucky for me, it got louder.

"I married your mother for love!" bellowed James. "Not money. And shame on you for suggesting otherwise! God rest her soul."

"Then where is it, you swindler? Where is her money?" the other man yelled.

"I don't have to stand here and listen to this poppycock. Excuse me, sir!"

That was my cue to get moving. I started up the stairs, slowly. From the landing I heard the sound of heavy feet and turned around to see James, oblivious to me, stomp off. Then, out from under the stairs, came the other man, thirtyish with a Pee-wee Herman look about him. He looked up at me snippily.

I smiled. It did no good. "Lover's quarrel?" I asked innocently.

He stalked off in full pique.

James McNichol had just climbed up my list of suspects. Was he truly a swindler? Where *was* Pee-wee's mother's money? And, God rest her soul, how did she die?

I proceeded up to the library on Deck Eight. Like last time, the room was almost deserted, a cool, peaceful respite from the fast-paced activity outside its doors. I chose a computer workstation and opened my e-mail account. I visually sifted through the contents, deleting spam (mostly X-rated) that had somehow gotten through my filter settings. I was looking for one message in particular, but there were two others I couldn't resist opening. The first was from Anthony, wanting to confirm the details of our arrival at his house in Tuscany. I replied, saying we were looking forward to the visit. The second was from my home e-mail address. Before leaving for Barcelona, I'd taught my reluctant Ukrainian mother a thing or two about the computer. I thought she might get a kick out of it while she was house-sitting. I didn't think much of my lesson had gotten through, but there it was, a message from my mother, sent just yesterday. I opened it with great anticipation, hungering for news of home sweet home. Instead, I got a curt inquiry, which I read in her voice: "Ya, uh-huh, hello? You dere? Mom."

I chuckled to myself, wondering how long she'd sat patiently in front of the computer screen, waiting for a reply as if this was some sort of electronic telephone call. I'd have to teach her about chat rooms. I wrote her a quick note, updating her on how the trip was going so far—having fun, weather is great, wish you were here—without elaborating on some of my more perilous experiences to date. I had doubts about whether she'd actually go near the computer again, but you never know.

Near the end of my row of messages was the one I was looking for, from my friend Mary in Toronto. I'd e-mailed her the other day asking for a favour. And, by her reply, I saw she'd come through: "Russell. Spink's is a local chain of fitness facilities, three locations, only in Toronto. According to them, there is no one by the name of Nick Kincaid who works or has ever worked for them. Hope that helps. The weather is here, wish you were beautiful."

Oh there's just something about that Mary.

Why would Nick Kincaid lie about his career? Was he out of work and ashamed to admit it? Yet, by the look of his wardrobe and the Rolex on his wrist, it seemed he wasn't suffering much in the financial sense. What about the rolls of cash I'd found in his room; were they his or Jackson's? And then there was the fight in Emerald City. He was definitely hiding something.

I was about to log off the computer when another thought hit me. I checked my watch. I still had plenty of time before I'd agreed to meet Errall back at our room. I returned to the browser, made my way to Google and typed in: Kismet.

342,000 hits. I added the word "yacht." 1,810 hits. I added the word "Benetti."

Four hits.

I quickly determined that each of the four hits referred to the same boat: a fifty-metre, Zuretti-designed, Benetti yacht with a nine-metre beam and cruising speed of fourteen-point-five knots. The same boat that rescued us last night. I spent the next few minutes scouring the four websites. I wanted to know what Sereena had been unwilling to tell me. Who owned that baby?

I clicked and clicked until finally I hit pay dirt.

The registered owner of the boat was A&W Incorporated.

A&W? A&W? Sereena was on a boat owned by a hamburger chain, the home of the Mama burger? Preposterous.

I searched a little more but there was nothing left to learn. This was one mystery that would have to wait.

I still had time before I was to meet Errall, so I began trolling the public areas (i.e. bars) for the whereabouts of some Wisers. I had a couple rooms left to search and if that didn't work out it was time for me to become more aggressive with my pool of prime suspects. Besides, I was feeling rather James Bond-ish in my tuxedo. I was hoping to find Nick Kincaid but instead found Jackson Delmonico in Curses, the bar next to the casino. Jackson was good enough. I had a few questions for him, too.

"Russell man," he announced loudly to the mercifully empty room when I sat on the barstool next to him. He had obviously been keeping the bartender company for a few hours. "Anything this good man wants, give him a double and pour me one too!"

I nodded politely at the cute bartender from *The O.C.* or somewhere like that and ordered a glass of champagne. I didn't want to get into a double rye drink-a-thon with this guy. He could really hold his liquor: me, not so much.

"I really enjoyed your playing the other night. Harry tells me you used to tour, and that you've spent a lot of time in New Orleans, playing with some of the best."

"I've been all over this world, man, even these parts before. But that's a long time ago, Russell man, loooooong time ago. Now I do the best I can, you know. It's really all I got, you know, the music, and Harry of course."

"She's a wonderful singer. It's obvious where she gets her talent from."

Despite being in the middle of a drink-a-thon, Jackson sipped at his bourbon on the rocks with the finesse of an English gentleman. "Not so obvious, it was her mama, Hy...you didn't get to know Hyacinth, did you? Naaaaahhhh, of course you didn't...but Hy, ooooo that girl could sing. Like an angel, a fuckin' angel—just like Harry sings now." Another sip and a signal for another. "But you're right about one thing, we are alike in one way. Just like I only got the music, same with Harry. It's all she got, Russell man."

I frowned. "What do you mean? What is she, twenty, twenty-one? She has a lot ahead of her." I tried to make light. "I wish I was that age again."

"This fuckin' family, this fuckin' Wiser family curse! Hy and me thought we had it beat, you know. We knew well enough about her mama and her granny dying when they gave birth to their daughters. But they were small women, frail-like women, you know. Now Hy, she was healthy as a horse, man, big hip bones. If there was a woman meant to bear babies it was her, man. But we were wrong, Russell man. We were so fuckin' wrong. And Harry, she'll be just like the rest of them. No babes for her. If she does, she dies. What a thing for a young'un to live with, huh? Since Hy's gone, all I got is the music, man and Harry's just like her old man. No babes for her, just music."

I was nodding empathetically in the silence that followed. Somehow I couldn't relate this sad story to the bright, energetic, optimistic girl I saw when I looked at Harry. But I also know that outward appearances can be deceiving.

"Fuckin' Wisers," Jackson concluded, as he gratefully took hold of his fresh drink before the Beverly-Hills-zip-coded bartender could place it on the counter.

"You're not a fan of the family obviously. Do you blame them for what happened to your wife; do you blame Charity?" Here goes.

"You wanna know if it's me trying to kill the old skeleton, right?"

Not so drunk after all.

"Where were you yesterday afternoon? Did you go ashore with the others? Were you alone?" It was a lot of questions to ask a drinking man, but I wanted to throw him off-kilter. It makes for better answers.

"I stayed on the ship, Russell man. Having some drinks. No way I went to town and hired lackeys to rig that boat you were on. How'd I know how to do that?" He'd just told me he'd been to these parts before. Maybe he knew someone. "Besides, I was here all day, ask this guy."

I looked up at the young Jason Priestley double.

He nodded. "Except for potty breaks, this big guy was my date all day long, yesterday *and* today."

I peered into Jackson's life-hewn face wondering how someone could drink so much and still be standing (or in his case, slouching on a stool) and, really, still be functioning pretty well. Practice, I guess.

He gave me a mile-wide grin that ballooned his cheeks and drew his lips thin, showing widely spaced, yellowed teeth. "See Mister Russell man, you got the wrong fella here." He winked at me. "So let me give you a hand."

"Okay," I agreed.

"Way I heard it, that boat's engine pooped out and had itself a leak, right?" There was a little more to it than that, but all right. "Now who is gonna know how to do that better than a mechanic, huh, I ask you? A me-chan-ic. Who you know is a mechanic here now, huh?"

"Are you talking about Ted?"

He took a deep pull of his drink, looking away then back at me.

"Why do you suspect Ted of the sabotage? Just because he would know how to pull it off?"

"And he needs money, man. People think just because I'm sitting here drinking I don't hear them when they're talking to me. Well old Tedding does some drinking too, let me tell you, and he tells me stuff over the years. He wants so far away from that woman of his that you can smell it on him. He wants money so he can run. And he won't be running with her, let me tell you, man. Nosiree."

"What else can you tell me, Jackson?" I asked, taking a sip of my drink, pretending to be only half listening to his rantings.

His big black eyes fell on me with sudden clarity. "I know lots, let me tell you, but that's all I'll tell you, Russell man. And you tell anyone I told you so...well, just don't do it, man."

Was this a threat or just a drunken slur? Ah, well, didn't matter. It was time to turn up the heat.

"I saw you, Jackson. I saw you in Tunis. You were in the medina when I was looking for Charity, right before she was attacked. You were supposed to be aboard The Dorothy."

His eyes grew darker and narrow and now I had my answer: threat. "You best be getting out of that seat, man."

I glanced over at the bartender to see if he had heard what I heard, but he was busily serving some newly arrived customers, two women who looked like twins and wore matching rings on their wedding fingers. Their formal attire consisted of unpressed golf shirts over jean skirts and well-worn sandals from a Wal-Mart discount bin.

I looked back at Jackson. Certainly he couldn't think I'd scare off that easily. "Tell me why you were in the medina, Jackson."

"There you are!" Phyllis' reedy voice rang out from the bar's entrance. "I've been looking all over for you." She sashayed over to us and laid a hand on my shoulder. She was wearing a sleeveless pink pantsuit and had her hair up in typical Phyllis style. "I want you to swear you'll be at the show tonight after dinner. It's going to be the best boys-will-be-girls-and-girls-will-be-boys show you have EVER seen!" She gave Jackson a little tap on the chest. "And you too, mister." She turned her head, curls jangling everywhere, and eyed up the twins with a scrunched up nose. "You two can stay home if you like."

Jackson grunted, heaved himself off his stool and stumbled for the exit. I debated following him but, in his state, I doubted I'd get much more out of him. He knew I was on to him. That was good enough for now.

Two more couples, the males in white jacket tuxes and the females in cleavage-baring gowns, entered the bar laughing. On their heels was the sextet of men I'd seen before who seemed inseparable. The most hulking of the bunch still had a black eye, compliments of Nick Kincaid. All were in black suits but each sported a different colour of the rainbow bowtie and suspenders. Curses was filling up fast. The evening's festivities were getting underway.

"Will you be there? Say you will," Phyllis was demanding to know, her grey eyes boring into me like a corkscrew.

I gave her a toothy one and said, "I wouldn't miss it for the world, Phyl."

"Oh thank God. Mary, that whore, thinks she's going to have the most supporters in the crowd. So when she goes on, do me a favour Russell? Don't clap, don't even breath. Her act stinks anyway. What's she gonna do, get up there and be nice?"

I got an idea, a hunch. "If you'll do me a favour."

"Anything. Do you need a foot rub? Full body massage, maybe? I have magic hands." This was delivered with a wink.

"There's a fellow who's part of the group I'm travelling with. Nick Kincaid. Do you know who I'm talking about?"

She raised an eyebrow. "You're talking about Tom Selleck mixed with...with...well, you can't add anything to Tom Selleck, he's got it all...you're talking about the big hairy hunk, right? I don't know him but I'd like to. Did he ask about me?"

"And do you see that guy over there? He just came in with all his friends, wearing an orange bowtie."

Phyllis nodded in the affirmative. "Sure. That's Mikey P. from San Diego."

"See, I knew you'd be the right person to do this. You are so popular on this ship. You know everyone and everyone wants to know you." I stopped there to let her savour the compliment and flutter her eyelashes a bit. She liked it, I could tell by the way her hand tightened on my biceps. "Well, you see, Nick and Mikey P. from San Diego got into a little fight in Emerald City the other night..."

She made a tsking sound and shook her head. "I know, I know, the hooligans."

"I was wondering if you could ask around. Find out what they were fighting about...and maybe anything else you can get on Nick, on the QT like?"

She eyed me with suspicion and said, "This doesn't happen to have anything to do with you having a crush on one of those two boys, now does it?"

I said nothing but let my smile do the talking.

"Consider it done." She kissed me on the lips. "I have to primp. Later." She was gone.

I was only five minutes late getting back to the room but Errall was already gone. The reason was in a handwritten note on my bed telling me she'd been invited for drinks and would meet up with me for dinner in Yellow Bricks. Drinks? With who? There was one other note, in an envelope I'd stepped on when I opened the door. It had obviously been delivered after Errall left. I ripped open the seal expecting another of the daily invitations for yet another cocktail reception. Not that I was complaining, mind you.

But I was wrong.

Mr. Quant
Can't explain now. Have found something out. Please meet me as soon as possible on the Pool Deck. Wait for me. I'll be there as soon as I can.
Flora

What had she found out? Shoving the note into a pocket, I grabbed the phone and rang her suite. No answer. I was about to dash out of the room when someone called me. It was Richard asking if I'd like to join him for a drink. I told him I couldn't, without telling him why, and tried to salve his disappointment by suggesting getting together at the drag show later that night. He agreed and I rushed off, barely setting the phone back on its cradle.

The Pool Deck was dark and deserted and even in my tuxedo I could feel a biting wind off the water. The seas were rough. For the first time since I'd set foot on The Dorothy I could feel her beneath me, the staccato vibrations of her toiling engines. I had to concentrate when I walked and keep my legs a little further apart than normal in order to keep myself from swaying along with the subtle shiftings of the ship. I wide-walked my way to the right side of the deck and, grabbing hold of the steel railing, peeked over the edge of the boat. I couldn't see much except for a few frothy waves as we sliced through the water from Sicily to the port of Salerno on the Italian mainland. State-of-the-art stabilizers and who knows what other high-tech gizmos, buried deep within the ship's mighty belly, were working hard to make it seem as if we were sailing through air.

I turned away from the sea and let my eyes cover the pool area in search of Flora. She wasn't there, no one was. All the other passengers were either at cocktail hour or prepping to go out for dinner or, for those non-formal types, settling down in their cozy cabins for a night of TV and snacks. Still holding on to the railing, I shuffled towards the shuffleboard court. Beyond it were two hallways, one running down each side of the remaining length of the boat. They were deep enough to allow for a row of chairs and plenty of room for passersby. And that was where I found Patrick Halburton, alone, in a light coat, cradling a cup of coffee in his hand.

"Mind if I have a seat, Mr. Halburton?" I asked, lowering myself into the one next to him. "Not going in for dinner?"

"Already had it," the man said, keeping his eyes trained on the invisible horizon where black/blue met black/green. "In my room. I've never owned a tuxedo or even many suits in my life. Don't like fancy things most times. Just having my coffee out here before I turn in." He gave me an assessing look that lasted about three seconds. "I like looking at the water. Reminds me of the lake."

"I'm glad you're enjoying the cruise."

"Didn't say that. I don't much like her highfalutin get-togethers."

"You're talking about Charity and her Charity Events?"

He nodded. "Stupid. Stupid woman with her stupid events. What we gotta do all this for? Why?"

"So why come?"

"For Harry. I love my granddaughter. She insists I come. She thinks it's good for me to get out, see the world. But I seen enough world on TV I tell her, and I don't like it any. But I'd do anything for that girl, and I got a responsibility for her, to make sure she's okay later in life. So if I have to come to these stupid events to make sure Harry gets what's coming to her, then I guess that's just what I have to do. Of course, now we're all here for nothing, aren't we? Stupid woman with her stupid charities. So, I'm just gonna have to work harder to take care of my Harry, aren't I?"

"Harry has a lot of fine men looking after her," I said. "I was just talking with her father."

"Drinks too much, that Jackson. He's all right I suppose, except

204

for the alcohol and all that."

"All that? What else is there, Mr. Halburton?"

He grunted in a way that told me he wasn't going to answer that question.

I decided to move on to something else. "You share your room with your father-in-law, James, right? Is he all right too?"

"Why wouldn't he be." It was more a statement than a question.

"I heard him arguing with one of the other passengers. Sounded kind of serious."

"Over a woman no doubt. He's a womanizer. Wasn't always, but once he started, couldn't stop. And it's cost him. He had money once. His own and what was left over from what Hope inherited from her father. Nothing of that left, damn fool. Nothing left for Harry. Women married him for it. And he gave it to them, gave it to them while they were married and even more after they were done with him."

"From what I heard, it was the other way around."

He shrugged, somehow guessing where I was going. "Yeah, yeah, I heard about it. The son thinks James married his mother for her money 'cause when she died there was none left."

"How did the mother die?" I asked at point-blank range.

"What do you mean how'd she die? She died. She was full of cancer. Detected it not long after they were first married. That James, always bad luck with the women."

In the interest of time—and likely futility—I decided to withhold comment on the insensitive remark. "So where *did* her money go to?"

"What the son doesn't know is that there wasn't any to begin with. The woman gambled it all away at one of those crazy casinos they got all over the place now. She died ten years ago for crying out loud, and the boy is still harping about it. James is just trying to save the son's good memory of his mother by not telling him the truth. But he should, I told him, he should, or else he's gonna end up in court, getting sued...or worse."

I didn't know if Patrick was telling the truth about his father-in-law, or just what he thought was the truth, but I did know that men who once had money and found themselves without it, could do some pretty desperate things to get it back. Was James

McNichol attempting to woo Charity to gain access to her millions? And if that failed, as it was sure to, what next would he try now that he knew about the change in her will?

Patrick raised his creaking body from his chair, slowed by an agedness greater than his actual years.

"You know about what happened to Charity and the rest of us yesterday?" I asked.

He nodded, preparing to leave.

"Do you have any idea who would want Charity dead?" Or should the question have been who wouldn't want her dead?

"All I know," he said, already moving off. "Is that she's made one hell of a lot of people madder than hatters. That's all I know."

That's all I knew too.

I was soaked, sniffly and feeling sickly and more than a little peckish by 9 p.m. The ride was getting rougher as the sea came alive around me and it had been lightly drizzling for the last half-hour. It was the kind of drizzle where no matter where you try to hide; it still gets you wet. All of this, along with the fact that I had not only missed cocktails and dinner but was being stood up by Flora, was making me a rather cranky fellow. How long did she expect me to wait? Couldn't she have chosen a more comfortable location? I finally concluded she'd either forgotten, changed her mind or, least desirable of all, some trouble had befallen her. I also knew that if I didn't get off the inhospitable Pool Deck soon I would spend the rest of the cruise in bed with a cold or seasick or both. I left.

I passed on the bank of elevators, all too busy ferrying passengers from deck to deck, party to party, and dashed down three flights of stairs and down the long corridor to Flora's Deck Five cabin. Just before I got there I passed one of the ship's multitudinous mirrors (this was a gay cruise after all) and was caught short at the sight of the disheveled wreck of a man I'd become. My rain-slicked hair was sticking out in countless directions like a duck caught in an oil spill, my once-spiffy tuxedo was wrinkled and damp, my bowtie and cummerbund were askew. I was not a pretty sight. Oh well. I marched up to Flora's cabin and rapped on the door.

No answer.

Again.

Nothing. I put my ear to the door. Nothing.

Frustrated and frumpy, I decided a change of clothing was in order, dress code be damned. I headed again for the stairs and ran smack into Faith and Thomas, looking superb in their evening finery.

"Mr. Quant," Faith exclaimed, laying a delicate hand on my wet log of an arm. "Are you all right?"

I laughed, pretending to be light-hearted, which was about as likely at that point as a gay man serving rump roast and mashed potatoes at a dinner party. "I got caught in the rain."

"Is it raining?" Thomas asked, surprised. "We've been at dinner."

I nodded rather than giving him the raspberry I felt that comment deserved.

"We're off to the casino to learn how to play poker. Care to join us?" Faith offered kindly. "After you change, that is. You're bound to catch cold, dear."

"Actually I'm looking for Flora. Have you seen her?"

"Oh yes, she was at dinner with everyone else."

Oh really.

Forgoing a wardrobe change, I stomped into Yellow Bricks, a pesky, squawky pelican that'd mistakenly stumbled upon a gathering of gentlemanly penguins and beauteous swans. The restaurant hosts stepped back, startled by my appearance, as I pushed my way into the room. The place was loud with the clatter and tinkle and sparkling chitter-chatter of late night diners at sup. I stopped about a third of the way in and tried to spot Flora. I didn't see her but I did catch sight of Errall and Captain Giovanna Bagnato at a table near the centre of the room. Errall was absolutely eye popping in a magenta ball gown I'd never before seen her wear and Captain Bagnato looked suitably impressive in full dress uniform. Although they were seated at a table for eight, it was obvious even to me half a room away, that they were dining *a deux*. Verrrrry interesting, I said to myself in the style of *Laugh-In*'s Arte

Johnson. I was about to intrude on their date when I saw a table of three young Wisers, Harry and the twins, closer by.

"Dude," greeted Nathan, going for the surfer-boy thing, his face hidden beneath a layer of overgrown bangs, "I think there's something wrong in your grooming regimen."

"Yeah, thanks," I said. "Have you seen your cousin Flora tonight?"

"Sure, Mr. Quant," the more serious Nigel answered. "We all had dinner together."

Nice. "Did she go back to the suite with Charity and Dottie?"

"Uh, no, Aunt Charity and Aunt Dottie weren't here."

"Aunt Dottie was feeling a little under the weather," Harry explained. "Probably from what happened yesterday. Didn't Flora meet you?"

Huh times two. "What do you mean?" I asked.

"That's why she left early," Harry told me. "She had a note from you asking her to meet you."

The words hit my brain like acid on skin. I had written no such note. "What are you talking about? She had a note from me? Did you see it? Do you know where she was going to meet me?"

Harry looked worried now. "Russell, what's going on? Is everything all right?"

No, it wasn't. Something was very wrong. "Harry, do you know what the note said?"

She stumbled a bit but got it out. "She was to meet you after dinner. At the aft end of the running track. She left like twenty minutes ago."

Shit. I had no idea what was going on or time to figure it out. All I knew was that Flora Wiser was in danger.

Chapter 14

I was back on the Pool Deck. The weather had worsened considerably since I'd abandoned my wait for Flora. Drizzle had turned into downpour making the deck flooring slick and nearly unnavigable in my spit and polished black patents, and the famed gentle Mediterranean breeze blew strong enough to rival any Saskatchewan windstorm. The pool, although swimmerless, seemed alive, its contents sloshing from side to side. The running track, where Flora had been lured to meet me, was most easily accessed via stairs at the far end of the pool area. So, lowering my head against the wind, I marched ahead, grasping anything nailed down that would help keep me upright and moving forward.

Bullets of rain hit me with the force of liquid BB gun pellets exploding against my skin and tuxedo. The onslaught of water flattened my hair against my skull. I pushed aside a swath of it from my eyes, only to have to repeat the action over and over again. I finally reached the stairs and, taking hold of both rails, hoisted my sodden self up each step. When I'd made it to the top

I wondered if Flora would be crazy enough to still be up here, waiting for me in such dreadful conditions. But as much as I wanted to, I couldn't leave until I was sure one way or the other.

From where I stood, three-quarters of the running track was visible. The rest of it, where the track led along one side, behind and out the other side of a large multi-unit storage area was not. The logical place for Flora to wait, assuming she would seek out as much protection as possible from the driving wind and rain, would be in one of the storage cubicles. I yanked off my tuxedo jacket, held it over my head like a Hugo Boss umbrella, and clipped down the length of the track until I reached the first bay. Except for stacks of deck chairs and chaise lounges securely fastened together and to the floor with bungee cords, the space was empty. No Flora. The same in the second bay. And then I heard the unmistakable sound of trouble.

I rounded the corner into the next storage bay and through the oppressive darkness made out the shape of a man and a woman. He was on top of her, grunting with his efforts to restrain her, she whimpering and then screaming out. Flora was being assaulted. I rushed forward yelling and, using my jacket as a kind of hooded lasso, tossed it over the man's head, tightening the collar around his neck and pulling back with all my weight. Flora screamed again and the man let out a strangled sound of alarm, muffled by the fabric of my coat over his face. We fell back, our drop softened by a pile of chaise lounge cushions. He struggled mightily to get away from me causing us to roll out of the storage area and onto the rain-pelted deck.

"Run!" I yelled to Flora. I couldn't see her. I had no idea how long her attacker had been at her or whether she'd been hurt. I just hoped she was okay and physically able to escape.

The man was tall and strong. I could feel legs and arms everywhere as he wrestled with me, screaming like a banshee for me to let him go, to get the coat off his face. As the rain covered us, it made us slippery as eels and I was having a harder and harder time holding my tuxedo noose in place. He used his greater size and leverage to flip me over onto my back, trapping me under him. Somehow the jacket was still covering his eyes and, fitfully blinded, his hands grew wild, fingers and nails mauling my face like an angry bear. I felt a tear in the skin at the corner of my mouth followed by shooting pain. I tasted blood mixed with rainwater on my tongue. I hate that.

I released my failing hold on the jacket, preferring to grab hold of the bastard's neck with my bare hands anyway. The sudden disappearance of the fabric from around his face took him by surprise, just long enough for me to regain some leverage of my own. I humped my hips and thighs up and to the right, with as much force as I could muster, and managed to sway him off me and onto his side, with me on him like salt on fries. Yes, he was bigger. But I was stronger. For a brief moment we were clasped together in a spooning position. With my front against his back, my right forearm around his neck, I reached down with my free hand to thread my arm between his legs, hoping to mount and subdue him once and for all. Instead, I felt the unexpected. My hand grabbed hold of a rather long penis. Everything happened so fast in so little light, I hadn't realized that the man was naked from the waist down.

It surprised me and then it enraged me.

This man hadn't just been attacking Flora. He was raping her.

With a growl of fury I grabbed onto his handy sack of accessories and squeezed as if I wanted juice. The man yelped like a blind dog running snout first into a porcupine, and his entire body stiffened like a board.

"Stop it! Stop it!" someone else was screaming over my shoulder, hands clawing at me, pulling me off the man.

"You sonofabitch!" I screamed at the man. I was now getting a better look at his face as I manipulated myself into a kneeling position over him, one hand full of scrotum, the other around his neck. Large, scared eyes were staring up at me out of a very young, not unattractive face. I loosened my hold on his privates just a bit. I didn't want him to pass out before I had a chance to yell at him some more.

Still the shrieking over my shoulder. "Get off him, you stupid! Get off!" I chanced a look and saw Kayla Moshier, wet, wild and wooly looking, her mouth flapping at high speed as she continued to berate me. Fortunately, the wind and rain stole much of what she was saying. I tried to ignore her and instead made a frantic search for Flora, desperate to see how she was. Had she survived? Or…wait a second…

It wasn't Flora this man had been attacking. It was Kayla. Ahhhh jeeeeez. It wasn't an attack…it was a…date?

"Let him go! You're hurting him!" I heard Kayla pleading with me, still pulling at my shirt, her voice at its whiniest peak.

Yup. A date.

I did as she instructed and as soon as I got off him the young man shrivelled into the fetal position. His hands were globed over his nether regions and he unsuccessfully fought back a deluge of tears.

I sat back on my haunches, letting rain wash over me, and watched in disbelief as Kayla threw herself at the boy's side, asking him if he was all right. He wasn't answering just yet. She glared back at me, smeared lipstick and mascara painting her face into an unattractive mask. "Why the fuck did you do that? You asshole! What do you think you're doing?"

"I thought I was saving…you…from an attacker," I said dumbly, noticing a large rip in my tuxedo shirt revealing most of my left pec. I lifted my hand to my mouth. I could feel a nasty cut, the blood still not completely clotted because of the sluicing rain that continued to pour over us. "Let's get him in here," I suggested, getting to my feet and urging the young guy to unravel. "Where it's a little drier. And maybe…his underwear is in there somewhere?"

I reached down and helped the young guy to his feet and into the storage bay.

"This is Aaron," Kayla told me when we were out of the rain.

"Fffffuck, maaaaaaan," was all Aaron could say for the first while. After we found his boxers and he gingerly pulled them on, he scuffled about the room, half crouched over, still trying to overcome that deep-in-your-stomach sickness, verging on nausea but worse, that overcomes a man when his goods have been…compromised.

"I'm sorry, Kayla," I said, meaning it. Sort of. "I thought you were in trouble."

"What were you doing up here anyways?" Good question. She glanced around. "Did you come up here with someone?"

"What are you talking about?"

"Up here is like where you go if you're like into having some fun with someone you shouldn't be having fun with," she told me, as if this had been part of our first-day orientation session.

"That's not why I'm here," I responded, wondering how she knew about this place. Did everyone know except me? Was it cruise ship etiquette? Had it been announced in our daily FOD newsletter or perhaps over the PA system by Judy Smythwicke: "Ladies and gentlemen, should you be desirous of a wee shag, please proceed—after dark only—to the storage area directly off the running track where we've created for you, our treasured FOD guests, a delightful atmosphere just for such shenanigans and rowdy romps."

"So why then?"

"I was looking for Flora. Did you see her?"

She rolled her eyes. "Uh, no, I was busy. Besides, this is the last place *she* would ever be."

I just nodded, still feeling unsettled about the whole thing and developing a healthy headache.

"You won't tell anyone about this, will you?" Kayla asked.

She was seventeen. Legal, as far as Canadian law anyway, for consensual sex. So I gave her an understanding, hip-uncle kind of look. "I'm not going to tell your mom and dad."

"Who cares about them," she snorted. "I mean the Dorothy people."

I gave her a puzzled look. I just didn't get this gal.

She pointed at the boy with her chin. "You can't tell them he's like straight. Nobody on the ship knows."

"Oh Kayla, it's okay." I knew this because Alberta told me so. "It's okay that he's straight. Anyone can work on this ship, gay or straight, as long as they're gay friendly. He won't get fired if they know he's straight."

She gave me another look, as if she couldn't believe how dense I was. "That's not it, jeeeeez. If the guy passengers think he's straight, they won't tip him. And that's how Aaron makes most of his money. He *wants* them to think he's gay."

Oh for crying out loud. I shook my head and wondered how many gay guys Aaron had suckered on this ship, giving them intentionally false hopes with an insincere smile or shake of his firm bonbon. Suddenly I didn't feel as bad about damaging his merchandise and decided to take off before I did it again—as payback from my people.

Four flights of stairs later I was back outside Flora's door. I knocked. Still no answer. I thought I could hear someone inside. I knocked again. Nothing. I debated breaking in—as I had most of the other cabins belonging to the Wiser clan—but decided against it. I'd learned my lesson some time ago: never break into a room unless certain it's empty. I clipped up one deck to my room to use the phone, thinking that maybe she wasn't answering the door unless she knew who was behind it. When I arrived, my message light was blinking.

"Mr. Quant, it's Flora. I waited as long as I could but it was raining and I was cold and I...well, anyway I'm in my cabin now. I thought I'd wait for you here, hoping you'd get this message." A pause. "But maybe you haven't? It's Flora...or did I tell you that already?" Another pause. "Anyway. I'm supposed to take Grandmother to the musical revue at the Munchkin Land Auditorium...anyway...I guess that's it. Bye."

What the hell was going on?

At least I knew she was okay. She had waited for me and left just because she was cold. But I still didn't know who sent her up there in the first place.

I dragged myself into the bathroom and stood before the mirror. I was aghast. Even worse than before—the debonair fellow who'd left here only a few hours ago had definitely left the building. My hair looked like the tangled, wet head of a dirty brown mop. My bow tie was still fastened about my neck but looked more like a drowned rat than an article of formal wear. In addition to the tear over my chest, my shirt was shredded in several spots and stained with dirt and my own blood. Never mind my jacket, which was a wretched, soaken, misshapen mess. (Thank goodness this was the last formal night of the cruise.) The cut at my mouth had clotted now and chips and blots of dry blood dotted my jaw.

But hey, at least the bruise I received compliments of the tender captain was almost gone. I gazed longingly at the bathtub, wishing I could shed my ruined clothes and immerse myself in hot water up to my chin. I wanted to soak away the cold that had settled in my bones after being wet for so long, and clean the wounds and scratches I'd gotten from my tussle with Kayla's loverboy. But there was no time for that. Something not good was afoot tonight on The Dorothy.

I dabbed away the worst of the blood smears from my face and left the cabin and its beckoning tub behind. I headed for Munchkin Land which, mercifully, was on the same level, across the central lobby and down a hallway. My legs were aching from running up and down those damn stairs.

"Sir, are you all right?" a box-shaped, uniformed woman asked me when I screeched to a halt outside the closed doors of Munchkin Land Auditorium, no doubt looking like Wile E. Coyote after the Road Runner had TNT'd him for the umpteenth time. *Beep! Beep!*

"Is it closed?" I ignored her question. "Isn't there a musical revue tonight?"

"Well, yes, sir, *Gays and Dolls*. But I can't let you in now. I'm afraid you're too late." She moved her made-for-overalls body in front of the doors to demonstrate her serious intent.

"Oh please," I begged. "I'm looking for someone. It's important."

"I can't, I'm sorry. Opening and closing the door during the act distracts the performers. But you can wait right here," she said, indicating a nearby collection of cushy looking couches and armchairs. "It should be over in a few minutes."

It was twenty-five minutes to be exact, but who was counting. At least it gave me time to catch my breath, do some thinking and practice my glaring technique with the usher who steadfastly ignored me the entire time.

When the doors finally opened I ran into the auditorium against the flow of guests, some heading back to their cabins, others to the casino or the Cowardly Lion lounge, but most to Emerald City where the big drag show was scheduled to begin. Eventually I spotted Flora, getting into the queue to leave. She was alone.

"Flora!" I called out as I wrestled to get by a gaggle of giggling gays. "Where is Charity?"

"Mr. Quant," she said when I reached her. She was wearing a long brown bag of a dress under a baggy brown sweater that stretched halfway down her thighs. "Where were you? I waited."

"Where were you?" I mimicked. "Your note said to meet you on the Pool Deck. You never showed."

Flora looked at me with confusion, her glasses migrating down her nose. "Mr. Quant, no, *you* sent *me* a note to meet you. I never sent you a note."

My face blanched. My heart turned over. "I never sent you that note, Flora."

"And I never sent you a note," she repeated.

I reached into the pocket where I'd stored Flora's note. From another pocket I pulled one of the notes Charity had received (which I'd made a habit of keeping on hand in case I got a chance to break into one of the Wiser rooms) Charity's note was in block letters, Flora's was also printed, but the letters were much less structured, almost messy. They were obviously prepared by two different hands—or made to look so.

She looked over my shoulder. "That's not my handwriting."

I returned the notes to my pockets and took hold of her thin shoulders, forcing her to focus on my face. "Where is Charity? I thought she was supposed to be here with you."

She nodded wildly. "Yes, she was. But I got a message from her…a note…saying she'd changed her mind and wanted to stay in the room with Dottie."

Charity and Dottie had been alone all this time. With slow dread the reason for tonight's confusion began to sink in. Whoever it was who'd orchestrated this symphony of fake notes wanted to ensure one thing: that Flora and I were out of the way. All night we'd been running around the ship like mice in a maze, too busy trying to find one another to pay attention to Charity.

He wanted us out of the way…so he could make his move on Charity!

We both reached the same horrifying conclusion at the same time. We had to get to Charity and Dottie's room immediately. The crowd in the auditorium had mostly cleared but the exit was still clogged with showgoers. We burst through them to a chorus of eeks and yikes from the guys and somewhat stronger language from the gals. We scrambled down the hallway to the lobby, weaving in and out of groups of passengers, and dashed up the stairs—again!—to Deck Seven where Charity and Dottie's cabin was. We raced down a seemingly endless corridor, Flora easily keeping pace in her hardy Birkenstocks, until we reached 702. My knuckles felt sore as they rapped on the door. It was only then that I realized how badly scraped they were, obviously from my scuffle with Aaron. Jerk. Again I knocked and Flora called out to the women.

"Let's get the purser," I suggested, an urgent tone in my voice.

But then, the door opened a crack. And then wider when Charity saw who it was.

"My goodness," she whispered. "Flora? Russell, what an unholy mess you are. I'd let you in but Dottie's just fallen asleep. Is everything all right?"

"Are you all right?" I asked, searching her face for any indications of trauma.

"Yes, of course. I'm fine. Dottie is a bit under the weather after yesterday's fiasco, but she'll be right as rain tomorrow, I'm sure."

From my recent perspective, there was nothing too right about rain, but whatever. "Nothing odd happened tonight? You didn't get any weird notes? No one tried to get into your cabin?"

Now she eyed me suspiciously. "No, of course not. Flora, I did wonder why you never turned up to escort us to the revue, but no bother. Now one of you tell me what is going on, right this instant."

"It's nothing, Grandma," Flora lied. "We can talk about it tomorrow."

Charity studied me, her eyes boring a hole into mine, knowing something was up but trying to conclude whether it was important enough for her to force it out of us right then or if it could wait. "Russell?"

"Just keep your doors and windows locked. Don't let anyone—a-ny-one—in. No matter who it is," I told her.

"Of course," Charity said.

When the door closed, Flora assured me she was all right, but I followed her back to her room anyway. I did a quick sweep of her cabin, found nothing amiss and, after saying our goodnights, I left her there. Once in the hallway, I fell back against the wall and spent a few moments trying to make sense of what had happened over the last few hours. Someone obviously wanted us out of the way. And they had succeeded. But then they hadn't taken advantage of it.

Or had they?

Could it be possible that Charity was not the target? Had something else of import been happening while Flora and I were running circles around the ship? Could someone be playing a hoax on us? Why? Or had something gone wrong with the plan? What had happened—or what was meant to happen—while Flora and I weren't looking?

My watch told me the passenger-participation drag show that Phyllis and crew were signed up for was beginning soon and that I was very late for my date with Richard. I knew that if I went back to my room to clean up and change, by the time I'd make it back, Richard would likely be long gone. My track record with him thus far had been less than stellar. I didn't want to take the chance. The better plan was to find him in Emerald City, torn shirt, bloody wounds and all, tell him to wait for me, and *then* go back to my room and make pretty.

Emerald City was packed to its gilt-edged rafters. I stepped into the room and felt that something perceptible that fills a room whenever people are waiting for a show to begin. A half-dozen coloured spotlights were dancing crazily over the stage area which was set up at the rear of the large room. The backdrop, simple but dramatic, was floor to ceiling plate glass overlooking the impressive vista of the passing sea. The crush of people was too thick for anyone to even notice my less-than-impeccable state, and for that I was grateful. I held to one spot near the door and began a scan for Richard. It wasn't going to be easy. The Dorothy crowd was a social one, and in the last few minutes before the show was to begin, they were busy mingling and milling and getting last rounds of drinks from the bar before curtains up (if there had been a curtain). Everywhere I looked was an impenetrable wall of people. Everyone was smiling and laughing so I couldn't get too upset at the situation, but I knew I wasn't going to get anywhere standing still. So I began a slow trip around the room.

The first familiar faces were a surprise to me; Ted, Marsha and Jackson were in a booth with the ever-glowing Harry. Ted and Marsha looked grim, Jackson was characteristically bleary-eyed and Harry was smiling wide, no doubt doing her best to canoodle the others into better moods. I passed by with only a wave. I didn't want Ted and Marsha asking me if I knew the whereabouts of Kayla.

Just as I moved on, Mary Richards/Mary Tyler Moore approached me, looking classy but demure in a beige pantsuit. She smelled of pansies and fresh fruit. "Oh Mr. Quant, are you all right?"

I was tired of people asking me that. I had to get out of these clothes.

"I kinda like the look." This from Rhoda, forever at Mary's side. She smelled like a tree. She reached out and slipped her fleshy hand through the rip in my shirt placing it on my bare chest. "You gotta try some-a-this, Mar."

"Rhoda!" admonished a wide-eyed Mary.

"Have either of you seen Phyllis?"

"I haven't. But she's probably where we should be, Mr. Quant," Mary said with an accusing but long-suffering glance at Rhoda. "She's probably getting ready for the show."

"Oh come on, Mar," Rhoda answered with a roll of her eyes. "There's plenty of time. Let's get a drink from the bar. Then we'll go."

"Why are you looking for Phyllis anyway, Mr. Quant?" Mary asked me. "Can we pass her a message?"

"I wanted to tell her I don't think I'll be able to stay for her show."

"What about our shows?" deadpanned Rhoda, looking decidedly unimpressed with me. "There something wrong with our shows?"

"I...no, not at all, it's just that...I..." Bugger. I didn't want to be in this conversation. "You see, I just want to find Richard and then go back to my cabin and clean up. It's nothing to do with your shows."

"I'm afraid I saw Mr. Gray have a drink and then leave," Mary told me with a doleful look.

Shit. This was turning out to be one crappy day, almost as bad as yesterday. Not quite, but almost.

The music suddenly got louder and the chatter in the room began to die off. The show was about to start. Mary and Rhoda looked at one another with horror and disappeared into the crowd. Once the room settled down the music faded away and was replaced with a voice loud enough to wake a circuit boy at an Anne Murray concert. Its owner welcomed us to Emerald City and introduced himself as The Great Oz. He wore a turban, but that's about as far as his similarity to the movie's character went. Our Great Oz was wearing hotpants and a flowing cape so purple it would make Prince (or whatever his name is now) green with envy. He was shirtless and his torso was a landscape of tattoos and piercings. It was a daring look but this guy could pull it off.

"Are you a good witch or are you a bad witch?" he bellowed the famed line from *The Wizard of Oz*, arching his dramatically plucked eyebrows. There were some rowdy responses from the frothed up crowd. Most wanted to be a bad witch. "Well there's no need to choose," he continued, his voice hinting that he had something spectacular in store for us. "Because we've got both!" The crowd went wild...I'm not sure why. "Here they are folks, straight from Ca-na-da!" Another rousing cheer.

Two tall figures mounted the stage. One was all lily-white taffeta and silk with sequins that sparkled brilliantly in the spotlights. On her head was the most humongous, diamond-encrusted crown I've ever seen. The other was all in black, with a fake hooked nose, pointed hat and green face makeup. Nigel and Nathan. Those two boys had the habit of turning up in the most surprising places.

The two young men began a dance routine that, although amateur, had enough twenty-year-old-straight-boy bump-and-grind sexiness to satisfy almost every gay male taste in the room. And then the women in the room began to howl when a very sexy Dorothy took the stage alongside them. She had the signature blue and white gingham apron dress, but had somehow forgotten the blouse that went underneath it. This was supposed to be a drag show, but Dorothy was definitely all woman playing a woman.

I watched in awe for a few seconds before deciding to back-track to Ted and Marsha's table. I couldn't resist catching a peek at their faces when they realized the two showgirls were actually their sons. But alas, the table was empty. I couldn't imagine what had driven them away.

When the witch routine was over, a hidden DJ immediately threw on an old Celine Dion remix and the men in the crowd rushed the dance floor as if it were a Harry Rosen fire sale. I was about to leave when a young man, wearing a snug muscle-T over a slender torso, came up behind me and tapped me on the shoulder.

"Oh gosh, thanks," I said, "but actually I was just leaving."

He quirked his head to one side and said, "Excuse me?"

I wanted to melt into the floor. "Throw water on me!" I'd have yelled if I was the Wicked Witch of the West. I realized—too late— that the young'un wasn't asking me to dance. And really, why would he? I looked like an extra from Michael Jackson's "Thriller" video.

As the guy wriggled to get by me, I felt something hard push into me. I looked down, startled, then back up but he was gone, the wake of his passage already flooded with fun-loving people danc-ing on the spot. I brought my hand up to see what he had pressed into it. It was a DVD in a see-through plastic cover. What?

I stood there for a moment, transfixed, not sure what to do. Should I chase the young guy down, try to find Richard, or go back to my room as planned? Nigel and Nathan were still boogying on stage, sopping up attention even though their number was over. I watched them for a bit until once again, the music died down and The Great Oz shooed the twins off the stage to much applause. He waited for the noise to subside then began his introduction of the next act.

That was when I heard it.

We all heard it; it was so loud it easily penetrated the thick plate glass behind the stage.

A scream, followed by a sight so terrible I hope never to wit-ness it again.

Behind The Great Oz, the floor to ceiling window acting as a kind of horror flick movie screen, we watched as a body whizzed by, plummeting to almost certain death.

I caught my breath, horrified, not only at the gruesome sight, but because in that one sickening instant, I was certain that the body belonged…to someone I knew.

Chapter 15

Although it happened quickly, there and gone in one horrifying instant, a surprising number of people witnessed the body plummeting past the window, limbs flailing about grotesquely. It then would have had to fall past four more decks, the hull of the ship and finally into the deep, dark waters below. What happened next was a scattered, confused flurry of activity. Everybody was moving and talking, and some were crying; as the news spread, people tried to react sensibly in a situation that made no sense. Almost immediately the man overboard siren we learned about at the muster stations on our first, innocent day aboard The Dorothy sounded its moaning, mournful wail. People began to scurry about Titanic-style.

I knew we weren't sinking or in any immediate personal danger, but another fear had taken hold of my heart. I'd barely caught sight of our fellow passenger on a speedy descent to an all-but-confirmed grisly fate, but I was certain I'd recognized something familiar about the victim.

I dashed headlong out of Emerald City, fighting my way through the dispersing crowd to the Deck Eight lobby. Everyone seemed to be making for the stairs or elevators. Who knew where they were going? Anywhere but Emerald City, I guess. Fortunately, where I was headed didn't require stairs or elevators. I had a clear path to the double doors that led outside. There was only one deck above Emerald City. The body had to have come from the running track above the pool.

I burst through the Pool Deck doors and ran for the steps that led up to the running track, the same route I'd taken earlier that evening to look for Flora. It was still raining, the wind was blowing, but I had been rained on and blown at all night, any more wasn't going to make much difference. I scaled the steps and loped towards the area I roughly guessed was above the Emerald City stage. It was near the same spot where I'd found Kayla and her half-naked Romeo, The Dorothy's unofficial Lovers' Lane. But when I got there, I realized I had no idea what I was looking for. Evidence of what had happened? Evidence that I hoped would disprove my guess about the victim's identity? But what could that be? I began a frantic search anyway, impeded by driving rain and darkness and found nothing. I knew I had to get out of there. It wouldn't take long for FOD security to piece things together and come to the same conclusion I had. And if they came up here and found me...well, I might as well have called ahead for a reservation in the ship's brig.

I abandoned my search and retraced my steps back to the lobby, still a swirling mass of people.

"Mr. Quant! Thank God!"

I turned to find the voice and saw Flora Wiser waving at me, attempting to make her way through the crowd.

I struggled towards her and she towards me.

"Someone's fallen overboard!" she screamed at me when we finally reached each other. "Who is it?"

I recognized the dread in her eyes and knew she suspected the worst. I grabbed her hand and together we ran down the stairs as best we could, heading for Charity and Dottie's cabin.

Judy Smythwicke had been called into emergency service and

the hallways and corridors were reverberating with her stoic announcements: "Ladies and gentlemen. There is absolutely no cause for panic or distress. As I'm sure you are all familiar with the rules, I expect each of you will be hastening to your assigned cabins in an orderly fashion. Please remain there until further notice." Her royal-wannabe voice had a much less pronounced singsong quality to it than usual, but Miss Judy was doing her headmistress best to instill confidence and obtain submission from her charges. "Might I suggest a calming beverage from your ice boxes, and I understand the movie channel is showing a wide variety of moving picture shows this evening that I most highly recommend. Very entertaining and good for a chuckle or two."

And then the floor began to shudder.

The atmosphere of barely controlled alarm began to falter.

Judy Smythwicke let out a nervous titter. Then nothing. Then, "Not to worry. Not at all," she finally said and clicked off.

People stopped in their tracks and an uncomfortable silence ensued while our cruise director no doubt checked things out for herself. Mercifully the PA system came alive again after less than a minute. "Not to worry. Please carry on to your rooms," she advised in a voice loud enough to be heard over the siren. "You may have felt a little shake. Nothing at all to worry about. You see, it appears that The Dorothy has...come to a stop."

The crowd got moving again, hopefully most of them to follow Judy's advice. Not us. Our progress was slow, but eventually we found ourselves back in exactly the same spot we'd been in only a short while earlier: outside Charity and Dottie's cabin door.

I banged on it. Hard.

Again. Then again.

"Who is it?"

Thankfully Charity had listened to me on this one bit of advice. "It's Russell. And Flora. Are you two all right?"

The door opened slowly and Charity gazed out at us, Dottie standing in the background.

"Come in, come in," she said, stepping back to allow us into the foyer of their suite.

"You're okay then!" Flora cried out. "I was so worried."

"What in God's name is happening out there? No one in management will take my calls. What is that infernal noise?" Charity railed on, ignoring her granddaughter's concerns. "And I think the ship has stopped moving."

"It's the man overboard signal," Flora explained. "Someone fell overboard."

"Oh my goodness, is he all right? Is..." She stopped and studied the expression on Flora's face more carefully. "You thought it was me, didn't you?"

We were silent.

"Oh you dear, sweet lovely," Charity cooed, pulling Flora into her grasp. "Your grandmother is just fine, just fine. We all are. Nothing to worry about." Then she said to me over Flora's nestled head, "Do they know who it is?"

I shook my head, deciding not to tell her that it was only Flora who thought it was she. I had been pretty sure it wasn't. "Not that I know of," I told her, my black heart feeling ill with my own suspicions about the true victim. "They're asking everyone to return to their cabins. So they can inventory the guests, I suppose."

"Of course. You should be going then." She patted Flora's back. It was still shuddering. Charity looked at me again. "I'll send her along in a minute. You go ahead. You should be with Errall now."

I nodded and left them. The hallways and public areas were quickly emptying out and I was able to make it to my cabin with little delay. I unlocked the door and was crestfallen when I saw that the room was empty. Where was she? Where was Errall?

There was nothing I could do. Judy Smythwicke's banter had been replaced by serious messages from the captain and other senior officers instructing all passengers to stay where they were, preferably in their own cabins. My legs felt like two columns of lead as I slugged over to the balcony doors and slid them open. I fell into a waiting chair, feeling beaten and exhausted and fearful for what the FOD officials would find out.

For a long time I sat there, as if paralyzed, staring into nothingness, hoping the impossible, that perhaps it had all been a bad dream, or that maybe, just maybe she'd be rescued. To believe she was down there, spiralling into the murky depths of the sea like a disappearing ghost, was too ghastly to comprehend.

I don't know how long I sat there before I finally got to my feet and took myself into the bathroom where I scraped off my filthy, tattered clothing and stood under a shower of punishingly hot water. I shampooed and soaped myself over and over until I felt some semblance of warmth and cleanliness. Afterwards, in a soft, white FOD bathrobe, I lay down on my bed to await the news I hoped would not come.

An hour later a call came to verify my presence in the room and that no one else was with me. I confirmed with a choked voice that indeed, Errall Strane was not in the cabin and that no, I did not know where she was. And that was it.

I must have fallen asleep because the sound of the phone was a clanging alarm jangling me awake. I grabbed at the receiver like a blind man, at the same time registering that Errall was still not in her bed. Where was she?

Where was she!

"Hello?" My voice came out shaky. I must have left the draperies open before I fell asleep and I could see that it was still dark out, but the rain had stopped.

"Russell?" It was Errall. "Are you okay?"

"God, yes, Errall, are *you* okay? Where are you?"

"I woke you."

"What time is it?" I asked, still trying to orient myself. I heard a splashing sound and realized the ship was moving again. Had they found the body already?

"It's after four, Russell, I'm sorry to wake you; I just thought you'd want to know what was happening, or at least what I know."

I sat up now, rubbing my face and running my hands through my hair that had dried into a fright wig. "Where are you, Errall? Do you know how worried I was about you?"

"I know. I should have called sooner...it's just that things have been so crazy here. I've been with...I was with Gio when...I was with the captain when the man overboard sounded and I just stayed around."

Uh-huh. Well, more about that later.

"We're moving. Did they find her?"

"You knew it was a woman?"

"Tell me. What's happened, Errall?"

"Well, no one immediately came forward to report a missing friend or family member or cabin mate, so they checked all the passengers...someone must have called you?"

"Uh-huh." Tell me for God's sake!

"Russell, I'm sorry, but it was Phyllis."

I was right. But knowing it did nothing to quell the sick feeling at hearing my suspicions confirmed. I felt numb. I felt too sad for words.

"Her electronic boarding card confirmed she was on the ship when we left Messina, and her friends and a number of other people she'd gotten to know on board reported seeing her on the ship after we left...but, she's gone now. So chances are pretty high she's the one who went overboard. That's what they think right now, anyway."

I was pretty sure they were right. When the body flew by the Emerald City window I was sure I recognized the bundle of hair, the big hoop earrings, and worst of all, the terrified face of Phyllis Lindstrom...or whatever her/his name really was. I wish I had asked. "And Mary and Rhoda...?"

"Those two were sharing a cabin. Phyllis was travelling alone. That's why they didn't identify her as missing right away. But the security people have searched her cabin and most of the rest of the ship. There's no sign of her."

"But the ship is moving. Are we just leaving her there?" I questioned, dismayed at the thought.

"Of course not, Russell. Members of the crew began searching the water as soon as the ship came to a stop and until the Coast Guard and other Italian authorities arrived on the scene. But eventually, The Dorothy, through Italy's discussions with FOD's owners and management, was ordered to continue on her way. There are hundreds of other passengers to consider." Errall's no-nonsense lawyer voice told me she agreed with the decision, but then she added, "Mary and Rhoda did get off though. They stayed behind on one of the Coast Guard vessels. For a couple of gals who really seemed to detest each other, they sure were a mess when they found out. Anyway, I guess if they find anything we'll hear about it, but G...the captain thinks the chances Phyllis survived or will even be found are slim."

"Why...why was she even up there?"

"Well, eventually another passenger came forward and admitted to agreeing to meet Phyllis up there at Lovers' Lane...did you know they have one of those on this ship?...anyway, he insists he never went. Stood her up, the asshole. I guess she must have been waiting for him up there when...well, when something happened."

I sat silent for a moment then asked, "Do they think it was suicide?"

"I...I don't know. Don't you?" She seemed taken aback by my question. "It would be pretty difficult to accidentally fall over one of these railings."

I shrugged without saying anything, then, "Thanks for telling me all this. Are you coming home soon?"

She was quiet, then, "I'm not sure."

"Okay."

"Okay."

We hung up.

My stomach rumbled and I remembered I hadn't eaten anything since lunch the day before. I didn't want to bother room service at that time of night (or rather morning), even though twenty-four hour service was offered, so I rummaged around in my airplane carry-on bag where I always stash something for circumstances just like this and found a package of Pull'n Peel red licorice and a bag of dry-roasted peanuts. I took my bounty with me outside onto the deck. It was cold and the ship seemed to be moving very fast, no doubt attempting to make up lost time. I let my thoughts flow into the blackness, remembering my shipboard friend and wondering what circumstances could possibly have led her to such a dreadful end.

And then a fiery explosion erupted in the sky.

I fell back, aghast. Now what? Was the whole world going nuts tonight? I blinked a few times to make sure I wasn't imagining it, but in the distance, seemingly suspended in air, I could make out a yellow and orange ball of fire, sometimes massive and angry-looking, sometimes almost disappearing into little more than a flaming matchstick. I watched in awe and disbelief, trying to iden-tify what it was I was seeing. Was it a distant lightning storm? Fireworks? The end of the world? Was it a bomb or some sort of missile launching? Were we passing by some war-torn country?

I ran back into the cabin, switched on the TV and clicked the remote until I found the channel that kept passengers abreast of our current geographical location. There was my answer. What I was seeing wasn't magic or some freak of nature or my imagina-tion, but rather something that had been happening almost contin-uously for the past two thousand years. The Dorothy was passing by the volcanic island of Stromboli.

We arrived in Salerno two hours late on Thursday morning. Because of our unscheduled stop during the night, our time in Salerno was cut short and longer land-tours, like those to Ravello and Amalfi, were cancelled and re-routed to Pompeii, only forty minutes away by bus.

It was a cool-ish, overcast day and the ancient town of Salerno with its heavy Romanesque architecture and dramatically arching cliffside bridges seemed dull and foreboding. I'd have given any-thing to stay in bed, close the curtains and watch movies all day, with the only interruptions being the steward bringing me treats and fresh champagne every two hours. But this was not to be. I had a case to attend to.

Just as I was locking the door to our cabin, Errall arrived from parts unknown...although I could make a good guess...and together we headed for the dining room. After a quiet breakfast with the Wiser clan, we lined up to get on one of the buses that would ferry us from the grey industrial port, crowded with mas-sive sea-faring transport containers, to whatever was left of the ancient city of Pompeii. The mood amongst the passengers, all aware of the previous evening's gloomy events, was decidedly sombre, a fitting match for the weather. En route, the rain began to come down, sometimes in spits, like a giant cat unhappy to see us, and other times in sheets so thick it threatened to overwhelm the wiper blades of the bus.

I love a good rain—when I'm at home under a blanket listening to music or reading a good book and looking out at it. But being caught in it while on a bus in a foreign country...not so much. And to be expected to tour a ruined city through it was just a miserable state of affairs. But, I kept on repeating to myself, how often do I get to visit Pompeii?

Despite the weather, the parking lot outside the walls of Pompeii was crammed to capacity. Our driver let us out near the front entrance while he circled around to find a place to stop. We were led inside by our FOD host and assigned a guide who must have been the last English-speaking one available, although to call him English-speaking was generous. He spoke in that mumbo-jumbo, garbled, hurried way that people do when they incorrectly assume they know how to speak another language but they really don't have a clue. As we took the first steps into the doomed city, the sky erupted, pelting the hoods of our umbrellas with such a clatter that it was almost impossible to hear him anyway. *Questa è la vita.* ("*C'est la vie,*" "*Que sera, sera*" or "Oh well," Italian-style.)

In 79 AD, a volcano called Mount Vesuvius, not far from last night's Stromboli, surprised the prosperous capital of Pompeii by erupting and burying the city under twenty feet of ash and pumice stone. The event created a hermetic seal about the town, preserving many public structures, temples, theatres, baths, shops, private dwellings and even some of its two thousand victims.

With its narrow streets of weathered rock, crumbling monoliths and leftover walls left standing like tombstone sentinels, it was an eerie, funereal place, made more so by the bleak weather. Yet at the same time, it was a truly remarkable picture of life in an Italian provincial city in the first century, if you're into that sort of thing. Although many of the other passengers were giving it a go, most of the Wisers weren't. Disappointed the town wasn't fully populated with lifelike volcanic ash mannequins caught doing laundry or having sex or taking their Roman cockapoo for a walk, they soon got bored and grumpy and eventually resorted to their favourite pastime: bickering.

I wasn't in a much better mood. At breakfast I had strongly suggested to Charity that she and Dottie remain on board. After the threatening events, direct and otherwise, of the past few days, I didn't believe taking another land excursion was the safest activity at this point in the investigation. Although Phyllis' death appeared to be wholly unrelated, it contributed to my general discomfort. It would be easier to ensure Charity's safety if she remained behind the locked doors of her cabin rather than out playing tourist in Pompeii. But, despite her promise to me on the Kismet, she paid my suggestion little heed and did what she wanted. Big surprise.

"You're a disgrace!" the words echoed down the rutted corridor.

Our group had become mixed with the general population of The Dorothy as we stumbled along en masse down the wrecked city streets of Pompeii. We were touring the town's once bustling red light district, bordellos and bawdy houses now little more than brick-and-mortar shells. According to my rough translation of what I thought our guide was muttering far ahead of me, whereas most of the structures were original, some were meticulous reconstructions. I couldn't tell the difference.

As we passed yet another closed-for-business brothel, I saw the target of the harsh admonishment. Jackson Delmonico was on his knees, in the doorway, hunched over with one hand braced against the crumbling façade, his back shuddering. He was being ignored by most passersby, except one. Standing above him was his father-in-law, Patrick Halburton.

"A horrible disgrace," Patrick repeated, spitting the words at the fallen man.

"What's happening here?" I asked, weaving my way through the parading crowd of tourists. "Is he all right?"

"Oh he's all right," Patrick told me, his eyes never leaving the heaving back of the man below him. "He's just drunk! Drunk as a skunk and it's not even lunch time. Look at him!"

I crouched down beside Jackson just as he let go of some rather unpleasant noises and a flow of bile. Fortunately there was still a steady enough rain to wash away the mess. I gently rubbed his back as my mother used to rub mine whenever, as a child, I had to throw up. I thought I could hear him trying to say something between retches so I leaned in closer.

"Not drunk." The words came out sounding more like he was trying to clear his throat rather than speak. "Not drunk. Sick. I'm sick."

I kept rubbing his back and tried to sound soothing but probably came off condescending as I said, "Of course, Jackson, I know, you're sick."

"Felt okay when I got up," he persisted, gagging a bit between each word.

I looked up at his father-in-law, still hovering above us like a menacing cloud.

"Right where everyone can see him," Patrick pelted out mercilessly, spittle flying. I guess he wasn't buying the "sick" bit. "He should have the sense to be a mess where no one can see. But here he is, for all to see, even poor Harriet. I begged Hyacinth not to marry him, but she ran off and did it anyway. This is what she got, what we all got. An embarrassment for us and for Harriet. Poor girl. Got no mother and barely got a father. All he cares about is his booze and his music. That's no career. Can't provide nothing for nobody with music. Poor, poor Harriet."

It was the most animated I had ever seen the old man and his performance left me speechless.

"Patrick, that's quite enough." It was Charity. She'd come up behind us, Dottie and Flora in tow. "I think that will be all the castigation Jackson will require this morning."

Patrick pulled his burning eyes from Jackson's quaking back to meet Charity's implacable ones gazing at him from below the rim of her black umbrella.

"Look at him. He's a disgrace."

"I said that will be enough," she ordered, her tone imperious.

Patrick stepped back, grumbled something and wandered off.

At about the same time Marsha and Ted with their children, a sullen, sodden threesome behind them, trotted by with only a "tsk"ing sound from Marsha. Not far behind came Thomas and Nick Kincaid who offered to look after Jackson.

"Get some food into him," Charity suggested. "He needs something to throw up other than his own gullet."

I lowered my head back down to Jackson's level. "You okay to walk yet?"

He grunted. "Helps to throw it up."

He did look ill, his features pale and waxen. I'd come to believe that if Jackson Delmonico was an alcoholic, as many of his family labelled him, he was a highly functioning one. I'd seen him that morning in the dining room. He hardly looked like a man who was drunk, never mind sick enough to be vomiting in the street a couple of hours later. I had noticed on the bus that he'd slept the entire way to Pompeii. "Were you not feeling well during the bus ride?"

"Not bad. Groggy though, groggy as all get out."

"Maybe it was something you ate for breakfast?"

"Nah, man. Never eat breakfast. I was just there for the company." He tried a gritty laugh.

"Nothing? Nothing to eat or drink or…"

"Nah, I …" Then something passed over his face like a shadow.

"What is it?"

"I did have some juice, Russell man."

"Juice. Did it taste funny?"

"It wasn't mine. I just had a sip."

"Who gave it to you?"

"Dottie."

By lunchtime the clouds had miraculously disappeared. The morning's deluge was settling into puddles and potholes of muddy water or flowing up and down the city's slanted streets and alleyways, looking for somewhere to go. A weak sun was doing its best to show its face through a haze of gray. As the day brightened, so, it seemed, did people's moods.

Our group congregated at a post-eruption building that housed a collection of souvenir shops and boutiques and a busy cafeteria-style restaurant. Hundreds of tourists were laughing and chattering away in a hundred different languages, enjoying the sunny respite. Even though there was an extensive indoor dining area, most were choosing tables in the outdoor courtyard, hoping the sun would last long enough to dry them off while they ate their authentic Pompeii hot dogs and pizza slices.

I also chose an outside table, situated near the restaurant's entrance. From there I could keep an eye on the counter and the door to the women's washroom through which I'd last seen Charity disappear. I scoured the courtyard for the rest of the family but saw only Dottie and Flora at one table, obviously waiting for Charity to return, Jackson, looking much better and sitting by himself near one edge of the courtyard, and Ted and the twins at the opposite edge shovelling down sandwiches and colas.

Many minutes passed. What the hell do women do in the can? Just as I was about to get suspicious the bathroom door burst open, expelling a huffing Marsha and then a few seconds later Charity. Marsha joined her husband and sons while Charity calmly proceeded to the cafeteria counter to order lunch. The bathroom door opened again and out came Errall.

"You'll never guess what I just overheard." Errall plopped herself down on a folding chair next to mine. "Aren't you eating anything?"

I looked at her, keeping Charity in my peripheral vision. "I was waiting for Charity to get done in the washroom. What did you hear?"

"First of all, if you need to do more than pee…well, I'd wait until I got back on the ship if I was you. Men are so frigging lucky they don't have to sit down. It was disgusting in there."

Yeah, yeah, tourist spot bathrooms are gross, no big news there. "Errall?" I prompted.

"Well, while I was in the cubicle, Charity and Marsha came in and they had a major blowout."

Now she had my attention. "They were arguing?"

"Not at first. Marsha started by saying how Charity had always been her favourite aunt—yeah, tough call there, girl—and how she hoped Charity would reconsider changing her will—get this—for the children's sake. Hah! She wants the money for a facelift."

"I take it Charity wasn't buying it either?"

"She was actually pretty quiet at first, listening to what Marsha had to say. And boy, did she have a mouthful to say. She said the kids needed the money for medical reasons."

"What?" This surprised me. Did the twins or Kayla have health problems? "What's wrong with them?"

Errall smirked. "According to their mother—and I'm sort of quoting here—Kayla is a nymphomaniac and Nigel and Nathan are burgeoning fags and they all need significant psychological and psychiatric help from expensive psychological and psychiatric-type doctors. End quote."

I choked back a laugh. "Oops. I bet that went over as well as a makeup counter in a lesbian bar."

"Yeah, uh-huh, but not funny, Quant. Anyway, when Marsha was done spouting, Charity clued her in on a thing or two. She told her in no uncertain terms that the boys were both straight as arrows, but even if they weren't, the only one who needed psychiatric help was their mother and that Kayla was only following in her mother's footsteps."

"Yikes." I winced, hearing every biting word in Charity's chilliest of tones. I glanced over at my client who was now carrying a tray of foodstuffs over to Dottie and Flora. She was a vision of tranquility. There was nary a sign of the recent fireworks in the bathroom. And I expected none. Charity was a woman used to that sort of thing.

"There's more," Errall told me. "Apparently Marsha pretended to be pregnant to get Ted to marry her then didn't have the baby for four more years.

"That's a rather lengthy gestation period," I commented.

"Unless she gave birth to an elephant," Errall agreed. "Anyway, when Charity reminded her of this, Marsha went off the deep end. She threatened her, Russell."

My heart did a little thrum in my chest. "What exactly did she say?"

"She said, 'If you change your will, you'll be sorry'." Errall recited. "And that's a direct quote. And then she left. Russell, Marsha Moshier could be the killer."

I nodded, thinking this over. "Kayla told me her parents are on the verge of divorce. Marsha might want the money to make a clean getaway and start another life somewhere."

"But Ted could get half of it with the right lawyer," Errall countered.

I nodded again. "Better than nothing at all, which is what Charity is giving them now."

"I'm getting some lunch," Errall told me, getting up. "You want anything?"

"Sure," I said, distracted. "Whatever you're having is fine."

As I watched Errall walk away, I pursed my lips and considered my suspects. Sure, Marsha Moshier wanted, maybe even needed the money. But who in this screwed up family didn't? Any one of them could have killed the damn cat. Any one of them could have sent Charity the threatening notes. Any one of them could have arranged to have Charity attacked in the medina and our tender sabotaged. Certainly some of the Wiser clan were higher on my list than others. Nick Kincaid had a secret I had yet to get to the bottom of. Jackson Delmonico had been skulking around Tunis and refused to tell me why. And one of those two men was carrying around an awful lot of cash. Patrick Halburton, although not fond of his son-in-law, seemed to be covering for him. James McNichol was growing more and more unhappy to have his romantic intentions towards Charity scorned, he'd been threatened by another passenger and reportedly was out of money. Ted Moshier knew the most about engines and could have orchestrated the problem with the tender. Marsha had just shown her true colours in the bathroom. And what of the others? Were they truly innocent, or was there something more about them I hadn't had a chance to uncover yet because I was too busy running around the ship or guarding Charity?

"Russell, look!"

I spun around and found Errall, empty-handed, crouching over me but looking off in the distance.

I craned my neck to see what she was staring at.

"There," she said, "by those crumbling Roman columns."

Oh yeah, good one. We were surrounded by Roman columns

and everything around us was half crumbling. "Where? What is it?"

"Didn't you say you saw Jackson snooping around in Tunis? Well, there he goes again."

At the mouth of a narrow passageway was Jackson Delmonico in a tête-à-tête with a local-looking youth. What was going on here? How could he possibly know anyone here? The two of them disappeared down the passageway, Jackson behind the young man. I jumped up from my seat and headed in their direction, trying not to run so as not to draw unwanted attention. But by the time I reached the entrance and peered in, there was no sign of them. So, in I went.

The hubbub of the courtyard was quickly replaced by stone-cold silence; towering thick walls on either side of me soaked up noise like gin into Auntie Mame. The tunnel-like passageway was only wide enough for maybe two medium-sized people to pass. Not that this was an issue, as there seemed to be no one else around. Hesitantly, I tripped along the uneven stone pathway as it zigzagged and slanted downwards, hearing only the echo of my own pattering footfalls. Every so often I passed a doorway or side alley and worried that Jackson and his cohort had taken one of these other routes rather than the one ahead of me. But a faint glow in the distance beckoned me. Something was up there.

The light ahead of me grew stronger and the rough walls defining the thoroughfare became brighter. Finally, I reached my destination. It was another courtyard, much smaller than the one outside the restaurant, much dirtier and smellier too. There were two dozen young men, also dirty and smelly, loitering in the area. And in the middle of one group of four or five of them was Jackson. He was handing over some cash, no doubt from one of the rolls I'd found in his room.

Oh.

It was a drug deal.

Immediately, I knew he had been in the medina in Tunis for the same reason. He hadn't been hiring thugs to kill Charity or following me for some nefarious purpose. He was scoring drugs to support a habit he had no way of feeding while on The Dorothy. A luxury cruise ship is a tough place to be for a dedicated drug addict.

His bloodshot eyes met mine as I stepped into the dusky light of the courtyard. We regarded each other. There was nothing to say. After a moment I noticed that the young men were all staring at me too, wondering if I was another buying customer or a source of trouble that needed to be dealt with. They were scraggly hoodlums but I knew I'd have no chance against all of them at once. With a menacing look on my face, I slowly turned around and headed back into the passageway. I'd gone about a hundred metres when I heard the running footsteps. Shit. They'd decided I was a problem and now I had one too. They were coming after me.

I took off like a jackrabbit. If only I could reach the restaurant, I knew I'd be safe. I could feel my adrenaline spike and the muscles in my calves and thighs pump. My breathing grew shallow and regular as I hit my stride. I listened for my pursuers, trying to figure out how far behind me they were and if they were gaining. But then, horror of horrors, I realized the steps weren't coming from behind me, but from in front of me! How did they manage that?

It was too late to adjust. Just as I zigged a dark figure zagged and ran directly into my arms.

It was Errall, out of breath and looking shaken.

"Russell," she said, barely able to speak between deep breaths as she pulled away from me. "Come back. I think something's happened to Charity."

"What is it?" I asked her as we both began jogging back to the courtyard.

"Charity left to take a walk and look at more ruins while Dottie finished her lunch. Then we heard screams," Errall explained, her breathing growing a little more regular as we ran.

"You let her go alone!" I yelled, quickly matching her level of distress as I heard the news.

"I threw myself down in front of her to try and stop her but she stepped over me...you asshole!" she yelled back.

Okay, I deserved that. She was a lawyer on holiday; I was the bodyguard who'd abandoned his client. Thinking Jackson might be the linchpin of this entire mystery, I'd left Charity's side to pursue my prey. I knew I'd made what might turn out to be a grave mistake.

"Flora went with her. I thought they'd be all right."

When we reached the entrance of the courtyard we came to a halt. Everything looked just as I'd left it. People were eating lunch and drinking coffee, enjoying the sun. I looked at Errall as if to say, what the hell are you talking about?

"I guess only some of us heard the yelling." She pointed towards a winding street to our right that inclined sharply upwards. "Up there, she headed up there."

"You stay here in case she comes back!" And with that I ran off to find my client.

I made my way up the path, ducking into alcoves, checking empty buildings and gutted structures, each one looking much the same as the last. Why had she come up here, I wondered, especially when she knew her life was in danger? But even as I silently scolded her, I knew Charity couldn't change her independent ways any easier than a Saskatchewan duck could resist migrating south in winter.

Eventually I stumbled upon a small, roofless enclosure: four walls of battered mosaics with dim tints of colour that hinted at past magnificence. This was probably what the two women had been studying when the dirt-filled clay urn came crashing down on their heads. When I found them, Flora was on the floor, her back against the wall, legs straight out, glasses off. Charity was hovering over her, ministering to a nasty-looking scrape on her granddaughter's forehead.

"Oh Russell, thank God you're here," Charity exclaimed when I dropped to the ground next to them.

"Are you all right?" I asked Flora.

"I'm okay," she answered. Her cheeks were flaming red but the scrape, although angry-looking, had only bled a little. Otherwise she appeared to be fine, just shaken.

"She got bonged on the head! She is definitely not okay!" Charity vehemently disagreed.

"What happened?"

"I wanted to escape that fool, James. He'd come by our table, to moo his pitiful love for me yet again. I've told him as plain as

I'm able that Dottie is my love, so he never could be, but it doesn't seem to help.

"I thought I'd come up here to get away, see more sights while the others finished eating. Flora kindly offered to come with me." She patted her granddaughter's hand and looked up at me. "But I'm obviously as much a fool as James, aren't I, Russell?" She shook her head as if disappointed in herself. "I'm sure that's what you're thinking, and I concur. I seem to be losing my capacity for learning from experience. I should have known this wasn't safe. I should have listened to you and stayed aboard The Dorothy. But I hate to be boxed up like that, especially when there are all these wonderful sights to be seen." She raised her arms to indicate the faded, patterned walls, gazing at them with sparkling, forever-inquisitive eyes.

"What happened here?" I asked again, giving the smashed pottery a pointed look.

"Someone pushed that pot on our heads. On purpose! Look at them up there!" Charity pointed a reedy finger at a row of similar pots on the top ledge of the wall where the ceiling should have been. "They are perfectly safe up there. None of them are sitting in anything nearing a precarious position. Someone had to have pushed it!"

I gave Charity a stern look and said, "Do not move. Stay right here."

I ran out of the enclosure and several metres further down the street until I found a set of uneven stone steps that led up to the roof level. I found the area above where the women were waiting and inspected what there was to see. Indeed the remaining containers, each partially buried in a thick red clay, seemed like they had been in their current position forever, heavy and immovable unless another volcano erupted...or a murderer did. Had James followed the women after being spurned once again? Where were the others? Other than Jackson, who I'd been with at the time of the incident, I couldn't be sure. I went back down.

"Can she walk?" I asked, inspecting Flora's eyes for signs of disorientation or dizziness.

"Yes I can," Flora answered for herself. "If it wasn't for Grandmother pushing me away, I'd have been killed, Mr. Quant," she told me with teary eyes, the eyes of someone who was just grasping the fact that they'd narrowly escaped a violent death. Again.

As we helped Flora into a standing position, a worrying idea came to mind. Was the murderer just a lousy shot with a clay pot? Sure, they were probably unwieldy, but enough to have missed Charity and nearly hit Flora? It was a niggling feeling, the kind that bugs me like an ill-fitting shoe with a pebble in it. Was this an unfortunate accident? Or was Charity not the true target of this attack?

Chapter 16

After the falling clay pot incident, I offered to escort Charity, Dottie and Flora back to The Dorothy in lieu of the rest of the tour which was scheduled to stop in Salerno for a couple hours of shopping before returning to the ship. We escaped Pompeii by cab—if only its former residents had had that luxury.

Back on board, Flora went to the infirmary to have her scrape looked after, insisting she didn't need company, while Charity led Dottie and me to the nearest bar. The Cowardly Lion was empty that time of day, but early afternoon sunshine filled the cavernous space with a lovely light. We took choice seats near the front of the room, allowing us an unobstructed view of the Salerno skyline, dank and bleak upon our arrival but now bordering on picture-perfect. Circumstances had not been as kind to my client. I studied Charity's face as she sank into her chair. After the trying events of the last several days, she seemed to have lost some of her larger-than-life bravado and bluster. Her hair looked lifeless and dry and her skin seemed to have loosened its hold on her magnificent bone structure. She looked…weary.

"An untenable situation to say the least," she decided, once we were comfortably seated. She regarded me, then Dottie, and, obviously not liking what she saw, proclaimed, "The worst time of any to remain sober!" She snapped her fingers and called out to a young man polishing glasses behind the bar in the back corner of the room. "Carlos, a bottle of anything white and cold and I don't mean water!"

Okay, perhaps she had some bluster left.

"Who is it, Russell? Who killed Morris?"

Was this still about the cat? I like cats, I really do, but there were issues of more import to concern ourselves with here.

Dottie, who had pulled out her knitting, seemed to be reading my mind. "You do recognize a euphemism when you hear one, don't you, Mr. Quant?"

So Charity didn't want to admit out loud that someone was trying to kill her. But hadn't she done it before? In front of her entire family? I gave Dottie a grateful nod anyway and turned my attention to Charity, wanting to get some work done before she got too deep into the juice. "Let's go through our list of suspects," I suggested without really wanting or waiting for an answer. "Beginning with Faith and Thomas."

"Oh no," Dottie exclaimed, scandalized at the thought, never missing a click-clack of her knitting needles. "Not them."

"I tend to agree," Charity said, though not nearly as quick to dismiss the idea as her spouse. "Faith is a former nun and Thomas a former priest. Not the most suspicious of characters, wouldn't you agree? The changes to my will that I announced would allocate much of my money to the Catholic Church." She stopped there and muttered, "Fat chance!" before continuing. "My sister and her husband are not wealthy people, poor even, but money has never been important to them. So for them, this would not be a horrible thing. If anything, they'd welcome it, imagining all the good it could do."

Fat chance? Huh? "Fat chance?" I croaked, somehow knowing I wasn't going to like what was coming next.

Charity's laugh rang out with the clarity of a church bell. "Russell! You didn't really believe that poppycock about me giving away half my money to those bleeding-heart charities and musty old churches, did you?"

I was astounded; I'm not sure why. Nothing Charity said or did should have surprised me by that point, but given her impassioned "Faith, Hope and Charity" speech, I *did* think she meant to change her will. But it was all a ruse, one of her games, a set-up to get what she wanted. "Do you mean to say you have no intention of changing your will?"

She huffed. "Of course not. Well, with one exception of course."

I cocked my head to one side.

"Well, I think it only reasonable that when you identify my murderer, he or she will be disinherited. Don't you agree, Carlos?" she said, with a crackling cackle over her shoulder to the approaching barkeeper.

Carlos, AKA Damien to everyone else, delivered a bottle of Ruffino Libaio Chardonnay. He offered a taste but Charity fluttered her hand to quell the suggestion. "Just pour the damn stuff," she ordered. "And quickly."

I gave the poor guy a smile, hoping to soften Charity's abrasive treatment. He smiled back, ever indulgent.

After he filled our glasses and gratefully retreated to his duties behind the bar, Charity downed a couple of ounces before pressing on. "Leaving aside Faith and Thomas, there is their son, Nick. Such a mysterious sort, that one. I've never gotten to know him well, but I do love to look at him. As for Marsha and Ted, oh dear, what a pair, dreadful couple. It has always confounded me that their children turned out as well as they did. Kayla needs a bit of refining, but I adore her spunk, and of course the boys are delicious in every way."

"I understand you and Marsha had words this morning, in the bathroom in Pompeii."

"Oh that! That was nothing. She's gives me the same speech, different version at every Charity Event—has for years."

"Does she threaten you every year?"

Charity tipped her head as if she were agreeing to something of little significance. "Every year, a boring blowhard.

"James is a dithering fool who doesn't know what century it

is," Charity moved on. "Patrick is a ghastly geezer, Jackson a hopeless case in a downward spiral. Harry the pleasant result of that questionable gene pool. That leaves Dottie and Flora, who, unless they are willing to commit hara-kiri in order to kill me at the same time as themselves, are as unlikely suspects as the rest of them."

"Are you saying that no one in your family could have done this? Are you saying you might have been mistaken about someone trying to kill you—the incidents in Tunis and Palermo and today in Salerno all simply bad luck?" I questioned, at the same time silently considering another possibility: could there be someone else aboard The Dorothy, someone not part of the Wiser clan, who wanted Charity dead?

Charity let out a mighty scoff. "Don't be ridiculous. Morris is still dead. Someone is responsible. And, of course, there is the matter of the notes under my door, the attack in the marketplace and the near drowning incident, as well as today's murderous flowerpot. All I'm saying, Russell, is that the homogeneity of their innocence makes them *all* the more suspicious."

"That's a very clever turn of phrase, dear," Dottie purred.

"I agree that *someone* is being very clever," I responded, studying Charity's face closely. "We simply must be cleverer."

After seeing Dottie and Charity to their cabin, I returned to mine. Errall had still not returned from Salerno—shopping fool. I tried calling Flora to see how she was but got no answer. Next, I dialled Richard's suite but he was also away, likely still on a shore excursion with other clients. I hadn't seen or spoken to him since I missed our date the previous night. I hoped he wasn't pissed with me. I slipped into a favourite pair of floppy white cotton pants and a bright red Lacoste and headed to the ship's library to check my e-mail.

When I got there, I was surprised to see Alberta. She was standing alone in an otherwise empty room, looking bored and very uncomfortable in a FOD uniform rather than one of her usual sparkly, jangling getups.

"What are you doing here?" I asked after a hug.

"Most of the ship's staff have at least two or three jobs on board," she explained. "To make our wages worthwhile, they fill our time as much as possible with whatever no-mind jobs that need doing."

"So you're not just the ship's psychic entertainment?"

"I'm also a sous-chef and library attendant." She rolled her eyes. "The ugly underbelly of my glamorous FOD career."

I smiled and shrugged. "It's not so bad, I guess."

She frowned at me. I'd seen the look before. Alberta has told me on countless occasions that my aura is one of the easiest to read. I am an open book to her. That's one of the reasons I don't hang out with her too often: I don't like being read.

"You're worried about the person overboard, aren't you?" she said in a hushed voice, even though no one else was in the room.

"It was a sad thing to happen. Phyllis was a great gal. I liked her. The whole thing makes no sense."

"Why is that?" she asked.

Good question. I was about to answer that Phyllis was one of the last people I'd expect to haul off and jump overboard, but could I really say that? I'd only known her a few days. I knew nothing about her background. Perhaps there were all kinds of crappy things going on in her life that drove her to suicide. I had no way to know. Mary and Rhoda were gone, so I had no one to ask.

About then, as sometimes happens with us curious detective types, a random theory jumped to mind. "Alberta, is it possible that Phyllis' death wasn't an accident? Could it be that the murderous vibes you were getting during your show were about her, not Charity?"

Alberta's eyes grew wide, two chocolate dots in pools of vanilla. For a moment she said nothing, instead pulling out one of the computer station chairs and dumping her heavyset body into it. I noticed that her uniform was rather tight and where it buttoned up in the front was a row of gaping diamonds through which I could see hints of a hot pink brassiere and pale skin.

"Oh Russell," she said in a quavery voice, taking hold of one of my hands, forcing me down into another nearby chair. She seemed to be going into some kind of trance, first staring into my eyes, then around my head, then into the far off distance before coming back to my eyes. All the while her hands were running up and down the length of my arms. She kept on repeating my name. "Russell, Russell, Russell." She was freaking me out.

"What is it?" I demanded to know, hoping the sound of my voice would snap her out of her psychic shenanigans. "Am I right? Was it Phyllis the voices were talking about?"

Her eyes fastened onto mine like white on rice as she spoke, very carefully enunciating each word. "Phyllis' death was no accident, Russell."

My blood grew chill. Whether you believe in psychics or not, hearing something creepy like that is still creepy. "So the voice in your head was really talking about Phyllis?" I stated, making sure I understood what she was saying.

She shook her head, locks of hair falling from where she'd tried to restrain them with pink plastic barrettes. She looked surprised at her own words. "No, I...it should be...but no...it wasn't."

Crap.

Sensing I was about to get up, her fingers tightened on my arm, her chubby knuckles turning white with the effort. "Wait...there's another thing...something else that was no accident."

I held my breath, my heart pounded in my ears.

"The other boat..." she blurted out, as if the words were coming to her as she spoke them, without knowing what she was saying.

"What other boat?"

"The other boat was not there by accident...it wasn't there for the reason she told you...she lied to you, Russell, the woman lied to you."

Other boat? She? What was Alberta blabbing on about? The only other boat I could think of was...the Kismet. The Kismet showed up just in time to rescue us. It was luck, good fortune. Wasn't it?

"It was not an accident, Russell," Alberta repeated, her face a crumpled sheet of features.

What was she saying? That the Kismet's fortuitous arrival was...planned? If that was true, then...was the woman who lied to me...Sereena?

A long-legged female in a serious-looking business suit walked into the room. She tossed a slim briefcase onto an armchair with one hand and released her voluminous hair from the confines of a bun with the other. She turned so I could see her face clearly for the first time. She looked like Lynda Carter from *Wonder Woman*, only blonde, complete with oversized eyeglasses and a chest to match. Exhausted after a day of toiling in the office, she collapsed on the couch, first bringing up one leg to remove a spike-heeled shoe (she must have a sit-down job, I thought to myself) then the other. She hiked up her skirt and, after releasing the garter tops with a snap, crackle, pop, she slowly began to peel off her sheer black hose from thigh to toe. Left leg, then right. She pulled the skirt up even more so that now it was a band of cloth around her tiny waist. I could feel a crimson rash begin to grow over my face. The woman was not wearing any underwear and was about to show me why.

"Russell?"

My head whipped towards the door of the cabin where Errall stood, hands on hips, staring first at me then at the TV screen where *Wonder Woman* was now in the process of releasing a couple litres of silicone from captivity.

"Are you watching a pornographic movie?" she asked with a look on her face I'd never seen before, a spicy mixture of astonishment and mirth. "Lesbian porn?"

My tongue was thick and useless.

"Are you pitching a tent in your shorts?"

My eyes shot to my crotch in horror. But it's *Wonder Woman*! All gay guys love *Wonder Woman*.

"Oh my God," she screeched, coming closer, her eyes riveted on the screen. "It's even worse than I thought! You're watching straight porn!"

And indeed, *Wonder Woman* had been joined by a suited man who looked amazingly like Lyle Waggoner. Talk about pitching a tent. He too had had a tough day at work and he too wanted to show us how he wore no underwear.

"Russell, what is going on here?"

Where was the damn remote? I fumbled around for it. "Errall, I swear I didn't know what this was when I put it in."

She sat on her bed and looked at me with heavy doubt. I didn't blame her. "Didn't the title *Debbie Does Dick* clue you in at all, Mr. Private Eye?"

I felt like a twelve-year-old boy caught with a nude Ken doll and didn't like it one bit. Why did I have to explain myself to this woman? You do, Quant, you just do. "This kid...last night at Emerald City...gave this to me."

"Uh-huh." More skepticism. She was really enjoying the whole scene.

On screen Lyle and Lynda were releasing their work-related tensions.

"I stuck it into my tuxedo jacket pocket right before Phyllis fell. With everything that's happened since, I forgot about it until now."

Actual dialogue was happening on screen. Our ears perked up. If it was important enough for Lyle and Lynda to stop what they were doing, it had to be important enough for us to listen.

"It's been a tough week, hasn't it honey?" Poor Lyle. Never was a great actor.

"Yes it sure has. I'm beat," Lynda told us, massaging her left breast nipple with a saliva soaked thumb and forefinger.

"So I brought you something." Lyle.

"Oh God, Russell," Errall whined, "can't we turn this off?"

I would have liked nothing better. "But why would some guy I don't know give me porn in a dance bar?"

Errall gave me a look. "God, you can be so dense. Maybe he was into you. Maybe he's in it. This could be a new trend. Maybe instead of giving out phone numbers, guys are doing porn videos and giving out copies, kind of like an audition tape. I wouldn't put it past the gay male population to come up with something like that."

I glanced back at the screen. Lyle was definitely not the guy who bumped into me. Lyle was older, tall and dark, with wide shoulders and slim hips. The guy in the bar was fair, young and slender.

"Oh, you shouldn't have!" Lynda exclaimed as she eyed her gift, doing an admirable job of acting surprised.

I, however, was not acting. Our mouths dropped as we watched the "gift" present himself to Lynda. Oh gosh, honey, you got me a human. Just what I always wanted. Lyle's gift to Lynda was a threesome.

But what was most interesting was that the "gift" wasn't just any human. It wasn't the fellow who passed me this DVD, but it *was* someone I knew.

There he was, naked as a jaybird (whatever that saying means—aren't all birds naked?).

"Isn't that..." Errall said with a dry swallow as she pointed to the screen, the cameraman having focused on Nick Kincaid's considerable charms. "He's...he's...okay, tell me the truth, as a lesbian I haven't seen many of these things but isn't that one just...well...is that normal?"

I was shaking my head, an appreciative smile on my face. I had suspected Nick of being gay all along. I assumed *that* was his big secret. Yet judging by his performance on screen, he was anything but. Nick had been lying to his family for years. Not about his sexuality, but about what he did for a living. He had to explain his money and lifestyle somehow. But he didn't make it by being a popular fitness instructor. He made it by having a world-class-sized dong and using it for financial gain.

"I've noticed a lot of guys on board paying attention to Nick. I thought it was because he was so good-looking and a closet case. But it was because they recognized him from his porn career. That's probably what happened with that guy in Emerald City who Nick had a fight with. He must have recognized Nick, thought he was gay, and made a move on him. Nick ended up having to use his fists to convince him otherwise."

And then I remembered something else. I'd asked Phyllis to ask around about Nick. The young guy in the bar was probably a friend of Phyllis' and passed me the DVD—probably from The Dorothy's own adult movie section in the library—because Phyllis asked him to. But did this have anything to do with Phyllis' death? Had I unknowingly put her in jeopardy? Was Nick more involved in all of this than I'd thought? Had he found out Phyllis was about to reveal his secret and followed her up to Lovers' Lane and pushed her off the boat?

"But he's a *straight* porn star," Errall countered, breaking my concentration. She was referencing Nick's rather convincing on-screen tongue work as evidence. "Why would a bunch of gay guys recognize him?"

"Well, I'm betting if we keep on watching this we'll see that Nick and Lyle have a little scene together too. This is a bi video."

"Are you saying the guys slobbering over Nick on this boat are bisexual?"

I shrugged. "Well, maybe some are, but watching bi videos is a real turn-on for some gay men."

"I don't get it." Errall found the remote and paused the video on a nice shot of Nick's muscular buns.

"Bi videos have straight guys...or at least very straight-acting guys...having a little action with other straight-acting guys. A lot of gay guys have fantasies about that. Don't lesbians fantasize about straight girls?"

"Is there anything gay guys don't fantasize about!" Errall asked as she got up and headed for the bathroom. "When do you guys have time to work, eat meals, attend family functions? Sheesh!"

I grabbed the remote to stop the film and the screen mercifully went blank.

"Mail," Errall called back at me, crouching down to pick up a white envelope that had just whistled under the door.

"It's from Charity," she said once she'd opened the envelope and begun to read. "We're invited to a Wiser family pre-dinner cocktail party at Tin-Sel." She looked at me. "Apparently the captain is going to attempt to reach the Amalfi Coast before sunset. Should be a nice view from there. Six p.m. sharp. Will you be done by then? Or should I leave you and Nick alone for a while?"

Not a wholly unpleasant idea.

I had no intention of missing the Amalfi Coast and Charity's party, but I had a couple things to attend to beforehand. There were two rooms I hadn't searched yet: Faith and Thomas' and James and Patrick's. Confirming that the two men were otherwise engaged, I started with the cabin belonging to Hope Wiser's widower and son-in-law.

The place was an unholy mess, so it took me a little longer than
I'd expected. And, in the end, beneath the piles of discarded clothing, magazines and books, I found absolutely nothing. So heading
into the room belonging to Charity's surviving sister and her husband, my hopes were low. My strategy of break-and-enter thus far
had resulted in little of use. None of the handwriting samples I'd
found in any of the rooms matched the notes Charity had been
receiving. Whoever it was who sent them had been careful. Sure,
I'd found the wads of cash in Jackson's room, but it turned out he
was using it to score drugs in our ports of call. And all the pricey
items belonging to Nick Kincaid had been paid for by his career in
porn. Even so, I went through the drill in Faith and Thomas' room.

Handwriting—no match. Communiqués with local thugs
arranging a hit—nada. Signed confession—nope. But then…

At first I almost missed it, rummaging through the bathroom's
cabinet and cubbyholes. But as I reached deep into a vanity draw-
er I felt something soft pushed into the farthest corner. I pulled at
it with two fingers and out came a white bundle, something
wrapped in Kleenex, maybe ten centimeters long and six wide.
There was a solid object at the centre of the package. I laid it carefully next to the sink and gently unwrapped it.

Inside was a glass vial with an eyedropper screw-on top. The
liquid was so clear, it was almost ice blue. I removed the lid and
took a small whiff. I didn't need a skull or triple X insignia to tell
me what this was.

Poison.

It was our last night aboard The Dorothy and although the dress
code for the evening was casual, when Errall and I entered Tin-Sel,
I noticed that many of the Wisers had made an effort to dress up a
bit, as had I. I put aside the dressy walking shorts I was going to
wear and went for a loose-fitting cream shirt with stylized fairies
dancing around the collar and cuffs and my tried-and-true won-
derpants—black, never out of style and tush-hugging. They'd
been sitting in my closet all week but came out as wrinkle-free as
Joan Rivers.

"Well, looks like the gang's all here," Errall, resplendent in a shark-coloured halter-top dress, said under her breath. "And Charity's managed to get through the cruise without getting killed. Congratulations."

"It ain't over yet," I responded in a low voice. "We don't reach Civitivecchia until seven a.m."

We helped ourselves to champagne offered by a passing Tin Man waiter and dove into the crowd. Most everyone was milling about near the windows, eyeing up the increasingly spectacular landscape. The Dorothy was chugging along at a fair clip, nearer to land than usual, in an attempt to reach the most scenic of the Amalfi's deep gorges and amazing Gothic-inspired cliffside resorts before dark.

"Charity Wiser?" a cultured voice called out from near the entrance.

Everyone turned. It was Mauro Corsaro, the ship's concierge.

"What is it Max?" Charity responded over the heads of her family.

"Er-hmm," he said, clearing his throat, obviously uncomfortable delivering a message in such a public matter. But Charity wasn't moving. "Your call from Rome has just come through."

A murmur rippled through the room. A call from Rome. Everyone knew it could only mean one thing. It had to be a call from the lawyer. This was the last night of the cruise. And here was a final, ugly reminder that when the cruise ended, so did their inheritances.

"We've put it through to your cabin?" Mauro added, a bit snippy—as befitting a concierge of his status. "Is that acceptable, Madame?"

"Oh dear," Charity answered. She looked at Flora. "Will you stay with Dottie? I need to take this call. I'll meet you later for dinner?"

Flora nodded dumbly. The room was silent as Charity made a good exit, the flowing sleeves of her pearl-white outfit and matching neck scarf flaring dramatically behind her as she went. For a moment the Amalfi was forgotten and everyone just stared at one another. I'd have given up my *Men's Health* subscription for a year to know what was going through the collective mind of the Wiser clan at that moment.

"Well, there's no use staying here," Jackson finally broke the silence. "I'm off to a real bar where they'll serve up something stronger than this damn champagne." And he marched from the room.

"The view from the upper deck is way better," Nigel announced as he and his twin ran for the door.

"What a good idea," someone else agreed.

Within seconds the room was cleared. I was quick to follow.

"Mr. Quant," Patrick Halburton greeted me with his old man rasp. He was ambling up the Deck Seven hallway and had caught sight of me in the small cubicle, halfway down it, where extra linens were stored and passengers came for ice.

Shoo fly, shoo, I wanted to say. I didn't have time for him right then. I nodded politely and pretended to be busy with something in one of my pants pockets. (Not that easy to do without seeming like a pervert.)

"What are you doing here?" he asked, looking wholly dumbfounded, as if he'd spotted a polar bear on Waikiki Beach.

Jeepers. I pulled him into the ice room and said in a hush, "Don't you want to be on one of the upper decks looking at the Amalfi coast?"

He shook his head. He was probably wondering why I was whispering.

"I'm a little busy right now," I told him, not whispering anymore but as quietly as I could. "Maybe we can talk later."

"What are you doing here?" he asked again.

My patience was running low. Patrick Halburton was about to spoil everything with his inane chatter. But I couldn't get angry with the old guy. He had no idea that he was standing smack in the middle of a trap.

It was the last night on board, and the murderer, whoever he or she was, had one last chance to make good on their threats against Charity and save their inheritance before she changed her will. Which meant I had one last chance to catch the culprit. I had some ideas. Now I needed proof. The party in Tin-Sel and the "call from Rome" had been set up to communicate to all the suspects that the change in the will was going ahead as planned and that Charity would be alone in her suite for the next while. If someone was going to hit her, it had to be now, while everyone else was too busy taking in the amazing Amalfi.

Time was short. If I couldn't get rid of him, at least I could get him out of the way. I pulled Patrick further into the room behind me so that no one—presumably the murderer—coming down the hall would spot him. Now if only I could keep him quiet.

At first, I felt only disbelief as the knife's blade slid cleanly into my back.

Chapter 17

He struck me hard on the head with something metallic (I know because it made a distinctive *dong* sound when it hit me)...maybe an ice bucket. And as I went down I heard him say in a falsetto that was probably his way of imitating Charity, "He's my advisor." Then in his own grouchy geezer voice, "Well, this is what you get for giving out bad advice. Shame on you."

My head began to pound with a dull, repeating thud, but it was the tearing pain in my back where I'd been stabbed that threatened my consciousness; it was incredible. What the hell had he used, a butter knife?

He stepped over my prone figure and left me lying there. I looked up and saw that his right shoe was leaving a mark on the hallway carpet. It looked wet...it was...blood. My blood. Ahh, jeez. I fought off an attack of nausea and tried to get up. But he'd beaned me harder than I'd thought. A psychedelic dizziness overtook me, the nausea came flooding back and I dropped to the floor like a bag of wet sand. I squeezed my eyes shut and took several deep breaths. After a few seconds I painfully forced open my right eye. I really didn't have to. I knew where he was going. He was heading to 702. Charity's cabin.

I used the wall to pull myself up, paling with the effort. I winced as my head and knife wounds screamed their combined irritation at the motion. I stumbled into the hallway, determined to catch up with Patrick. But I was too late. He'd already found her unlocked door and thrown it open. All I saw was the green and black pattern of his flannel shirt as it disappeared inside. I did my best to jog the distance, holding my side in a half-assed effort to stem the bleeding and the pain.

It seemed to take a week for me to reach Charity's cabin door. When I got there, I saw her on the deck, facing the water, a phone to her ear. In the foreground was Patrick Halburton, walking determinedly in her direction, knife in hand. He was probably debating whether he should stab her or simply rush her and throw her overboard. A millisecond later he chose the latter and, at a run, began bellowing, "You can't do this to my Harry!"

The figure on the deck turned around just in time to expertly ward off Patrick's flailing attack and revealed himself to be not Charity, but rather one of the ship's security officers in drag. As he felled Patrick as sure as a lumberjack on an aged birch tree, five other security men jumped out from various hiding spots throughout the room, all yelling and screaming for Patrick to yield. Perhaps a bit of overkill—I'm sure it almost gave him a heart attack—but it did produce the desired result. His assault died as quickly as it took him to hit the floor. He didn't struggle, not even a little. He did, however, begin to weep.

"I don't believe it!" This from the real Charity, being escorted into the cabin by Captain Bagnato along with Flora and Dottie and two more of the ship's officers. "Patrick, oh Patrick, why have you done this? Why is it you?" She turned to the lead security officer. "Oh let him up. He's a sixty-three year old man for goodness sake."

The security men hauled Patrick up into a standing position facing Charity, but were careful to keep his hands secure behind his back. He was wet-and-wild-eyed but semi-coherent.

"I couldn't let you and that advisor fellow of yours take away from Harry what's rightfully hers. What's she got, poor Harry? You tell me that," he spewed. "She can't marry 'cause she can't have kids. No man'll ever want her. She has nothing because of this family's disease! You promised me once, Charity, you promised me you'd take care of her. You said you understood how badly she'd been done by. Her father's got nothing, I've got nothing, her great-grandfather's got nothing. We got nothing to give her, to make up for all of this. 'Cept you. And you promised."

"Yes," Charity agreed in a still voice. "Yes, Patrick, I did."

"And now you're going back on that promise," he said accusingly. "I couldn't let it happen."

"I'd never go back on a promise like that. I care deeply about your family, Patrick, most especially about Harry. You should know that," she told him.

"How?" Patrick shot back, tears collecting in the deep crevices of his face. "How would I know that?"

And to that, Charity Wiser had no answer.

According to Errall, most of the Wiser clan, except of course for Patrick who was locked up somewhere until we arrived in Civitivecchia, and Harry, who kindly asked and was allowed to sit with him until then, showed up at Yellow Bricks for dinner that night. Later, they even attempted some weak-hearted last night celebration at Munchkin Land by taking in the entertainment, including Alberta's psychic show. But nothing cheered them as much as when, at the end of the evening Charity made the announcement that she had no intention of changing her will and that there'd be many more Charity Events in the family's future. Talk about sweet and sour news.

After a visit with the ship's doctor, I spent the night alone, recuperating in my cabin, licking my wounds, old and new. I was feeling a little sour myself. There was nothing satisfying about seeing a man driven to uncontrollable fury. All for an altruistic, although misguided, purpose: to protect and provide for his beloved granddaughter.

I actually wasn't too worried about Harriet Delmonico. If

someone had the spirit and verve and tenacity to survive the curse of her family line, it was she. And someday she'd have some of Charity's money as added succour. Until then, I guessed, she'd be just fine. Of all the Wisers, she probably needed the money the least to make a good life for herself.

When Errall walked in quite late that evening, I was in my bathrobe, sitting on our beautiful teak-floored deck staring out at the sea, stewing. Although I didn't know I was stewing.

"A euro for your thoughts," she said, slipping soundlessly into the chair next to mine.

"Oh nothing," I answered. "Just thinking about Patrick Halburton."

"And?"

I hesitated, thinking, then answered, "And how, despite all that's happened, I've really enjoyed this experience. Being on this ship I mean. I think this prairie boy has fallen a little bit in love with the sea. I'm sad to see our trip come to an end."

True as it was, she wasn't buying it. "And?"

I thought some more. It wouldn't come.

"Richard's gone," she told me flatly in her Errall way.

I shifted in my seat, catching a sharp intake of breath from the pain that came from disturbing the bandage around my torso. Richard was gone? This was a surprise. I thought he was giving me the cold shoulder. We hadn't talked since Wednesday night when he'd called asking me out for a drink. I put him off until later and then never showed up. I could see him being pissed, but enough to leave the ship, forgo the last part of the trip? What about the rest of his clients on board?

"Giovanna told me," Errall said softly. "She knew about...well, that you and he were spending time together. She received a note from him before we left Salerno. It said he was staying behind to catch a flight back to the States to attend to a personal crisis."

"I...I didn't know...he didn't tell me."

"That's what I thought."

"It's odd he wouldn't have," I said. "Or at least leave me a note too."

She shrugged. "It sounded serious. Maybe he had no time."

Hmphf. "I guess."

"Sorry."

"Thanks for telling me." I gave her a smile. "You should get back to your captain."

She smiled back. "It's good, y'know."

This was a rare personal admission from the steely Errall Strane. I took a second to study her face. I thought to myself how very pretty she is when she allows herself to let down her guard and relax the muscles in her face and neck, as she had now. "I know."

"Were you and Richard getting close?"

I considered the question, but not for long. "I liked him. We were having fun. No big deal." Big, strong, unemotional man.

"You should try it. Getting close to someone I mean."

I looked away. Was it bad that I didn't want to? "You should get back."

"To Giovanna?" She snuggled deeper into her chair. "She's kinda busy right now...the whole steering the boat thing. I thought I'd hang around here for a while if you're serving something good. After all, it's our last night. Any champagne left in the fridge?" She got up to check then stopped. "Oh, I suppose you're on pain medication or something? You shouldn't mix drugs and alcohol."

I shook my head, disappointed.

"Well then, we'll indulge in the next best thing," she told me, heading inside for the phone. "I'm going to order everything off the room service menu that has chocolate in it."

Errall did sneak out to the captain's quarters later that night but returned bright and early the next morning. I think she thought I wouldn't notice, having left after I'd fallen into a deep drug and chocolate induced sleep. But I did notice she wasn't in her bed when at 7 a.m. a rather curt Judy Smythwicke addressed the ship's passengers one last time.

"Good morning all," she began. "It is now seven a.m. on a bright and beautiful Italian morning. If you take a peek out your windows you shall see that The Dorothy has arrived in Civitivecchia. As this is the final day of your cruise, you will be expected to vacate your rooms no later than eight-thirty a.m. and be off the ship no later than nine-forty-five a.m. So please, budget your time accordingly. For those of you heading into Rome, have a pleasant day in one of the world's most exciting and stunning cities and for the rest of you, safe travels wherever they may take you." In other words, get up and get out. When Errall came sneaking back in moments later, I was wide awake and packing my bags.

"Did I thank you enough, Russell?" she asked as we finished our last cup of coffee on the deck before leaving our cabin and The Dorothy for the final time.

"Of course," I answered absentmindedly, still half-brooding over something I couldn't put my finger on. It didn't help that I hadn't slept too well. I wasn't sure if it was the persistent headache that was ailing me, or all the chocolate Errall and I had tossed down our throats before going to bed.

"Good. I want you to know how grateful I am." She pinned me with the full force of her blue, blue eyes, a look meant to reinforce how serious she was. "This has helped."

Neither of us wanted to say the "K" word, but it hung in the air for a while before floating harmlessly off on a passing wisp of sea breeze. Then, just as we were about to get up, a wave of water washed over us, as shocking for its cold wetness as for its unexpectedness.

"What the fuck was that?" Errall yodelled. She hopped up and over to the railing to see what had caused the sudden tidal wave.

Then another splash. Fortunately Errall got the brunt of that one.

"Oh my God!" she yelped, jumping back.

"What? What? What?" was about all I was capable of, not knowing if I should laugh or run for my life jacket.

Errall fell back in her chair, holding her tummy and chortling.

"What?" I stared at her, wondering if she'd lost her mind. Or had I? Were we still at sea? Were we sinking? Was all my earlier blathering on about falling in love with the sea about to turn around and bite me on my drowning ass?

"They're washing the ship," Errall managed to tell me through bursts of laughter. "They're washing the fuckin' ship!"

And indeed, once I garnered enough courage to stand up and steal a look over the deck's railing, I saw a large mechanical thingy bob, (I'm nothing if not knowledgeable about machinery) making its way up and down the length of The Dorothy giving her a bath. I pulled back and went for a last sip of coffee, which turned out to be mostly dirty ship-cleaning water. Blech.

I shook my head with incredulity. First the 7 a.m. wake up call, now this. There was no doubt; when the cruise is over, it's really over.

Anthony and Jared had generously offered to host all of us, Errall, Charity, Dottie, Flora and myself that first night off the ship. The next morning Errall and I would head south to Rome to catch a plane for home while the others made their way to Florence and other points north for an extended holiday.

After disembarking from The Dorothy, Charity and Dottie and I remained shipside, collecting luggage and saying our fare-thee-wells to the rest of the Wiser bunch and Alberta (who gave me a hurried hug before having to dash off with the rest of the departing crew). Flora and Errall caught a shuttle into town to find the Europcar office. In surprisingly short order we were packed up and on our way to Tuscany in matching blue Golfs, Errall and me in the lead, with Errall driving (I was still rather stiff).

Our route took us north through Grosetto, then inland towards Siena. The beginning part of our journey was unremarkable and rather disappointing scenery-wise, with flat, uninspired parcels of land, ramshackle farm houses and dilapidated, industrial-looking towns devoid of colour or character. But at some point, almost imperceptibly, the landscape transformed, caught in the beauty of summer meeting fall. Browns turned into yellows and oranges and reds and countless shades of green—olive, pea, chartreuse, viridian. The land heaved up to become softly rolling hills dotted with picturesque homesteads and miniature castles and grazing cows and sheep. There were endless vineyards, fields of olive trees, plots of spent sunflower and lavender, majestic cypress trees and wind-breaks of stately poplars. Tractors without cabs pulled rickety wagons and worked hard at the business of harvest.

A couple of hours later we arrived in the village of Castellina in Chianti and stopped to stretch our legs, buy water and consult the map Anthony and Jared had provided. It was hand-drawn and points of reference included a ruined mill, an overgrown mud hole, something called a *casalta* and a power transformer. These were our guides to the temporary country home of our friends. Studying it I began to imagine I'd somehow been magically trans-ported into some sort of fairy-tale land; take a left at the dragon's lair, beware the troll as you cross the moat. Archaic, yes, but accu-rate, as only fifteen minutes later we were rolling up a steep, heav-ily rutted, stone-pitted, overgrown, dangerously winding, narrow road and found at its end the little bit of Italiano heaven we were looking for. Surrounded by a lush growth of trees and overlooking endless acres of grape vines ripe for the picking was a rambling, two storey stone house and emerging from it two handsome Canadian men, arms wide open.

"Welcome, welcome, welcome," Anthony greeted us warmly, his Robert Redford good looks burnished gold after weeks beneath the Tuscan sun. "And what remarkable timing. Jared and I were about to make for town to do some shopping for dinner. You must all come along."

Following a flurry of introductions, movement of luggage into guestrooms and freshening up, we piled into a jeep and headed back to Castellina. Dottie chose to remain behind to rest and Flora offered to stay with her. Anthony drove, with Charity taking the passenger seat next to him. Errall, Jared and I were squeezed in the back, me in the middle.

"Russell," Jared spoke into my ear as Anthony did his best to tra-verse the bumpy road without shaking us up too badly. "Are you sure you want to come along? You look a little pasty. Are you all right?"

"He's right," Errall said. "You do look a little off."

Although the spot where I'd been stabbed didn't hurt nearly as much as it first did, the headache I'd had since being attacked by

Patrick Halburton was still a doozy. Perhaps it was from being beaned on the head with an ice bucket? Or maybe from being punched and throttled by the Sicilian tender captain and Aaron the fake gay guy? Regardless, it was becoming a real bother and I suspected I was developing a fever too. I put it down to the travails of strenuous travel after suffering a rather serious wound. The ship's physician had counselled me to see my own doctor as soon as possible after getting off The Dorothy—just to keep an eye on things. Something about infection setting in or something like that. Yeah, sure, I'll get right on that.

But more discomfiting than my physical aches and pains was a growing apprehension I couldn't shake. Something was bothering me. What made it even worse was that I had all these crazy ideas in my head but none of them seemed to fit together. There was Richard leaving without so much as a so long, thanks for the memories. Alberta's prediction that someone was lying to me, possibly Sereena. The possibility that Phyllis' leap off the deck of The Dorothy was not an accident. And the poison I'd found hidden in Faith and Thomas' room. Was it truly poison? What about Jackson's illness?—was he poisoned?—by the juice given to him by Dottie?—by Faith and/or Thomas?—by someone else?—and why? Patrick claimed that he wanted to kill Charity to protect his granddaughter's inheritance, yet, if Charity was to be believed, all this began with Morris the cat being poisoned. That happened long before Charity announced her bogus intention to change her will. The same with the "I'm going to kill her" voice Alberta kept hearing. And what of the wild goose chase Flora and I had been sent on? There had to have been a purpose for that. Patrick Halburton certainly didn't use the opportunity to carry out his killing plan.

But reality couldn't be ignored. The man who attempted to murder Charity Wiser was caught and incarcerated. And the rest of the Wisers were gone, they'd scurried off The Dorothy like ants, back to their everyday lives.

"I'm fine," I assured Jared and Errall. "But maybe instead of the market, is there someplace in Castellina with internet access where Anthony could drop me off?"

"Me too," Errall piped up.

Jared nodded. He'd let his copper tresses grow long over the summer and now they fell into haphazard plaits across his forehead and over his brilliant green eyes. "Sure." He called up to Anthony, "Hon, can you drop Russell and Errall off at the internet café first. We can meet them there for a drink when we're done at the market." Anthony barked his affirmative reply over the din created by the truck's body and tires as they struggled over the rough terrain. Jared looked me in the eye, as if assessing my well-being. "You're sure? We could take you back. You could have a rest before lunch."

"I'm good," I told him, not sure if I was telling the truth.

The internet café was the small Italian village version of a fast food cafeteria. Instead of bloated hot dogs on a rotisserie, greasy hamburgers and runny milkshakes, they were serving hearty slices of mouth-watering osso bucco, spicy olives stuffed with garlic, exquisite million-layered torts, and a cheap but tasty Chianti by the glass. Errall ordered wine and a coffee for me and we were directed to a group of four or five bistro tables in one corner of the dining area. Except that each had a computer on it, this could have been any charming European eatery in any charming European village. Traditional meets modern.

I decided to start with Richard. It was selfish and immature of me to be feeling miffed that he hadn't left me a note as he had Captain Bagnato. If indeed he'd had a personal emergency to attend to at home—serious enough to leave The Dorothy—then the least I could do was express my concern. Except for the keyboard having a few keys in unfamiliar places I quickly mastered it, found Google and typed in a search for GrayPride Tours. My request returned hundreds of hits. I was looking for the URL for GrayPride Tours but halfway down the first page something more intriguing caught my eye. I had found what it was that had likely beckoned Richard home.

I clicked on a link that took me to a news article from a popular west coast U.S. gay news weekly with the snippy headline:

"Beleaguered gay travel company cruising into bankruptcy?"

I scanned the article but found little detail. The news was too fresh and no one was talking much. But apparently Richard's business, GrayPride Tours, had infamously been in financial trouble for years. The not-quite-objective author of the article made thinly veiled accusations suggesting that Richard, as president and sole owner, used company dollars to fund an extravagant personal lifestyle far beyond what he or his company could sustain for any length of time.

I sat back in my chair and sipped my coffee. So, I wondered, had Richard run off to try to save his business? Or had he just run off?

I navigated back to the hit list and punched the appropriate buttons to get to the GrayPride homepage, hoping there'd be an e-mail address or "Contact Us" button I could access to send a note to Richard. Instead I got a blue screen telling me the website I was attempting to reach no longer existed. I assumed I must have done something wrong and tried again, then a third time, always with the same result.

Thinking that perhaps I was at an old website that wasn't linked to a more recent version I went back to the hit list and searched for another web address. I found nothing for GrayPride Tours, but I did find something else.

The missing link.

My gasp was audible to Errall and several others in the tiny internet café.

Errall poked her head around the corner of her computer where, at my request, she was trying to contact Captain Bagnato about the results of the investigation into Phyllis' death. "What is going on over there?" she whispered, loud enough for only me to hear.

In a low voice I told Errall what I'd uncovered about GrayPride Tours' financial situation.

"That's interesting but surely not worth a gasp."

"There's more."

Hearing the ominous tone of my voice, she scurried over and, crouching at my side, studied the screen of my computer. "What's this? It looks like...an obituary?"

"Yes. I typed in Richard Gray as a search parameter and one of the links took me to a British Columbia newspaper archive site and the obit for Virginia Wiser...nee Gray."

It took my intelligent friend about two seconds to put it together. "Flora's mother?"

"Yes. Flora's mother and, according to this obituary, sister of Richard Gray."

"How can this be? How can Charity and Flora not have recognized him?"

"From all accounts Charity had little or nothing to do with her son, John, after he moved away from home. She may never have met Virginia, never mind Virginia's brother, Richard Gray."

"And Flora?"

"Well, I'm only guessing here, but John and Virginia were reputed to be serious alcoholics, and perhaps not the most interested in maintaining close familial ties. Flora, too, may have never met Richard, her uncle, or only as a small child."

"So what does this mean, Russell?"

"I've been perplexed by the fact that Patrick Halburton admitted to wanting to kill Charity *after* he heard about the change in her will. Yet the voices Alberta heard and the death of Charity's cat happened long before. But neither were proven or provable signs of a plan to kill Charity. Maybe Alberta is a charlatan and the cat died of natural causes. Maybe they meant nothing. But if they did..."

Errall's eyes widened. "If they did...there's another murderer out there!"

I nodded. "The real murderer...or rather, the first murderer...had to have had his plan in place as far back as last spring, in May when Morris was poisoned." My eyebrows referenced the obituary. "Richard Gray."

"But why?"

"Vengeance for his sister's death," I theorized. "He must somehow blame Charity for Virginia's death, which, according to Kayla Moshier, was more like a suicide by drunk driving than an accident."

"How could he possibly believe Charity was responsible for that?"

I shrugged. "Responsibility by way of inattentiveness?" I took a shot. "By being a bad mother, shunning her only son, ignoring him as if he was unworthy of her love…her money…her help when he needed it…she drove him, and by association, his wife Virginia, to an early death. John and Virginia Wiser died horrible, senseless deaths. Deaths like that can cause loved ones great anger."

Errall shook her head. "Oh dear God. I suppose it's possible. And if so, he's unhinged."

Richard Gray was unhinged. How could I not have seen it? How could I have…? My headache was growing worse at the thought. I'd dated jackasses before, but never a murderous jackass. I felt betrayed, disappointed…ashamed.

"But we can't be sure of any of this, Russell. It's all conjecture, possibly wild coincidence. We can't prove any of it."

Errall was right. But I didn't believe it for a second.

"And even if he did try to kill Charity," she continued, "he failed, thanks to you, and now he's gone. Maybe that's why he left The Dorothy early. His attempts to have her knocked off flopped and he finally gave up and decided to call it a day, before anyone could suspect him of anything."

Not good enough, I growled to myself. If Richard Gray was guilty of this, as my gut told me he was, I wanted him to pay. And, somehow, I would see to it that he did.

As a travel professional, it wasn't hard to believe Richard Gray could secure connections in foreign ports of call to commit the acts of violence we'd experienced. But each attempt had been foiled. So when Patrick's threatening notes started to show up, Richard realized his great stroke of luck—there was another murderer on board, spurred by Charity's announcement, who would do his dirty work for him. So Richard orchestrated the wild shipboard goose chase to keep Flora and me occupied and Charity without protection to give the killer a chance to do the deed. When that also didn't work he resorted back to poison, his original weapon, but somehow poisoned Jackson instead of Charity. And then he planted the poison in Faith and Thomas' room to point suspicion at them, the poor relatives living hand to mouth, who'd just learned they'd get nothing from their rich sister.

I knew it was the truth—or close to it—but I couldn't prove any of it.

"Are you just about done over there?" Errall had returned to her own computer station and was slugging back the last of her wine.

The coffee seemed to be helping my headache, but I was still feeling uncomfortably hot. And uncomfortably bothered. Something, something, something more...

But there was nothing else I could think of to do on the internet to help me bring Richard Gray's actions to light or the man to justice. "Just a sec..." I was about to log off when I remembered yet another niggling bit of unfinished business. I returned to the search engine and typed in the words: A&W Incorporated—the registered owner of the Kismet.

One hit. It wasn't a website for the company, but rather some kind of public notice, referencing the initial incorporation of the company several years earlier. It was mostly legal mumbo-jumbo that made little sense to me. Except for two words that jumped out at me, hitting me in the face with an almost physical force. I jerked back from the computer screen, the legs of my chair screeching against the cement floor. I stared at the two words: names.

I now knew what A&W stood for.

The first name was hauntingly familiar, a name I knew I should recognize.

Ashbourne.

Where had I heard that before?

The second, I knew very well.

Wistonchuk.

My mother's maiden name.

Chapter 18

"Russell, you've got to settle down. There's nothing you can do right now."

Anthony and I were alone on a two metre by two metre stone pad, a private outdoor seating area just outside the doors to my bedroom on the side of the house that faced a grove of fruit trees and an unruly patch of overgrown grasses.

"But how can it be, Anthony?" I stared into the movie-idol eyes, taking in the greying blond of his boyishly shaggy hair, the deepening lines of his handsome face, the familiarity of it somehow a comfort to me so far away from home. In deference to the dry early afternoon heat, he was wearing a pair of loose shorts and an unbuttoned shirt that showed off his still shapely torso. "How can my sixty-three-year-old Ukrainian mother from Howell, Saskatchewan, be the owner of a fifty-metre yacht sailing around the Mediterranean? With Sereena Smith on it!"

"Russell," he said in his cultured, Englishman's voice, "you don't know that the Wistonchuk you saw on the ownership docu-

271

ments was your mother. It could be anyone. I grant you it's not the most common of names, but surely there are a few others in the world," he reasoned. Anthony was more than my friend. He was my mentor, my teacher, my Obi-Wan Kenobi.

"That's true," I admitted. "And I thought the same thing…"

"Until?" he said with narrowing eyes, reading me well.

"Until I remembered where I'd heard the other name."

"Ashbourne?"

"Yes. Anthony, when Sereena and I were in New York City last year a man called her Ms. Ashbourne."

Anthony's brow furrowed with interest. "Really."

"When I asked him about it he apologized, said it was a mistake, but there was something about the whole thing that didn't seem right."

"Who was this man?"

I cleared my throat. "Well…he was an elevator operator at The Sherry-Netherland hotel."

Anthony regarded me for a moment, not saying anything.

"I know what you're thinking."

"Doubtful," he shot back. "Anyway, it doesn't matter what I think. You'll be home soon enough and you can ask Sereena and your mother directly if they happen to be co-owners of a luxury yacht that they forgot to tell you about."

He was making fun of me in that genteel way of his that made it seem as if he wasn't doing it at all.

"Listen, puppy," he said, slipping his tanned bare feet into sandals and getting up. "The others have lunch preparations well under control. We'll eat around two out back. Why don't you get some rest until then? You are the walking wounded after all." He laid his right hand gently against my cheek, registered a look of concern and moved his hand up to my forehead. "You're a little warm, Russell. Perhaps we should fetch a doctor."

"No, no, no," I scoffed at the idea. "It's just the after-effects of all the pain medication. I think I will lie down for a while though. I'll be fine after some shut-eye."

I knew Anthony was right. There really wasn't anything I could do until I got home. It probably was nothing anyway. My mother owning a yacht? Ha. She was more the old Russian barge type. And I did need rest. I hadn't had much since being stabbed. (Now there's a sentence I don't say every day.) I needed time to think about Richard and how we could prove his attempts at murder. As soon as we had returned to the villa after our trip into town, I had a short private meeting with Charity and Flora and told them what I'd found out at the internet café. They were appreciably shocked and, like me, doubted that it was all a big coincidence. And, also like me, they were flummoxed over how we could bring Richard Gray to justice.

Anthony left, softly closing the door behind him. I didn't even bother to take my clothes off. I felt irresistibly drowsy. I crawled under the blankets of my bed and fell fast asleep listening to the soothing sound of a light breeze playing in the orchard.

Jared appeared like a hazy version of himself floating on top of me.

"We didn't know if we should wake you," he said, smiling. He was sitting on the bed next to me, one hand resting on my chest. "Are you all right? Do you want to eat or would you like to sleep a little longer?"

"What time is it?" I said in a voice that I didn't recognize, feeling disoriented.

"It's close to three."

"Three? How long did I sleep?" I said, startled further into wakefulness.

"You needed it, Russell. The gals have been telling us about all you've been through this last week. Your body needs time to recuperate." He stopped there, brushing a stray lock of hair from my forehead. He was even more beautiful than Anthony, more beautiful than most men. Jared was nearing thirty-five. But in his line of work, modelling, he might as well have been eighty-five. His life and career as he knew them were slowly but surely coming to an end, but he was handling the disappearing job offers, the fewer phone calls, the flight of fame, as he did everything else, with distinguished and incomparable grace. "But it also needs food. Do you feel like joining us?"

I sat up, a little quicker than my brain wanted me to. I felt dizzy and a little sick to my stomach. "I'll be right out," I mumbled, trying for a smile that likely looked more like a grimace. "But I'm gonna get cleaned up first. You and the others go ahead and get started."

He laughed lightly, showing his perfect teeth and voluptuous, shiny lips to their best advantage. "We already have." He patted me affectionately on the shoulder as he got up. "You take your time. We'll be outside. It's a beautiful afternoon. We thought after lunch we might go to Radda. It's a cute village not far from here. Very pretty drive."

Jared left and I felt a renewed energy. He often had that effect on me. I needed a shower badly. I stumbled out of bed and began to strip. As is my habit, I patted down my pant pockets to ensure I didn't leave anything in them before tossing them into the laundry pile. I'd lost way too many twenty-dollar-bills that way. And indeed, I felt the familiar feel of crumpled paper in my left pocket and pulled it out. But it wasn't money. It was a white piece of stationery, folded in two. I opened it to see a hand-written note. At the bottom was Alberta's signature. She must have slipped it into my pocket that morning when she'd hugged me on the pier before rushing off to catch up to the rest of the disembarking staff.

Russell,
I don't know whether I should tell you this or not, and I'm not sure if I'll have the chance to before you leave. I hope that by the time you get this note it won't matter any more.
During my show last night on the ship, I heard the voice again, angrier, saying the same thing, 'I'm going to kill her.'
I'm sorry for having to give you this news.
Maybe it means nothing.
But I doubt it.
See you in Saskatoon.
Love
Alberta Lougheed

My ears began a rhythmic pounding like an African drum solo as my blood pumped double time through my veins. Why did I feel so unsettled? During Alberta's last show on the ship, when Patrick Halburton was already behind bars, there was someone else, another murderer, thinking about killing my client. This news changed nothing. It reinforced what I'd already suspected. Patrick was not the only murderer out there. But something…something…not right…. I staggered against the bedpost. Why did I still feel so tired? I just needed another minute of rest…just forty more winks…

"Dolly Parton is here to see you."

Huh?

At first all I could see was a brown and gray shape in front of me. I tried to open my eyes wider, then rubbed at them to wipe away the sleep. I saw that the brown thing sitting in a chair pulled up next to my bed was Flora Wiser. I had fallen asleep…again.

"Huh, what was that?"

"Dottie made some tea for you."

Still a little discombobulated, I dutifully turned my head to the right and saw a steaming cup of liquid on the bedside table. I was parched. I felt as if I hadn't had anything to drink in days. Tea is not usually my thing, but at that point I would have drunk anything. I struggled to release my arms from under the covers and sat up into a drinking position. The first thing I noticed was that my headache was gone. The dull throbbing that was slowly driving me insane had mercifully disappeared and I felt cooler. My fever must have broken. Ah, the healing properties of sleep.

Flora carefully handed me the cup of tea on its saucer and watched as I blew on it to cool it. "Thank you," I said. "Tell Dottie thank you."

Flora's thin mouth curved up into a small smile, causing her glasses to slide a millimeter down her nose. "Dottie believes that a good cup of tea cures just about anything."

"Did I miss lunch?"

"Oh yes," she said. "But I brought you some cheese and crackers and an apple."

These too were on the bedside table.

"What time is it? How long have I been sleeping?" I was beginning to sound like Sleeping Beauty or Rip Van Winkle, but Flora most definitely was not my prince come to kiss me awake and I was pretty certain I'd yet to sprout a long beard.

"It's about four-thirty. Everyone else went on a drive, to another town...I forget its name." She nodded a little. "I didn't feel like going, so I stayed here to look after you."

"That's so nice of you." I meant it. Why wouldn't she want to go for a drive in the Italian countryside rather than babysit me?

"I don't mind at all." Flora's cheeks grew unusually pink. "I owe you. Without you I don't know what would have happened to us out there adrift in the sea. I suppose we wouldn't even be here. We'd have all drowned."

Oh shucks, ma'am. So that was it. She felt beholden to me for saving her life. Nice, but unnecessary. "I didn't do much other than hold onto the boat with the rest of you," I countered. "Sereena and the Kismet deserve all the credit."

"But you fought off those men. You kept our spirits up and watched out for us and made us believe we'd be okay, whether you truly believed it or not. And it was especially brave of you to dive in after the captain when you're so afraid of water."

I looked at Flora.

Suddenly I knew.

My heart began to dance wildly in my chest and my head exploded with renewed pain. I tried to remain calm and hoped Flora did not notice any change in me.

Like Jell-O into a mould, a story began to pour into my mind, slipping and sliding until it reshaped itself and settled into place.

"Are you all right, Mr. Quant?"

Darn, she noticed. "I'm fine. Just a little tired, that's all."

"Maybe some food would help?"

"Water?" God I was thirsty. "Cold water."

"Of course." She got up and left the room to get me some water.

I wanted to get out of bed, but didn't. I felt my forehead. Still a little warm. I guessed I wasn't fully recovered yet. I lay there trying to think of something to convince me that I was wrong, that what my gut was telling me couldn't be true. But it was all there.

Alberta's note said she heard the voice in her head saying: "I'm going to kill her" on the last night on the ship. The voice couldn't have belonged to Patrick Halburton. He was in The Dorothy's brig. It couldn't have belonged to Richard either, for he abandoned ship in Salerno. Of course the voice could have been talking about someone else on the boat, or Alberta could have been out to lunch, but suppose not?

"Here you go." It was Flora, back with the water.

Setting aside my teacup, I took the offered water and drank down half of it before saying, "Flora, do you remember the night on the boat when we both received messages to meet each other, messages neither of us sent?"

"Yes," she said, quietly lowering herself back into the bedside chair.

"Someone wanted both of us out of the way."

She nodded. "Yes. You already told us. It was Richard."

"If Richard wanted the murderer to get to Charity it would make sense to keep you preoccupied—everyone knows you're always at your grandmother's side. But why me?"

"Well," Flora responded slowly, as if she were trying to figure out where I was going with my comments. "You're a detective, grandmother's bodyguard—although I know you don't like that term...everyone knew..."

"Not true," I countered. "As far as the rest of the family was aware, and Richard, I was your grandmother's financial advisor, on the way to Rome with her to help effect the changes to her will, nothing more. Richard'd have no reason to suspect I'd be physically protecting her unless...unless somehow he knew exactly who I was and why I was really on the boat."

"But how could he have found that out? Do you think maybe your friend...Errall...told someone?"

I shrugged as if accepting that as a possibility. "I suppose."

Flora stared at me, unmoving except for her nose, quivering like a rabbit's on the scent of a carrot. "I suppose," she finally spoke, repeating my words as if agreeing to an unalterable fact. She reached for one of the pillows that had ended up at the foot of my bed and began to knead it with her bony fingers.

"The tea Morris drank was poisoned during a Charity Event when the entire family was present on your grandmother's estate. But Richard wasn't there, was he?"

Flora said nothing but continued to mush up the pillow.

"Does Richard know your grandmother's habits well enough to know that she drinks tea every night before going to bed? I don't think so. He had to have inside information, inside help."

Flora's eyes grew wide with dawning shock and her voice trembled as she answered in a tiny voice, "Dottie."

I held her eyes for a long moment before I said, "There is someone else though, isn't there?"

Flora had just told me how brave I was the night our tender was sabotaged in Palermo, especially since I was afraid of water. The problem with that was that I'd admitted my fear of water to almost no one, not even my closest friends. But I had told one person: Richard Gray. The only way Flora would have this information was if Richard had told her. And why would he share pillow talk with a girl he supposedly hardly knew? Only if they were in cahoots and in constant communication with one another. I'd have to confirm it with Charity, but I was betting the whole FOD cruise, arranged by GrayPride tours, was likely Flora's idea, inspired by Richard. It's true the information was weak on its own, but the more I thought about things, the more I found to support my theory…a theory that was fast revealing itself as the truth. The pieces were beginning to click together.

Flora's face fell flat. She just sat there, watching me now like a cat waiting for a mouse to pop its head out of a hole.

I glanced pointedly at the cooling cup of tea on the bedside table, most of it gone. Slowly I moved my eyes to Flora's face. I'll never forget the smile on her lips.

It was a smile, but there was nothing joyful or happy in her dull, wan face. Her eyes looked dead, her skin was pallid. Yet the corners of her lips were turned up in a look of…satisfaction? Just then my eyelids drooped as if an irresistible weight was attached to them, an invitation to unconsciousness. I was showing the same signs of drowsiness as Jackson Delmonico had experienced on the bus ride to Pompeii after he mistakenly sipped a poisoned glass of juice. But it wasn't Charity's juice he drank at breakfast that morning. He'd told me it was Dottie's. A glass of tainted juice that I happened to see being delivered to Dottie by none other than her spouse's caring granddaughter, Flora. It was the second time Flora's evil mixture had met the wrong lips.

I focused on Flora's face. "The poisoned tea that Morris drank, it wasn't meant for Charity, was it? It was meant for Dottie."

No reaction. No denial.

"All this time, we thought it was Charity who was being targeted for murder. But it was really Dottie all along. Why? Was it because you and Richard blamed your grandmother for the death of your parents? You wanted her to suffer the same punishing loss, the loss of someone she loves dearly, just as you had, just as your uncle Richard had. You were in it together from the start, weren't you?"

Nothing.

"And then your first attempt to kill Dottie failed," I said to her. "So you came up with the idea of the cruise on The Dorothy." It had been Flora's voice Alberta heard that first night and every night on the boat.

"No one will believe you, Mr. Quant," Flora said, her voice surprisingly calm and even.

There it was.

The admission.

Flora was no longer playing a game with me, no longer denying that she was the queen of a murderous scheme, and Richard the king.

"I was in the tender with the rest of you when it was sabotaged and attacked. I could have been killed just as easily as the rest of you."

"That's true," I agreed, giving my head a sobering, stay-awake shake. "But that was part of the plan, wasn't it? To divert suspicion away from you. You knew who I was and that I would be looking for someone to accuse of murder. So although you were desperate to finish what you'd already attempted once, you knew it wasn't going to be easy." My voice began to slur. I kept on, determined to get at the truth. "You and Richard wanted three things—to kill Dottie, to get away with it and to keep me out of the way. By pulling the little stunt on the tender you reinforced both the idea that Charity was the true target and that you couldn't possibly be responsible."

Flora's forehead creased into a frown as if she was considering my theory for the first time, or at least a portion of it. Maybe some of what had happened during our cruise was not as it should have been, or not as Flora expected it to be. Flora's fingers continued to mutilate the pillow. "People might believe your ideas about Uncle Richard, but never about me."

"How much did you pay your uncle to help you? You could afford to offer a lot because you'd already received a hefty endowment on your twenty-first birthday. And Charity's will promised you more to come. GrayPride Tours is in serious trouble. Richard needs the money, badly."

Flora bristled. "He wasn't in it for the money. He was in it for the same reason I was—revenge, for my mother's death and my father's."

"So no money changed hands?"

Again with a frown. "I did give Uncle Richard some money out of my birthday money," she admitted. "But that had nothing to do with this. It was a loan, to help him with his business problems."

"With more to come as soon as you got the rest of your inheritance—when Charity was dead. The sooner the better as far as Richard was concerned, I'm sure," I goaded her.

"That's not true! We wanted Dottie dead, never Grandmother. Never her! I couldn't kill my own grandmother. But I did want her to suffer and so did Uncle Richard, so Dottie had to die. After the poisoned tea didn't work, I began replacing her heart medication with sugar pills. We thought her heart would eventually weaken to a point where any stressful situation might cause a heart attack and she'd die."

"Stressful like being set adrift on the tender when she couldn't swim?"

"That's right."

"Then why was it Charity that Sicilian was trying to pull off the boat? Why was Charity attacked in the marketplace in Tunis?"

Flora winced. I nervously eyed the pillow in her hands, now a well-worked piece of dough. "I remember you yelling, Flora. You screamed, 'This can't be happening! It isn't right! It's all wrong!' At the time I just thought you were upset about the boat sinking. But it was more than that, wasn't it? Your and Richard's plan had gone awry and when you saw The Dorothy leaving without carrying out a rescue, you began to suspect Richard."

"Of what?" Flora asked, the whites and pinks of her face turning ruddy.

"Of wanting your grandmother dead as well as Dottie." I let her glare at me for a moment, remembering the argument I'd witnessed between Flora and Richard on the Kismet. I kept at her. "The Dorothy didn't rescue us because he didn't want to risk anyone witnessing his real plan: the murder of Charity. I'm sure he had full intentions of coming back for you later. After all, you are his meal ticket. But the Kismet coming along was just convenient happenstance which he used to his advantage.

"You didn't know that Patrick was planning murder. You didn't know it was Patrick sending the threatening notes. Richard probably told you it wasn't him, but after what happened in Tunis and Palermo and the wild goose chase on the ship you couldn't be sure." I rubbed at my slacking face, moulding it into alertness. "You were right. He did plan all those things. He did want Charity dead more than Dottie, but he couldn't afford to let you know that. He suspected you wouldn't go along with it."

Flora remained attentive, but silent.

"So you arranged to meet him on the running deck to confront him with your suspicion that he was double crossing you." I pulled in more oxygen and struggled with keeping my eyelids open. "You fought and Phyllis overheard you. She was visiting Lovers' Lane and heard everything. So you and Richard killed her."

Flora let out an indignant squeak. "That is not true. We did not kill anyone! When I left Richard there was no one else there!"

Not that *you* saw. "Then it was…" And suddenly my voice faltered and grew weak. I made a sound as if I might throw up but didn't. My hands fell limply to my sides as my eyes fluttered. "Rich…"

"Mr. Quant?" I heard Flora's voice washing over me, testing to see if I was still responsive. "Mr. Quant?"

"D-don't," I managed to get out, begging for a life I didn't want to end. My hands and arms and feet quivered, as if trying against impossible odds to resist her, to flail against her, to beat her off. Instead I lay there, trapped in a body that was useless to me.

"I'm sorry, Mr. Quant," Flora said, slowly bringing the pillow up to my face. "You know too much. The others may know about Uncle Richard, but I can't let them find out about me...at least, not until I make Grandmother pay for what she did to my parents."

"You...can't...get...away...with..."

"I can," she answered matter-of-factly. "You were ill, still hurting from being stabbed, and you took too much pain medication. Or maybe someone else, the real killer...perhaps Uncle Richard, followed us here and killed you. I'll say whatever I have to. But don't worry, Mr. Quant, this should be painless."

Painless? What was she talking about? She was going to press a pillow over my mouth and nose and hold it there until I stopped breathing! The pillow was coming closer. It was getting so dark. Maybe...maybe she was right...maybe it would be painless...

"Get off of him, you fucking crazy bitch! Or I'll tear your fucking head off!"

I love Errall.

Through half-lidded eyes I was barely visually aware of what was going on around me, but I could still hear. A blur flew over my bed like a hawk descending on prey and suddenly it wasn't so dark anymore. Yowling and screeching and colourful curses ensued—all from Errall.

Then I heard someone else. Charity. "Why? Why would you do this?" Her voice sounded like walking on broken glass. "I love you!"

"You only love me out of guilt!" This from Flora, somewhere below me. Errall had her pinned to the ground. "You only love me to make up for the love you denied your own child. You pushed my father away, like a stranger you wanted out of your house. He never went back. Not because he didn't want to, but because he knew you didn't want him there. It was the horrible realization that his own mother didn't love him that drove him to drink.

That's why he killed himself! That's why my mother died! And that's why I wanted to kill Dottie! I wanted...I need you to feel what that feels like, the horrible loneliness that never goes away."

"Stop it, Flora!" Charity screamed in outrage. "It was because of your mother that your father drank, and because of your father that your mother drank! Not because of me. They were both alcoholics, raving mad alcoholics. When they got in that car that day they were both so drunk they had no idea what they were doing."

"He did know!" Flora spat. "He knew he wasn't loved by his own mother. He knew he was a failure in life. That's what drove him to drink, drove him into that car and over that cliff. There was nothing left for him."

"Of course there was, you foolish girl!" she cried. "He had you!"

For a moment there was silence, then, "By killing himself," Charity said quietly, "he abandoned you, Flora."

"I wonder," Flora asked her grandmother, "where he learned that trick?"

And there it stopped.

"Shut up! All of you!" A new voice. But a familiar one. My new boyfriend was back in town. Richard Gray. He must have slipped in through the garden door. Through the narrowest of slits, I could see that he was holding a gun pointed at Charity. He was out to finish what he started.

"Let her up!" he called to Errall who was still on top of Flora.

"You can't get away with this," Errall told him. "The others are right behind that door. They'll hear the gun fire. Then what, are you going to kill all of us?"

He grinned. "Thanks for the idea. Massacre at the Italian Villa. I can see the headlines now. Now let her up!"

Errall slowly rose to her feet and Flora followed suit.

"What are you doing?" Flora's voice was plaintive. "He said you killed Phyllis. He said you wanted to kill Grandmother, not Dottie."

Richard slowly approached my bedside, his gun unwavering in its target. He stole a glance down at my near-comatose face. "I see that damn poison finally did what it was supposed to do. Too bad about the victim." How sweet. Special treat for him next

Valentine's Day. Then he turned his back on me as if I was already dead and of little remaining interest.

"He said you wanted to kill Grandmother," Flora repeated herself.

"I've always been there for you, Flora, no one else. Me! Not her! You know this is the only way now that we'll ever see any money. I know it's your money, but you've always been so good about helping me out. I simply can't wait any longer. Do you know GrayPride Tours is being thrown into bankruptcy as we speak? I can't wait for your grandmother to die. And now, with this ridiculous change in the will...you have to understand. We can't let it happen."

"But she's not! She's not changing her will!"

Richard shook his head as if he didn't want to hear it. "It's too late. Too late!"

"No. No. No you can't." She sounded near tears.

I guess Flora was willing to administer poison, fake heart medication, even try to frighten someone to death, but she wasn't into guns. She was willing to off her grandmother's spouse but not her grandmother. Apparently all murderers are not indiscriminately evil. But I can say one thing: they *are* all dumber than mouse shit. Did she really believe I'd drink any tea *she'd* serve me? I'd tossed most of it out when she went to fetch my water.

Using my excellent position of supposedly being in a poisoned tea–induced coma and behind the guy with the gun, I rose like a phoenix (well, that may be a little overstated) and jumped him, screaming like a banshee (not overstated). Richard fell to the floor and his gun went sliding out of his hands towards Errall's feet. She picked it up, pointed it at our pile of struggling man flesh, and the fight was pretty much over before it really got started. After being misled into a fake relationship with this jerk in order to keep me occupied and pump me for information (and other things), I really wanted to get in a few good jabs, but managed to resist. I knew I'd get him back as a witness for the Crown.

I awoke feeling amazingly refreshed. It was dark outside so I knew I'd been sleeping a long time. After a long shower, I spent a few minutes reminding myself of all that had happened before I nodded off. We kept Richard at gunpoint until the authorities arrived. Flora had grown rather sedate after the confrontation in my bedroom, barely moving or talking to anyone. The police interrogated all of us and then lawyer Errall strongly suggested they leave us alone until tomorrow, especially me who was still fighting an infection I'd gotten as a result of my stab wound. Anthony sent for a doctor friend who examined me, gave me some pills and told me to go to bed. Which I did.

I heard the buzz of voices outside my door and eventually a light tapping.

"Come in," I called out.

The door opened and Charity Wiser stepped into my room.

"Russell," she said. "I heard the shower. I'm glad you're awake. Everyone is worried about you. Are you all right?"

I nodded, surveying her for telltale signs of the emotional ordeal she'd no doubt been through since learning her granddaughter had tried to kill her beloved Dottie. But there was nothing. She looked as put-together and confident as always, as if this was just another fine day at the beach. "I'm okay."

"Good, good. Glad to hear it." She closed the door and came closer to where I was standing near the French doors.

"Tell me what happened," I said. I wanted information, not sympathy. "Why did you come back?"

"It was Errall. That girl saved your life, Russell."

Well, not really. Sure she pulled Flora off me as she was trying to suffocate me. But I had it all in hand. I expected Richard was somewhere nearby and would make an appearance, so I only pretended to be poisoned, copying the symptoms exhibited by Jackson when he was poisoned. Even so, I could only imagine what Errall's heroics were going to cost me.

"We were talking about things on our afternoon drive to Radda, what you'd learned about Richard, when she suddenly got it into her head that he might still be in Italy, that he might have left The Dorothy early not to go home but to plan one last attack.

She thought he might have followed us to the villa, still after me and, since you'd figured out his involvement, after you too. Of course that meant you and Flora were in mortal danger and she insisted we go back."

Well, she was only half right. Flora wasn't *in* danger...she *was* danger.

Charity turned away then, giving me her intimidating profile to look at for a while. "Oh Russell," she finally blurted out. "You'll think me awful."

Now what? "Does it really matter what I think?"

She turned towards me again, a tiny smile flirting with her lips. "No." She took a moment to straighten her shirt collar. "I need to ask you one more favour, Russell."

Uh oh.

"I'd like you to recant all that you told the police earlier...about Flora and her involvement in this...this sordid affair. You can say whatever you wish about that despicable man, Richard Gray; he should burn in hell, but Flora...not Flora."

Certainly Charity understood that this was more than just a simple family misunderstanding. It was murder. I was done putting the fractious pieces of my case together, including Flora's not insignificant role in it, and now it was time to let the authorities take over. "Charity, there has been a murder and several attempted murders, of you and Dottie."

Her breathing was jagged and her eyes darted around the room. She knew what she was about to beg for was all wrong, but she was desperate. "Russell, please no. There must be another way."

"Charity, no. No." Sure Dottie hadn't actually come to physical harm, but that didn't excuse Flora for wanting it so, no matter how tough a childhood she or her father had had. I hadn't heard the rest of the confrontation between Charity and her granddaughter before she'd been taken away, but I could guess it had been filled with bitter recriminations, guilt and festering anger, some called for, some not. But in the end, there was no defence for what Flora had done or intended to do. She and Richard had set in motion a plan that led to Phyllis' death and much violence. "Flora must be held accountable, Charity. You know I'm right."

Charity lowered her chin in one last offensive move, setting her bright eyes on mine. "Russell, do you remember what I told you in Barcelona, on the Ramblas? About the tapas?"

I gave my head a shake and shrugged my shoulders. What was she getting at?

"Tapas," she reminded me, "were created to keep a lid on things. That's what I want to do now. Can't you understand?" she pleaded, her voice scratching against its naturally poised grain. "This is a family matter. I'll deal with it in the family."

Did she think she was Tony Soprano or The Godfather or someone like that? Get real! Did she really expect me to agree to cover this up? As I searched her eyes, I knew the answer was no. She was simply in denial over how this had ended. When she hired me and then agreed to the plan for the Charity Event on The Dorothy, this was the last result she ever expected. It could not have been easy to admit to herself that not one, but two members of her family had wanted her dead or to suffer. She was reeling from that knowledge, wanting to somehow make it all go away, wanting to protect her granddaughter, to somehow preserve Flora as she once believed her to be.

"Murder," I said, "does not belong in the family, Charity. Tapas were created to keep things out, not to keep them in. They were never meant to hide things."

It was not until the Saskatoon Blue Line taxicab dropped me off in front of my house days later that I realized how wrong I might be. In front of the house next to mine was another tapa, one last cover-up, like a lid pulled tight over something I was not allowed to see. It was one last mystery left unsolved. The house itself was dark. Abandoned. On the front lawn was a sign.

For Sale.

Sereena was gone.

Acknowledgements

I love the office where I work each day, poking away at my keyboard, the peacefulness, solitude and deep quiet of it rarely broken by two little dogs who keep me company (or I them). Then comes the time to reveal what I've been toiling at. There will always be a special place in my heart for each of you who share this with me…those who show up at events, bring friends, read these books, recommend them to others, surprise me with your generosity, the cards, e-mails, thoughtful gifts, notes of support…I am so fortunate and truly grateful…you are amazing.

To each incredible bookseller, store manager, event coordinator, festival and awards organizer: I am forever in your debt—and to my special team of Deneen G, David R, Bill S, Sharanpal R, Megan, Louann S, Holly M, Janine, Jackie, Billy A, Ron G, Larry B, Adrienne, thank you for the continuing support.

My gratitude to the reviewers, interviewers, columnists and news reporters who spend time with writers and their books—you help keep our words alive.

And then one evening at the Saskatoon Club…talk about starting things off with a bang…I realize now I cannot say it enough: Shelley Brown is a gem…Murray, my fellow E&Y alumni, what a fantastic group of people you are.

Special thanks to: Patty-o Lantern, Lynne, Rhonda, Kelly, Catherine, Karen for sitting around in witch hats; Grant Park for the giant martini glass display; the Opus cocktail partygoers; Jilly Bird for edible flower pots; David Rubin of DavidTours—a man who truly knows luxury travel; the incomparable Robert Taylor for his graciousness in allowing me to hop aboard his mighty coattails for a ride down America's beautiful west coast; to all our friends aboard the Silverseas; the many who became the voice of my Sicilian tender captain; Eldeen for making RQ one of her picks; Moo's stew; Paul J for sharing with me Cadbury's Caramilk Bar Secret and the fate of Sour Cream and Onion Flavoured Rings; Paul & Jan for my very own MVA shrubs; Dori, I love my wall hanging; Fran—pahmyatie meneh, and, Johanna, the best mom ever.

Insomniac Press—thank you for keeping Russell alive.

Michele Karlsberg—for opening up new doors, answering all my questions and keeping it going—my thanks.

Excerpts from an editor's letter: "...Anyway it's late, my handwriting sucks and my eyes hurt...remarkable how you have intertextualized the RQ series...with a little more treatment you can colour the characters up a touch...ultimately I can't picture it... your use of language is, as always, particularly intriguing...that plot line comes out of nowhere...just a thought...you've achieved an incredible pique of interest here...maillot? What's a maillot?... Russell is certainly developing a larger-than-life-of-his-own...You have my support and sincere affection." *And you, Catherine Lake, have mine.*

Thank *you* for being a reader.

And Herb.